Forbidden Forest 3

AMBER ARGYLE

Book Cover Design by Melissa Williams Design

First Edition: December 2020
Library of Congress Cataloging-in-Publication Data
LCCN: 2020920387

Argyle, Amber
Wraith King (Forbidden Forest) – 1st ed
ISBN-13: 978-0-9976390-5-6

TO RECEIVE AMBER ARGYLE'S STARTER LIBRARY FOR FREE,
SIMPLY TELL HER WHERE TO SEND IT:
http://amberargyle.com

For all my fellow ADHD girls and boys out there,

You are weird. You are wild. You are witty.

And that is what makes you wonderful.

CHAPTER

MIRROR

Surrounded by ancient, corroded mirrors, Larkin braced herself as her grandmother, Iniya, wrenched a brush through her curls until they resembled a very robust weed. Iniya muttered curses as she pinned down each wayward bit of fluff; Larkin's head was heavy with pins that poked and pulled and weighted her down.

That finished, Iniya pasted thick makeup on every inch of Larkin's exposed skin. She dusted her eyes with gold flakes and painted her lips vermilion. It all seemed a bit much for so early in the morning, but they had over three hundred embedding ceremonies to get through today, which would put them finishing late in the night.

Finally, Iniya stepped back. "There. Now you look like a princess instead of a wild thing, though no amount of finery can hide those hideous scars."

A long, ragged slash across her neck and the pitted scars on her arms were the most noticeable. But there were others. A thin, crooked line on her palm. Numerous sword kisses. Not to mention the ones her father had given her for the sin of being a girl. She also bore a chipped tooth from gritting her teeth too hard the night the wraiths nearly turned her husband into a monster.

Larkin was neither ashamed nor proud of her scars. They just were. And she would not let her grandmother bully her into being self-conscious of them.

"Remind me why I let you help me?" Larkin muttered.

"Because I know what it takes to make you a queen."

"Do you?" Larkin immediately regretted the bite of her words, but it was too late to take them back.

Iniya stiffened. "I kept my end of the bargain. I got you into the druids' palace." Never mind that Larkin had been captured shortly after. "You have yet to keep yours." To return Iniya's title as queen of the United Cities of the Idelmarch.

Larkin bit back her groan of frustration. "We're working on it."

Iniya gathered up her things. "Work on it faster." Cane tapping out a steady rhythm, she left in a huff.

To her right, the tiara stared Larkin down from its green silk pillow. With a steadying breath, she reached out, a thousand copies of herself doing the same, and traced the splay of sacred tree branches that wove to a sharp point, where a single emerald had been set.

Larkin had been born and raised in the mud with a drunkard for a father. There had never been enough food, and her clothes had been little better than rags. Now, she wore a fancy Idelmarchian dress, a priceless cream piece with a gold, opal, and emerald belt cinching her waist. Around her neck hung two amulets—one a stylized version of sacred tree and the other a leaf.

And of course the dress was backless to show off her monarch sigil—raised white lines that formed a geometric copy of the White Tree. A sigil she was the only woman in three centuries to bear. A sigil that proclaimed her a princess and gave her more magic than all, save her husband, the prince.

I'm not sure I can do this.

She didn't have a choice. She'd been hiding for the past two months, ever since she and Denan had returned to the Alamant after the battle that had come to be known as Druids' Folly.

It was time to stop hiding.

She reached for the reassuring power of her magic. The sigils—including the two on her left arm and one on her left hand—flared opalescent, the edges trimmed in gold. They were all in geometric patterns of leaves or flowers. Her favorite were the wedding sigils—vines that twined up her hands and wrists nearly to her elbows like lacy gloves.

The comforting, somewhat painful buzz reminded her that she was not the helpless girl she'd once been. She took the tiara between her fingertips and centered the emerald on her forehead. Another steadying breath, and she turned to face her reflection.

All that light—all that refinery and beauty—couldn't disguise the dark circles under her eyes. The paleness that made her thick freckles stand out like a constellation of dark stars against a bright sky.

She'd come to accept herself as Denan's wife. And then as a warrior. But a princess?

"You look lovely."

Denan leaned against the doorframe to her left. He was dressed in the simple manner of the pipers. Backlit by the rising sun, her husband's dark gold skin and black hair paired nicely with his forest-green tunic and trousers embroidered all over in gold. A wild crown of branches and opals graced his head. His leather mantle—embossed with a three-headed snake knotted in a circle—had points at the shoulders and front and back, precious cabochon stones hanging from each. On his chest, his monarch sigil gleamed golden through his clothes, a sigil that marked him as prince, as much as hers marked her a princess.

Like her, Denan bore marks of strain. For him, it was in the stiff way he carried himself. The way he sucked in a breath if he moved the wrong way. Though the wound the wraiths had given him had closed, it had never truly healed. And the way he sometimes stared south—toward the fallen city of Valynthia—with a look of hopelessness and dread.

Tonight wasn't a night for such thoughts.

Larkin forced a smile, crossed the room—a hundred other reflections following suit—and hugged him. "And you, my Piper Prince, look just as lovely."

He held out a velvet bag. "I brought you something."

He'd bought her so many things over the last month, including this dress. As if he were trying to make up for the nightmares that kept her up most nights. Nightmares of her friends turning to mulgars. Of men she'd killed. Of living shadows that snatched at her, drawing her into the dark that lives beneath the grave.

Shivering, she took the bag, something clinking delicately inside. She tugged open the drawstring and carefully upended a pair of emerald earrings into her palm. The stones dangled from a geometric pattern of delicately wrought gold vines that perfectly matched her wedding sigils.

"You had these made." More than once, she'd caught him sketching her. Sketches he would never show her. He'd been capturing her sigils to have a jeweler remake them.

She tipped up on her toes and kissed him. His lips smiled against her mouth. "Do you intend the whole of the Alamant to see me wearing your lipstick?"

She pulled back and gave him a wicked grin. "Maybe." She slipped the earrings in her ears and admired them in the closest mirror. "They're beautiful."

He offered her his arm. "Shall we?"

I can do this. She eased her hand through the crook of his elbow and passed through the magic pane that kept out the weather. There was the cool feeling, like walking through glass, and the taste of stardust on the back of her tongue. Then she stepped from the platform onto a branch of the White Tree. The opalescent white bark hummed with magic that echoed beneath her skin.

They made their way down to the main platform—a curved, bowl-shaped depression where the trunk met the boughs. On the far side was a delicate arch; beyond it, circular stairs led down to the lake, from which a city of enormous hometrees grew.

Almost directly beneath Larkin was a dais. At its center, the font gleamed with the wicked thorns that granted magic. Behind the font, the musicians were almost set up. Servants laid colorful platters of food onto tables that circled the perimeter. Most of the Alamantian dignitaries had arrived. The Idelmarchian delegation—nearly all of them Black Druids—wouldn't be far behind.

Druids who'd locked her in a dungeon and then sold her to the wraiths in exchange for dark magic. Now those same druids would receive magic from the White Tree.

"Larkin?"

She'd stopped walking to glare down at the party. "You know we can't trust them, Denan. Especially with something as powerful as our magic."

He trailed the back of his fingers down her cheek. "Little bird, we do what we must."

It was an old Alamantian idiom. One the pipers used to justify any number of sins. For instance, stealing Idelmarchian girls—like herself—for wives. She'd hated those words, but over these last months, she'd also learned that fighting the curse that spawned the wraiths justified many lesser evils.

The simple truth of it was that the Alamant was desperate for more fighters, and the druids were their only option.

"We wouldn't have to rely on them if I had found Eiryss's amulet." But the Curse Queen's tomb had been empty, and they didn't have any clues where to look next.

Larkin's thoughts broke apart as a leaf twirled delicately through the air. She caught it, gently holding it in the cup of her palm. The leaf's normally opalescent white trimmed in gold had turned to yellow, the edges crisp and brown.

In the long centuries of the tree's existence, it had never shed its leaves. Its magic had never allowed it. But all the magic in the world wouldn't prevent it from dying. And if the tree died, so would the magic. The same magic that protected them from the wraiths. The same magic that prevented the poisoned wound in Denan's side from spreading.

And if it spread, a fate far worse than death awaited the man she loved.

The breeze picked up, the branches around her sounding like rushing water. The leaf was ripped from her palm to spin out into the day.

She pressed the amulets into her skin, leaving an imprint that gave her comfort. Denan's words echoed through her. *We do what we must.*

CHAPTER 2

UNTIL THE STARS FALL

More leaves fell, showering Larkin and Denan with dying gold.

"Larkin?" Denan's brows were crinkled with concern. He had enough to worry about without adding her to the list.

She gave him a bright smile, and they continued their descent. More Alamantians arrived on the platform. The men outnumbered the women three to one, as the curse had robbed the pipers of the ability to bear daughters.

Just as Larkin and Denan had orchestrated, the men wore the simple piper tunics and robes, over which went the embossed mantles of their family crest and swinging jewels, while the women were all dressed like Larkin, in the Alamantian style, with fancy dresses bedecked with gems.

They'd hoped the differences might make the druids feel more at home and therefore be less likely to commit violence.

Though Larkin didn't really believe anything would stop that, she'd endeavored to try.

Sitting sideways across the bottom step, his elbows on one cocked knee, Tam watched them with spring-blue eyes beneath blond curls. He winked at Larkin and nodded a greeting to Denan. "You're in trouble."

Denan frowned. "Why?"

Tam hopped up and tipped his head toward the current king of the Alamant, King Netrish, who stood at the food tables with his wife, Queen Jaslin. Succession in the Alamant was different than the Idelmarch. The White Tree chose the next prince at his embedding ceremony. Once the prince was married and his stolen bride settled, that prince became king. But King Netrish had made no move to step down.

The king had clearly been waiting for them to appear. He stormed over, his wife in tow. A vein stood out on his bald head, as he shook a letter at them. "I've already told you; the people aren't ready."

Larkin had helped Denan compose the letter the king held, a letter which formally asked the king to step down. She shot Tam a flat look that said, *You could have given us a little more warning.*

Tam shoved his hands in his pockets and shrugged, clearly unconcerned.

"The law is clear, Netrish." Denan's tone was almost bored. "When a prince's wife is settled, he becomes king."

Netrish pointed his fat finger at Larkin. "She escaped the Alamant—damaging our trees and the barrier in the process. She managed to get herself captured by the druids. Then she managed to get captured a second time. Hundreds of our pipers have died because of her actions. She is as willful and wild as a wraith!"

Jaslin nodded in agreement.

Tam's nonchalance faded away. His hands came out of his pockets, and he stepped closer, a murderous look on his face.

Denan's gaze sharpened. "Larkin isn't the one who will be king."

King Netrish's gaze flicked to Denan's hidden blight mark. "And who do you think will rule when the blight takes you?"

All Larkin's life, men had insulted and threatened her. They would not insult her husband. Her sigils for her sword and shield flared bright enough to make the king blink. "This willful and wild woman is about to make you apologize."

The king's mouth opened for what she was sure was another insult.

Denan took a step closer to the king, his expression thunderous. "Larkin is the only reason your son survived. The only reason our entire army wasn't overrun by the Idelmarchians. The only reason those same Idelmarchians aren't tearing down our defenses while the wraiths wait in the wings to destroy us all." He swallowed hard. "When the blight finally takes me—"

"If," Larkin interrupted. She'd contained his blight with her own magic—a barrier in the shape of an orb, which she'd discovered later was called a weir, old magic that the enchantresses were only just beginning to grasp. He was in no danger.

"If," Denan agreed, "the blight takes me, you'd be lucky to have her."

In the beat of silence that followed, the king's guards circled closer. Tam shifted so he was between them and Larkin. The queen glared at her. The powerful of the Alamant stilled to listen. Even Denan's ever-present pages watched.

What would happen if Netrish refused to cede? The pipers wouldn't survive a civil war. Would the White Tree itself intervene? Could it?

The king took a deep breath and straightened his fine vest. "Try me if you wish, Denan, but you'll find most of the council and our people feel the same as I about your wife. Come along, dear." He turned on his heel and marched off, his wife right beside him.

Larkin watched them go, wishing she could use the magic buzzing under her skin. Wishing she could explain herself to those still watching her. *Yes, I made mistakes, but those deaths were not my fault.* The fault lay at the feet of the wraiths' and druids' foolish alliance.

As if sensing her impulse, Denan wrapped his arm around her waist and held her tight. "Don't," he murmured. "It will make you look weak."

"I'll make *him* look weak," Tam grumbled after the king.

The tinkling of the amethysts in Alorica's gown announced her arrival. She glared at the king's back. "May the shadows eat him." Her lovely, pale purple gown contrasted with her dark skin, eyes, and short black curls.

"You look beautiful," Larkin said.

Alorica shrugged. "Of course I do."

"Thanks for the warning." Denan punched Tam's arm, then winced as his blight twinged.

Tam sidestepped the worst of it and sidled up to his wife. "Not my fault you decided to challenge the king on a day he can verbally flog you in front of everyone."

Denan grunted. "Hiding behind your wife, you coward."

"Wouldn't you?" Tam said. Alorica shot him a glare. "See? She's scary."

Alorica rolled her eyes.

Insulting each other was a game between the men, a sparring match to work out their tension. Larkin was stuck with taking a calming breath and closing her sigils.

Denan pressed on his blighted side. "Let's find Gendrin. See if he can talk some sense into his father."

"You two go ahead," Larkin said. "I need to speak with Alorica about our defenses."

Denan nodded distractedly. He and Tam moved through the crowd, which bowed respectfully to their prince. Some still watched Larkin, but most returned to their own conversations, which was a relief. She hadn't liked the attention of crowds since one tried burning her at the stake.

Larkin eyed the women around them. Hidden beneath fine dresses and sparkling jewels were their best enchantresses. They'd been drilling with the White Tree Sentinels for weeks. "Have they docked?"

"Come see for yourself."

Alorica slipped through the crowd. Larkin followed. The enchantresses bowed to her. Most of the men did not. Larkin tried not to notice. What the pipers thought of her didn't matter and shouldn't bother her.

She hated that it did.

Alorica glared at them. "They'll learn to respect you. Like I did."

That brought a crooked smile to Larkin's face. She and Alorica had hated each other once, but being kidnapped and forced through the Forbidden Forest together had made allies of them. Over the last couple months, that alliance had deepened to a bond as strong as any Larkin had with her sisters.

Shifting through the bodies clogging the entrance, they passed under the archway opposite the dais. Squinting against the bright morning light, they peered at the sudden drop below. Twenty stories down, the three hundred or so Idelmarchians had already disembarked. Their all-black Black Druid uniforms made them look like beetles instead of people. In contrast, the White Tree Sentinels wore white livery with their gold-and-silver armor.

Black and white. Black like the screaming shadows that had torn apart the Alamantian defenses. White like the light pulsing from a raised fist. Even now, Larkin felt herself being sucked back into a vision of the Curse Queen's memory of that horrible day. When a massacre had occurred on this very platform. A massacre that had preceded the curse.

Already, she could hear the screams...

"Larkin!" Alorica tugged Larkin's hand open. The echoing screams abruptly stopped. Without realizing, she'd gripped her amulet too hard. One of the branches had pierced her skin, activating the vision of the day the curse had come into being. Alorica pressed a handkerchief to the spot of blood on the side of Larkin's palm.

They had perhaps thirty minutes before the druids reached them. Larkin had to get control over herself. She slowed her breathing. Slowly, her panic eased. "Did you see Nesha?"

Alorica dabbed away the last of the blood. "Twenty stories is too far away to pick out one person."

Larkin tucked the amulet inside her dress and passed a hand down her sweaty face. It was barely morning, and already the sun felt hot and the air heavy.

Alorica frowned. "You'll smear your makeup."

Larkin tried to laugh her friend's concern away.

Alorica clearly wasn't buying it. "Do you want me to get Denan?"

"No!" Larkin said too quickly and too loudly. Light, she didn't used to be such a mess.

Alorica dragged Larkin back under the now-empty arch and didn't pause until she'd pushed her way through the press crowding a table of delicate crystal glasses filled with golden champagne. The instant the crowd recognized Larkin, they backed up a step, giving them the space her position demanded.

Alorica pushed a flute into Larkin's hand. "Drink."

"I don't want—"

"I don't care what you want. You cannot fall apart in front of the druids." She took a long drink of her own. "Or the Alamantians, for that matter. All these men need to see us as equals. Not hysterical women."

And just like that, Alorica had shoved a dagger into Larkin's fear and twisted.

I will not fall apart when I see Garrot. I will keep it together. Despite the strangeness of drinking champagne so soon after breakfast, Larkin threw the glass back, the bubbles burning her throat and nose and sending her eyes watering. A burp burbled out, earning her disapproving glances. A man to her right gave her a hostile stare and marched off, many in the crowd following him.

She hated champagne.

"Larkin." Iniya stepped into the place the man had vacated, her voice holding more than a touch of scorn. She pulled Larkin away from the table and off to one side, Alorica trailing.

"Champagne is an ornament," Iniya whisper-shouted. "You do not throw it back like a barmaid!"

Alorica crossed her arms. "She needed something to settle her nerves."

"Nerves?" Iniya sent Alorica a scathing look. "A princess doesn't have nerves. Nor does she keep company with her guard."

Larkin set down her glass. "I—"

Iniya banged her cane on the bark. "I don't want your excuses. Circulate among the crowd. Be the delight they need to see."

"I don't like you," Alorica said through clenched teeth.

Iniya huffed. "You don't matter." She shot Larkin a piercing look and then fixed her gaze on the king. She shooed Larkin. "Off you go. I have work to do." Her expression transformed into serene gentility as she limped away.

Alorica stared after her. "Why do you listen to her?"

Larkin started to rub her face, remembered the makeup, and dropped her hands. "She survived in an enemy court for decades. If anyone can help me, it's her."

"She's wrong." Alorica studied her. "You're not duplicitous enough to be the kind of person Iniya wants you to be."

Yet still the pipers ignored her. "Who I am hasn't swayed them."

Alorica looped her arm through Larkin's. "It takes a bit of time getting used to you is all."

Larkin would have laughed, but one of her enchantresses signaled that the Idelmarchians were through the inspection.

Following her gaze, Alorica began ticking off their precautions. "The druids were all excised of the wraiths' thorns. Your Arbor father-in-law and I checked them over when they entered the city; if I never see another hairy druid, it will be too soon. We tested them under enchantment to make sure none were planning anything. The White Tree Sentinels have done a thorough search for weapons. And if those druids are idiot enough to try anything…" Alorica lit her sigils. "Well, I would hate to get blood on this dress, but I will if I have to."

No one was allowed to bring weapons to this ceremony, but it wasn't as if the enchantresses could put their sigils down. Larkin was counting on the druids dismissing the women out of hand, as they always had.

It had worked once. Perhaps it would again.

They were as ready as they could be, yet a knot of tension still burned in Larkin's belly.

An enchantress approached Larkin, her head bowed deferentially. "No weapons were found. There are no women among them."

Larkin was both relieved and disappointed. Relieved because she didn't want Nesha here in case things went badly. Disappointed because she'd yet to speak with her sister or even meet her baby. Larkin wasn't even sure if the child was a boy or girl. She'd only ever seen them from a distance when they'd entered the Alamant a week ago.

Larkin signaled to the band. They began to play a variety of masterfully carved wind instruments made from the sacred wood of the White Tree—instruments that were as varied as the men who played them. An enchantment rode on the melody, one that exuded calm.

The leaf amulet Larkin wore was a dampener; it blunted the enchantment enough that she could fight it. She didn't want to fight it.

She let the magic settle against her skin and sink into her pores like the first real sunlight after a cold winter. The tension she always bore eased. Her mind emptied of everything except the sound. When she opened her eyes, calm had settled into her heart. It was a false calm, but it would keep pipers and druids from killing each other.

At least at first.

"Let me know when the delegation is nearly here," Larkin said.

Her eyes on her husband, Tam, Alorica nodded—apparently, she didn't want to use her dampener to fight the music any more than Larkin did—and slipped away.

Across the crowd, Gendrin spoke with Denan, their heads bent together. Denan. Her husband. The man who had married her against her will. Taken everything from her. And yet, she had fallen in love with him all the same. Fallen in love with his kindness and determination and confidence.

Also, he was gorgeous.

Larkin wove through the people—the music had all of them looking for their loved ones, same as Larkin—until she came to a stop before Denan and Gendrin.

Gendrin was barrel-chested and dark, hints of russet in his beard. He was not handsome, but quiet power exuded from the man.

"I'm sorry, Denan, but my father is right." Gendrin noted her and stiffened in clear embarrassment before bowing. "Princess Larkin."

Gendrin always wore his emotions on his face. It was part of the reason Larkin had immediately trusted him. And Larkin trusted very, very few people.

"Even you have turned against me, Gendrin?" After all, she'd saved his life.

Gendrin stepped closer. "I'm simply telling the truth, princess."

She pointedly snubbed the man and held out a hand to her husband. "We never got to dance on our wedding night."

Denan smiled wryly. "If I remember right, that's because you begged me not to."

Gendrin cleared his throat. "My prince, if you'll excuse me, I have my mother to attend."

Why hadn't his wife, Caelia, come?

Larkin took one of her husband's hands and settled it on the curve of her hip. "Denan, will you dance with me?"

He looked deep into her eyes. "Until the stars fall."

He took her other hand in his. A push sent her spinning under his raised arm. He pulled her close and dipped her. He spun her. The gown twisted and flared around her legs, the earrings and amulets spinning, the belt sparkling. He pulled her back, holding her firm against him. They twirled about the room. In his arms, she felt beautiful, treasured. Her body responded to the slightest pressure, the gentlest tug, until they moved as one.

Larkin had never felt such synergy with anyone but him. And with the magic of the melody, she forgot everything but his hands directing her and the feel of the music moving through her.

Denan abruptly stopped. Larkin turned to see why and found Alorica behind her.

"They're nearly here."

The druids. The music had made her forget. She'd let herself forget.

Now it was time to remember.

CHAPTER 3

BLACK DRUIDS

It was a strange feeling, purposely stepping out of the enchantment. To turn away from the gentle caress toward the sharpness of reality. Larkin blinked as if coming awake. She suddenly realized she was breathing hard. A slight sheen of sweat slicked her skin and made the short hairs along her neck curl tight.

A tug of Denan's hand, and she moved beside him through the crowd. Most of the enchantresses were still glassy-eyed with enchantment. The pipers only had fifteen dampeners—all from the time before the curse.

Denan and Larkin fell in five steps behind the king, who shot Denan a look that said he better keep his wife under control—a look they both ignored. Queen Jaslin was somewhere tucked out of sight and safe, something Denan would never ask of Larkin.

Denan's parents, Arbor Mytin and General Aaryn, were already waiting at the top of the dais, which was around ten yards across and surrounded by stairs on all sides. Just to the left of the central font, Aaryn wore her full ceremonial armor, while Mytin wore the Arbor mantle, an embossed and painted White Tree at his chest and cabochon gems hanging from the four peaks at the shoulders as well as the front and back. He also carried a staff made of gnarled sacred wood.

Both bowed to the king and gave little nods to Larkin and Denan. Just before Larkin took her first step up the dais, Larkin passed Iniya, who stood in the first row before the sentinels, who stood with their backs to the dais. The woman caught Larkin's attention and pointed at her hair.

Larkin nervously touched her curls only to find them frizzed, a few pinned locks slipping out. She hurriedly tucked them back up and smoothed her hair.

Feeling self-conscious and out of sorts, Larkin moved left and took her place beside Denan to the font's right. A servant handed her husband and the king their crowns of branches. Larkin searched out Alorica and Tam, who stood next to the branch that led to where Sela waited above. If things went bad, they were to take her down the ropes to a boat waiting below. They were the only ones Larkin trusted with keeping her sister safe.

Larkin would have preferred leaving Sela at their hometree with Mama, but Sela had insisted that the White Tree needed her present. Mytin had reluctantly sided with her, effectively ending the discussion.

A moment later, conversations stilled. Knowing what that meant, Larkin tightened her grip on Denan's hand. She forced herself to look up. A hundred yards away, the first of the Alamantians came into view beneath the archway. The rising sun behind them threw dark shadows over their features, so they looked almost like wraiths. So much so that Larkin drew in a breath, the urge to run making her insides twist.

She was purposefully not looking for Garrot. But even with the distance, her traitorous gaze zeroed in on him. He strode at the head of the druids, a thick tooled belt with a large silver medallion about his waist proclaiming him the Master Druid. The cravat was new. Probably wore it to cover his blight.

A sudden memory reared up and struck Larkin.

Her boots slipped on a blood-smeared floor. She knelt beside her grandfather—the Master Druid who had orchestrated the coup that had killed Iniya's father, the king, along with the rest of her family and forced her from the palace, who had ruled the United Cities of the Idelmarch with lies and the iron fist of the druids. The man had been a monster. But his being a monster hadn't dulled the horror of his blood soaking through Larkin's dress. Of his mouth opening and closing as he struggled for breath that wouldn't come.

Through blood and betrayal, her grandfather had left power the same way he'd come into it. And now, standing in the sacred tree, was his successor. The new Master Druid.

Don't panic! Larkin couldn't lose control in front of all these people. She closed her eyes in a futile effort to banish the images. But the iron smell of blood remained in her nostrils. As did the gurgling sound of her grandfather gasping his last breath in her ears.

"Larkin," Denan whispered from beside her.

He had protected her for months—letting her stay home while he and the king had met with the druids. But she couldn't avoid this ceremony. Not if she wanted the pipers to take her seriously. Steeling herself, she made herself face the druids.

They were halfway across the platform. Close enough that her gaze met Garrot's, and everything disappeared. He was haggard and thin, shadows like bruises filling the pale hollows of his face.

The price of the blight he bore? If so, he deserved that and more.

Her ears rang as another memory swarmed her. Her shoulders and wrists ached as she fought the men holding her. Garrot dragged Bane up the scaffolding steps and wrapped the noose around his neck.

"No!" The word had ripped from her throat. Bane could not die. He was a childhood of fishing in the rivers and teaching her to overcome her fear of the water. Of warm bread and jam when she could never get enough to eat. Her first love. The man who saved her over and over again.

How could life exist without Bane?

"Don't watch," Bane said.

Garrot glared at her. "Make her watch."

And then the trapdoor snapped open.

At the edges of her awareness, the druids marched closer. Words without meaning passed over her.

"Get her under control," King Netrish snapped under his breath.

Standing on her tiptoes to see over the tall sentinel's shoulder, Iniya watched with a furious frown. She shook her head in disgust and mouthed, "Do not embarrass me."

"Larkin." The brush of Denan's nose against her cheek brought her back with a start. All her sigils were alight; the only thing keeping her sword and shield from forming was Denan's bruising grip over her sigils. He left his place to stand directly in front of her, his body blocking her from view.

"He should die for what he's done." She would either charge Garrot or fall into a puddle of sobbing. She wasn't sure which would be worse.

"Breathe with me. Listen to the music."

She turned her face into the hollow of his neck, breathing in the scent of him, letting him shield her, letting the music flow through her body, find the dark tension and fear, and turn it to light.

He tucked her smaller hands into his large ones. "Feel the power coursing through your sigils."

The buzzing pain filled her like a river overflowing its banks.

"You are stronger than he is. He can't hurt you. Not anymore."

Denan was right. Larkin had all the power here, and Garrot would do best to remember it. Five deep breaths, and the fear had abated enough for her to leave the safety of Denan's body. To face the man who had taken so much from her.

He would take no more.

"I'm ready."

Holding her hand tight, Denan shifted back to his place. Larkin forced herself to meet Garrot's gaze. And this time, he was the one to look away. A tiny victory. Yet it expanded in Larkin's breast, forcing her back to straighten and her jaw to tilt up.

She surveyed the rest of the druids. The robes and belt made it obvious that of the three hundred men present, all were Black Druids. The ruling class of the druids. The warriors. The men who knew the secrets of the Forbidden Forest and refused to tell their people, instead letting them believe some insatiable beast called their daughters into the forest to their deaths.

They stopped a dozen steps before the dais.

For a long moment, the groups stared like two armies sizing each other up. It was as if the ghosts of the dead pipers swirled about the druids, crying for justice. But just as strong was the grief of the druids, the fathers and brothers of generations of girls who'd been stolen from their homes.

Garrot looked to their king. "We will not come a step further until your music has ceased, Piper King." His voice was low, but it carried. A voice that had remained gentle even as he'd bound Larkin's chained hands to the crucible.

Every one of the druids was probably wearing a dampener gifted them by the wraiths. The music could not control them, only influence them. Garrot would be far better served by fearing the enchantresses and their warrior magic than the pipers' music.

Frowning, King Netrish motioned to the band, who stopped playing. The comforting magic faded, leaving only fear and anger sharp enough to cut.

It was into this sharpness that Larkin's little sister stepped down the stairs of one of the side branches. At five, Sela's strawberry blonde puff of hair framed her face like a halo. With her emerald eyes and willowy build, she was a beautiful girl. But her bearing was not that of a child, but a woman grown. A woman with all the power of the White Tree at her beck and call.

Not yet, Larkin wanted to scream at her.

Larkin tugged Denan's hand to get his attention and tipped her head toward her sister. His mouth tightened.

Sela stepped through Alorica and Tam, who were too busy watching the crowd to notice until the Alamantians parted reverently for Sela—as they had never for Larkin. For not only was Sela the voice of the White Tree, she had accomplished what Larkin could not: she had broken the curse. At least in part.

Enchantresses casually repositioned themselves to protect the girl if the druids made any aggressive moves. Hurrying to catch up, Alorica bent down and whispered something to Sela, but the girl ignored the woman and kept marching. Alorica shot Larkin a look—should she stop Sela?

By then it was too late.

Iniya caught sight of Sela and rolled her eyes, her head in her hands, as if she couldn't quite believe she had such idiots for granddaughters.

Sela stepped directly into the path of Garrot and his Black Druids, her hands folded behind her back, her expression exuding a serenity Larkin could only hope for. "Garrot of the Black Druids, the White Tree is most eager to see what kind of man you are."

Alorica and Tam shifted close enough to snatch her out of harm's way in an instant.

Garrot's brow furrowed as he studied the little girl in confusion. "Sela?" He glared at the king. "What is the meaning of this?" Judging from the tone of his voice, he was clearly offended that a child had been sent to greet him.

Larkin released Denan's hand in case a fight broke out.

"She is the Arbor in training," King Netrish said. "And she has found ways to communicate with the White Tree no one has ever managed before."

All the Alamantians present were strung tight—each would fight to the death to protect Sela. Larkin would fight at their head. Denan's hand twitched toward the sword missing from his waist. Enchantress sigils flickered, the light catching on the jewels of their gowns and throwing prisms across the crowd.

The druids shifted uneasily, their gazes flitting to the enchantresses surrounding them. As if they'd just realized that the women wearing a king's ransom of jewels and fine gowns could kill them where they stood.

Sela pulled up the sleeves of her simple green dress, revealing the sigils curling prettily up and down her arms. "Though I appear as a child, my mind bears five centuries of memories and knowledge."

Knowledge a child shouldn't have.

Garrot blinked in surprise.

"It is because of Sela that the curse was lifted from the women of our kingdoms, Master Druid," Mytin said.

"There are refreshments." King Netrish gestured to the tables in an obvious attempt to diffuse the tension. "The band could perform a song if—"

Garrot held out his hand. "We came here for the embedding ceremony. Not a party."

King Netrish stiffened in affront. "As you wish."

Turning her back to the druids, Sela lifted her hem, climbed the dais steps, and took her place beside Mytin. Larkin hadn't liked this arrangement; she wanted Sela with her and Denan. But Sela was technically an Arbor, so Larkin had been overruled. She took comfort in the dozen enchantresses—Alorica and Tam among them—at the base of the steps who could flare their shields if the druids tried rushing the font.

Netrish nodded for Mytin to begin.

"The White Tree chooses who will receive their thorns," Mytin said by rote, as if he'd given this speech hundreds of times. He probably had. "If the thorns take root and become a sigil, the magic will grow as they do. But you should be aware that each sigil is its own sentient being. You will have to train them, as you would a child, communicating with them using the music played from instruments made of the White Tree."

"The enchantresses don't use music," Garrot pointed out.

"Enchantress magic is warrior magic," Aaryn said. "We have no need of pipes or flutes in order to flare our swords and shields."

Garrot glanced at Larkin again before quickly looking away. Was it possible he was afraid of her? The thought was heady enough to smother her fear, leaving only righteous fury in its wake.

Mytin stepped back and dipped a chalice into the font. "Only the Arbors, royalty, and an initiate seeking their thorns may step onto the dais."

The king shifted to the side, leaving the way up clear.

The Arbor held out the dripping cup. "Who will go first?"

Garrot didn't even glance at the men around him before climbing the steps. Iniya shot him a hateful glare—she despised Garrot even more than she despised everyone else. In this hatred, Larkin and her grandmother were one.

As he drew even with Larkin, her hackles rose. She was glad Denan stood between her and Garrot. If he wasn't, she would have killed the druid where he stood. As it was, Denan took her hand; she wasn't sure if it was to show support or to pin her sword hand in his. Maybe both.

Garrot took the cup, peering suspiciously into the liquid. "Now what?"

"You drink," Mytin said. "Then push your palm into the conduit thorn." The thorn was as thick as her wrist at the base and culminated in a wickedly sharp, hollow point.

The whole ceremony was somewhat different from when Larkin had received her thorns—Sela's doing. Apparently, with the breaking of the curse, some of the old ways were coming back.

Garrot tipped up the chalice and drained it in a couple enormous swallows. Gaze hungry, he pressed his hand into the conduit thorn and gasped. His blood rolled through the font like angry thunderheads.

"Mm." Sela's eyes danced beneath closed lids. "There is darkness within you, Master Druid. Darkness battling with the light. It is too soon to see which shall win." She opened those eyes, which shone with preternatural light. "The White Tree will give you no thorns."

Larkin let out a breath in relief. Nothing good could come of a man like Garrot having more power than he already did.

Garrot pressed his thumb into the bleeding wound and glared down at Sela. "I am the Master Druid."

She tipped her head to the side. "And Master you shall remain, though you will have no magic."

He took a step toward her. Denan let go of Larkin's hand, and she flared her sigils. If Garrot took another step toward her sister, he would die, treaty or no.

Sela's sigils pulsed white, casting a brilliant glow. "Spill blood within this tree, and every single Idelmarchian will die where they stand."

Larkin waited for Garrot to make a move. From the crowd came the gentle tinkling of jewels as the enchantresses moved into a fighting stance. This was the moment she had been dreading, the moment when Garrot finally revealed how selfish he really was.

But something shifted in his hard expression. Something like regret. "I will, of course, acquiesce to the White Tree."

Larkin didn't relax—surely this was a trick. But Garrot stepped to the side and motioned for the next man to take his place before the conduit thorn. Mytin motioned for Garrot to step down. He shook his head, clearly refusing to go. For a tense moment, no one knew what to do.

"Let him stay," Sela said without taking her gaze off the druid.

Denan shot Larkin a baffled look. Maybe the battle they had been anticipating, planning for months, wasn't going to come to pass. Larkin released her hold on her magic. For the first time since the druids appeared, she allowed herself to sink back on her heels.

A sudden warm wetness splattered against her right side and clouded her vision. She blinked, rubbing her eye to clear it. Her fingertips came away red with blood.

That's when the screaming began.

CHAPTER 4

LONG LIVE THE KING

To her right, King Netrish stumbled. A bolt shaft stuck out of his chest, blood quickly spreading. Larkin reached for him. Pain flared in her right forearm. Another bolt appeared in the king's chest. He staggered back.

"Larkin, shield!" Sword out, Denan turned to face Garrot, who held up his empty hands.

Flaring her shield, Aaryn stepped before the king and Sela.

Her body sluggish with disbelief, Larkin mirrored Aaryn's movements, her shield lifted to protect from above. Mytin dropped beside the king and pressed his hands against the wound. Tam bounded up the steps and stood before Sela with his weapons drawn. Gendrin rushed to his father's side and took the man's other hand in his.

Aaryn called out commands to her enchantresses. With a precision born of weeks of drilling, they snapped into position. Alorica and two dozen enchantresses spread their shields over and around the font, effectively locking Larkin and the others inside a nearly impenetrable barrier. Other enchantresses created a shield wall and trapped the druids in a long column. One of the sentinels tossed Iniya over his shoulder and carried her to safety toward one of the upward branches, where ropes were waiting to take her down to the boats.

The Black Druids bunched together, looks of defiance on their faces.

Denan gestured to the White Tree Sentinels standing guard at the six sets of stairs leading up into the boughs. "Find who did this!"

They raced up the steps.

King Netrish made a gurgling, gasping sound. The horror in his eyes... Larkin had seen it many times—the look on the face of a man who knew he was about to die. Gendrin gripped his shoulder and hand, murmuring reassurances.

"Magalia!" Mytin called for the healer.

There was nothing the healer could do, not for a man with an arrow in each lung. The king was as good as dead. *Light, what will this do to his family?*

"We are unarmed!" Garrot shouted from behind her.

Larkin rounded on him. "You did this." He had orchestrated this attack on their king. She should never have allowed this monster into the city. Never allowed him the chance to hurt her or anyone else she loved ever again.

She happily stepped into her role as a warrior—a role that fit her far better than that of a princess. She flared her sword and swung horizontally toward his neck.

"Don't!" Denan cried at the same time Sela said, "Larkin, no!"

Garrot threw himself back. Her sword cut through his cravat. It gaped open, revealing black, forked lines crawling up his neck—the mulgar blight he'd earned by his own foolishness. He ran down the steps, but Alorica whipped her sword toward him in warning.

Denan grabbed Larkin's shoulder. "Stop!"

Queen Jaslin pounded on the shields around the dais and begged to be let in.

Garrot scrambled back, his gaze searching for escape. There was none. He bared his teeth and faced Larkin. "I did not do this."

A lie. Larkin jerked out of Denan's grasp and put her shield between them, flaring it so it touched Alorica and another enchantress's shields, effectively locking Larkin and the two enchantresses inside with Garrot. When he made no move to defend himself, she hesitated. Light rippled past her and stuck to Garrot's skin before melting away.

What had just happened?

"Larkin," Denan shouted.

Garrot gestured to the panic around them. "Is this some elaborate ploy to justify murdering me? Murdering your own people? Why? Vengeance? To keep us from magic?"

The Idelmarchians were not her people—not after they'd turned their backs on her. Her people were the Alamantians. "You think *we* did this?"

His cold blue eyes drilled into hers. "You and your husband are the ones who stand to benefit from the king's death."

Garrot was evil incarnate. Just like the wraiths he'd served, every word that left his mouth was poison. If he had his way, he would turn every piper against her. She thrust, but her sword did not sink into his guts. Instead, it glanced off. A faint light rippled across his skin.

Larkin stared. What kind of enchantment was this?

Farther back, some of the druids rushed the enchantresses blocking the only exit. Their shields sent out a pulse of light, which threw a dozen druids to the ground. They came up, rabid fear etched on their faces.

Weapons or no, the druids were about to attack. It would be a bloodbath.

"You will stop!" Sela roared, and somehow her voice vibrated with power.

Her sigils flared streamers of light, the details of her face lost in its powerful gleam. Liquid, iridescent gold shimmered across everyone's skin before going transparent. Just as had happened to Garrot. Somehow, her sister had saved Garrot. Spared him from paying for his crimes.

"Sela," Larkin hissed furiously.

Ignoring Larkin, Sela held up a bare arm. Before Tam could stop her, she raked a small knife down its length. Larkin made a cry of alarm, released her shield, and stepped toward her sister.

But the blood that should have been there... wasn't. Not even a scratch. Larkin stared, not understanding.

"I have armored you all," Sela said. "You can't hurt each other now even if you tried. You will all return to your home-trees. The embedding ceremonies will continue in small groups."

If Sela had the ability to protect everyone, why hadn't she just done that in the first place?

In the silence that followed, Larkin became aware of Netrish's rattled breathing. Of his wife pounding on the shield and sobbing her husband's name. Of Gendrin's low murmurs to his father. Of Aaryn calling out to her enchantresses to stay calm.

When no one moved to obey her, Sela's eyes narrowed into a fierce glare. "Idelmarchians, you may go first," she said in a deathly quiet voice.

The druids hesitated.

"Go," Garrot said.

The enchantresses slowly parted. Eyes still wary, the druids passed between them and then hurried down the winding stairs.

Garrot's sharp gaze bored into Larkin. "We did not come all this way to be tricked and murdered."

It took every bit of self-control Larkin had to lower her shield.

Denan came to stand beside her. "No one tricked you."

"If we wanted to keep you from the magic," Larkin said through gritted teeth, "we would have never let you into the city. If we needed an excuse to slaughter you, we would have done it already."

"You just tried to kill me!" Garrot cried.

"If I thought it would work, I'd try again." She meant every word.

"Larkin," Denan breathed, clearly aghast.

Sela marched over, Tam in front of her. "Go now, Master Druid. Or I'll drop your armor and let my sister do whatever she wants with you."

Larkin glared at the druid.

Garrot paled and backed down the steps, pausing just out of reach from Alorica's sword. She ground her teeth, clearly not wanting to let him go any more than Larkin had.

"Alorica," Sela said. "All of you, release your shields."

"Now I'm taking orders from children," Alorica grumbled, but she released her magic and stepped aside.

The other enchantresses did the same. Queen Jaslin rushed onto the dais, tripped on the last step, and crawled through her husband's blood to take his hand from Mytin. Larkin's father-in-law stumbled back from the carnage, seemed to realize there was nothing he could do, and came down the steps, which left the top of the dais to Netrish and his family.

Casting a final parting glance over his shoulder at Larkin, Garrot stepped past Alorica, who let him go, and hurried after his men.

Aaryn trotted past them. "I'll make sure the druids return safely to the Enchanter Academy." Motioning for her enchantresses to fall in behind her, she followed half a dozen steps behind Garrot.

Standing on the second to last step, Larkin itched to follow him and settle this once and for all. "We can't let him go. Not after what he did to Netrish."

Sela, Mytin, Tam, and Denan gathered around her. At Larkin's back, Alorica continued watching the crowd.

"The White Tree saw into Garrot's mind," Sela said. "He didn't plot the attack on our king."

Larkin rounded on her sister. "Having the White Tree whisper in your head doesn't change the fact that you're a child! Setting a trap in a crowd is exactly Garrot's style."

It was how he'd captured her, after all.

Tears sprang into Sela's eyes, and she turned away. Tam shot Larkin a reproachful look.

"Larkin," Mytin chided.

Larkin instantly regretted her harsh words, but she was too angry to apologize.

"Who then?" Denan asked.

Sela glanced into the boughs, in the direction the arrow had come from. "I don't know."

Larkin threw out her hands in frustration. "Who else would it be?"

There was censure in Denan's eyes. "If Garrot did this, he'll pay for it. But we don't know that yet."

Larkin had summarily been overruled. Again. Anger buzzed through her. She needed someone or something to lash out at. She rounded on Tam. "How was that protecting her?"

"How was I supposed to know she'd try to cut herself?" Tam cried.

He had a point. "She stepped right between you and Alorica!"

Tam threw his hands in the air. "I wasn't watching for danger *from* her!"

"Are we going to turn on each other now?" Denan rubbed his eyes in exasperation or exhaustion or both.

A beat of guilt tore through Larkin. "Sorry," she mumbled.

His trousers and sleeves wet with blood, Mytin crouched before Sela. "Are you all right?"

"Of course," she said, as if she hadn't just witnessed a man take two arrows to the chest *and* single-handedly stopped a massacre.

A sentinel jogged toward them, stopping just short of the dais steps. "We didn't find anything, my prince. We're going to make a second sweep."

Denan nodded. "Tam, make sure they search everywhere. Take Alorica with you."

"What about Sela?" Alorica asked.

Denan motioned to Sela. "Thanks to her shield, we don't need you."

Why didn't Sela just shield us all from the start? Then we could have avoided all this.

Tam seemed about to argue, then glanced at Larkin. Muttering about obstinate women, he stepped down by Alorica, and the two left together.

Carrying her bag, Magalia finally managed to push through the last of the crowd. She took the steps two at a time and shouldered the king's grieving son out of the way. She retrieved a pair of scissors and cut the king's fine tunic down the center, revealing the black bolts piercing a canvas of blood and magic.

Denan crossed to the other side of the dais, the others trailing behind. "What do you need?" he asked Magalia.

Magalia sat back on her haunches, her head bowed. "I'm sorry, my king. The arrows are buried to the haft in your lungs—if I remove them, you'll only bleed out faster."

"No," Jaslin begged. "No, please."

Larkin felt a swell of pity for Jaslin, who believed that if the king fought, if he wanted to live badly enough, that he could survive this. That he could bargain or fight or steal his way out from under death's cold grip. But there was no running from death. Not once it had you in its sights.

Death was blind to strength and deaf to pleas for mercy.

The king knew this too. He'd commanded the armies before Denan. He'd seen strong, hale men cut down in moments. Men who fought death with every bit of their considerable strength. Netrish brushed his fingers down his wife's face, murmuring something too softly for Larkin to hear.

Then the king's gaze shifted to Denan. "Are you really so eager to be king?"

Denan's brow shot up. "You think I did this?"

"Father—" Gendrin began.

Netrish coughed, blood spewing onto his wife's pale blue dress. His lips and teeth were painted a garish red. "Garrot was right. You're the only person who benefits from my death."

"You can't believe Garrot," Larkin said, aghast. "If anything, he plotted this with the wraiths!"

"I told you—" Sela began.

The king's sigils flared brighter, so bright Larkin raised her hand to shield her eyes. And then all that light was suddenly gone. King Netrish's face was slack, his body unnaturally still. Jaslin threw herself on his chest, sobbing. Gendrin buried his face in his hands.

"The king is dead," Mytin intoned. His gaze shifted to Denan. "Long live the king."

CHAPTER 5

DEADWOOD

Death was an intimate thing. And in this death, Larkin was an interloper. Denan, Magalia, and Mytin seemed to sense it as well. With a shared look, they all moved off the dais completely, leaving the man and his family alone with their grief. Larkin was nearly past the sentinels before she realized Sela wasn't following them. She remained, watching the queen grieve over her king.

"Sela." Larkin held out her hand for her sister.

Sela turned reluctantly away and glided down the remaining steps toward them. She didn't take Larkin's hand. "I will never understand why mankind craves darkness more than light."

Those were not the words of a child. Or even a human. They were the words of an ancient, alien being. Sela, translating the White Tree's thoughts—thoughts that had changed Sela so much that Larkin wasn't sure how much little girl even remained. A different kind of grief threatened to pull Larkin down.

She couldn't let it. Not while there was still an assassin to deal with.

A dozen guards surrounded Larkin, Denan, and Sela the moment they left the dais. The enchantresses flared their shields above and to the sides.

Denan led them to the center of the platform. "Are we still armored?" he asked Sela.

She continued past them without looking back, six guards breaking away to surround her.

Larkin gestured to the slight sheen of gold at the edges of her own body. "You can see it if you know where to look."

He scanned her and then his head came up in understanding. He stepped forward, taking her arm; the armor prevented her from feeling his touch, aside from the warmth of it. He examined a gash on her forearm. "You're hurt."

Only then did Larkin feel the sting of it. He sent one of the guards for Magalia with a tip of his chin. Larkin tried to recall when it had happened. Not with Garrot; he hadn't even bothered to draw a weapon.

Then she remembered. "One of the bolts nicked me."

The guards stepped aside to let Magalia approach them. She glanced at Larkin's arm and reached into her bag.

Denan nodded for one of the enchantresses to shield Larkin. "Sela," Denan called. "Release her shield."

The faint outline of gold around her faded.

Denan's brow drew tight with worry. "You were a target."

She shook her head. "It was when I reached for the king."

He didn't look convinced. "What if the bolts were poisoned?"

Larkin hadn't even considered that. A new kind of fear wormed its way inside her.

Magalia pressed a hand to Larkin's forehead. "Are you feeling sick to your stomach?" Larkin shook her head. Magalia looked somewhat mollified. "If she'd been poisoned, she'd either be sick or dead by now."

"You're sure?" Denan said.

"I can't know all the poisons in the world," Magalia said. "But she should be fine."

Larkin breathed out in relief.

Magalia poured a tincture over the wound, which set it to stinging. Larkin hissed through her teeth and looked away as Magalia pulled apart the edges and peered inside. It started bleeding again. Larkin watched the blood drip on her lovely dress. The dress Denan had given her. Would the stain ever come out?

Magalia reached back into her bag. "It's only skin deep. Needs stitches though." She pulled out a needle and thread.

Stitching would take too long; they had an assassin to find. "Just wrap it for now. Mama can fix me up tonight." As their village's midwife, she'd stitched plenty of women.

Magalia frowned in displeasure but handed Larkin a couple tinctures, showing her which needed to be drunk and which to wash the wound with. She set about bandaging the wound.

One of the sentinels rushed toward them, lowering his voice when he came close enough. "Your grandmother has had some kind of fit, princess."

Iniya might be a bitter old woman, but she'd been a child once—a child who'd witnessed her family's slaughter before being driven out of her own home. Pity welled within Larkin. "Violence triggers them." Violence that made her relive that dreadful day and rendered her nearly catatonic.

"Your Majesty," Magalia said to Denan. "If I may be excused to see to Iniya and round up ice to pack the king's body." Netrish would be laid out on the dais for days so the populace could pay their respects.

It was strange, seeing someone besides his soldiers ask for his permission. But as king, he commanded all of them now.

King.

Light and ancestors, that made Larkin the queen. A queen with absolutely no power of her own. She and Denan had made plans for that to change when he took over the monarchy. Until it did, she was little more than a decoration for Denan's arm and a mother to his children.

Denan motioned for Magalia to be excused.

"Send someone for Harben," Larkin said. Her father would know what to do for Iniya.

Magalia nodded and hustled after the guard.

Denan started toward Sela, who waited for them at the base of the stairs that led into one of the upper boughs.

"What you did," Denan said to Sela, "it was like the magic of old. Like what Larkin did." When she'd created the weir that had saved his life. "Though the weave was different."

"It's called armor," Sela said. "Only magic blades can pierce it—and only when it's weakened."

With magic like that, the wraiths wouldn't stand a chance. "Why didn't you tell us about it before?" Larkin asked. "We could have used it at the outset and avoided all this." *King Netrish would still be alive.*

Sela watched her as if debating what to say. Finally, she sighed. "Come with me." She started up the stairs.

Larkin made to follow her, but Denan stepped in front of her. "Go back to our hometree with the guards."

Her brow furrowed. "What? Why? I'm better prepared for an assassin than you." To prove her point, she flared her shield.

He stared at the bloody bandage wrapping her arm. "The assassin targeted you. Until we find him, you're not safe."

"It was just a stray bolt."

He took hold of Larkin's hand. "Little bird, don't make me order you."

She pulled her hand from his. "Try it."

Larkin glared. He glared back. Neither budged.

Tam crossed the platform and approached warily. "The assassin is gone, Denan." He held out a rope and pulley. "This was all we found."

We failed, Larkin thought.

Denan turned the rope over in his hands. "He's in the city."

Mouth in a grim line, Tam nodded.

The White Tree was the safest place in the city now. Larkin shot him a look that dared him to try to stop her now and stepped past him with a huff. Grumbling, Denan started after her, Tam following.

Larkin hurried to catch up to Sela, sliding past the guards to walk beside her sister, who never acknowledged her presence. Not that Larkin blamed her.

"I'm sorry for snapping at you," Larkin said.

Sela nodded but didn't say anything.

Larkin sighed. "You can release the armor now."

Sela still didn't say anything, but a glance back at Denan and Tam confirmed it was gone. They climbed until Larkin's breath came short and her arm throbbed to the beating of her heart. Morning had given way to midday, the heat building like a miasma. Sweat ran down Larkin's back into her dress, which clung to her; it was well and truly ruined.

Halfway up the White Tree's branches, Sela motioned for the guards to wait behind and stepped onto a branch.

Tam mopped his brow. "Where is she going?"

Denan shrugged and stepped after her. Larkin exchanged an exasperated look with Tam before following. From here, they had a clear view of the city. Below, the sun reflected off the lake, making Larkin squint. The hometrees that ringed the White Tree didn't so much as shift on a nonexistent breeze. A distant figure whooped and jumped from a lower bough, slicing into the cool water.

Obviously, word of the king's death hadn't yet spread.

They traveled along the branch until it bowed under their weight. Denan and Tam paused, uncertainly.

"Sela," Larkin asked. "What are you trying to show us?"

After a few more steps, Sela finally paused. "Look down."

Larkin followed her gaze. There was nothing beneath them but more branches and a twenty-plus-story drop.

"Ancestors save us." Denan gazed at the branch itself.

What was he seeing that Larkin wasn't? She bent down. The golden sheen at the edge of the bark was gone. The colors had stopped moving.

The entire branch was dead.

Tam gasped. Denan's nostrils flared, his hands opened and closed. He was a man of action. But what action could he take against this?

Larkin looked between them. "Don't branches die some-times?" She knew the answer before she asked, but she needed to hear a different answer. Needed it desperately.

Denan shook his head.

Sela knelt, resting the flat of her hand against the deadwood. "The old enchantments take more magic than the White Tree has to give."

Denan's brow furrowed. "Are you saying this happened as a result of you armoring everyone?"

"The more magic I use," Sela said, "the faster the White Tree will die."

All this beauty—all this life—would be corrupted. Twisted to death and decay. This is why Sela hadn't used the armor from the outset, but only as a matter of last resort. Larkin covered her mouth in horror.

Sela folded her hands in her lap and bowed her head. "The White Tree gave up so much trying to counter the curse. And now she's old and weak. She can't regenerate as she once could."

Tam eased a little closer. "How much time do we have?"

Sela seemed to look inward. "A year. Maybe less."

A year until the White Tree would be dead. "What about our magic?" It felt selfish to ask, but Larkin couldn't lose her magic. She just couldn't.

Sela lovingly stroked the bark. "Most of our sigils are saplings with their own consciousness. They will live on, as will the magic they've woven. But some—like the Arbor and monarch sigils—are grafts. They will diminish, become mere saplings again."

Which meant Larkin and Denan would no longer be stronger than the others. Larkin rested a hand on one of the branches that spread across her shoulder. After this generation, there would be no more thorns. No more embeddings. The magic that made the Alamant what it was would be gone. Where did that leave them?

Denan stared out over the city. "Will the barrier around the wall hold?"

Sela shook her head.

That barrier was the only thing preventing the mulgars from overrunning the city.

Tam interlocked his fingers behind his neck. "So in a year's time..."

The barrier would die when the tree did.

"Oh, light." Larkin felt like she might pass out.

"Can we fix it?" Denan asked desperately.

"The White Tree will show Larkin how," Sela said.

Larkin didn't want this responsibility. Didn't want the fate of the Alamant on her shoulders. "And if I can't?"

Sela didn't answer.

"We have to strike first," Tam said. "End the curse once and for all."

"How?" Larkin asked.

"We have to kill the wraiths," Tam said.

"They can't be killed," Larkin said.

"The Black Tree can," Sela said.

"And if the Black Tree dies—" Larkin began.

"So do the wraiths," Denan finished for her.

They would have to cross the Forbidden Forest, battle through the mulgar horde, reach the dead city of Valynthia—where the wraiths themselves would be waiting—and then destroy the tree.

Larkin reeled at the impossibility of it. "But aren't sacred trees nearly indestructible?" They were more mineral than wood; they wouldn't burn, and only the dead branches gave before an ax.

"There is a way," Sela said.

If that was true, then they had no choice. They would have to go to the dead city. Larkin cradled her forehead in her hand.

"Ancestors save us," Tam said.

CHAPTER 6

STITCHES

Past the empty space around the White Tree were rings of hometrees, all interconnected by a network of woven branch bridges. Beyond, a tall wall made of evenly spaced trees grew together in curving sheets. By themselves, they weren't much of a defense, but they were encased by an impassable magical barrier.

Beyond that... the Forbidden Forest and the wraiths.

In a boat packed with guards, Larkin shivered despite the oppressive heat. On her left, Sela stared back at the White Tree, her brow furrowed in concentration. On her right, Denan dipped his quill in the inkpot she held and wrote a missive on his lap. Alorica and Tam sat facing them.

"How far is Valynthia?" Alorica asked.

Denan rubbed his forehead, smearing it with ink. "It's not the distance that's the problem."

"It's the thousands and thousands of mulgars plaguing the Black Tree's forest," Tam said.

"It's not just the mulgars," Denan said. "It's a logistical problem. We can't possibly forage enough to provide for an army ten thousand strong. And even if we do use the Idelmarchians' stock animals—"

"And that's if the Idelmarchians join us," Alorica interrupted.

Denan went on as if she hadn't spoken. "There are no roads, so we'd be limited to what our soldiers can carry on their backs, which we can only stretch out to a week at most."

They would have to fight their way through, which would take months. Memories of Larkin's only battle reared in her head. Men and women crying for their mothers or their spouses. How many thousands would they lose on the way? How many grieving families would she have to face?

"What if we went in with a smaller force?" Larkin asked.

Tam and Denan exchanged heavy looks. "It's been tried before," Denan said. "None have ever made it back."

Silence rained down at the gravity of what they had to do. Of the thousands upon thousands who were going to die in this campaign.

"Then we go in with a larger force," Larkin said. It was the only choice.

"I will go with you," Sela said.

They all looked at her aghast.

"Absolutely not," Larkin said.

Sela locked eyes with Denan. "When the time comes, you'll need me."

He didn't seem to know what to say to that. Larkin didn't care what anyone had to say. Her sister wasn't going anywhere.

The boat slowed as it approached Larkin and Denan's hometree, which contained five chambers—large clusters of bedrooms with an attached bathing room. The chambers were made of a frame—some square, others round. The round ones reminded her of upside-down flowers. At the top center of each frame was a medallion, not unlike the one Larkin wore around her neck. These medallions created a magical pane, the density of which could be adjusted by a twist of the hand.

Presently, all but the doorpanes were opaque, which meant they were impassable by even a breeze. The hometree had been locked down.

Light, it's going to be hot inside.

West waited at the dock that spread out from the hometree's roots. He'd trimmed down his once-bushy sideburns. The wind made his glorious mustache snap like a flag. The three fingers on the outside of his right hand were gone, taken by the Wraith King. Unable to grip a sword with that hand, he'd been practicing with his left.

He still wasn't good enough to hold his own in a fight, but being a soldier was the only thing he knew. Larkin owed him her life, and he was one of the few people she trusted implicitly. So despite Denan and Tam's disapproval, she'd named West one of her personal guards—a job he took just as seriously as his previous job as her jailer.

"The tree has been thoroughly searched, my king," West called out to them.

King. Word had spread of Netrish's death. The guards maneuvered the boat into the dock. Denan sent his pages off with the missives.

West's arched mustache covered his lips, but she could still tell he was frowning at the blood on Larkin's cream dress. "My queen, I should have been there."

Queen. Larkin's guts twisted at the title. "You couldn't have done anything." He was a night guard. He should be sleeping.

Denan's jaw clenched hard enough to break teeth. "An attempt was made on Larkin's life. I want security doubled."

"It was just an errant bolt," Larkin protested.

"I'm not taking any chances," Denan said.

The soldiers tied up the boat. Tam paired them up, and they headed to their destinations at a jog. By the time they were all in place, there would be thirty-four guards in their tree. The thought of all those people watching and judging her behind their implacable masks made her uneasy.

Alorica handed Sela up to West. Sela started up the dock without waiting for Larkin, a pair of guards on her heels. She was obviously still angry. Denan held out a hand and hauled Larkin up. Tam and Alorica bent their heads together, murmuring something too soft for Larkin to make out.

Denan searched the faces around him until he found their butler, Unger, coming down the dock toward them. He was a tall, thin man with hollow cheeks and a sickly pallor. "See Cook Viscott prepares food and hot water," Denan said. "Bring it to the common room."

Unger bowed. "Yes, sire." He directed another pair of servants as he headed for the cooking platform.

Tam nodded to Alorica and hopped back into a small boat. "We've decided to move in. I'm going to round up a couple friends to help bring our things here."

Alorica's expression dared them to argue.

Denan seemed about to do just that—Tam and Alorica had their own hometree—but then he thought better of it and shot Larkin a questioning glance. She couldn't deny that having Tam around would make them both safer. And at this point, what was two more people? At least these two people cared about her.

She shrugged. "I suppose we have plenty of room."

Denan wagged his finger at Tam. "All right, but no waking me up for your late-night mischief."

Tam gave a playful scoff. "Late-night mischief is always better with friends."

Denan rolled his eyes. "We're not in the academy anymore."

"Old man!" Tam shot back.

Denan was trying hard not to smile—it was part of their game. Whoever smiled first lost.

"We're going to need a raise." Tam shot Larkin his customary wink. Gratitude swelled for this friend of Denan's who'd become just as dear to her. And not just for his protection, but for his bright burst of levity in the dark.

Alorica rolled her eyes, but she was clearly trying not to laugh.

West turned to Larkin. "If you don't mind, my queen, I haven't slept yet this morning." West insisted on the night watch. Said that was when he was the most useful.

Larkin liked that he asked her instead of Denan. "Of course."

He bowed and took his leave, heading to his small platform in the higher boughs.

Alorica took the lead as Denan and Larkin headed up the stairs.

Denan dropped his voice so the others couldn't hear. "Larkin, you attacking Garrot, that cannot happen again. You risked everything."

He was right. Shame slammed down on her. "It's just... seeing him again. And I was so sure he killed the king." Part of her still was, no matter what Sela said.

"I know. And I'm not angry. But we cannot be the aggressors. We cannot be the reason this alliance fails."

"I'm sorry." She meant it.

He nodded.

Where the trunk met the boughs was the main platform. The curving roof peaked around an ahlea medallion that created the magical panels. Two guards stood on their side of the doorpane; there was always one enchantress and one enchanter. Both bowed.

"Which chambers would you like us to take?" Alorica asked.

Denan shrugged. "Pick an empty one."

Alorica nodded and set off. Larkin and Denan stepped through the doorpane, a feeling like walking through liquid glass. It was swelteringly hot inside. From the supports hung a chandelier of potted lampents, their soft, sweet scent as soothing as their light. More lampents hung before the supports.

There was a long, rectangular table by the door, comfortable couches and chairs around the fireplace, a game table by the far pane, and a few chests of games, toys, or blankets scattered around the room. Four-month-old baby Brenna wiggled on a blanket, brightly painted wooden toys around her.

Across the room, Sela looked out a transparent pane, the sight of the towering White Tree taking up the view. It also let in a breeze, which licked across Larkin's sweat-damp skin. She sighed in relief.

Sela clasped her hands behind her back, eyes narrowed like some great lady with the weight of their survival on her shoulders. Larkin bit back a sigh. Sela should be on the floor playing with Brenna.

"We need to keep it shut, Sela," Denan said. "There's still an assassin out there."

Larkin wanted to argue, but he was right.

Frowning, Sela closed the pane but didn't move away.

Kit in her hand, Mama stepped into the room and marched toward Larkin. Her eyes caught on the blood splattered on her side and soaking into her hem. Her mouth tightened into a thin line.

"I'm all right, Mama."

Mama set her kit on the dining table and tugged at the bandage knots over her daughter's upper arm. Larkin winced as the bandage stuck to the wound.

"Change Brenna, will you, Denan?" Mama jerked her chin toward the clean swaddling on the chair—clearly what Mama had been intending to do before Unger had her fetch her kit.

Denan shot Larkin a sympathetic glance.

Mama poured water into a shallow basin. "Whose blood is on your face?"

It was on her face? Larkin saw it again. The king's expression. The terror of a man who knew he was dying. His warm blood blinding her. She'd completely forgotten it in the ensuing chaos.

"The king is dead," Denan said. "Killed by an assassin."

"I heard." Mama pulled out a chair at the table, motioned for Larkin to sit, and settled her arm in the hot water. She poured water over the stuck bandage to soften the dried blood.

Denan knelt before Brenna. "Hello, sweet. Are you ready for a change?"

Brenna kicked her feet harder and let out a coo. She startled, as if the sound surprised her. Denan chuckled softly and unwrapped her.

"Who else was hurt?" Mama mixed up a pain powder in a cup.

Larkin drank the bitter draft, which left her nauseous. She stared blankly at the twisting grain of the wood beneath her hand. "No one. Thanks to Sela." She quickly told Mama about the new magic Sela had displayed, as well as the cost. Denan spoke softly to a fussing Brenna; she didn't much like being undressed or the cool water. Mama poured more water over Larkin's wound and shot worried looks Sela's way.

Shushing Brenna, Denan wrapped her in clean swaddling. Larkin watched her husband with her baby sister, a tenderness swelling within her. He'd always been so sweet with the little ones. He would be a wonderful father.

If he didn't fall to shadow first.

Larkin wouldn't let that happen. She would take the fight to Valynthia and destroy the Black Tree, which would free her husband of the blight and secure her family's safety.

"Garrot is behind this." Mama pulled things out of her kit. "Mark me."

"It was the wraiths," Sela said without turning from the opaque window, "working through druids or pipers. I don't yet know which."

Larkin knew from his expression what her husband was thinking. "If that's true, then one of our own people could have murdered the king." *We may have a traitor in our midst.*

"And no clues as to who he or she is." Denan washed his hands, lifted Brenna onto his shoulder, and stood. Halfway up, he winced. A beat later, the pain was gone from his face.

It was too late; Larkin noticed. "Denan?"

He avoided her gaze and rubbed Brenna's back to settle her fussing. "It's all right. Lots of men have injuries that never fully heal."

But most of those injuries didn't carry the risk of turning them into a monster. Larkin fiddled nervously with her amulet.

Pouring more water, Mama tugged carefully at the bandaging, which made the ache spread up Larkin's neck and down her fingertips. The stained cloth finally came away, fresh blood running in trickles and drips into the basin. It swirled like dancing ribbons that dissipated, leaving the water pink.

The pain made Larkin remember Magalia's tinctures. Larkin retrieved them from her pocket, drank one, and handed the other to Mama. "Magalia sent these."

She tugged off the cork and sniffed. "I'll have to ask her for the recipe." Thumbs planted on either edge of the wound, Mama pulled it apart and poured the tincture. Larkin dug her fingers into the table to keep from jerking away.

"Twelve stitches or so should do it," Mama proclaimed.

Unger came in with a tray filled with the stiff, glossy leaves of the hometree, which the pipers used for everything from plates to shrouds for the dead. They even pulped the fibers to make clothes.

Taking a leaf, Denan loaded it with flat nala bread, smoked fish, and crunchy lake greens. He drizzled a tangy cream sauce and took a bite. Larkin's mouth watered, but there wasn't any point in eating until Mama had finished.

Unger set about pouring them each a glass of rainwater.

Brenna on his lap, Denan ate hungrily—neither he nor Larkin had bothered with the lunch waiting for them after the ceremony. He looked over his shoulder at Sela. "Cook Viscott made you some sugared berries."

Sela didn't seem to hear him. With such plentiful food, Larkin and Mama had put on weight since coming to the Alamant, while Sela remained painfully thin.

"Want me to get her to eat?" Denan asked Mama.

Mama didn't trust men; her cruel father and abusive husband had made sure of that. But Denan had proven himself worthy of her regard in a thousand tiny ways. From his gentleness and patience with her children to his adoration of her daughter.

So it meant a lot to Larkin when Mama didn't hesitate to smile her thanks at Denan.

But Unger stepped up. "Let me, my lady. Our king has so much he needs to do."

Mama reluctantly nodded. Unger took the baby, crouched before Sela, and murmured a few words. In a moment, he had her seated at the table, dutifully eating. He brought Denan paper and a quill. Her husband set about writing up calculations of supplies a sizable army would need.

"Thank you, Unger," Mama said. "I don't know what we'd do without you."

Glowing with the praise, the man gave a little bow. Mama searched through her kit until she came up with a numbing salve, which she smeared on the wound. Then she threaded a bone needle with catgut. Watching her, Larkin's stomach knotted.

"I can play the pain away for Her Majesty while Lady Pennice stitches," Unger offered.

At first, Larkin's overwrought brain couldn't fathom who Her Majesty was. Then she realized he meant her. "I—Thank you, Unger."

Setting Brenna down on her blanket, Unger took out his strange pipe—curved like a ram's horn—and played, his song high and piercing. It carried through Larkin, finding an ancient part of herself. She imagined her soul was a shooting star caught up in a body. And when she laid that body down again, her soul would continue its journey across the never-ending night sky.

The music stopped. Larkin waited for it to pick up again. Waited for the sound to bear her up and away. But it did not. Instead, she came back to herself. Feeling dizzy, she looked down to see twelve neat stitches, black against the paleness of her skin.

Another scar. "At least that means less freckles." She laughed at her own joke, not caring that no one else did. Her arm burned and throbbed—but the pain was a distant thing. Rainbows flared from every source of light, and her head felt floaty and heavy at once. "I think the medicine is working."

Denan took the tincture she'd drunk and sniffed it, a single eyebrow rising in amusement. "Yes, I think it is."

Mama picked up Brenna. "How's my baby? Have you been a good girl while I patched up your sister?" Brenna smiled a huge, gummy smile and cooed. "That's right. Brenna is Mama's good baby."

Brenna nuzzled Mama's neck and grinned at Larkin. Ancestors, babies were such a light in the dark. Sela finished her food and left without a word. Mama sadly watched her go. Unger cleared away the dirty dishes and left.

Fully armored, Tam stepped into the room and set down a large chest. "Denan, the chief constable is here, as you requested." He bent down to eye level with Brenna and tickled her feet. She rewarded him with a startled laugh.

Larkin sniffed. "She's such a sweet, precious thing. I love her so much."

Tam shot Denan a baffled look. Denan mimed drinking.

"I'm not drunk!" She tried hard not to slur. Gah, she sounded like her useless father. "It's the medicine." Medicine that obviously had White Tree sap inside. It promoted healing and reduced pain, but there wasn't a lot of it to go around. It was usually reserved for soldiers in the forest.

Denan grabbed the paper full of calculations. "We're going to need to start rationing the populace and have quotas for each family to produce so many pounds of dried fish, fruit, and nuts. Whatever grains we can get too."

"Let the quartermaster deal with that," Tam said.

Groaning tiredly, Denan pushed to his feet. "Let me get my armor."

Tam started after him. "I'll help milady with her straps."

Denan punched Tam's arm. Always teasing each other.

"Where are you going?" Larkin asked.

"To fetch my armor and start preparations for the campaign," Denan said patiently.

Her fingers tightened around the armrests. "What if the assassin's after you?"

"They didn't target me before," he said gently.

"Doesn't mean they won't," she said. "Especially now that you're king."

"I'll see some of your enchantresses shield me," he said.

"I'm coming with you." She tried to stand, but her legs weren't working right.

"No you aren't," Mama said.

Denan placed a firm hand on her shoulder. "When you're up to it."

He was right, curse him. She collapsed in the chair. "Fine. I didn't want to go anyway."

Tam nudged Denan with his shoulder. "Come on, man."

The two of them headed to Denan and Larkin's chambers. Mama watched Tam go with narrowed eyes. She might trust Denan, but that trust hadn't extended to his personal guard yet.

"He's a good man," Larkin said.

"Your father was a good man too. For the first few years."

At the mention of her father, Larkin rubbed her tired eyes. He'd been writing her letters, asking to meet Brenna and see Sela. Mama refused. Larkin didn't blame her. As far as she was concerned, Harben had lost the rights to his children when he'd abandoned them for his new wife.

And yet he'd helped Larkin when she'd asked for it—at great risk to himself. It didn't make what he'd done right, but it did make her feelings more conflicted.

"Hold her while I wash her swaddling." Mama set Brenna in her arms and left.

Brenna was all simple smiles, baby coos and giggles, and the sweet smell of new life. She didn't worry about the mulgars and wraiths lurking in the Forbidden Forest. Didn't worry about curses or bargains or life and death. All she worried about was warm milk and cuddles and clean clothes.

Larkin stroked her back and blew bubbles against her feet. She took a bite of her food and suddenly realized how hungry she was. Her favorite part was the waternips. They were the size of grapes, the flesh as white as new snow. The flavor was juicy and mild, with a bit of heat at the end. She was nearly done when Tam and Denan stepped back into the room.

Instead of his embellished gold armor, Denan wore the dull set, riddled with pounded-out dents and deep scratches. Both were family heirlooms; both had caged dozens of living heartbeats. But this armor had felt those heartbeats still.

The forest take her, Larkin just wanted him to be safe. Why couldn't they just be safe?

Denan knelt to press a kiss to her forehead and another to Brenna's cheek and left with Tam.

Larkin stared after him long after he'd left. She'd always felt safe in the Alamant. But now, little bits of danger were worming inside her safehold. And she had a sinking sense that it was all just beginning.

CHAPTER

RUINS

*L*arkin was in the White Tree of centuries ago. She knew this vision. She'd had it a hundred times before. It was the night the curse came into being. The night the mulgars had been born.

All around her, creatures made of torn shadows ripped apart the barriers to reach the people inside. To tear down their throats and turn them into monsters. The mulgars, with their solid black eyes and forked lines marring their skin, turned on each other.

Larkin didn't watch. She'd seen enough death. She didn't want to be here. She wanted rest. Peace. Maybe she wasn't meant to have such things.

Instead, Larkin went to Eiryss, who stood on the dais around the font. She wore her wedding dress, her gold-and-silver hair spinning about her as she wove the magic with her bare hands.

This was Larkin's ancestor, though Larkin could find no part of herself in the woman. Fighting beside her was Larkin and Denan's shared ancestor of centuries ago. King Dray had sharp features and dark skin and hair.

She watched Dray collapse. Watched him go to the font, beg the White Tree to help him. Watched as he died, all his sigils alight. Between Eiryss's and his palms, light flared. Blood ran between their entwined fingers.

"Use my light," he gasped. "Drive out the wraiths." His eyes rolled up, and he went perfectly still. He was dead.

The queen panted, looking at the bloody thing in her hand in horror—an amulet that looked like an ahlea.

"Little bird, let me in."

Larkin blinked awake to the darkness of deep night. Her hand gripped her amulet, blood settling into the creases of her palms. She released it, the branch slipping from her skin, and set it on her nightstand.

"I don't need visions," she muttered, aware she was speaking to an inanimate object. "I need sleep."

She sat up. Her damp nightdress clung to her; without a breeze, the room was stifling. Across her bedroom, the doorpane rippled like a stone tossed into still water.

Careful not to move her injured arm, she tapped the potted lampent on her nightstand, which sent bright colors racing along the edges of the petals, casting a faint light. Her room came into focus. Like almost all chambers, it had a large bed in the center with an armoire across from it and a pair of chests at the foot. On the far side of the bed were two doorways—one that led to a bathing room and the other to a nursery, which Larkin was eager to keep empty for a few years at least. A dining table took up the space by the main door.

Larkin slipped out of bed and stubbed her toe on one of the dining chairs. Muttering curses, she twisted open the doorpane. West and Maylah stood on the other side, the corridor keeping the rain off them. Both guards kept their eyes respectfully averted.

Denan stepped inside. Water trailed down his face. His hair was plastered to his head—it had grown since their wedding, so it covered his forehead. It made him look younger, less severe.

"Sorry I woke you," he whispered.

"I'm glad you did." She sealed the doorpane with a twist of her wrist.

He studied her, his gaze lingering on her blood-stained palm. "The vison with Dray and Eiryss?"

She nodded. "If only we had found that cursed amulet."

He sighed. "The druids scoured the Idelmarch. We searched everywhere we could think of."

She sighed and changed the subject. "You're soaking the floor." When had it started raining?

He slicked his hands down his head and then flicked water at her.

"Hey!" She blinked and wiped her face.

He grinned, tugged off his shirt with a wince of pain, and tapped a lampent on the table. With the medicine still affecting Larkin, pulsing rainbows flared across the room. Everywhere except the angry, puckered scar and the jagged forks of black just below Denan's ribs. His blight mark seemed to suck in light and color.

Even now, the wraiths haunted them.

But she would not let them stay. Not here. Not between them.

She sat on one of the dining chairs; it was too hot to go back to bed. "How did your meetings go?"

"I spent most of my time with the quartermaster, writing decrees for food production. Everyone is going to have to pitch in."

"Any sign of the assassin?"

Denan unbuckled his armor. "The constables are conducting interviews—hoping someone saw something—and making lists of everyone who attended. Chances are, it's an Alamantian. The Idelmarchians were too tightly controlled."

The thought made her sick.

He dropped his trousers. The light reflected off his damp skin; an aura of color danced around him. Soft shadows lingered in the valleys of his body, which highlighted the hard planes of muscle. Light, he was beautiful.

She swallowed hard. "We'll find them. And then we're going to march on Valynthia and cut that cursed tree down."

He stared in the direction of Valynthia, and she knew he was thinking about his blight. About the wraiths. But there was something new there too. Toweling off, he sat beside her.

She rested her chin on his shoulder. "What is it?"

"Just rumors. Whispers, really."

"Tell me."

He shivered. "You're warm." He pulled her into his lap and nuzzled her chest.

Reveling in the cold damp of his skin, she stroked his hair. "Denan?"

He sighed, his breath tickling the tiny hairs on her arm. "Gendrin and I grew up together; he's like a brother to me. His father was at all our tournaments and ceremonies, cheering me on as much as my own parents."

She hadn't realized how long the Denan had known the king. "You're grieving him."

"It's not just him. It's the horrible way he died. Gendrin and Jaslin saw his murder. Jaslin couldn't get to him. They're both devastated and angry and—"

"Surely they don't really believe we had anything to do with it."

"Not Gendrin. Jaslin, though. And the populace... I am the king now, Larkin, and people must always have someone to blame. I have to find Netrish's killer."

Before the populace started to blame him. The assassin posed more than one kind of danger to them.

She held her husband close, drawing every bit as much comfort as she gave. She stroked her fingertips up and down his back and arms and hummed one of the calming songs the pipers played.

Soon, he turned toward her. But now it was a different kind of comfort he sought. His palms skimmed up her sides and pulled her closer still. The tip of his nose trailed along her jaw. He inhaled the scent of her and moaned. "Light, you're perfect."

Something hot and shivery settled in her lower belly, something that grew hotter still as he kissed her neck, his lips so soft against her sensitive skin. Enough of teasing. She wanted his mouth—the taste of him on her tongue.

She tipped his jaw back and kissed him, gentle and slow like the drizzle of honey. He tasted like rainwater and summer nights. She nipped his bottom lip, pulling it back before gently releasing.

His searching fingers found the edge of her nightgown, slowly pulling up. His touch left a burning trail up one pale calf and then curving around her thigh. Higher still. She gasped.

He paused. "Your arm. Maybe..."

She pinned his wrist in place. "I don't need my arm. Not for this."

Pipe music winnowed through the trees like cold, clean water through trailing fingers. It tugged Larkin along, spinning her this way and that beneath the dense canopy of trees. Crisp leaves crunched under her feet. Beams of light speared slantwise

through the high canopy, the brilliant emerald dazzling Larkin's eyes, blinding her.

She spilled out of the trees into a deep meadow, the tall grass swaying gently. The light grew murky, blocked by a dirty, smoky sky. Larkin nearly turned around and went back to the forest, but the music had its hooks in her deeply now.

And it was reeling her in.

In the middle of the meadow, a man sat on a rock. His back was to her, but the breadth of his shoulders, the sheer massiveness of him was achingly familiar.

Talox.

Talox, who had saved her life at far too high a cost.

Talox, who was now a mulgar.

Larkin dug her heels in, her feet sliding in the muck. She grabbed handfuls of meadow grass, but it was soggy, coming apart into a slimy mess in her hands. She clawed at the ground, her fingers leaving deep gouges.

Faster and faster, the music reeled her in until she lay at Talox's feet. He lowered his pipes, then slowly rose to his full height and looked down, down, down at her.

She'd seen him as an ardent before. But she still wasn't prepared. How could she be prepared for solid, beetle-black eyes in Talox's gentle face?

"You can stop this, Larkin."

She panted hard, the mud bitterly cold beneath her body. "Stop what?"

"It's in your blood. In his blood."

If she just held still enough, maybe he wouldn't attack. "What's in my blood?"

Talox's eyes met hers. In an instant, he wasn't Talox, but the Wraith King. Robes like torn shadows and a crown like black, broken glass. The blackness where his face should be sucked her in.

She screamed and clawed, trying to escape. The wraith bent over her, reached toward her. "You're mine."

Larkin woke to a whimper. Her whimper. Denan held her tight. Tears leaked from her eyes onto his chest. Their bed dipped and swayed with the wind. The soft gray of early morning filtered through the branches, sending crisscrossing shadows across the top of the panes that made up the roof.

"Easy, Larkin. It was just a nightmare."

The nightmares came every night. This was the latest she'd managed to sleep in weeks.

Denan squeezed her tighter, his voice gruff with sleep. "Are you awake now?"

She buried her head into his chest and nodded.

"What was it this time?"

She shook her head. She didn't want to talk about it. Didn't want to remember. She wouldn't risk going back to sleep—doubted she could if she tried.

He stroked her hair, and she loved that he didn't pry.

"How do you deal with it all?" she whispered.

"What do you mean?"

"You've sent men into battle—your friends. Watched them die. But you've never let it break you."

He sighed heavily. "I imagine locking my fears and worries in a chest. If that doesn't work, I throw that chest to the bottom of a deep, dark lake. Then I seal them inside with a layer of ice."

She turned in his arms. "Really?"

He pushed up on his elbow. "When I need to deal with them—when I have time to deal with them—I pull them out. If not, they stay put."

"And it works?"

He kissed the side of her face, his hand stroking up her bare side. "It's... one of the things that helps."

She bit her lip to hide her grin. "What's the other thing?"

He kissed her mouth, his hands moving lazily over her skin. "Can't you guess?"

She giggled. "Nope. No guesses."

He grinned. "Well, let me show you."

CHAPTER

MURDERS IN THE NIGHT

L arkin lay tucked against Denan's chest. On a normal day, she would slip out of bed, dress, and pad down to the training platform. She'd been working on her archery skills; she was terrible.

When Denan woke, he'd join her, and they'd spar. Unger would bring them breakfast. Then they'd dive into the lake to cool off and bathe in one of the cordoned-off nooks. They'd try to keep their hands off each other. Most likely fail.

But not this morning. This morning, they would don their armor and plan a war. But for now, she let herself hold and be held by the man she loved.

Denan's bare skin pebbled. She reached down to tug the blankets over him when her gaze caught on his blight. Even as she watched, it moved, the shadows sharpening and digging deep. Denan's breathing abruptly tightened as if he were in pain.

Even here, we're not safe. Maybe we never were.

She pulled the blankets under his chin and sat up. A sharp shout brought her to her feet. Denan was out of the bed in an instant—years of surviving in the Forbidden Forest had honed his instincts. He snatched his tunic from the floor. Larkin reached for her trousers, ignoring the sharp tug in her arm.

"Breech!" a familiar voice shouted.

The sounds of running feet. The tree shivered beneath their steps. *Where are my cursed boots?*

"Healer!" the voice again, this time a wail. "I need a healer!"

Larkin recognized the speaker that time. It was Tam.

Ignoring the sharp twist of her arm, Larkin hauled on her tunic. Denan was already fully dressed. No time for her boots now.

He grabbed his sword and shield from their hooks by the doorpane. "Stay here."

"Healer!" Tam cried again.

Tam, who had saved her life more times than she cared to remember. She would answer his call, no matter the consequences. Larkin shoved past Denan and through the doorpane.

West moved to block her. "Majesties, please go back inside."

"Are my mother and sisters secure?" Larkin demanded.

"As far as I know, Majesty," Maylah said.

"Now please—" West began.

"Lead the way," Denan barked.

West and Maylah jogged through the paneled colonnade toward the guest chambers on the other side of the tree. The colonnade's passageways were all sealed panels. There was no danger from bolts. It irked her that the guards had argued with her and obeyed Denan without question.

Another pair of guards left the guest chambers at a run and headed toward the main bridge. Where were they going?

Larkin reached Tam and Alorica's chambers twenty or so running steps later. A crush of guards jammed the entrance.

"What happened?" Denan asked.

"Two people were injured," a tall enchantress said. "The attacker disappeared. We sent for a healer and are searching the tree."

Attacked who? Tam? Alorica? Both of them? Are they all right? How did someone get in? "Move!" Larkin demanded. They scattered, and she burst into the room.

Tam knelt on the bed, his hands pressed into Alorica's middle. Blood seeped through his fingers, soaked Alorica's nightgown and the sheets beneath her, and puddled on the floorboards. She was unconscious. Tam didn't appear hurt.

Tam's desperate gaze met Larkin's. In a flash, she remembered all he had done for her. All the times he'd made her laugh so she wouldn't fall apart. The times he'd cheerfully followed her into danger on nothing more than her word. She could not let him lose Alorica. Could not watch him bear the burden of his heartsong's death the way Talox had.

"Denan." Larkin pushed him toward the door. "Fetch my mother." She was a lot closer than any healer from the healing tree. "And stay behind to protect my sisters." Mama wouldn't leave them with anyone she didn't trust.

Denan clearly wanted to argue. Instead, he stepped outside. "You two, come with me. West, Maylah, stay here and don't let anyone else in. The rest of you, search for intruders."

The floorboards trembled with their departing steps.

Larkin stepped closer to Alorica. Mama would know what to do. The guards had said someone else was injured. "Are you injured?" she asked Tam.

Tam shook his head, a spasm of guilt shuddering over him. "I was showering. I heard a fight. Her screaming. Unger is hurt." He motioned to the other side of the bed.

Unger! Why hadn't anyone told her? She rounded the bed in time to see Unger fist the sheets with his hand and haul himself up to his knees. A wicked knot bulged from the side of his head.

The attacker must have hurt the two of them and fled when they heard Tam coming. Larkin went to help Unger, but he shoved her so hard she fell on her backside. Only then did she notice the knife in his hand. A bloody knife. Larkin's mind tried to fight it—deny it. But his gaze fixed on Alorica with a predatory focus Larkin knew all too well.

Unger had hurt Alorica. Was trying to hurt her again.

Larkin's weapons automatically filled her hands. Lunging to her feet, she slammed the edge of her shield into Unger's face. Alorica moaned in pain as the bed shifted beneath her. Unger skidded half a dozen feet before coming to a stop before the desk.

Larkin charged after him, her sword cocked behind her shield. But she hesitated to kill the man who had so gently tended her and her family all these months. He was her friend.

He's not a friend. He's an assassin.

But Unger wasn't a threat. Not anymore. Judging by the impossible angle of his head, Larkin's blow had broken his neck. But even with such a grievous injury, his eyes still fixed on her.

She lowered her sword. "Do you know who killed the king?"

"No," Unger said.

West burst into the room. "What's going on?" He hustled up behind her. She blocked him from doing anything to the assassin.

"Why have you done this?" she asked Unger.

Despite the horrible pain he must be in, he made not a sound. And then Larkin noticed that the trickle of blood sliding from the corner of Unger's mouth was not red.

It was black.

West swore.

All the air left Larkin.

This was not Unger. At least not anymore.

"He's a mulgar," West said.

A cut from a wraith blade poisoned people. Turned them into mindless monsters that were little more than puppets for the wraiths. But some retained their cunning. The curse twisted those mulgars into something different, something wicked: ardents.

But all ardents had one thing in common—solid black covering even the whites of their eyes. Yet Unger's were the same pale blue they'd always been. Such a thing wasn't possible... unless... "You're like Maisy."

Larkin still didn't know what Maisy was. She'd been a mulgar once—that had been clear from the tined scars on her body. The girl had always been in the periphery of Larkin's life. Helping Larkin one moment and condemning her the next. Seemingly driven by both the wraiths and her own twisted desires.

What if Maisy wasn't the only one of her kind?

"What are you?" Larkin asked.

Unger coughed, more black blood splattering from his lips. "We're like you, Larkin—children of the Curse Queen." Larkin's ancestor, Eiryss. The woman who was rumored to have inadvertently created the curse, though Larkin had seen visions of her trying her best to prevent it. "We've come to save you."

"Save me?" *This is the wraiths trying to get to me. This... thing stabbed my friend because of me.* "What does saving me have to do with Alorica?"

A peaceful look stole over Unger. "We know the truth, Larkin. Soon, you will too." And then his blue eyes swirled with black.

"You're ours." It was not his voice that said it, but a voice born of shadow and hatred. It was the voice of the Wraith King, Ramass.

West stepped past Larkin. She turned away, but that didn't prevent her from hearing the meaty thwack.

If Unger had been able to hide among them all this time, how many others had? Was it possible another ardent—for lack of a better word—had killed the king? At a sudden cold wetness against her bare feet, she looked down. Black blood seeped around her feet, between her toes. She staggered back, horrified. Would ardent blood affect her like poisoned wraith blood? She waited for the sucking darkness, the rage and despair. But nothing happened.

"Larkin!" Tam shouted.

It was not the first time he had called her name, she realized.

"Guard the door!" Larkin shoved West.

"Not till I search the rooms." West checked the panes.

"Larkin," Tam cried. "You have to help me!"

Alorica was awake now and writhing in pain, fighting to push off Tam's hands, which was causing her to bleed even more. Larkin felt as helpless and cold as when her father had thrown her into the river, knowing full well she couldn't swim. As helpless as when she'd been splayed on the crucible before the dark forest. As helpless as when she'd been locked in the dungeon deep beneath the druids' stronghold.

Where was Mama? She should be here by now. Why hadn't Denan brought her? Larkin didn't know. All she knew was that she was all Tam and Alorica had. Whatever was going on with her family, Denan and the guards would have to take care of it.

She crossed the room in half a dozen strides, knelt on the other side of her friend, and took her pale, clammy hand. Alorica's desperate, pleading eyes locked on Larkin's.

"Hurts," Alorica managed.

It was hard to believe Larkin had ever hated Alorica. They'd been through so much since then. Those first terrifying days after they'd been ripped away from their homes by strange men with stranger magic. The heartache of losing Venna. And then later, Talox.

So Larkin knew Alorica well enough to know it was the panic more than the pain that was affecting her.

"Stop acting like a child," Larkin commanded.

Alorica bared her teeth at Larkin, but her pride kicked in, and she stopped fighting. Larkin didn't have the skills to save Alorica. But maybe she could save her from this pain.

"If I stanch her bleeding, can you enchant her?" Larkin asked Tam.

"No," Alorica snapped. "I won't spend my last moments out of my senses."

"You can't think like that." Tam's voice broke.

Alorica's hard gaze locked on his. "People don't survive gut wounds, Tam."

"Magalia has saved a few," Tam said.

The wound was well below Alorica's belly button. Low enough it might have missed her guts and the gruesome death that would certainly follow.

"Tam, get your pipes. I'll take your place." She batted at his hands.

He pulled back, and she replaced him, pressing the balled-up sheet against the wound. Even as quickly as they had moved, a surge of blood welled up between Larkin's fingers. Alorica's back arched in pain, her hands shoving at Larkin's.

Larkin held fast. "Just hold on, Alorica. Tam's going to enchant you."

"I don't want it," Alorica panted.

Tam threw clothes from the armoire, bloody smears marring the fine fabrics. He stared at the lump of clothing, his hands buried in his curly hair. "Where is it?" He rushed out of sight into the bathing room.

Larkin looked around for West, but he must have finished his search and gone to guard the door.

"Alorica," Larkin said as calmly as she could muster. "The wound is low enough that I think it might have missed your intestines."

"What?" She lifted her head to look at the wound. "No. Not my baby."

Baby? What ba— Larkin's gaze went to her hands. Hands that pressed down on Alorica's womb. Her gaze slid to the place between Alorica's legs. More blood.

Larkin's eyes involuntarily closed against the horror. "Does Tam know?" she whispered.

Alorica shook her head. "I've been sewing a baby gown. I wanted to surprise him with it."

Larkin imagined shoving the knowledge into a chest and slamming the lid like Denan had taught her. When she opened her eyes, her expression was calm. "Don't think about it now."

A sob caught in Alorica's throat. "What should I think about?" she snapped. "Dying?"

"Tell me about the first time you kissed Tam."

Tam burst into the room, his pipes at his lips. He played, and the music wove through Larkin, making her think of soft summer nights and warm fires in winter. Of full bellies and cheeks tired from laughter.

Alorica relaxed into the bed and stared at the ceiling. "I hated him so much after he forced me to marry him. I was horribly cruel to him." She chuckled breathlessly. "So he let me go."

If Denan had let Larkin go, he would have never seen her again.

"He knew I had an interest in healing, so he took me to Magalia. I lived with her and worked with her. And I hated it." Her eyes squeezed closed. "I didn't realize how pampered I was with my family. How sheltered. I helped saw off arms and legs of men infected with the curse. I watched them die. I watched them live. And I began to understand the terrible cost of protecting us from the wraiths.

"Tam visited me every day. He brought me lunch and made me laugh. And eventually, I started to look forward to his visits.

"Then one day, I watched a boy die. It was his first mission outside the Alamant. His first time being a man instead of a boy. And all I wanted was Tam. He cried with me and rubbed my back. And somehow he made me laugh."

Alorica smiled at the memory, but that smile was short-lived. "So many people died before they ever had a chance to know love. The kind of love Tam was offering me. So I took a chance. I kissed him. I'm so glad I did."

Tears streamed down Tam's face, and his music wavered before growing steady again. He sat on the bed beside his wife, and she rested her forehead against his thigh.

Watching the intimate moment, Larkin felt like an intruder for the second time in as many days.

Arguing sounded from outside.

"Let us in, you big lug!" Magalia shouted.

"I have orders—" West began.

"The forest take you, West," Larkin said. "Let them in!"

Magalia burst into the room wearing little more than a nightgown. Five orderlies hustled in behind her, one of them drawing a two-wheeled cart. Magalia assessed the room in a single glance and directed one of the orderlies to take over playing for Tam.

She stepped in beside Larkin, who leaned in and whispered, "She's with child. Tam doesn't know."

Magalia's mouth pressed in a tight line. She pulled linen cloths from her bag. "Has the bleeding slowed?"

Larkin stared at her hands, trying to remember when the blood had stopped seeping between her fingers. "I think so."

Magalia wrapped the linens around Alorica's middle, tying a knot tight over the crumpled bedsheet. Larkin slid her hands out from under the bandages. Magalia stepped back and motioned for the orderlies, who eased Alorica from the bed and onto the cart while she groaned in pain.

Larkin touched Magalia's arm. "Will she live?" she asked softly.

Magalia frowned. "I don't know."

The orderlies wheeled Alorica out, an anxious Tam by her side. Denan still hadn't come with Mama.

Something was wrong.

ANCIENT MAGIC

L arkin stepped through the doorpane of Tam and Alorica's rooms into the morning light. West and Maylah eyed her. The corridors were flooded with guards. A sharp chemical smell mixed with burnt hair assaulted her.

West eyed her bandaged arm with a tight expression. It was bleeding. The stitches felt tight and hot; she hadn't noticed before.

"Stay inside," he said.

Ignoring him, she leaned over the leftmost railing to look down one level to Mama's chambers. Two guards stood at the doorway—one with a hand on his sword, his gaze darting. The other, an enchantress, leaned over the railing and vomited into the water below.

Light. These were the best soldiers the Alamant had. They'd lived through hard combat. Yet something in Mama's rooms had rattled them deeply.

"My family," she called down to them.

The nervous guard looked up at her. Only then did she realize he was covered in black blood.

Another ardent like Unger.

"They're all right," the nervous guard said.

Then why was he so upset? She tensed to run down the colonnade to the stairs, but Alorica and the healers blocked the way. There was an unused chamber beneath this one. Larkin could jump on it and slide down the panel. She swung one leg over the railing.

West caught her injured arm, drawing a hiss from her lips. He didn't let go. "You heard what that thing said."

Ardents are killing people to keep me "safe." How could I forget it? She fixed him with a glare, her sigils flared in warning. "I will pulse if I have to."

He shared a tense look with Maylah before releasing Larkin. She swung, letting go at the last second. She landed on top of the pane, her feet smarting. The panel shimmered beneath her feet. Lying flat, she slid down and landed on her feet. West swore, and the two of them rushed to try to slide around the healers.

Not bothering to wait for her guards, Larkin started across the corridor. "What is it? What happened?" she called to Mama's guards.

The vomiting one wiped her mouth. The other held out his hand. "They're fine."

"What aren't you telling me?" she demanded.

He turned toward the chamber. "Your Majesty, we need you."

Denan stepped through the hazy barrier. His chest heaved with exertion. "Larkin." She heard the heaviness in his voice— the kind of heaviness that told her something had gone horribly wrong.

She came to a stop before him. He held his sword in his hand. The blade was black.

Ardent blood.

There had been another one. A servant? A guard?

And her family. Her family... She couldn't bear to let her mind wander that dark path.

"Denan..." Words sticking in her throat, she pointed at his blade.

"One of the assassins was in your mother's room. He tried to kill Sela."

A small, wounded-animal cry wrenched from Larkin's throat.

He held out his hand. "They're all right. Sela stopped it."

Larkin shook her head against the impossibility of her five-year-old sister stopping any attack, let alone an ardent one. But Sela wasn't just her sister anymore. She was an Arbor.

"They're all right?" she asked in an impossibly small voice.

Denan nodded. "The baby didn't even wake up. Your mother's more upset than anyone."

"Who was it?" she asked.

"One of the new guards stationed in the boughs. I didn't even know his name."

Larkin didn't want to know his name. Perhaps it was selfish, but she didn't need another face to haunt her nightmares. She had to see for herself. She tried to move around him. He blocked her. "You need to prepare yourself; the body is in pieces."

Light. Oh, light! "Mama! Sela!" She pushed past him and rushed through the barrier. Mama met her on the other side, her expression haggard. Larkin launched herself into Mama's arms, reassuring herself with the warmth and solidness that she was all right.

Eyes watering at the haze of smoke and chemicals, she searched the room to find her sister sitting primly on the edge of the bed. Her hands rested in her lap, her head tipping to the side as she stared at the walls with empty, strange eyes.

Following her gaze, Larkin turned, only to step on something jagged and sharp. Stumbling, she sidestepped into something squishy and cold, something that made her shudder.

And then she saw what Denan had meant. Singed bits of flesh and bone were splattered across the floor and the lower portion of the barrier. A trail of black blood led to what remained of the smoking body. The upper half was burned so badly that the armor and clothes were nearly gone. Bones peaked through the ridges, and burnt flesh filled out the hollows.

Fresh stab marks pierced the char—Denan's doing. So the blast hadn't killed the ardent. And judging by the blood trail, he had dragged himself toward her cowering family. The legs were gone—splattered on the wall behind Larkin. And under her.

Crying out in horror, she jumped out of the mess. Light, there were pieces stuck to her bare feet. She kicked them off and pressed the back of her wrist to her mouth to keep from vomiting.

Sela had done this. Seen this. Light, what would that do to a little girl?

Larkin swallowed hard and crossed the room to kneel before Sela. She reached for her, but Sela flinched away from her blood-covered hands. Dried blood had settled into the grooves and lines of Larkin's skin—like a river delta seen from high above.

Alorica's blood.

But there was other blood too. Black ardent blood had soaked into her bare feet and splattered against her green tunic. Larkin fisted her hem in her hands.

"Sela?"

Her sister continued staring out the window as if she hadn't heard. But Larkin had to believe her sister was in there somewhere, devastated by what she'd done to save herself.

"Sela, you saved Mama and Brenna and yourself. You did what you had to." *Light, how did she do it?* Old magic. Had to be. And if they could just harness it, they could defeat the wraiths. Blast them to pieces.

Sela focused on Larkin. A strange glow emanated from her eyes, washing away the emerald, like streams of light through stained glass. "No, you couldn't."

Had… Had Sela read Larkin's thoughts? How was such a thing possible? Larkin fought not to recoil from her sister. "What do you mean?"

"It won't kill them," Sela said.

She's just in shock, Larkin thought. *That's why she's acting strange.* And her eyes were just a trick of the light.

Larkin longed to run her hands up and down Sela's arms, to check for blood or other obvious signs of injury. She shot a panicked look back at Mama, who paced and wrung her hands.

"She's not hurt," Mama said.

Larkin nodded in relief. Denan stepped back into the room—when had he left? He wore his full armor. West and the nervous guard came in behind him. The two men took hold of the ardent's arms and dragged his body from the room, his head dangling, teeth a startling white against the black. And then he was gone, the hazy pane hiding him from sight.

Larkin turned away quickly, only to find Sela staring at all the blood.

"Sela." Larkin shifted to block her sister's view. "Look at me." Sela's gaze fixed on the black stain on the floor. "We need to get her out of here."

Mama bent down and picked her up, keeping her head tucked into her chest so she couldn't see.

Larkin suddenly realized the baby was missing. "Where's Brenna?"

"In the bathroom." Mama headed that way with Sela.

Larkin followed, but Denan called after her, "I have to go."

He was leaving them in this state? Her family had been attacked! She shot him an incredulous look.

He stepped closer. "I'm going to test our guards for ardent blood."

How was he going to manage that?

Denan gestured toward her family. "They need you."

"Denan, these aren't ardents. Unger's eyes weren't all black. They're human. Like Maisy."

His expression was troubled. "They are ardents; their blood is black. They're just a higher form than we've seen before."

"He said he was a child of the Curse Queen. Like me." Light, was she a monster too? But the wraiths had cut her with their cursed blades; only, it hadn't turned her. Tears welled in her eyes. "He tried to kill Alorica to hurt me. He spoke in Ramass's voice. Ramass was here."

Denan's nostrils flared. He grabbed her and pulled her tight to him. "The wraiths won't have you."

Denan had his own strength, plus his magic and an army. If anyone could keep her safe, it was him. "Whatever they want me for..." They would use her for evil, as they used everyone else.

"I won't let them take you," Denan said.

She gave him a watery smile. "I know you won't."

From beyond the pane, one of Denan's guards hollered, "We're ready, sire."

He studied her, searching for the truth of her statement. Whatever he saw made him relax a bit. He kissed her forehead. "I'll be back as soon as I can."

She nodded for him to go.

Denan started toward the doorpane and called over his shoulder, "Make sure they're safe."

Her family. It pleased her that he knew she was up to the task.

"West and Maylah are just outside the door." He stepped through the doorpane.

Inside the bathroom, Sela sat in the corner, holding a sleeping Brenna.

"You're covered in blood. Get in the shower," Mama ordered.

Larkin tugged her tunic over her head. The cut on her arm burned at the movement. The bandage was bloody. She stepped under the faucet and opened the spigot. A stream of cool water hit her in the face. She gasped and leaned into it, letting it spread over every inch of her.

From outside the room came the sound of a bucket being upended and someone scrubbing. Good. Larkin didn't want Sela or Mama to have to see that carnage again.

Mama stepped in and shut the water off. "We'll all be wanting baths," she said by way of explanation.

Larkin soaped up a woven horsehair pad and scoured her feet. "What happened?"

Mama shook her head, as if she still couldn't believe it. "I woke to bright light. That thing was standing over Sela. She built a lightning ball and threw it at him—"

"It's called an orb," Sela supplied.

"It hit him and shredded his legs. Burned him to the bone." Mama shuddered and knelt beside Larkin. "He got up and came at us like he didn't even feel it." She brushed the tears from her face with the back of her wrist. "Sela wove an arch of light around us. He couldn't cross it. She kept us safe long enough for Denan to come and finish it off."

"It's a dome," Sela said.

"What is?" Mama asked.

"The arch of light," Sela said. "It's a dome."

Larkin had seen those domes of light in her visions of the day the curse came into being, had made a modified one when she'd created Denan's weir. Sela had used ancient magic. A lot of it. "How damaged is the White Tree?"

"It had to be done." Sela blinked hard, and suddenly her eyes were emerald again. She looked around in confusion, and then that confusion cleared. She set the sleeping baby on the floor and stood. "I'm supposed to bathe now too."

What exactly was going on with her sister?

"Will you get us some clothes, Larkin?" Mama asked.

While Sela showered, Larkin toweled off, dressed, and stepped into the main room. The mess was gone, and the room smelled of sharp soap, though the stains remained. Maybe they'd never go completely away.

Larkin crossed the room and risked lowering a panel. Beyond, the White Tree gleamed moon-bright. Purple waves crashed against the base—purple because of the algae that glowed when disturbed. Rainbows of light pulsed in the lake. The Alamant was always full of color, even at night.

Would all that color go forever dark when the White Tree died?

She turned the panel opaque, grabbed some clothes for Mama and Sela, and went back to the bathroom. Pale and shivering, Sela stood outside the shower, a towel around her.

Larkin set the clothes down on the floor. "The room has been cleaned. I didn't see any damage to the White Tree." Which didn't mean it wasn't there.

Mama nodded in relief and turned off the water.

Larkin studied Sela's eyes. Still their lovely green. She must have imagined the change before. "Sela, ask the White Tree if we could defeat the wraiths with ancient magic."

Sela looked inward and shook her head. "Maybe once. Not anymore."

The White Tree had been forever weakened when the ancient Curse Queen, Eiryss, had used up most of its magic to create a countercurse. Her actions were the only reason mankind had survived for the last three centuries.

But Larkin had seen what Sela had done to that ardent. If they could use it on the wraiths... "The orb and the dome—could you teach me?"

"It's barrier magic." Men's magic. Sela rested her head against the panel as if it were too heavy for her to hold up. "And their magic isn't strong enough. Not anymore."

"If it's men's magic, why can you use it?" Larkin said.

"Because I am not a woman."

Then what are you? The hairs on Larkin's body rose.

Dressed in a clean shirt and skirt, Mama bent and touched Sela's face. "She's fevering."

Larkin sighed in relief. That explained Sela's strangeness.

"Probably from the stress." Mama tugged a simple dress over Sela's head. "I'm going to wrap her up and ring Unger for some feverfew tea. Bring Brenna."

At the mention of their butler, the events of the day slammed into Larkin all over again. She picked up her baby sister, glad she'd slept through all this, and followed Mama into the main room. "Unger is the one who tried to murder Alorica."

Mama laid Sela on the main bed. "What?"

Sela stared blankly at Larkin.

"He's dead," Larkin whispered. *Light, I killed him.* Even killing monsters exacted a payment from her heart.

Mama shook her head. "But he seemed so normal."

Larkin had dismissed him as a quiet man. A solitary one. He'd been with them for months. Held her sisters. Played his pipes for Larkin when she was hurt. She'd never have guessed the wraiths controlled him.

She jumped when Denan barged into the room with the chest containing her armor.

"What is it?" Larkin didn't want to know, but not knowing was worse. "Is it Alorica?"

He set down the chest, flipped open the lid, and handed Larkin's armored skirt to her. "It's Iniya. She's taken a turn for the worse."

CHAPTER

BETRAYAL

Larkin and Denan hustled through the network of bridges that connected the hometrees on their way to the healing tree. Two guards cleared the way before them, two more bringing up the rear. Four of Denan's young pages trailed behind, ready to deliver his orders.

Denan's eyes never stopped searching for an enemy. "I still think we should have taken the boats."

They'd been over this. It would have been easier to shield them from a boat, but with the contrary wind, it would have taken them twice as long. Larkin glanced over her shoulder at the guards following them. "You tested them?"

Denan tugged up his tunic to reveal a scratch on his arm. "Every last one of them bled red."

"Clever man." Larkin breathed a little easier knowing Mama and her sisters were safe. Her cut arm throbbed to the beat of her heart. It was swollen, the stitches divoting the skin.

He pulled down his sleeve, but not before she noted the veins in his arms standing out. His skin was flushed. And though the day was hot, he shivered.

"Are you all right?" she asked.

"Just tweaked my side during the fight," he said. "It aches."

"It hasn't spread?" she asked breathlessly. He shook his head. She itched to look at it, but not here in front of his men. "Have you taken any pain powder?"

"Hasn't been time," he answered.

If he wouldn't take time for himself, she would.

She searched the trees all around them, trees filled with unsuspecting Alamantians going about their day. "Any one of them could be an ardent."

"Which is why I've called my council; they'll be waiting for us in our hometree. We're going to test every person inside the Alamant."

Her eyes widened. "What about planning the invasion of Valynthia?"

He frowned. "Sela said we have a year. That gives us time to grow our army with Idelmarchians and stockpile our supplies. So for now, this will take priority."

She didn't like it, but the ardents were the more immediate threat.

At the next intersection, they bore left, and the healing tree came into view. Small platforms like upside-down flowers dotted its boughs from top to bottom, all connected by rows of colonnades enclosed in magic panes. Healers in dusty blue traversed the lengths.

Market stalls lined both sides of the bridge—mostly food vendors who serviced those going to and from the hospital, as well as those inside.

The tantalizing smells coming from them reminded Larkin that she had yet to eat lunch. The owners smiled and bowed to her; she often bought food for her friends when she came to visit.

She stopped at one of her favorites, which sold sautéed defin bird and crunchy tubers wrapped in crispy bread.

Luckily, he had enough prepared for Larkin to buy some for their entire company. They ate as they walked under the archway onto a covered platform. The pages wolfed their food down so fast she wondered if they even tasted it.

An older woman sat at a desk, a dozen ledger-filled shelves boxing her in. She looked up at them. "And who is it you wish to see?" Her voice warbled with age. She made no move to bow—Karaken was nearly blind to anything beyond arm's length.

"I'm here to see Iniya," Larkin said.

"Oh, Majesty, forgive me." She started to push to her feet.

There was no need for that. Larkin rested a hand on her arm. "Where is she, Karaken?"

The woman pointed. "Level three, room forty-seven."

The guards marched into the colonnade and turned right, Larkin and Denan on their heels. The corridor circled the boughs, rooms branching off on both sides. She would have liked to stop in and check on some of the enchantresses who were still inside—the women whose wounds had been grievous enough that they hadn't been discharged, though it had been nearly three months since Druids' Folly.

It would have to wait for another day.

As they passed an orderly in gray, Larkin called out, "Would you mind bringing me some pain powder mixed with tea? I've a throbbing headache." Denan would drink every drop.

"I'd like some too," Denan said with a look that said he knew exactly what she was doing. He leaned in close. "Retaliation, little bird."

She elbowed him playfully. His face went red, and he hunched over. She'd accidentally hit his blight. "Oh! I'm sorry!"

A chuckle burst from his lips. "You win. I surrender."

She choked back a laugh. "I really am sorry."

He straightened with a wince and cocked a wink at the orderly. "Might want to get something a little stronger than pain powder."

The orderly bowed even lower. "Certainly, Majesty."

He waved him away. "I'm joking, man. The pain powder is fine."

Taking Larkin's arm, he led her to room forty-seven. The guards had taken up positions on either side of the doorpane. Denan went in first and immediately set about shifting all the panes to opaque, which cut off the cooling breeze and the sounds of birds above. It would also protect them from bolts.

Larkin's father and his new family were already there; this was the first time she'd seen them since her grandfather's assassination. With blonde hair and brown eyes, Raeneth would be easy for an artist to draw. A round face, two round breasts, a round waist. But her usually flawless skin was marred with worry, her pert mouth turned down in a frown.

Harben held his son, Kyden, in his arms. The boy had his mother's roundness and his father's curly red hair and freckles. Larkin felt a flare of anger toward her half brother. The son her father had always wanted. The child he fussed and cooed over, while Larkin and her sisters had been little better than servants at best and burdens at worst. The same hands that bounced Kyden had hit Larkin more times than she could count.

Not Kyden's fault, Larkin reminded herself.

Iniya lay in the bed, her withered frame looking more shrunken than ever. Had the druids' coup failed, she would be queen of the Idelmarch now. Larkin would have grown up a princess instead of scraping out her existence from the mud.

This was her family, but Larkin felt like a stranger among them. Maybe even an enemy. She was glad when Denan finished with the panes and came to stand beside her, his hand finding hers.

Drawing strength from his presence, Larkin crossed the room and leaned over her grandmother. "Iniya?"

The woman stirred, her beady eyes locking on Larkin. She reached out with one hand, grasped the front of Larkin's armor, and pulled her down. "I'm not dying, do you hear me?" Her words were badly slurred, one side of her face drooping like it was made of melted wax. "I'm too close to the throne to give up now."

Her strength deserted her, and she lay back, panting.

Dying? Larkin looked back at Harben. "It wasn't just another of her attacks?"

He shook his head. "That healer friend of yours said she will never fully recover. If she lives at all."

He had to mean Magalia. Larkin didn't know how to feel. She hadn't even known her grandmother existed until a few months ago. And their relationship hadn't exactly been friendly.

Iniya waved dismissively at Harben. "A drunkard cannot take my place. I will live until Kyden is ready for the throne."

The baby who was sucking his thumb? It would be nearly two decades before he was old enough to be king. But then, he was the only option she would consider. Larkin was already a queen, and Sela an Arbor. As far as Iniya was concerned, Nesha was a traitor.

Harben ground his teeth. "And you wonder why I started drinking in the first place."

She pinned him with a hate-filled glare. "You have never lived up to even the smallest expectation. You were never a warrior or a leader. You couldn't even manage to be a decent father."

Raeneth stepped forward. "And why would that be, hmm? 'Cause he had a harpy of a mother! A woman so vile she drove her own husband to kill himself!" She grabbed Harben by the sleeve and marched him toward the doorpane. "You'll die alone, old woman. And you'll deserve it."

Larkin swore her children would never face the same discord, no matter what she had to sacrifice to see it done.

"Denan," Iniya pleaded. "You're king now. Make my ascension part of the requirements for the druids' sigils."

Denan only stared at the woman and didn't answer.

Larkin knew her husband. He wouldn't lie to Iniya, even if it would spare her feelings. Wouldn't promise something he would never deliver. Larkin wanted to protest—what harm was there in letting a dying woman hear what she wanted? But then, Iniya was a wily old bat. She would probably survive this just to spite them. And then where would they be?

"Larkin promised me I would be queen in exchange for my help." Tears slipped down Iniya's cheeks. Larkin pitied the child she'd once been—the child who'd watched her family die, watched everything be stripped from her. But the woman could have made different choices. Could have chosen happiness over hate. Family over the crown.

Now she would have neither.

"Are you in pain, Iniya?" Larkin asked gently.

Iniya fiddled with her blanket. "You will never make it as queen, Larkin. Not without me to guide you."

Larkin reared back as Iniya's words struck one of her deepest fears.

"She's already a fine queen," Denan said.

Iniya ignored him. "Talk to that healer friend of yours. Make her help me."

Here it was again. Someone believing they could cheat death. Could bargain or fight or steal their way out from under its cold grip. But there was no running from death. Not once it had claimed you as its own.

"Magalia has done all she could for you," Denan said.

Iniya's hateful gaze swung to Denan. "What kind of king—what kind of man—breaks his promise?"

"If you were queen, what would happen to the druids?" Denan asked.

For once, Iniya remained silent. But Larkin could see murder in the woman's eyes.

Denan must have seen it too. "Better to break a promise than let a despot be queen."

"I curse you," Iniya said, her voice shaking with rage. "The same curse as that of old. All your happy memories will turn to bitterness. Your own magic will turn against you. And everyone you love will come to hate you."

Larkin gaped at her grandmother in horror. How could she wish such things upon anyone, especially her own family?

Denan took hold of Larkin's arm and steered her out of the room. She stepped into the corridor, reveling at the feel of the breeze against her damp skin.

She shifted her amulet side to side on its chain. "Is it wrong that I'll be glad when she's dead?" she whispered.

Denan pulled her into his embrace. "If you're wrong, then so am I."

"You don't think her curse meant anything?"

"She's just an angry, bitter old woman."

He's right. Of course he is. Larkin vowed again that she would be nothing like her grandmother.

Muffled sobs sounded to her right. Her father had only made it a dozen or steps down the corridor before he'd broken down. Raeneth stood beside him, her arm wrapped around him. Oblivious, the baby kicked at the banister.

Here was another conundrum. Her father had abused her, badly. For years. But it really did seem like he was trying to change. Larkin could hold on to her anger, as her grandmother had. Or she could let it go.

She looked up at her husband. "Give me a moment."

Denan looked from her father back to her. "Are you sure?"

She nodded. He motioned for the guards to hang back. She crossed the corridor toward her father. Raeneth noticed her coming and shot her a warning look. Larkin still didn't like the woman, but she was fiercely protective of Harben. And she'd risked her life to help Larkin and Iniya on their search for Eiryss's tomb. That alone made Larkin soften toward her.

"I'd like to speak with my father alone."

Whatever Raeneth saw in Larkin's eyes made her relax a fraction. She took their son and backed away. Larkin leaned against the banister beside her father. His face was all blotchy from crying—one of the unfortunate traits she'd inherited from him.

He wiped his cheeks. "If you've come to rail against me, don't."

Larkin laced her fingers together. "I'm sorry she said those things."

Harben glanced at her in surprise, which was fair. Larkin hadn't made any effort to see him since she'd returned to the Alamant.

He looked out over the water. "She wasn't wrong."

"You didn't want to fight in a civil war that would most likely kill you long before you could ever become king. That isn't a failing. It's wise. And you weren't always a drunk. When I was little, you were hardworking and playful."

He shook his head. "That doesn't excuse what I've done to you and your sisters and... your mother." He choked, barely managing to get himself under control. "And others."

He'd mentioned hurting someone else once before. What exactly had he done? She'd no doubt he'd stolen from half the town.

"No," she admitted. "But you've been trying to do better, to take responsibility for what you've done. That counts for something."

They both fell silent. Larkin didn't know what else to say. It seemed he didn't either.

"All right, then." He awkwardly patted her arm, and she tried not flinch.

Denan crossed the dozen steps to her, the guards fanning back into position. He handed her a cup of pain powder. They clinked cups and drained them, identical grimaces crossing their faces.

He glanced at Harben. "I don't know if you'll want to visit your mother again. But if you do, demand that she speaks to you respectfully. If she doesn't, leave."

Harben didn't raise his gaze. "And let her die alone?"

"That's her choice." Denan passed the cups back to an orderly. "We should check on Alorica and Tam." He gestured for the guards to move out, and they took their place a few steps behind.

"Larkin," Harben called after her. "Where does that leave us?"

She looked back at the man who had raised her. "Maybe we could start slow. You could write me a letter."

He nodded, his expression hopeful. "I'd like that."

Alorica's older sister, Atara, paced the corridor before her sister's room. Both women had tightly curled black hair and dark skin. But where Alorica was lithe, Atara was stocky. She wore healer blue, and a huge bruise was visible on her arm—probably from the weapons training all enchantresses were required to attend.

"How is she?" Larkin asked.

Atara blinked hard, obviously trying not to cry. Before she could answer, a wail rose from inside the room.

"Our parents should be here," Atara whispered.

Would travel between the Idelmarch and the Alamant ever be safe? Maisy had destroyed the portable wards, so probably not.

"Will she live?" Larkin asked.

"I don't know," Atara said.

Another wail rose. Larkin glanced back at Denan; this was no place for a man. "Stay with her." He nodded.

Steeling herself, Larkin stepped through the doorpane. Immediately, the smell of blood hit her hard, drawing her back to the day Garrot had slaughtered the Black Druids who refused to cow to him, including her grandfather.

She fought against the horror and fear that clawed up her throat. Forced herself to focus on the here and now. Magalia stood at a table, pouring herbs into a pipe. Alorica lay on her side, her dark skin ashen and shiny with sweat. Pain drew deep lines across her skin. She was naked but for a wrap around her breasts.

Without her clothing, the gentle mound of her belly showed beneath the blood-soaked bandages. Tam held her hand, worry stamped across his face

Alorica groaned and doubled over. Fresh blood soaked the sheets beneath her. Mama was a midwife. Larkin had seen enough women in labor to know what was happening. Alorica's womb had been punctured. With each contraction, she'd lose more blood.

Magalia lit a pipe and held it out for Alorica. "Here, take a puff when you need it."

Alorica took it, puffed the smoke, and coughed. Either the contraction subsided or whatever was in that pipe started to work because Alorica relaxed onto the bed.

Looking broken and lost, Tam rubbed her back.

Larkin crossed to Magalia. "What can I do?"

Magalia's mouth thinned. "There's nothing anyone can do. The baby has to come out before the bleeding will stop."

And if not, Alorica would bleed to death. "Mama might know what to do." Maybe even Nesha; she'd been trained by Mama, after all.

"There's nothing your mother could do for her that I haven't." Magalia held a cup of tea to Alorica's mouth. "Just a sip."

Alorica sipped and lay back, clearly exhausted. Her eyes focused on Larkin, and she reached out. Terrified, Larkin hesitated before taking Alorica's hand.

"Promise me," Alorica whispered. "Promise that you'll be there for him."

"Alorica…" Tam trailed off.

Another death loomed, but Alorica knew better than to bargain. Larkin wanted to assure Alorica that she would survive. That everything would be all right. But she might not. It might not. And Larkin wouldn't lie to her.

"He's my brother," Larkin said. "And he always will be."

Tam began to cry.

Alorica's eyes fluttered shut in relief. A handful of beats later, she groaned, the muscles in her neck standing out. She puffed hard on the pipe.

From her position between Alorica's legs, Magalia gave a cry of relief. "I have it."

She held a bloody baby that fit neatly in her palm. A child that would never draw its first breath. She brought it to Alorica. "It's a girl, I think."

The first girl in nearly three centuries to be born to the pipers, and she'd been murdered before she'd ever been born. Murdered by the wraiths.

"Oh!" Alorica cried, her eyes shining with love and grief. "She's the first. The very first."

"She's a miracle," Larkin said.

Alorica held her close. "That's it. That's her name. Miracle."

Tam climbed on the table behind Alorica, reaching around her to lay the very tip of his finger on his daughter's back. "Miracle."

Larkin and Magalia shared a look, wordless communication passing between them. In sum, Magalia still didn't know if Alorica would survive.

"Tam," Larkin said. "I'll send some food in for you." The hospital didn't provide food if the patients could buy their own.

He nodded without looking at her.

Larkin backed out the door. "I'll leave one of the pages here as well. If you need anything, they'll fetch it for you."

She left the three of them curled up, Magalia doing her best to clean up the blood. Beyond the doorpane, Denan stood beside Atara, who had managed to calm down.

"The baby didn't make it," Larkin said before they could ask. She turned to one of the pages and instructed him to bring enough food for everyone, including Iniya, and then be at Tam's beck and call.

Atara wiped her cheeks. "Denan told me what you did, that you saved her life."

It took Larkin a moment to understand that she meant by killing the ardent that had attacked Alorica. "Tam would have taken care of it if I hadn't." And she wouldn't have saved anyone if Alorica didn't survive.

"That's the second time you've saved her life," Atara said. "I won't forget it." She pushed past them, stepping into the room.

Denan held her gaze. "You can stay if you like, but my council is waiting for me at our hometree."

Larkin looked back at the room. Alorica and Tam didn't need her. And Iniya... didn't deserve company. "I'm coming with you."

Side by side, they left the healing tree.

CHAPTER

11

SELA

Denan's library circled the entire trunk, with deep alcoves full of books and comfortable chairs. Potted lampents and crystals hung at regular intervals, and the supports were lined with mirrors to increase the light.

The effect was bright and airy. The sweet scent of the lampents and the musty smell of paper reminded Larkin of the long, comfortable nights she and Denan had spent here while he'd taught her to read.

That bright, cheery atmosphere was a stark contrast to the mood of the council waiting for Larkin and Denan in the largest alcove, and she couldn't help but feel like her sanctuary was being invaded yet again.

A large, circular table took up the center of the room. His back to them, Gendrin slumped in a chair. He looked hollow and worn out—his father's funeral was in three days. On the opposite side of the table, Arbor Mytin and General Aaryn pored over lists of the Alamant's stockpiles.

Denan gestured for Larkin to sit beside his father. He took the seat on the other side of her. "As king, I'm required to stand down on all military matters. Gendrin will take my place as general until a new prince is embedded."

Gendrin must have suspected this was why he'd been called to a council meeting. It was a smart move—one that would placate King Netrish's supporters—and Gendrin was respected as a brilliant military commander.

He bowed before his king but said nothing.

"Before we begin," Denan said, "I want to talk to you about security for Wyn."

Larkin hadn't even considered Denan's young brother. The boy could be a target simply because of his parents and brother.

"He's furious he missed the excitement." Aaryn said. "Which is why your father and I sent him to live with your uncle Demry until this mess is over."

Demry would certainly be able to keep Denan's precocious younger brother out of trouble.

Denan nodded approvingly. "As you've probably heard, we've ardents among us. For now, this is our most pressing concern. We'll leave the logistics of planning our invasion of Valynthia to our subordinates."

Jaslin marched into the room. The woman's eyes were swollen and her nose raw. She took an empty seat beside Gendrin, who didn't seem surprised to see her. Larkin's eyes narrowed with distrust and suspicion. They'd planned this. Why?

Denan shot Gendrin a questioning look, which Gendrin returned with a helpless one.

Denan frowned and leaned forward. "Lady Jaslin, again, my sincerest condolences for your loss, but—"

"A former queen may take her husband's seat at council," Jaslin interrupted.

Denan took his time answering. "The position is customary."

"As is hers." Jaslin motioned to Larkin. "Four of the five members of this council are immediate family. My presence will even it out a bit."

Aaryn picked up a ball of purple yarn and started knitting, which she often did when she was thinking. Or angry. "Are you suggesting that we would elevate our own agendas over what's best for the Alamant?"

"Perhaps not deliberately," Jaslin said.

Mytin hummed in disapproval.

Why did Larkin get the feeling this was a bad idea?

Denan considered her. "I will allow your presence on *my* council, but only if you can be an asset and not a hindrance."

Jaslin gave a curt nod.

Denan studied the other members. "As I was saying, we were attacked by our butler and our guard. Both ardents who were able to seamlessly blend in among our people."

Like Maisy. A sudden memory clawed its way to the forefront of Larkin's mind.

The blight was tearing through Denan's body. She was losing him. She looked up at Maisy. Begged her for help.

Black tears streamed down Maisy's cheeks. "Magic black. Magic white. Magic binding up the night." She turned and ran.

Larkin hadn't known what it meant, but it had been the clue that helped her figure out the weir. The clue that saved her husband and hundreds of others since then. Many who would have become mulgars were now living normal lives thanks to Maisy.

"For how long?" Gendrin asked.

Gendrin's words snapped Larkin back into the present. Everyone looked at the new general in confusion.

"Ardents are infected by wraiths," Gendrin explained. "Wraiths who can't cross the water to reach the Alamant. So it would follow that the ardents were infected the last time they were in the Forbidden Forest."

Denan nodded. "The guard would have been at Druids' Folly. Unger... I've no idea."

That meant that the guard had hidden among them for three months, and no one had been the wiser. And Unger had been among them for even longer.

Gendrin swore. His mother shot him a scathing look, which he ignored.

"The assassin who killed my father was an ardent," Gendrin said. "And ardent who could be anyone. And there could be scores of them."

At least he didn't believe she and Denan had anything to do with the king's death.

Denan pulled up his sleeve, revealing the scratch there. "I've tested all my guards and servants. We've all bled red. Now it's your turn."

Gendrin was the first to act. He took a small knife from his pocket and nicked his arm. The blood welled red. Mytin and Aaryn followed suit, with Mytin borrowing his wife's sigil blade. They were all clean. That left only Jaslin.

Jaslin set her chin. "What about her?" She nodded to Larkin.

"She bled all over herself at the embedding ceremony," Denan said.

"So the rules don't apply to her?" Jaslin said.

The woman obviously hates me. Why? Because I took her place as queen? Or did she truly believe Netrish's accusations?

Larkin sighed loudly, pulled up her sleeve, and picked at the scab under her stitches until it bled. Jaslin harrumphed and used her magical blade on herself. Larkin was a little disappointed when the woman bled red; being a mulgar would have been a solid excuse to banish the woman from the council.

Denan leaned back in his chair. "We have to test everyone. The whole city."

"If they find out about the search," Gendrin said, "any hidden ardents will start a killing spree."

"We start with the leadership and work our way down," Larkin said.

Aaryn unraveled some of her knitting. "At Copperbill Island." The enchantress training grounds. "The border is easily contained. We can test in small groups."

The six of them worked for over an hour, arranging the logistics of the operation.

When they finished, Aaryn packed away her needles. "We'll wake the enchantresses in batches and test them through the night."

"I'll bring soldiers to be tested first thing in the morning," Gendrin said.

Denan looked around the room. "Questions?"

No one said anything. Denan pushed back his chair as everyone filed out. He rested an arm on his mother's shoulder. "I'll accompany you to the island."

"Denan," Larkin interrupted with a meaningful look at his side.

"I'm all right, Larkin."

Aaryn swung her knitting bag over her armor. "She's right, dear. No point in all of us losing sleep. My enchantresses and I will handle it. Then you can take over in the morning while I sleep and Gendrin's men are tested."

Denan pursed his lips unhappily.

Mytin pushed in his chair. "Your mother is more than capable of handling her enchantresses, son."

Aaryn kissed Denan's cheek. "Cross me, and I have an army to back me up." She hugged Larkin. "How's Alorica?"

"Alive, but she's lost a lot of blood."

Mytin made an unhappy sound. "I will see some of the White Tree sap brought to her."

Larkin nodded and saw them off. Back upstairs, she and Denan went to check on Mama and the girls. Her skin flushed with fever, Sela lay sleeping in the bed. Mama sat in a rocking chair, nursing Brenna—she was always changing or nursing the baby. It was one of the reasons Larkin took her maidweed tea religiously every morning. She wasn't ready for children of her own. Maybe she never would be.

"I hadn't time to ask before," Mama said, "but have you heard anything about Nesha?"

Larkin shook her head. "Not since I saw her entering the city last week."

Mama rocked faster. "She hasn't answered any of my letters."

And Mama had written every day. Denan's pages had delivered them all to the Enchanter Academy, where the druids were staying, and then returned empty-handed.

Mama looked worried. "Garrot is keeping them from her."

Nesha might ignore a letter from Larkin—not that she'd written any—but not Mama.

"I'm sure of it," Larkin said.

Mama looked to Denan. "There has to be a way to reach her."

He passed a hand down his face and sat heavily in one of the chairs. "That's the one point Garrot wouldn't budge on."

"You're the king now. You could make Garrot give her up. Deny the druids thorns!" Mama's cry startled Brenna, who began to fuss. Mama patted her bottom and made soothing noises.

"We need them, Pennice," Denan said. "We lost too many men in the fighting last spring."

Mama placed Brenna over her shoulder and burped her. "There has to be a way.'

"What if Nesha asked for help?" Larkin said.

Denan leaned forward and braced himself on his knees. "She's Idelmarchian."

"Technically, so are we," Mama said. "Are Idelmarchians not subject to Alamantian laws while in the Alamant?"

He studied her. "As you can imagine, the Alamant has very strict laws about wives staying with their husbands." They would have to, what with all the wife stealing. "But if he were to harm her in any way... We're very protective of women."

"She's not his wife," Larkin said. "With her clubfoot, she's not allowed to marry."

Denan sighed and turned to Larkin. "The druids are accustomed to seeing my pages in the academy. I'll have them scout around a bit. See if they can figure out where she's staying."

Larkin felt a spike of apprehension—the pages were mere boys. "What if Garrot catches them?"

Denan's gaze hardened. "Garrot got where he did because he knows which lines he can and cannot cross. If he hurt one of my pages, his life would be in my hands."

"So we're betting on Garrot's restraint?" Larkin said uneasily.

Denan shot her a look. "They aren't just boys, Larkin. They're warriors in training. Being in danger is part of the life they're born to." He pushed himself up. "I'm going to take a shower." He left the room.

Mama worried her bottom lip.

"He really is doing everything he can," Larkin said.

"It's just... she's my baby, Larkin."

"I know." It really wasn't that late—the sun hadn't even set yet—but Larkin was exhausted. "I'm going to bed."

She crossed the room to kiss Sela good night, but even through her hair, Larkin could feel the heat radiating off her. "She's burning up," Larkin said.

Mama's brow creased with worry. "She was better after lunch." She pushed to her feet. "I'll make her some feverfew tea." She left the room without another word.

Sela opened liquid eyes and looked up at Larkin. Her bottom lip trembled. "Larkin, I'm scared."

"Why are you scared, little one?"

Big tears streaked down her cheeks. "Because the wraiths want you."

What had her sister overheard? Or had she learned something from the tree? Heart breaking, Larkin wrapped Sela up in a blanket and settled with her in a rocking chair.

"They're going to get you." Her little body shook with sobs.

Sela must have overheard Denan's worry that the assassin had targeted her. "We've checked all the guards. None of them are ardents. And I have my magic and Denan. There's a wall around the city and an army inside it. I'm the most protected person in the Alamant."

"Promise you'll stay with me," Sela said to Larkin.

Larkin couldn't stay in the hometree forever; she had responsibilities. But Sela was too young to understand that. "I promise."

Sela burrowed into Larkin's arms. She tugged out Larkin's amulet and held it in her hand as if she took comfort in its presence.

Relieved at Sela's display of affection, Larkin pressed her cheek to her sister's head. "I love you, Sela. I love you so much. I'm sorry for being so short with you before."

"I love you too," Sela said, voice shaking.

Larkin stroked her curls. "I miss telling you stories and tickling you and having you leave me little presents on my bed. I miss you, Sela."

"I never left," Sela said.

But she had. "Would you like me to tell you a story?"

Sela nodded. Tears filled Larkin's eyes. Maybe she hadn't lost her sister, after all.

"Once," Larkin began, "a toad fell in love with a fish. He loved the fish's silver scales, lithe body, and whip-fast movements. But the fish didn't love the toad's warts. So the toad cut them off. But the fish didn't love the toad's voice. So the toad cut it out. But the fish didn't love the toad's fat body. So the toad cut off his sides. But the fish didn't love the toad's mutilated body. So the toad ate the fish, and that was the end of it."

Sela giggled. "Why did the toad care what the fish thought?"

"Because sometimes we want to be everything we're not." Like Larkin thinking that her grandmother covering her freckles with makeup and taming her wild curls would make her a queen. Larkin was the toad. Cutting herself to pieces to become something she could never be.

Mama returned with Cook Viscott, who bore a tea tray. He was no more than twenty-five, the single braid behind his ear proclaiming that he'd yet to marry. He walked with a measured limp, a wound that had ended his career as a soldier. And probably ended his chances of ever braving the forest to find a wife of his own.

Larkin felt a stab of pity for Viscott. But then, things were changing. The Idelmarch had promised to send girls who wished to come. Maybe he would get his chance, after all.

"I told him I could manage," Mama said.

Larkin doubted Mama would ever really be comfortable with servants.

"It's what I'm paid for, lady." Viscott set the tray on the table. "Would you like me to pour her a cup, Majesty?"

Larkin nodded.

The man brought Sela a cup. "I always make it strong and then add lemon and honey. Very soothing."

Larkin helped Sela drink it all down.

"Another, please," Sela said.

Viscott brought her another.

"You should go home to your family." Larkin would never feel comfortable with servants either. "Please feel free to take the rest of the evening."

Viscott took the cup. "Oh, I couldn't. Without..." He trailed off awkwardly. "Well, we're a bit short staffed. There's a lot to do. And I can't fight anymore. This way, I'm still doing my part."

Because Unger had turned out to be a murderous ardent.

"Well," Mama said, "be sure to take some of our supper home with you."

Viscott smiled. "That wouldn't be proper, lady. But I thank you. Please ring if you need anything else. King Denan doesn't like you wandering with an assassin about." He bowed again and left.

Sela finished her second cup. "I feel better now." She closed her eyes and within moments was back asleep.

"Maybe we haven't lost her, after all." Mama looked as relieved as Larkin felt. "Maybe she's just trapped by all the tree's memories."

Larkin wouldn't mind rocking Sela for a long while more, but she'd been worried about Denan's weir since the healing tree. She laid her sister on the bed and kissed her forehead. "Sweet dreams, sunshine girl."

Larkin said good night to Mama and stepped outside. The sun was just setting, casting the world in orange and gold. She climbed a level to her own chambers. West was back on guard, a great bruise on his cheek.

"The new trainees still beating you senseless?" she teased.

He puffed out his mustache in consternation. "I'm still too slow."

She patted his arm. "You'll get there."

She passed through starlight to her room. Denan lay on the bed, a warm compress over his blight. He'd done that a lot in the early days. There was another pot of tea on the table. She sniffed the spout. Feverfew and pain powder.

She sat beside him on the bed and rested her hand on his forehead. He didn't feel warm, but his normally golden skin was a bit ashen. "Are you fevering?"

"No. The tea just helps with the pain."

She peeked under the warm compress. The blight looked the same as ever, the forked lines about the size and shape of a handprint. She breathed a silent sigh of relief. "You pushed yourself too hard today."

"I'll be all right. I just need a good night's sleep."

Not buying it, she stripped off her armor and placed it back in the chest. "Sela's sick."

He finally bothered to open his eyes. "How sick?"

"Fevering."

He made an unhappy sound. "We'll have to test her and your mother's blood tomorrow."

"She's just a child," Larkin said.

"She's been exposed to the forest and the wraiths. We can't make exceptions. Not if we want the people to cooperate."

She mimicked his unhappy sound.

He crooked a little smile that quickly slipped away. "How is she?"

Larkin sighed. "Worried about me." Afraid to look at him, she studied the scar on her palm. "What could they possibly want with me?"

He motioned for her to sit beside him. He took her hand and held her gaze. "Whatever it is, I'll stop them. And you know I never break my word. Do you believe me?"

This man who was as undaunted as a mountain. How could she not? She nodded. He kissed her hand.

He finished his tea while she stripped the rest of her armor and checked her stitches. The wound was a little puffy. She swiped some ointment on it, drank her own cup of tea, and un-dressed for a quick shower.

By then, Denan's breathing was deep and even. He looked so peaceful sleeping, his body gilded by the light cast by the set-ting sun. Light, she'd never get tired of watching him sleep. Un-able to help herself, she crossed to him and kissed his forehead. She turned to go, but he caught her arm.

"You're naked."

She grunted. "It was miserably hot today. I'm going to wash the sweat off."

He tugged her hard enough that she landed half on him.

"I thought you were sick!" she protested.

He grinned. "Larkin, if ever I'm too sick for this, you should start to worry."

She tipped back her head and laughed.

CHAPTER

COPPERBILL ISLAND

*A*ll around Larkin, enchantresses and enchanters stood side by side. They wore strangely cut clothing—their armor familiar in a way she couldn't place. She turned in confusion, and someone walked through her as though she wasn't there.

The White Tree was showing her a vision.

She walked to the edge of a colonnade and looked over the lake to the distant shoreline. She was on the city wall in the Alamant. Sometime before the curse fell. But there was no gathering army to defend against. What was the White Tree trying to show her?

A horn sounded. Enchantresses and enchanters lit their sigils. From the tower above, a note rang out. The men lifted their intricately carved, jeweled flutes and began to play. The music tugged at the enchantresses' magic, pulling it from their bodies in gleaming ribbons. Those ribbons wove intricate patterns in the air—a repetitive symbol that looked almost like a snowflake.

A reverberating drum beat from the tower above, and the enchanters shifted seamlessly to another melody. Larkin rushed up the tower's winding steps. At the top was a flat platform. A handful of young boys in livery waited at the back. A young man and woman leaned over the banister.

Larkin immediately recognized them.

"Signal the chorus," King Dray said.

"Not yet." Eiryss pointed. "There's an error with the weave."

Dray squinted at the spot she pointed out. "Good eye, my queen."

"I'm not your queen yet," she teased.

Dray kissed her cheek. "Soon."

This must have taken place right before their wedding, the day the curse came into being. Oh, how Larkin wished they'd been able to find the woman's amulet.

Sending him a shy smile, Eiryss stretched up on her toes, ran her hand over the enchantment, and smoothed a ruffled edge. "There." She sank back onto her heels. "Now it's ready."

Dray nodded to the drummer, who beat out a single note. The weave shrank, fitting around the barrier like a second skin. It flared bright and then faded to nothing.

The White Tree had shown Larkin how to weave the barrier around the wall.

"Good," Larkin said. "Now show me how to make an orb or armor."

Sharp pain in her hand. She watched as a single bead of blood welled and then rolled down the lines in her palm. It broke away, falling to the ground.

Larkin sat up with a gasp. She released her grip on her amulet and pressed her thumb to the prick in her palm to stanch the bleeding.

"Probably have blood all over the sheets," she muttered.

The chamber shifted with the wind like a ship in a storm. The panes moved with a liquid shiver as the wind and rain pelted their surface. The movement was mesmerizing. Larkin imagined this is what the surface of the lake must look like to a fish.

She pushed out of the bed and then realized she really had bled all over the sheets. Her monthly had come during the night.

At least I'm not pregnant.

Groaning, she went to the closest pane and twisted it to partly open. It was light enough to see the churning mass of clouds above—morning wasn't far off. A cool breeze touched her, a breeze that smelled of rain.

Twisting the pane back to impenetrable, she shuffled to the bathroom and cleaned herself up. When she came out, Denan sat at their table, eating breakfast. Their sheets had already been stripped and taken.

"I can do that." Larkin's cheeks flamed at the thought of Viscott washing the blood from her bedding.

"So can he." Denan handed her a letter. "I've word from my mother. They tested all the enchantresses in the night, but one is missing. Hurry and eat; we need to go."

Larkin scanned the letter while eating her breakfast. When she set it down, she caught sight of another letter on the table— or rather, the signature on the bottom. She picked it up as if it might bite and started reading.

"Garrot is demanding we give him and his men their thorns," Denan summarized for her. "He doesn't care that the king is laid out in state before the font or that the White Tree is filled with mourners."

She dropped the letter and wiped her hands on her tunic. "Three days won't make a difference to the war. Garrot will just have to wait."

She had to figure out a way to make sure Nesha was all right. "Have the pages found anything yet?"

"I forgot to tell you; they haven't found her, but they know where Garrot sleeps."

Larkin mulled this over. "Any way for them to reach her?"

Denan shook his head and picked up another letter. "This one is for you."

She unfolded it. It was from her grandmother, written by one of her healers.

"Aloud, please," Denan asked.

Larkin cleared her throat and read, "'If my words offended you, I apologize most sincerely. It is only that I watched my parents' and sisters' blood staining the halls of my home. Watched them breathe their last breath. Lived on while my heritage and my home was stolen from me. If my father were alive to see his murderers treat with his own great-granddaughter... But then, my life has always been the worst kind of irony.'"

Larkin threw the letter down in disgust without bothering to finish it. "I swear upon my life that I will never become a bitter old woman like my grandmother."

"Your reading has improved tremendously though." He took the letter and scanned it.

Larkin's chest felt warm with his praise. He'd only had to help her on some of the larger words.

"Light, the woman goes on and on."

"I know what happened to her was awful. Nothing will change that—including her being hateful."

"Magalia made a note at the bottom. Iniya hasn't been able to swallow. She likely won't live for another day."

No longer hungry, Larkin stared at her plate. "Her whole life, she only wanted one thing. I promised her that. She's going to die hating me."

Denan sighed and bent over a fresh sheet of paper, his quill scratching across the surface in his crisp handwriting. When he finished, he blew on it and held it out to Larkin.

She quickly scanned it, her eyes closing at the emotion that welled within her. "You made her queen."

"Let's hope Magalia is right," Denan said dryly. "Or we'll have the whole of the druids to contend with."

She folded the letter, dripping wax to seal it. "I should be there with her, but I can't leave. Not today."

"You are a queen. Your people need you."

He was right. "I'm not sure I can live with not being there though."

"Why don't you write to your father? Tell him to be by her side as she dies."

She mulled his offer over and then nodded. "Will you write it for me? My handwriting... It looks like a child's."

He covered her hand with his. "You should be proud of that handwriting. Three months ago, you couldn't read, let alone write."

Feeling better, she pushed aside her unease and wrote to her father. When she was done, Denan gave her letters to a page. She and Denan set about buckling their breastplates and backplates, as well as armored skirts. Beneath, Larkin wore black, which would be hot, but it would hide any stains.

She was just tying her cloak into place when someone knocked on the doorframe. "Larkin, Denan, it's me."

"Tam?" Larkin's heart fell.

She twisted the doorpane open. Tam stood between the guards. His eyes were haunted, his normal smile nowhere to be found.

"What is it?" Denan came up behind Larkin. "Is Alorica all right?"

"She threw me out," Tam said. "Said my pacing and worrying was driving her crazy and that I needed to be useful." He shuffled awkwardly. "I think she's right. I need something to do."

Denan embraced his friend. "Glad to have you."

Tam hugged Denan and then shoved him away. "None of that. I'm a married man."

Larkin snorted. If Tam could still crack jokes, everything would be all right. She wanted to hug him too, but he was barely keeping his tears in check. Any more affection might throw him over the edge. He wouldn't thank her for that.

She settled for punching his arm. "You're late for duty."

"There goes my raise." He gave her a grateful smile.

They stepped outside, and Denan studied the sky. "Wind's in the right direction."

Bracing herself, Larkin stepped to the edge of the colonnade and peered at the white caps beneath them. She remembered the feel of the lethan's tentacle gripping her ankle and wrenching her beneath the waves—the feel of being dragged into the depths, more tentacles wrapping around her chest and squeezing the life out of her.

"I'm not going out on that lake," Larkin said.

Tam leaned into her. "Ah, come on, Denan and I have run the lake in storms far worse than this."

She glared at him. "I'll go out when the lake is calm. But definitely not in a storm." Nor at night, when the lethan prowled.

"We don't have much of a choice," Denan said. "Bridges don't go all the way to the island."

She made an unhappy sound. "Fine. While you ready the boat, I'm going to check on Sela."

On the next level, the men continued down while Larkin stepped past the guards at Mama's chambers. They were all still asleep in bed. Sela lay on the far side, an empty pot of tea on the nightstand, the cup still steaming. Larkin laid a hand on Sela's brow, grateful that she didn't feel as hot as yesterday.

"As long as she keeps the tea in her," Mama said sleepily, "she does all right."

"I'm going to leave you in charge of bringing on a new butler," Larkin said. "Just make sure the guards test him first."

Mama mumbled something that sounded like an agreement.

"Send one of the pages if you need anything," Larkin said.

Mama made the noise again before her breathing deepened, and she went back to sleep.

Larkin moved to leave when Sela's hand gripped her wrist. Her eyes were strange again; they had lost their emerald hue, turning pale in the dimness. "Where light is, shadow cannot go." Her voice was strange. Whispery and faint.

"What?" Larkin asked in surprise.

"Remember." Sela's eyes slipped closed.

Sela often communicated with the tree, but this felt different. It hadn't felt like Sela was speaking at all. Larkin stared at her, breathing hard. *I'm just tired. It's a trick of the light.* But she couldn't shake her fear—fear that she dared not look at too closely for the truths it might reveal.

Moving fast, Larkin slipped out and made her way to the dock, where Denan, Tam, three other guards, and four of Denan's pages were waiting for her. She took the seat directly in front of Denan, who took the helm.

They rowed away from the tree's spreading roots and set the sail, the boat launching forward fast enough to throw her backward. She held the bench with a white-knuckle grip as the wind sent the boat skittering up and down waves that grew larger by the minute.

Above, the sky grew darker with thunderheads. Lightning traced across the heavens, followed by a protracted, rumbling growl of thunder. The boat slammed into a wave, spraying Larkin. She gasped and pulled her cloak tighter. The boat began its laborious climb up the wave, crested, and pitched over the other side before slamming into another wave.

Larkin's stomach roiled. A fat raindrop smacked her directly in the eye. "We need to take down the sails!"

"He won't let you die," Tam said.

Denan tipped his head up, welcoming the rain on his face with a grin, the exhaustion of yesterday completely forgotten. The cursed fool was going to get them all killed.

She grabbed her husband's shirtfront. "Take down the sails before the whole ship breaks apart."

He gave her a bemused look. "There's no chance of that. Besides, we're nearly there." He pointed ahead.

Through the rain, Copperbill Island came into view. The wind scoured the island, trees and grass bowing under it and enchantresses ducking into it, their clothing streaming to the side. At the top of the central hill, three large buildings stood unbent by the storm—the few land-built buildings in the Alamant.

Larkin's relief at sighting land was short-lived, as she bent over the side and heaved her breakfast into the lake. Humiliated, she pushed away from the gunwale. Thankfully, Tam pretended not to notice. Denan handed her a handkerchief to wipe her mouth. She slumped in relief as her nausea faded.

When they were nearly to the island, Denan ordered the guards to take down the sail and handed Larkin a paddle. "This is the tricky part."

"Tricky part?" Larkin echoed in a high, disbelieving voice. She gestured to the cresting waves behind them. "What was that?"

"That was the fun part," Tam said.

Denan dug his oar in. "If we weren't on the leeward side of the island, we wouldn't be able to dock at all."

Without the sail, the boat slowed. Denan called out commands, and they paddled hard. When they were nearly to the dock, Tam threw a rope to the men working the dock and missed.

"We should have brought your grandma," Denan said. "I bet she could hit it."

"Shut it!" Tam threw again.

This time, the men caught it, looped it around a piling, and drew them in. A wave caught the boat and tried to drag it back into the lake. The rope and paddlers strained.

"Hang on," Denan said.

As soon as the wave passed, they sidled in hard. They slammed into the dock. Larkin banged into the gunwale, the breath knocked out of her. She gasped and sat back, her hand going to her chest. The men, all former soldiers, tied off both ends of the boat. The guards stepped out as if nothing had happened.

Denan looked down at her as if he wasn't quite sure what to do with her. "We used to go out in storms all the time at the academy."

"Why?"

"Because one day we might have to fight mulgars on the lake," Denan said.

The idea made her shudder.

"A little mint tea, and you'll be fine," Tam said.

She sent him a scathing look, which he accepted cheerfully as he hauled her onto the dock. The men bowed. They all bore signs of old injuries, limps, missing limbs. One appeared to be blind.

Tam directed the guards into position. Larkin and Denan climbed the hill that bisected the island. The first building was the enchantress headquarters. It was rectangular, the walls made of magical barriers. The supports were not elegantly carved, but utilitarian and varnished to an almost black. With all the lampents inside, it resembled a stately greenhouse.

The moment they passed the corner of the building, the wind cut off. Larkin sighed in relief and smoothed her damp hair out of her face. It was warm, but the lake water had chilled her, and she shivered.

The guards fanned out around the door. Denan and his pages went inside the building. Larkin hung back to watch the enchantresses drilling on the field. Moving as one, they flared their sigils. The resulting pulse knocked down the first row of dummies. They rushed forward, stabbing the dummies through the hearts, before charging on to the next group.

Larkin felt a swell of pride and loss, for she would never fight beside them again. When General Aaryn had been injured, Larkin had led these women into battle. Together, they'd knocked their stubborn fathers and brothers on their backsides with that maneuver. Then they'd removed their helmets, letting the breeze flare their long hair to the side. They'd stared down at the men from their families as those men realized they'd been attacking the very daughters they sought to avenge.

Larkin had demanded they stand down.

And they had.

When the mulgars and wraiths inevitably turned on the druids, the enchantresses had fought beside their husbands to save their fathers.

They'd won that battle too. It was the first time in her life she'd felt powerful.

Now, standing on a different hill on a different day, Larkin felt a kinship, a oneness with her fellow enchantresses.

"We are not our fathers' daughters." Denan stood behind her. "We are not our brothers' sisters. We are not our husbands' wives. We are our own. Warriors who fight for what's ours."

"You heard that?" And then made the effort to memorize it.

"I've never been prouder of you than in that moment." He gestured to the women. "They repeat it every morning before drill."

Her eyes widened. "They do?"

He nodded.

A part of her wished she was still leading them. But it was not her place, any more than restoring the magic had been. The glory would always go to others, but she'd played her part as best she could.

That had to be enough.

"Come on," Denan said gently, as if he sensed the loss of the warrior she'd been. He probably did. He'd suffered that same loss.

They stepped past the guards huddled next to the building, Tam cracking a joke about one of their broken noses. Inside, there were seven rooms—three on either side with a large room in the center. Light came from the lampents that hung from five great chandeliers. The air smelled of damp soil and sweet blossoms.

The pages lined up with a dozen others against the far wall, all of them waiting for any messages that might need to be delivered. Enchantress commanders worked over a large table in the center.

Larkin took off her sopping cloak and hung it from a peg next to a dozen others just like it. Shivering in her damp clothes, she approached the unit commanders. On the table were maps, ledgers, and scattered papers. The women's eyes were bloodshot, their fingers stained with ink—they'd been up all night.

"Where's General Aaryn?" Denan asked.

The conversations cut off, the enchantress commanders bowing as they noted their king and queen. Larkin was surprised to see Caelia among them, her unit commander mantle over her shoulders. After all, she was still in mourning for her father-in-law, the king.

Caelia had the same dark hair and hooked nose as her brother. The eyes were different though. Caelia's were blue where Bane's had been a mesmerizing gold ringed by brown.

A beat of sorrow pulsed through Larkin at the memory of the boy she had loved. The boy she had failed to save. Another emotion to stuff in a chest and sink in the lake.

Someday, they would all burst open and drown her.

"Waiting for you in her office, Majesties," Caelia said.

Larkin wondered if Denan's mother felt as strange being called General as Larkin felt being called Majesty.

She was relieved when she left the main room for Aaryn's office with Denan. There were chests and bureaus along most of the walls, bits of cloth or yarn sticking out here and there. Aaryn sat behind her desk, looking nearly as wet as they were. She held a steaming cup of tea in her hands and wore a purple knit shawl around her shoulders, probably the same one she'd started at the council meeting.

She stood when they came in. "Oh, you both look half drowned." She opened a chest and carefully rifled through the contents.

"Have you found the missing enchantress?" Denan asked.

"Varcie," Aaryn supplied.

Larkin was relieved she didn't know the woman.

"She hasn't been seen since yesterday." Aaryn pulled out two beautifully woven cloaks. The knotted, three-headed snake of Denan's house took up the back. She placed one around Larkin's shoulders and the other around Denan. "I've been meaning to give you both these anyway. Had I more time at my loom, they would have been done months ago."

Beeswax had been rubbed into the fabric to make them waterproof. Larkin had spent every planting barefoot in the mud and soaked to her skin. What she wouldn't have given for a cape like this and a pair of sturdy boots.

Larkin burrowed into it for warmth. "They're wonderful. Thank you."

Denan sat in one of the chairs, draped the cloak over him like a blanket, and tucked his hands under his armpits for warmth—strange, as the man was always hot. "Where have you searched?"

Aaryn shut a drawer and searched another. "Her hometree and the barracks. We started on the edges of the island as soon as it was light. We didn't want any assassins escaping into the lake. I'm hoping—"

"General," someone called from the other room. "They found her!"

Aaryn slammed the drawer shut as a young page darted into the room, pulled a damp missive out from under her shirt, and handed it to the general.

CHAPTER 13

LETTERS

The silence in Aaryn's office was loud enough to choke on. Aaryn scanned the missive, dropped it onto her desk, and leaned against it for support. "She was my best unit commander."

Denan leaned forward and picked up the missive.

"What happened?" Larkin asked. *Maybe it was an accident.* A foolish hope. But maybe.

Aaryn seemed incapable of answering.

Denan swore. "He was my trainer at the academy."

Unable to stand the suspense for another moment, Larkin snatched the missive.

The search party had followed two sets of tracks across the island. The first set was Varcie's. The second belonged to her weapons trainer—another ardent. Varcie had tried to hide from him in a bunch of rushes. A fight ensued. She killed him, but he'd mortally wounded her. She managed to drag herself nearly a league before she died.

Aaryn hadn't been exaggerating when she'd said the girl was one of their best.

Aaryn sank into her chair. "She was so eager to prove herself—first in the ring and the last to leave. Her trainer would have known that."

"So the ardent killed her early last night?" Denan asked.

"Must have," Aaryn said.

"She repaid the favor before she died," Larkin said.

A fierce pride shone in Aaryn's eyes. As there should be. Varcie was ambushed by someone she trusted. But even dying, she'd managed to take down an ardent. And now she was gone. They'd have to replace her with someone lesser. *Curse the wraiths.*

Denan stared into nothing. "King Netrish, Alorica, Sela, and now Varcie."

"They're picking off our most powerful," Larkin said. "Our leaders."

"Alorica was only a guard," Denan said.

Larkin's instinct was to defend her friend, but Denan wasn't trying to insult Alorica. Only stating a fact.

"Perhaps they thought Alorica and Tam were you and Larkin?" Aaryn said.

The thought of Alorica losing her baby and facing death in Larkin's place knocked the breath from her. She should have seen this coming. Should have realized Maisy wasn't an aberration. That other ardents like her were possible.

"The wraiths are demonstrating abilities we've never seen before," Aaryn went on. "All these long centuries, they've been holding back. Until now. Why?"

Denan glowered. "Because they knew that as long as we had the White Tree, they could never completely defeat us. They've been biding their time."

And now the tree was dying. Memories swarmed Larkin. The taste and feel of rot as their king caught her. The sucking sensation as he dragged her into the shadows... She shuddered.

We're not going to win this fight, she thought. *Not against creatures who can never die. Not without the White Tree.*

If Denan and Aaryn were thinking the same thing, none of them said it. It simply wasn't the kind of thing one said.

A page stepped inside. "General Gendrin and his commanders are here. They're removing their weapons now."

"He's late," Aaryn mumbled as she pushed to her feet.

Larkin and Denan stepped into the main room. The enchantress commanders were clearly crestfallen—with tear-streaked faces they were trying to hide. One of their own was dead. A woman they'd trained with and strategized with and fought with.

Caelia stood with her back to them at the windowpane, watching the enchantresses drill in the rain.

"Varcie knew what being an enchantress meant," Aaryn said. "We all do. Cry if you must, but don't let your enchantresses see you scared." She looked at each one in turn until they met her gaze and nodded. "Now, what are we going to do so this never happens again?"

"Set a watch," Caelia said.

"Build a watchtower," said another.

"See both begin immediately," Aaryn said.

"We should have set a watch after the king's death," a woman muttered.

Aaryn whipped around and fixed the woman with a sharp stare. "Why didn't you bring that up at the time?" She didn't look away until the woman did. "You will oversee the watchtower, Nelury. Fail, and you lose your command." She waited.

The woman shifted her weight ever so slightly.

"I'm waiting," Aaryn said.

"Understood, General," the woman said.

It was strange to see Aaryn as a commander. When Larkin had met her, she'd been a wife and mother. A woman who took great pride in her weaving and her two children. And now, she led all the enchantresses. But she hadn't tried to change who she was—she still knitted and wove. And she didn't put up with people disrespecting her.

Why couldn't Larkin be more like her?

Gendrin stepped in, half a dozen men filing in after. His eyes were a little less lost, if still bloodshot. But his shoulders were back, and he moved with purpose.

He bowed to Denan. "The first two boats of my men are docking now. All they know is they're here for training exercises. More will be arriving throughout the day."

Denan nodded in approval.

Aaryn motioned to one of her pages. "Bring the enchantresses in."

The boy ran out. A few minutes later, over a dozen enchantresses came into the room. They were mostly dry, so Larkin guessed they'd been waiting in the barracks.

"Everyone know what they're doing?" Aaryn asked her commanders.

A chorus of "Yes, General," and her leaders started moving. The commanders took three enchantresses and split into each of the four rooms. Caelia moved into Aaryn's office.

Gendrin's men looked about in confusion.

"What's going on, sir?" one asked.

"Training exercise," Gendrin said.

The men exchanged uneasy glances.

Aaryn stepped close to Gendrin and dropped her voice. "My commanders will test your men. If they're clear, they'll take over. All goes well, and we'll expand to testing more men in the other buildings."

Gendrin nodded.

Denan moved toward the door. "We'll start with Tam. He hasn't been tested yet."

If anyone is human, it's Tam, Larkin thought. Denan must have thought along the same lines, or he would have insisted the man be tested earlier.

Gendrin directed four of his men into the other rooms and followed the last one in.

Denan and Tam returned, deep in conversation.

"Do you think his wife suspected he was an ardent?" Denan asked.

It took Larkin a moment to realize they were referencing Varcie's killer, or rather, the man he'd once been.

Tam wiped a drop of water off his nose; he was making a puddle on the floor. "Maybe we shouldn't have played all those tricks on him."

Denan chuckled. "He was furious when we put all the birds in his office."

Tam sniffed. "How were we supposed to know he'd be gone for two days?"

"Gah," Denan said. "I still gag every time I smell bird droppings."

Light, how much troublemaking did these two get into at school? Larkin shook her head in disbelief. "So that's why Aaryn is a good commander. She kept you two in line."

Denan tipped back his head and laughed.

"Anyone who could manage those boys could handle an army." Aaryn pointed to her office. "Go, so you can see how it's done."

Inside, Caelia sat at Aaryn's desk with a ledger open in front of her. Three enchantresses waited in the wings. They'd removed all but one chair, which sat in the center of the room.

"Name?" Caelia asked.

Denan pushed an unsuspecting Tam toward the center of the room. "Tamrel Bordeck, captain of His Majesty's guard."

Tam glared at Denan. Larkin shot Tam an amused look; she hadn't known his full name was Tamrel.

Caelia flipped through the pages until she found what she was looking for. She gestured to the chair. "Sit."

Tam hesitated. "What's this about?"

"It'll be all right," Larkin said.

"Well, now I'm really worried." But Tam did as he was told and sat.

The enchantresses stepped forward, shields coming to life to trap Tam within a shield wall. He darted to his feet. "What's—"

"You're being tested for ardent blood," Caelia interrupted. "Take the knife you were allowed and scratch your right forearm. Just until blood appears. Do not cut too deep."

The way she said it made Larkin think it had been a problem.

Myriad emotions crossed Tam's face—hurt, betrayal, anger, and then reluctant understanding. He took his knife, which was made of sacred-tree wood that never lost its edge, and scratched his arm. He held it out for them to see.

Denan let out a breath. Larkin hadn't been worried—no ardent could fake Tam. Caelia's quill scratched across the paper. The enchantresses released their magic and stepped back.

Tam placed his knife in its sheath and glared at them. "Always a good day when your friends ambush you with plans to kill you if things don't work out."

Denan elbowed his ribs. "Want to do it to someone else?"

Tam grinned. And just like that, all was forgiven.

Larkin rolled her eyes. *Men.*

Caelia wiped her hand down her face, her exhaustion clearly showing. She pushed to her feet and headed toward the door. "Nothing too difficult. My commanders and I are going to get some sleep in the barracks. Don't wake me unless something's on fire."

Larkin flinched when Caelia rested her hand on Larkin's arm. The woman's gaze locked on Larkin's. Less than a year ago, the two of them had conspired to help Bane escape. A few months after that, Larkin had told the woman how her brother had died. How Larkin had failed to save him. To even realize he'd been sentenced to death.

"I couldn't stand going to the embedding ceremony to face him." Caelia had to mean Garrot. That explained why she hadn't been there with her husband, Gendrin. "I'm glad you were there."

She moved on without another word. Larkin exchanged glances with Denan. Maybe... maybe Caelia was on their side.

Tam eyed the scratch on his arm in distaste. "And if we find an ardent?"

"Kill them," Denan said simply.

"But they might tell us something," Larkin said.

Denan's gaze grew distant. "They never do. Not in all our years of trying."

"Maisy did," Larkin said softly. Enough to warn them. Give them hints. Keep them safe.

"What if she's one of them?" Tam asked.

"Maisy wouldn't do this," Larkin said.

"How do you know?"

I just do. Aware of how mulish it sounded, she didn't say anything at all.

"All the ardents we've found so far have been men," Denan said. "A woman would have too hard a time hiding in the Alamant."

He was right. Larkin relaxed in relief.

He eyed them both. "If either of you find an ardent, kill them."

Larkin wanted to argue—she still thought they could interrogate them—but Denan was far more familiar with ardents than she.

"And after we've proven the army?" Tam asked.

"We'll move on to the constables and then the populace," Denan said.

Larkin thought of his intentions to test her sister—had he ever done it? "Even the children?"

"Everyone." He rounded on Larkin. "You can handle this?"

She bit her lip. "I'm not a fast reader."

"Tam will help you," Denan said.

Larkin gave a reluctant nod.

Denan strode out. "I'll be in the room next door if you need anything."

One by one, enchanters filed into the office. One by one, they bled clean. Larkin and Tam ate lunch and then supper in Aaryn's office, only pausing long enough to use the privy out back.

Five times, she heard a scuffle in one of the other rooms. Five times, that scuffle was followed by the thud of a body. Five times, one of the pages reported that an ardent had been found and killed.

By the time night fell, Larkin despaired. Exactly how many assassins were they dealing with and how deeply entrenched were they? A warning buried deep in her heart burned like an ember: whatever the wraiths had planned, they hadn't seen the apex of it yet.

Denan stepped inside. "The constables are taking over."

He moved aside as one of the constables stepped into the room, his own ledger under his arm. Relieved to be leaving the stuffy office, Larkin entered the main room. Denan, Gendrin, and Aaryn all gathered around the table.

Tam hung back as Larkin moved to stand between Denan and her mother-in-law. A lovely map of the Alamant lay on the table. A stylized White Tree painted white and gold took up the center. Beyond stood the hometrees, with smaller bridges leading to the main bridges. Around it all was the defensive wall, which had four gates and numerous guard towers.

Beyond that was the uneven shore, and beyond that... the Forbidden Forest.

"How many ardents did you find?" Larkin asked.

"Seven." Aaryn braced herself over the table. She looked more rested than she had this morning. "Their bodies will be burned."

Relief washed through Larkin that she hadn't had to witness any of it.

Gendrin gestured to the map. "When the remaining ardents find out what we're doing—if they haven't already—they'll either try to escape, mount a defense, or hurry to complete their missions."

"The constables will see all Alamantians remain in their hometrees until the search is completed," Gendrin said. "My men will guard the bridges."

Aaryn tapped on the Enchanter Academy, which was situated on the second ring of hometrees. "What are we to do about the druids?"

They were all busy with their own tasks.

"Larkin and I can do it," Denan said.

Cold dread slithered down Larkin's spine. She didn't want to see Garrot. Ever again. But for Nesha... "It will give us a chance to find my sister."

Gendrin called for one of his pages and whispered something to him. The boy took off.

Aaryn nodded. "I'll send you with a hundred of my best enchantresses. Just in case." She wrote something on a slip of paper, sealed it with wax, and marked it with her signet ring. "I'll have Mytin meet you there. He can use embedding as leverage to get what you want."

Aaryn locked eyes with one of the pages and lifted the letter. The boy came at a run.

"Take it to my husband," Aaryn told him.

The boy took off at an even faster run.

Gendrin's page returned with a heavy ledger, which Gendrin handed to Larkin. "A copy of the Idelmarchian manifest."

Denan leaned over her shoulder as she scanned the list of names, ranks, and physical descriptions.

"Anything else?" Denan asked. No one said anything. He nodded. "All right, everyone get some sleep. The search begins at first light tomorrow."

Ledger tucked under her new cloak, Larkin followed her husband outside.

"Wait." Aaryn hurried to catch up. "Be careful with the druids; they're snakes in the grass. And not the good kind." She shot a meaningful glance at the knotted snake on Larkin's new cloak to show what she meant.

Acting on impulse, Larkin hugged her mother-in-law. Her armor made it awkward, but Aaryn didn't seem to mind. Larkin was just so glad to have more people who loved her. Who would stand beside her if she ever needed them.

Larkin, Denan, and Tam left the building, stepping out into the evening air. It had finally stopped raining. The ground squished beneath her boots. Bits of sky peeked beyond the clouds. Below, boats departed the overcrowded dock.

Tam took the lead with Maylah, two other guards falling in behind. The breeze picked up. Larkin breathed it in, glad to be out of doors. Denan shuddered and huddled in his cloak. He winced, his hand going to his side.

"What's wrong?" she asked.

"Just my blight mark."

It was more than that. She opened her mouth to press him when Maylah flared her shield and moved to block a woman who was headed straight for them. "State your business."

Larkin shifted to get a look at the approaching woman. "Atara?"

"Is it Alorica?" Tam asked. "Is she all right?"

Atara frowned at her brother-in-law. "She's fevering."

Tam flinched as if her words had landed a blow.

Light, Alorica.

"If you hurry," Atara said, "you can catch the same boat I came in on." She pointed down the dock. "That one there. *Deluge* written on the side."

Tam shot Denan a pleading look.

"Go," Denan said gently.

Tam took off at a run. Atara squared herself before Larkin. "I'd like to take my sister's place as your personal guard."

Larkin's brows rose in surprise. "But you're a healer."

"I'm an enchantress first, same as any of us." Atara cleared her throat, clearly trying to keep her emotions in check. "You saved her life. Twice now. I want to repay that favor."

Denan and Larkin exchanged loaded glances.

"That's not necessary—" Larkin began.

Atara stepped closer. "You don't understand. I-I need this."

Denan shot Larkin a questioning look.

"I know how hard it is to be helpless against something," Larkin whispered.

Denan motioned to Maylah. "Test her first."

"Hold out your arm," Maylah said.

Brow furrowed in question, Atara obeyed. Quick as lightning, Maylah nicked her, red blood welling.

Atara pressed on the wound. "What was that for?"

"Just making sure you're not an ardent." Maylah looked to Denan for orders.

"It's Larkin's decision." Denan motioned Maylah back into position. They started back down the hill.

Atara fell in beside Larkin. "Well?"

"West will test your skills in the morning," Larkin said. "If you pass his inspection, you'll be my guard. For now, take Tam's place up front."

With a look of profound relief, Atara moved up beside the other enchantress. The wind gusted, and Denan shivered.

Larkin leaned in and pressed her hand to his forehead before he could duck away. He was fevering. "You're sick."

He and Sela clearly had the same illness.

"It's just being in wet clothes all day," Denan said. "I'll be better by morning."

"Denan," she chided.

"I can't be sick," he said stubbornly. "I have assassins to find."

"Maybe we found them all," Larkin said.

He huffed. "We can't afford to hope for that. We have to know."

How was she going to keep this man in bed? "The plan has been set in motion. We'll go home, get some supper, and retire early. You're no good to us if you're too sick to get out of bed."

They stepped out onto the dock when one of their pages leaped out of a boat, darted through the crowd, and handed Denan a letter.

"Another letter from Garrot." Denan tore it open and read. "If he can't go to the White Tree," he summarized, "he wants the thorns brought to him."

Larkin rolled her eyes. "That's not how it works."

Denan, Larkin, and their guards climbed into their boat. They used their oars to push off other boats and rowed into open water. The lake was calm, so Larkin dared sit beside Denan at the rudder.

It would be dark soon. She eyed the water suspiciously. "Is it possible that the druids snuck ardents in with them?"

Denan rubbed his eyes. "You think they're still in league with the wraiths."

Clear of the press of boats, the guards dropped sail, and the boat picked up speed.

"The assassinations started when they arrived," she said.

"Every single one of them was counted and recounted, Larkin. No one else came in with them." He shivered again. "And all the ardents we've found have been in the Alamant for months."

She wanted him to be wrong, wanted to blame the druids. But he was right. She rubbed his arm. "How about, when we get home, I make you a pot of feverfew tea and rub your feet?"

He moaned. "That sounds wonderful."

"King Denan." One of the guards pointed to a boat headed toward them. One of their pages stood at the prow and waved another letter at them.

"I'm starting to hate letters," Larkin muttered.

They dropped sail, both boats slowing as they passed each other. Two guards helped the page jump from the other boat into theirs. He handed Larkin a letter. With shaking hands, she tore it open and read the single line.

"What is it?" Denan asked.

"Iniya is dead. My father and Raeneth were with her." She waited for the grief. The loss. But all she felt was pity for a woman who had chosen misery.

CHAPTER 14

TIME

*S*hadows stalked Larkin. Relentless black shadows that smelled of the rot and freshly turned soil of an open grave. She stumbled through a thick forest of moth-eaten trees with sticky, tattered sheets of spiderwebs instead of leaves. The sky above was black, the ground beneath thick and tangled. With each step, she broke through brittle roots. When she tried to pull her foot out again, it tangled in the undergrowth.

She opened her sigils, adjusted her sword to a razor's edge, and hacked her way forward. She managed to make it a dozen steps before her foot caught fast. She caught herself on a tree.

When she tried to pull her hand away, it stuck. She pulled harder, but it sank into something the texture of rotted flesh. She braced her other hand and tried to pull back, but it, too, became stuck.

She struggled, throwing all her weight backward. But it seemed the harder she pulled, the further she sank. And then a face appeared in the tattered bark.

Bane's eyes and tongue bulged with rot. "You left me to die."

A sob caught in her throat. She glanced to her left. The black nothingness had stalked closer, devouring everything in its path. When she looked back, another face appeared in the bark.

Venna, marked with jagged lines, her eyes a soulless black. "If you would have listened to Denan, you could have saved me."

"I'm sorry," Larkin cried.

The darkness was close enough now to reach out and touch it. With her hands trapped, she couldn't form a sword.

A new face appeared. Talox's. He didn't say anything, only looked at her sadly. As if to say that he'd suffered a fate worse than death to save her. To save the woman who was meant to break the curse.

Only that woman wasn't Larkin. It was Sela.

It was then that Larkin understood the truth.

She was the shadow.

Always had been.

The tree became the Wraith King. Larkin didn't try to run or fight. She simply sank into his arms. Let his icy touch creep into her. Through her. Her body dissolved into shadows. Shadows that rolled relentlessly forward. Devouring everything she touched.

When she was finished, there was nothing left.

"Larkin."

Arms wrapped around her, bringing the nothingness of her back together. The heat radiating from those arms chased away the cold. She left the shadows behind. Became herself again.

It was morning. And she was not a shadow. Not a monster. For the space of a breath, relief washed through her. But then she realized the arms that held her raged with fever. She turned to face her husband, the color high on his cheeks.

"Denan?"

He pulled the blankets higher but didn't open his eyes. She had to get his fever down. She slipped out of the bed and shifted open the doorpane, wrapping a rob over her blood-stained night-dress, though thankfully she hadn't stained the sheets again. West and Atara stood on the other side. A couple pages waited on the connecting colonnade.

West eyed her in her robe and then quickly looked away again. "My queen."

"Aren't you on night shift?" she asked.

"Tam's late," West said.

Larkin shot Atara a concerned look.

"Still fevering," Atara said softly.

Larkin's eyes fluttered closed. *Light, please let Alorica be all right.*

She made to step onto the colonnade, but West blocked her way. "You're not wearing armor, Majesty."

"Denan's very ill," she said.

"You're a queen," Atara said with a roll of her eyes. "Have something brought up."

Feisty, just like her sister. Larkin decided she liked Atara, but she hated feeling like a prisoner in her own home. "My ho-metree is crawling with guards. The panes are closed. No one could get close enough to see me, let alone take aim."

"A guard's job is always to assume that other measures have failed," West said.

"One of you fetch their breakfast and a pot of feverfew tea," Atara said to the pages.

They shot Larkin a questioning look. She made a disgusted sound low in her throat and waved one of them off. "I take this to mean you passed West's testing," she said to Atara.

The woman nodded.

The other page edged closer. Larkin held her hand out for the packet of letters in his hand, but the boy hesitated. He clearly had something to say.

She raised an eyebrow. "What is it?"

"I found your sister, Majesty."

Nesha. Finally. "You know which room she's staying in?"

The boy nodded eagerly. He was young with big brown eyes edged with thick lashes, acne, and a breaking voice. Despite his youth, he'd put himself at risk to help her.

Larkin rested her hand on his shoulder. "What's your name?"

"Farwin, Majesty."

"You could find it again?"

"Yes, Majesty."

"Well done." The boy grew under her praise. "Don't go anywhere. I'm going to need your help today."

He nodded vigorously. She took the packet and hurried back inside her chambers. Letters from Garrot, Gendrin, Aaryn, Magalia, and a dozen other people. She set them on Denan's nightstand and went to the bathroom. She came out with a wet rag that she laid on Denan's forehead.

"Oversleeping, are we?" She forced her tone to be light instead of worried.

Denan shifted under her ministrations as if struggling to wake. She reached out and kissed the top of his head.

"Save those for later," he said in a rough voice.

Her lips curved into a smile. "One of the pages, Farwin, found Nesha." Denan finally opened overbright eyes. He made to swing out of the bed. She didn't move, effectively blocking him. "You've been working too hard. You need to rest."

His gaze searched hers. "I can't let you face Garrot alone. Not after what he's done to you."

She'd been so worried about her husband that she'd forgotten all about Garrot. As they always did, the memories assaulted her. She flared her sigils, grounding herself in the painful buzzing, in her strength.

"He doesn't frighten me. Not anymore." It was a relief to realize she meant it. "Besides, your father will be with me."

Denan studied her as if trying to assess her truthfulness. "You're sure?"

"Save your strength for the funeral tomorrow. Gendrin and your mother can handle searching the populace. Let Mytin and I handle the druids and Nesha."

Frowning, he stared at his hands. "You'll take Tam with you?"

"He hasn't come in this morning—Alorica is still fevering. I'll take West and Atara instead."

Denan clearly wasn't happy, but he didn't argue. "You'll send me updates if you find any ardents?"

Knowing she had him, Larkin stifled a sigh of relief. "If you promise to let me send in a healer."

He shivered and pulled the blankets higher. "Fine. But we still need to come up with a plan for you to get a message to your sister."

The new butler asked for admittance. Larkin noted the red scab on his arm with relief as he set breakfast on Denan's nightstand. After he left, Larkin mulled over how to reach Nesha.

She poured Denan a cup of feverfew tea. "Farwin found her room. He could sneak something to her."

"Failing that, we could bribe someone."

Oh, she liked that idea. "West might know someone willing to take some gold in exchange for delivering a message." After all, he'd worked with them for years. She tested the tea with her upper lip. Too hot. She blew across the surface. "And if she wants to leave with us?"

He studied her. "I studied the law on the subject. They aren't married, she is not his heartsong, and her child isn't his. He has no legal claim on her."

That was all she needed to hear.

"But I don't need another incident to rile up the druids and my council. Keep it quiet."

She nodded.

Denan was silent a moment. "I want you to take some gilgad venom—just in case."

Someone pricked with a dart dipped in gilgad venom would be paralyzed within a minute. It was how Denan had *almost* captured her the first time—*almost* because she'd repaid the favor.

Denan's gaze shifted to worry. "But what if you're caught?"

She tested the tea again. Still too hot, but better. She handed it to him. He took an obedient sip and tried to hide the trembling in his hands.

Trying not to let her worry show, she busied herself eating her breakfast. "You said yourself that Garrot knows which lines to cross when. Do you really think he'd risk harm to the Alamant's queen?" No matter how much of the populace disapproved of her.

Denan was silent as he considered every outcome, every option. Finally, he nodded. "At worst, he would use you to try to gain some leverage, but he's surrounded, so I still have the upper hand. Send one of my pages to purchase the venom and darts."

"You don't keep it on hand anymore?" she teased. "What if I escape?"

He chuckled softly. "I'd come for you."

"Always." She finished the last of her food and settled his breakfast on his lap. "Try to eat something."

She sent Farwin to purchase venom and darts and meet them at the academy. She took a quick shower, dressed in her full armor, tucked the druid ledger into a satchel, and swung it over her shoulder.

"Apparently, there are people sick all over the Alamant." Denan lifted one of the letters. "Mother said twenty-three were too ill to show up for duty. Gendrin had thirty-three. Three of them are bad enough to be in the healing tree."

"We can't afford a plague in the middle of the war," Larkin said.

"I'll write Magalia. See if we can quarantine the sick at the healing tree."

That would give him something to occupy his time while she was gone. She kissed his forehead and headed for the doorpane.

"Larkin," he called after her.

She turned back to him.

"You're a queen. Remember it."

She lifted her head high and nodded. West and Atara waited outside. It would be dawn soon. And judging by the cloudless sky, hot. Light, she missed afternoon swims.

"No sign of Tam?" she asked.

West eyed her armor in approval. "I'm going with you."

"I'm counting on it." She started down a level.

"The bridges will be faster," Atara said, clearly thinking Larkin was heading to the docks.

"I need to check on my sister." Larkin relayed their plan for the druids as they went.

Atara and West waited outside while Larkin slipped past the guards and into Mama's room. Brenna slept in her crib. Mama was nowhere to be seen.

Larkin sat beside Sela, whose forehead didn't seem as hot. "How are you today?"

Sela opened her eyes. "You've seen it, haven't you?"

"Seen what, Sela?" Larkin tried to smooth out her sister's matted hair. It would be painful to brush out. The old Sela would have run screaming and hid somewhere by the river. The new Sela would endure the yanks and tugs without a word—as if she couldn't even feel it.

"The weaves."

Larkin's mouth fell open. "How do you know about that?"

"They're the shape of music. The language of it." Sela tugged Larkin's amulet out from her tunic and rubbed the edge of her thumb against the sharp branch. "The White Tree wants you to practice the weaves."

Did the White Tree know how exhausted Larkin was? How desperate for sleep? Larkin rubbed at the headache she could feel forming across her brow. "We have a year."

"Less now that I've used up so much magic."

"How long?"

"Maybe nine months."

Nine months until the source of their magic winked out. Nine months to prepare. Feeling completely overwhelmed, Larkin breathed out. She put her worry and fear into a chest like Denan had taught her and locked it up tight. She'd deal with it later.

Right now, she had the druids to deal with. "After all this mess with the assassins is over, I'll practice every day. All right?"

Sela nodded.

The butler entered with a breakfast tray.

"Stay with her until my mother returns."

Nodding, the man handed Larkin a wrapped parcel. "Your lunch, Majesty."

Larkin tucked it into her pocket. "Thank you."

The man nodded.

Larkin stepped back out to her waiting guards and glanced at the sky, blue overtaking the gray. "We're going to have to hurry."

CHAPTER 15

ENCHANTER ACADEMY

Twenty minutes later, Larkin, Atara, West, and a handful of pages left the main bridge for the smaller one that led to the Enchanter Academy. The hundred enchantresses Aaryn had sent parted to let them through. Above, the Enchanter Academy came into full view. Larkin had been here a couple times to see Wyn, Denan's younger brother, before all the boys were sent home to make room for the druids.

Three colonnades formed a triad, with three massive trees at the ends. Facing them was the point of the triad, the Hall of Ivy, where the students were taught. The tree on the back left was the Hall of Althea and served as the barracks and dining hall, with the kitchens on the lowest levels, the smell of beans and baking bread rising like heartburn.

The last tree on the back right was called the Hall of Thorns. It had a large practice area on the main floor and sleeping chambers on the upper levels. It was also the tree most likely to hold Larkin's sister, though they hadn't been able to spot her before Farwin.

Below was a lake garden, where boys usually tended their lake greens. Now, it stood empty, the leaves waving forlornly with the current.

This was where the Alamant trained her sons to become soldiers in a never-ending war. To become men who would someday steal their wives. Men who would do what they must to protect their people.

Larkin, Atara, and West passed through the last of the enchantresses, who snapped back into formation. Caelia stood at their head. The woman hadn't even come to the embedding ceremony to avoid confronting Garrot. Larkin could only think of one reason she'd be here.

"I know you want justice for Bane," Larkin said. "Believe me, I know."

Caelia gave a hard, brittle smile. "I'm not going to kill him. Just make sure he can't hurt anyone else."

Larkin studied the woman, trying to decide if she believed her or not. She didn't *seem* murderous. But then, who did? "I mean to rescue my sister from him. Killing him will make that hard."

"Nesha was only a few years younger than me; she was always tagging along with me and Atara, much to our chagrin." Caelia's gaze was distant, troubles. "I won't risk her."

Larkin gave a curt nod.

Mytin strode out of the Hall of Ivy's rotunda to meet them, a pair of guards trailing a step behind. Her father-in-law wore his mantle of office, the heavy jewels dangling, and bore a staff—a simple, gnarled branch taken from the tree.

Farwin trotted ahead of the Arbor, the boy practically bouncing on his heels in excitement. Maybe bringing him wasn't such a good idea—he wasn't nearly as nervous as he should be—but it wasn't as if she had a choice.

He stopped before her and opened his light jacket, revealing a hollow tube and blow dart.

Larkin pushed the boy's jacket shut before the druids noticed.

Caelia raised a brow. "For Garrot?"

"For whoever stands between me and my sister," Larkin said.

Caelia grunted. "Do me a favor. If you do hit Garrot, don't give him the antidote."

Larkin eyed her. "You're sure you can handle this? I won't judge you if you can't. I almost lost control the first time I saw him again."

Caelia ground her teeth. "How do you stand it?"

"Don't think of it as needing him," Larkin said. "Think of it as using him."

Caelia frowned.

"Can you do it or not?" Larkin asked.

"I can do it," Caelia said.

Mytin rested a hand on Larkin's shoulder in greeting. "Where's Denan?"

"He's fevering."

Mytin frowned. "Poor timing, but then, sickness always is." He shot meaningful glances at her guards. "Atara and West, be alert."

West certainly doesn't need the encouragement, Larkin thought.

Mytin gestured to his own guards, an enchanter and an enchantress. "Devon and Jenly."

Nodding in greeting, Larkin handed Mytin the satchel. "It's the druid manifest." He was a much faster reader, and besides, she had a sister to rescue.

Nodding, Mytin settled the satchel over his neck.

Larkin pulled Farwin aside. "You understand that this is dangerous?"

His eyes widened. "Yes, Majesty." She didn't quite believe him. He withered under her scrutiny. "I promise to be careful, Majesty."

"Which tree is she in?" Larkin asked. He gestured to the Hall of Thorns on the back right. "Don't say a word to anyone about the darts. Keep them out of sight and wait until I call for you." She pushed him toward the pages behind her.

The boy opened his mouth as if to argue before remembering himself. Head hanging, he joined the others.

"We need to test the men in the Hall of Thorns," Larkin said.

"Easily done," Caelia said.

Larkin turned to Mytin. "Denan told you about Nesha?" He nodded. "If a fight breaks out, your priority is to get out. Garrot doesn't need both of us as hostages."

Mytin frowned, but he knew he wasn't much of a warrior. "All right."

The guards spread out around them as Caelia, Larkin, and Mytin strode past the Alamantians stationed at the outer archway. They entered the rotunda. Larkin's light-blinded eyes were slow to adjust to the dimness.

Above, the pattern of the beams reminded her of a spiderweb. Below her feet was a seven-pointed star in shades of gray and black. The arched windows were bare of either glass or panes. Lacking any decor and robbed of light, the atmosphere was austere, unwelcoming.

Larkin imagined Denan crossing this space as a young boy. Was he frightened? Excited? Both? Well could she imagine such a place producing a man as undaunted as her husband.

The three of them stopped before two stern druids guarding the hazy doorpane. She could only make out vague shapes moving on the other side, but she knew from experience that beyond, colonnades veered to the right and left.

Larkin was grateful for the presence of their guards around them, as well as Mytin and Caelia beside her.

"We're here to see Master Garrot," Mytin called.

Garrot's second-in-command, Met, stepped through the doorpane; he'd clearly been waiting for them. He was young and handsome, but for his constant sour expression. He'd wanted to beat her after Garrot had murdered her grandfather. West had stopped him.

Met's gaze met hers. She didn't look away. Didn't balk from the simmering rage in his eyes. Beside her, Caelia subtly shifted her weight to the balls of her feet.

Larkin hoped the woman didn't do something stupid. "After all his letters, I thought Garrot was eager to speak with us. Perhaps I was wrong."

Met gestured to the hundred enchantresses behind her. "Why them?"

"'Why them, Majesty,'" Caelia corrected.

Met glared at Caelia, who met his gaze without flinching. He lowered into a mocking bow. "My apologies, *Majesty*. Would you like to give a reason for this… visit?"

"I would not," Larkin said.

Garrot walked through the doorpane. She hadn't thought it possible for him to look worse than the last time she saw him. She'd been wrong. He'd aged ten years since she'd seen him last. He'd gone from thin to skeletal, his skin sallow and sagging. Despite the heat, he wore a cloak drawn close about his shoulders, and he was slightly breathless, as if he'd come at a run.

He was obviously ill. The same illness Denan had? The druids had probably brought it to the Alamant. She never should have made this foolish bargain. The druids couldn't be trusted, not even to keep their sickness to themselves.

Larkin felt an all-consuming rage. If he'd done something to Nesha or her baby, Larkin would kill him.

"Garrot—" Met began, concern clear on his face.

Garrot held out a hand.

"You're sick as well?" Mytin asked.

Garrot raised a brow. "As well?"

Larkin wanted to kick her father-in-law. Garrot didn't need to know Denan was also sick. "There are quite a few people ailing," she said quickly.

Garrot grunted. "Majesty, Arbor." He nodded to a greeting each of them, the cravat covering his blight firmly in place over his neck. He looked expectantly at Caelia.

"Unit Commander Caelia," she responded, her demeanor and voice betraying nothing of the turmoil she must be feeling.

He nodded to her as well. "I assume this is about all the letters your king has ignored."

Larkin could flare her magic and lunge, her blade slicing through his neck faster than he could scream. But she'd promised Denan she wouldn't. Instead of answering, she let out a long breath.

Mytin shot her a sideways look. "We've spent the last few days testing our leaders, military, and constables for ardents. Today, we begin with the populace, starting from the top down. Will you submit yourself and your people to be tested?"

Garrot folded his hands behind him. "Tested how?"

Caelia pulled up her sleeve to reveal a scratch just above her wedding sigils. "If your blood runs red, you are clean. Black and you die."

She sounded a little too eager. Larkin tried to catch the woman's gaze, but Caelia didn't look away from Garrot.

Garrot looked between the two women. "Why has your king sent his wife and father to tell me this instead of coming himself?"

That was none of Garrot's business. She ignored the question. "I have other tasks requiring my attention. Will you submit or not?"

He studied her. "We were promised magic. You have yet to deliver. I see no reason to submit until you do."

"I will not risk giving ardents magic," Mytin said. "Only the men who pass the test will receive thorns."

"When?" Garrot asked.

"Two days." Mytin's gaze narrowed. "After the king's funeral. Taking thorns before then would be highly disrespectful."

Garrot considered them. "I will test my men myself. If we find any ardents, we'll inform you immediately."

"You don't know who to trust," Mytin said.

"My enchantresses have all tested clean," Caelia said. "We will guard your men in the Hall of Althea's dining hall. One at a time, they will be taken across the bridge to the Hall of Thorns's training hall. We will encircle the man to be tested in a shield wall, and they'll cut their own arms."

Garrot's eyebrows were halfway up his forehead. "I politely decline."

Larkin gave a humorless laugh. "You misunderstand, Garrot. We will test your men or escort you from the Alamant. You choose."

Mytin shot her a flat look. Removing the druids was not something anyone had discussed. They needed all the Idelmarchian fighters they could get. But not at the cost of ardents destroying them from the inside out.

Garrot shifted his cloak forward over his shoulders, as if he were chilly even in this blistering heat. "When are we going to learn to trust each other, Larkin?"

"Never," she said.

Mytin's lips thinned in disapproval. She probably should have said something diplomatic, but this was the man who'd nearly murdered her. Twice. Had murdered Bane and her grandfather. The man who'd turned her own sister against her. He was not to be trusted.

"Then the wraiths have already succeeded in dividing us," Garrot said.

She stood her ground. "Do you really believe we mean to slaughter you? We could have done that right after we stripped you of weapons."

Garrot let out a frustrated huff. His gaze shifted to Larkin. "I want your word that my men will not be hurt."

"So long as you do not threaten us or try to escape," Caelia said, "your men will not be harmed."

"Met," Garrot finally said. "Round up my high druids and have them wait in the training hall. Make sure all the men are in the dining hall. Inform them that the enchantresses are there to see they don't escape. Anyone who tries to run or puts up a fight will be killed on suspicion of fraternizing with the enemy."

Met stepped closer. "They could slaughter us. We can't allow—"

"Met," Garrot barked. "Now."

Met shot them a hateful look and went.

Garrot stepped back and gestured for Larkin to go ahead. "I will hold you to your bargain."

All the hairs on the back of Larkin's head stood up at the idea of turning her back to Garrot. "After you."

He rolled his eyes and crossed the doorpane.

As soon as the man stepped out of sight, Mytin leaned in. "Are you trying to provoke him?"

"You don't know Garrot like I do," she said. "Haven't seen the depths he'll sink to get what he wants. We go in with a show of strength or we don't go in at all."

Mytin made an unhappy sound. "I hope you know what you're doing."

So did she.

CHAPTER

BLOOD

West and Atara stepped through the barrier first, followed by Mytin and Larkin, then Mytin's guards, Devon and Jenly. They made their way along the colonnade toward the Hall of Thorns. Behind them came four pages and two dozen enchantresses.

Larkin motioned to Farwin, who jogged ahead of the other boys to catch up to her. "Where is she?"

"Third level." Farwin looked pointedly ahead. "Left of center."

Those were the rooms the professors had used. There had to be fifty chambers scattered through those boughs. She'd never figure out which one without the boy. "Stay close."

He nodded and dropped back, just behind the guards. Larkin glanced across the thirty feet separating her from Caelia and the other enchantresses, who left the colonnade and entered the Hall of Althea.

The druids were already on their feet, their breakfast forgotten, as the enchantresses circled the dining hall. They'd been stripped of all weapons upon entering the Alamant. Larkin wondered if that left them feeling helpless. Powerless. She hoped so.

Focusing on the path in front of her, Larkin motioned to the pages. "Wait just outside the doorpane."

The boys nodded.

Taking a deep breath, Larkin, along with Mytin and their four guards, stepped into the Hall of Thorns. A hundred yards across, the empty training platform took up the whole main level. The roof was disc shaped, the panes clear, giving her a view into the tree above. Different-sized circles had been painted on the floor. Along the edges of the hall, scars marked where chests of equipment had once sat. Near the far wall, a spiraling staircase disappeared into the canopy.

Midway down on Larkin's left, six high druids conversed with Garrot and Met before the archway that led to the Hall of Althea. They turned as Larkin's group entered the room. The druids ranged in age and size, but the heft of the silver medallions adorning their belts marked them as high druids.

The druids had been lying to her people for centuries—telling everyone that the girls taken by the forest were devoured by a beast. These men had had the power to change that. Instead, they'd perpetrated the same poisonous lies that had kept her people helpless and afraid. All so that they might hold all the knowledge—and therefore all the power.

"She shouldn't be here," said a druid with scraggly black hair as Larkin's group stopped before them.

She recognized him. Recognized all of them. They were the men who had made an unholy alliance with the wraiths, taken thorns from the Black Tree, and wielded its forbidden magic. Men who had slaughtered any druids who'd opposed them—including her grandfather. All while she'd watched, a helpless prisoner.

And then... then had come Druids' Folly. So many had died needlessly that night. All deaths she'd been blamed for.

Larkin had a hundred enchantresses throughout the academy and more magic than any living woman. The druids couldn't hurt her. But she could hurt them. Very badly. The urge rose so strong within her that she had to clench her fists to keep from filling them with her weapons.

Mytin shot her a concerned look.

Denan's words echoed back to her. *You're a queen.* The Alamant needed more soldiers.

"We do what we must," she murmured. Even if that meant allying themselves with murderous fools. So instead of taking her sword in hand and bathing these men in their own blood as they deserved, Larkin squared her shoulders.

"Are you quite in control of yourself, Majesty?" Garrot asked far too lightly.

"If she wasn't, you'd all be dead," Atara said dryly.

Mytin glared at Atara. West rolled his eyes.

To their credit, none of the high druids reacted to the threat, though they clearly all knew themselves at her mercy.

Mytin frowned at her before turning back to Garrot. "Best to be done with this quickly."

"We'll be conducting the tests ourselves," Garrot said.

"Fine," Mytin said before Larkin could argue. "I'd like a table and chairs."

The men looked back at Garrot, who nodded to Met. "Tables and chairs for all of us. I have a feeling it's going to be a long day."

The man stepped into the colonnade that led to the dining hall.

"Let's start with you," Mytin said with a pointed look at Garrot.

Garrot grunted and removed a small knife from his boot—so apparently some weapons had gotten through—and scratched himself. Larkin was disappointed to see it red.

"Line up by rank," Garrot ordered.

The six commanders obeyed without question, their backs straight and their hands tucked behind them.

Mytin motioned to the first man. "Name and rank?"

"High Druid Ballis," the first man said. "It's in the back."

Mytin flipped to the end of the ledger—the names must have been listed in order of rank, with lowest rank first.

Garrot stepped before the first of his men. "Bare your left forearm."

The man's brow furrowed, but he unbuttoned and rolled up his cuff, revealing pale flesh. Garrot scratched, just deep enough for a line of red to appear. Mytin checked off the man's name. And the next. And the next. All the high druids bled red.

A shame. Larkin would have liked an excuse to end them.

"Have the men line up on the colonnade and enter one at a time," Garrot said.

His men started toward the door.

Hours later, Larkin had seen more hairy forearms than she'd ever hoped to. Every single one had been clean. The table she sat at had been brought straight from the dining hall. It was covered in carvings—some of them rather boorish—and more than a little sticky.

She glanced over at the ledger Mytin held and tried to figure out how many pages were left. A couple, maybe. All the highest-ranking druids.

The more druids who passed the test, the smugger Garrot and his high druids became. She wasn't sure she could endure another couple pages.

Garrot kept surreptitiously sipping from a metal flask—probably whiskey—before dozing off in his seat, a testament to how sick the man was. Met and three men entered with baskets of bread and a pot of what smelled like beans. A pair of high druids took their seats at the table across from Larkin's and shook Garrot awake.

He looked about blearily. "Have the men wait until we've finished eating."

Met stepped outside long enough to give the order. The two servers gave each druid a piece of bread, a ladle of beans, and a cup of water.

Larkin was sweltering inside her armor. She fanned her tunic. "Weren't supplies arranged for you?"

"We prefer to see to our own needs," Garrot said as he dipped his bread in his beans and stirred it around without really eating anything.

Meaning he didn't trust the pipers not to poison him. It wasn't a bad idea, really. The men approached Larkin's table. She held up the lunch Viscott had packed for her. "We have our own food, thank you. Just some water, if you don't mind." She'd nearly drunk all hers in this oppressive heat.

Larkin pulled out a small loaf of bread, a hunk of creamy cheese wrapped in isuit leaves, and a gobby. She flared her sigil and used her magic to cut the loaf and spread the cheese across the slices; it was handy to always have a knife. She alternated bites of bread with bites of gobby. It was simple but delicious.

"I brought you something special, Queen Larkin." One of the servers, a rail thin man, set a flaky pastry on the table before her. "Because of you, my daughters are safe from the Forbidden Forest."

West's hand shifted to his sword hilt.

Larkin shot him a glare and offered the man a smile. "Thank you, sir."

The man bowed.

Licking her lips, Atara eyed the pastry and then the man. "I helped, you know."

"I didn't bring more preserves, but—" the man began.

"That's quite enough," Garrot snapped.

Met stormed up behind the man and grabbed his tunic. "Why are you so intent on being close to the queen?"

Larkin hadn't thought the man dangerous, but then, she'd never suspected Unger either. She pushed to her feet and flared her weapons. West and Atara flanked the man. Devon pulled behind him. Jenly flared her shield.

The server's gaze darted about. "But you said—"

Met hauled him closer. "Roll up your sleeve!"

The man paled. "I don't do well with the sight of blood, sir."

"What kind of soldier can't handle blood?" Met released him and pulled out a knife. "Just roll up your cursed sleeve and let's be done with it."

"I'm not a soldier," the man said. "I'm a cook."

Met pushed the knife toward the server's arm. The server smacked Met's hand away. Met pinned him on Larkin's table, scattering their lunches everywhere. "Lousy piece of forest-grubbing—" But his gaze wasn't on the man squirming beneath him. It was locked on Mytin.

Larkin recognized the predator's gaze just as Met threw his knife at Mytin. It clattered against Jenly's shield, sending faint ripples across its surface.

Suddenly, everyone was scrambling. Met leaped over Larkin's table and slammed into her shield. Releasing her sword, Larkin braced with both hands and gathered her magic to pulse. But Garrot and his high druids appeared behind Met, knives in one hand and chairs in the other.

Pulsing now could very well kill them, which could very well start a war. *Cursed, idiotic druids!*

Atara charged Met from Larkin's left. He danced back from her sword and Larkin's shield. Met had left to fetch the tables when the other high-ranking druids had been tested. And as Garrot's second, his name would have been on the last pages of the ledger.

"We didn't test him," Larkin growled.

The druids weren't the only idiotic ones.

"Larkin, get back," Mytin cried and tried to come toward her.

"Stay behind me!" Jenly demanded as she backed him toward the closest exit—the archway that led to the Hall of Althea—and the enchantresses waiting on the other side.

"Larkin!" West motioned her toward the exit.

She ignored him and advanced on Met with Atara and the druids.

"The forest take you," West growled as he took his place on her right. "My job is to keep you safe, woman. Stop making it impossible."

Larkin ignored him.

Met must have known he'd soon be trapped. He pivoted and threw another knife, which embedded in one of the druid's shoulders. He threw two more knives in quick succession, one hitting the other druid and the other piercing Garrot's chair. Atara lunged. Her sword punched through his arm, the bone breaking with a snap. The arm dangled, black blood pumping.

Confirmation for what Larkin already knew. Met was an ardent.

Garrot threw his knife, which slammed into the ardent's back. Met simply drew another knife with his other hand and charged Larkin again. She ducked behind her shield while Atara and West stabbed him. West's blade went through Met's sternum and out his back, severing his spine.

Out of the corner of her eye, Larkin caught sight of movement behind Mytin. "Behind you!" She gestured toward the doorpane that led to the Hall of Althea, where six more druids—ardents?—poured into the room.

All of them angled for Mytin. Ardents, then. Where had they got the swords?

Working together, the druids and pipers met them. Devon shoved Mytin out of the way and met an ardent's sword with his own, then bashed the creature in the side with his shield. His sword whipped up and down, cutting off a chunk of the ardent's head.

"Enchantresses!" Atara cried.

Where are they? But in a beat of silence, Larkin heard fighting going on beyond both doorpanes. The enchantresses on both colonnades had been attacked.

"Seal the doorpanes!" Garrot cried, but no one could fight their way to seal them off.

Garrot grabbed a sword from the fallen ardent and stood shoulder to shoulder with West. Jenly hauled the Arbor to his feet and herded him toward Larkin. Atara and Larkin ran to meet them. Larkin, Atara, and Jenly flared a shield wall around the Arbor.

"Are you hurt?" Larkin asked her father-in-law.

Mytin held a dagger in his right hand, his eyes scanning for danger. "No."

An ardent stumbled into the room, black blood streaming down the side of his head. Garrot stabbed him in the guts, West through the neck. Another ardent charged through. Garrot lifted his sword to meet the creature's blow, a blow which easily toppled him. Garrot tried to rise, only to fall back.

Taking his place, West ducked behind his shield, wrenched the ardent's shield up, and swiped his sword across the ardent's chest. The ardent tried to lift his sword again, but his muscles had been cut. West dropped back and beheaded him.

Larkin ached to join the guards—to help before one of them died—but she couldn't leave Mytin unprotected.

An ardent battling Devon broke free and tried to lob a knife into the opening above their shields. Larkin pulsed, sending the ardent and his knife flying.

Within seconds, enchantresses entered the fray, Caelia at their head. Larkin gritted her teeth to keep from breaking formation to help. Within seconds, it was over.

"Secure the panes." Caelia strode into the hall, blood dripping from her scalp down her temple. "And double-check that the ardents are dead."

Enchantresses twisted their fingers against the numerous panes, turning them opaque and cutting off the breeze. Within seconds, sweat dripped down Larkin's body and soaked her tunic.

Caelia surveyed the room, enchantresses standing arm's length apart throughout, and stormed over to Larkin and Mytin. "Are either of you hurt?"

They both shook their heads.

"What happened?" Larkin asked.

Caelia's mouth thinned. "The ardents planned the whole thing. Nearly every high druid waiting on the colonnade was one. Had to have been at least thirty of them. They all rushed toward the training room at once. We held most of them off."

The druids would need new leadership after this.

An enchantress jogged up to Caelia. "We're secure, but two of our enchantresses are badly hurt."

"Send a runner for healers," Caelia said.

Larkin released her magic, her shield winking out. "Send one of the pages—they're the fastest runners in the city." She pointed toward the exit leading to the Hall of Ivy, where the boys were. Light grant they were all right.

The enchantress bowed and took off.

"Atara," West called as he dragged an injured enchantress into the room. "Help me."

Atara and Mytin hurried over. Larkin started to follow but then caught sight of a lost-looking Garrot staring down at his two dead high druids. He tipped back his flask and drained it before moving to crouch beside not-Met, a look of betrayal and loss on his face. Not-Met shifted, his mouth moving.

The ardent was whispering with Garrot. Telling him lies? Or giving him instructions? Larkin marched over to him, her sword filling her hand. "What did he say to you?"

Garrot noted the sword in her hands. "I'm interrogating him."

"You can't interrogate ardents."

He pushed to his feet and swayed a bit, but his gaze remained fierce. "I can try." She was surprised that his breath didn't smell like alcohol but medicine.

She huffed. "Met is gone. All that's left is a bit of his cunning. The rest is all wraith."

"Hello, Larkin," said a voice that sent Larkin's teeth clenching. She recognized the preternatural darkness in Met's eyes— the kind of darkness that sucks in all light. The Wraith King was here.

"I'm going to find a way to kill you," Larkin said. "I swear it."

Not-Met chuckled. "Soon, Larkin, we will come for you. And you will willingly join us."

Larkin pushed Garrot out of the way, shifted her sword to an ax, and buried the blade in the center of not-Met's skull. Her vision ran black with the blood that sprayed across her.

"No!" Garrot shoved her.

Larkin stumbled but managed to keep her balance. She blinked hard to clear her eyes. Within moments, West was at her side and Atara was between Larkin and Garrot, with more enchantresses edging closer.

"The wraiths' words are poison." Larkin let her magic fade, the blood falling like rain from where her ax used to be. She wiped her sleeve across her eyes. "Haven't you learned that by now?"

Garrot opened his mouth to berate her, turned, and paced away before rounding on her again. "You enjoyed killing him!"

She hadn't killed a man; she'd freed him. "I did not."

He tore up his shirtsleeve, baring his arm and the horrible scars where his dark sigils had been excised. "You think I don't know the joy of a righteous kill when I see it? You think I don't crave it still?"

"I'm nothing like you," Larkin bit out.

Garrot bared his teeth. "Aren't you?"

Atara shoved him. "I'm feeling pretty joyful, druid!"

Garrot ignored her. "What did the wraith mean? Why are they still after you?"

I don't know! Larkin wanted to scream.

"Stop it!" Caelia marched over to them. "What is all this about?" Then she caught sight of the blood soaking Larkin's face and shirt. "Light save us, you're covered in ardent blood."

Larkin felt it then, the blood rapidly cooling against her skin. Tasted the iron in her mouth. She bent over and spit, the movement pushing her damp collar against her throat.

Caelia grabbed her arm and dragged her away. "Ardent blood is just like wraith blood. You have to get it off."

Larkin shot her a bewildered look. "No it isn't."

Caelia pinched her. "Go find your sister," she whispered. "I'll keep him occupied as long as I can." She rounded on Garrot. "We're going to test the rest of your men—and we're going to do it my way." She herded him toward the Hall of Althea.

Caelia had just given Larkin the perfect excuse to find her sister. But first, she cast about for Mytin. He was pale but looked unharmed. Larkin addressed his guards. "Take a dozen enchantresses and get him somewhere safe."

Larkin turned on her heel and hustled toward the exit that led to the Hall of Ivy and Farwin.

"Larkin," Mytin called after her, worry plain in his voice.

"They're not after me," she called without looking back. And even if they were, the wraiths wouldn't allow her to be hurt. *I'm probably the safest person in the Alamant.*

"You're not going anywhere without us," Atara said. Beside her, West wore a stubborn look that said it would be easier to overthrow the curse than shake him.

She motioned for them to follow her as she stepped through the doorpane leading to the Hall of Ivy. A dozen enchantresses and double that in dead ardents clogged the colonnade. Most of the enchantresses bore injuries. Five lay completely prostrate. The others were helping them. There was blood everywhere.

"Where did those ardents even get the weapons?" West asked.

"Probably from other ardents." Larkin looked him up and down. "You did pretty well fighting with your left hand."

He grinned.

Farwin and the two remaining pages hauled the ardents' bodies out of the way. One of the boys limped.

"Light," Atara said. "They're just children!"

What had Denan said? Something about there being no place in the Alamant for children. Better they become men now and have a chance at survival.

"Boys," Larkin called.

Farwin smacked the other two pages to get their attention. Leaping over bodies, they came running over.

Larkin directed one to report to Denan, the other to continue helping the enchantresses. Frowning, they rushed to do as they were told. "Farwin, lead the way."

Farwin stepped onto the railing and hauled himself onto the roof of the training room. "It's best way to come up from under the chamber."

Good thing the enchantresses had turned the panes opaque.

"Where are we going?" West asked suspiciously.

"To fetch my sister," Larkin said.

West groaned. Atara smiled wolfishly.

"Nesha better appreciate this," Larkin grumbled as West interlocked his fingers and hoisted her up.

CHAPTER 17

NESHA

L arkin, West, and Atara followed Farwin as he scrambled from branch to branch until they reached the base of a colonnade on the second level. Farwin leaped onto a vertical branch, pushed off it, and caught hold of the bottom railing. He dangled over the training room's roof—a fall that would break him to bits.

Larkin gasped and hurried to reach him. But he was already pulling himself up. She rested her hand over her heart and tried to squelch the horrid panic twisting her insides.

"Huh." West's mustache twitched. "Who knew such a scrawny kid had the strength for that?"

"You obviously don't know children," Atara muttered.

Farwin peeked between the railing to confirm the way was clear, rolled over the top, and signed for them to wait. He disappeared. A minute later, he returned and motioned them up.

Instead of trying what Farwin had, West boosted Larkin again.

"Ugh," he cried. "You stepped on my mustache."

Trying not to laugh or think of the fall, she scrambled up the railing. Atara followed. They both lay on the colonnade, stuck their hands through the bottom of the railing, and helped West up.

"Maybe you should trim that thing," Atara puffed.

"Who would I be without my mustache?" he said, clearly offended.

Atara rolled her eyes. Larkin bit off a laugh.

The three of them hurried to where Farwin peered around a branch. He pointed to a single guard on a side colonnade before a three-room chamber. The guard was young, a boy with a blotchy beard. He faced away from them, watching below, where healers were helping the injured.

Larkin bit her lip. "All right. We dart him and—"

"He'd call for help before the venom took effect," Atara said.

"You need to act helpless and distraught about the blood," West said. At Larkin's unsure look, he grunted. "Trust me. Men love a woman in distress."

Farwin nodded emphatically.

The tips of Larkin's ears felt hot. "And then what?"

"Then dart him," Atara said. "Make it look like an accident."

"Why am *I* the one doing this?" She was supposed to be a queen, after all.

Atara raised her eyebrows. "Because you're the one covered in blood."

Grumbling, Larkin started on her armor straps; it was hard to look helpless when wearing armor. Atara helped her.

"If it isn't working," West said, "take off more clothes."

Farwin blushed furiously.

Larkin stood in nothing but her long tunic, which wasn't an uncommon a sight in the Alamant but scandalous in the

Idelmarch. She tucked in her amulet, reached into Farwin's coat, and palmed a dart.

She shot West a glare. "Don't let the boy see."

West gave Farwin a little shove back the way they'd come. "Watch the other side of the colonnade. Tell us if anyone is coming."

Farwin slipped away.

Muttering under her breath, Larkin took a deep breath and then staggered into view. Standing in only her damp tunic, she scrubbed at the stains on her skin. "I have to get it off."

She pretended to see the guard—whose mouth had fallen open—and stumbled toward him. "Ardent blood is poison. I have to wash it off." She reached for him, gripped his robes in her hands, and pulled his body flush with hers. "Please. I have to get it off."

He swallowed hard. "All of these chambers have a shower."

She stepped toward the chamber behind him. He caught her arm. "Not this one."

She broke down into fake sobs and launched into his arms. He staggered back into the railing. She stabbed him in the back with the dart and quickly dropped it over the side.

"Ah!" He twisted to look behind him. "Something poked me."

Larkin folded her arms around herself, making sure to push up her breasts, and pretended to cry some more.

His grimace softened. "The next room should be open."

She nodded and moved down the colonnade.

Behind her, she heard him stagger. "What—why am I dizzy?"

She kept walking, waiting for the sound of a thud. When it came, she hustled back to him. He lay sprawled across the colonnade. He blinked up at her, fear in his eyes. This was going to get the poor boy in trouble. Feeling bad, she crouched at his side.

"I can't move my legs." His hands fluttered. "It's climbing down my arms."

The boy could still call for help. "It's the ardent blood—sometimes it affects people like this." She pulled out the antidote vial. "Take this. It will cure it." She poured it down his throat so he wouldn't die of the venom and rose to her feet. "I'll get water."

She slipped through the barrier and found herself in a large chamber set up like most Alamantian rooms. A bed, armoire, and table, plus an extra room and a bathroom. Not daring to call her sister's name for fear of alerting the guard to her true purpose, Larkin eased toward the first room.

A soft snuffing brought her up short. She knew that sound—the sound a baby makes before it's fixing for a good cry. She followed the sound into the side room. There was a bed and a cradle. And inside the cradle was a three-month-old child. The face had just started to plump out, the soft spots filling in, and there was a shock of black hair against pale skin.

The baby looked just like Bane.

He would have taught the child to swim and fish in the river. Played the game where you had to guess what he held in his hand. Spent hours tending the animals together. The boy's grin would have been sticky with Venna's jams.

But for a twist of fate, Larkin would be married to Bane now. She could have a child of her own on the way. She wouldn't be embroiled in politics and facing a war with the wraiths.

The baby squirmed and let out a little squawk.

A song came to her mind—a song of loss and longing.

Blood of my heart, marrow my bone,
Come hear the saddest story e'er known.
A cursed queen, her lover lost,
A forbidden magic and dreadful cost.

Consumed by evil, agents of night,
Seek the nestling, barred from flight,
Midst vile queen's curse of thorny vine,
Fear not the shadow, for you are mine.

In my arms, the answer lie:
A light that endures so that evil may die.

She sang it for the child, but also for herself. For her grief at the loss of the life she might have led. For the lives that Bane, Venna, Talox, and countless others should have led.

"Larkin," someone breathed from behind her.

Larkin knew that voice as thoroughly as she knew her own. It had been the voice that had risen to her defense time and again. The voice that had called Larkin's name a hundred different ways—from exasperated to gentle to desperate. It was also the voice that had condemned Larkin to burn, even if she hadn't known it at the time.

Larkin faced her sister. The last time Larkin had seen Nesha, she'd been heavy with child. Larkin had finally been able to convince Nesha of the truth: that the druids' unholy alliance with the wraiths was going to get Larkin killed. Going to get them all killed. That Larkin had never betrayed her. Nesha had gone behind Garrot's back to free Larkin so she could warn Denan.

Now Nesha's stomach was flat, her breasts fuller. She wore a simple dress of black, which made her striking features even more vivid. With her violet eyes, auburn hair, and fine features, she was the most beautiful woman Larkin had ever seen.

No wonder Garrot hadn't been able to resist her.

"The forest take me," Nesha said. "You're covered in blood. Are you hurt?"

"I'm fine. Ardents masquerading as druids attacked. We killed them all." Larkin swallowed back tears. "Do you ever think what our lives might be like if Sela hadn't gone into the forest?"

Nesha sagged. "All the time."

So many horrible things had happened because of that moment. But then, so had many beautiful things. Things she would have missed had that moment never happened. Talox's gentle protection. Tam's teasing. Aaryn's strength and Mytin's kindness. Magalia's skill and Alorica's wit. Just to name a few.

Denan.

Larkin might wish Bane and the others were still with them, but she wouldn't go back to the way things were before. She wouldn't wish Denan away.

Larkin stooped and inhaled the baby's sweet scent. "Boy or girl?"

Nesha twisted her hands. "Boy."

Larkin smiled. Bane would have loved that. Loved a son to fish with and swim with and love. "He's beautiful, Nesha. What's his name?"

"Soren."

A scuffing sounded from outside the room. Alarmed, Larkin pushed past her sister and stepped into the main room. West dragged the limp guard through the doorpane. Nesha gasped.

Atara followed, her arms loaded with Larkin's armor. She set it on the table. "Good. You found her. Let's go."

"What's taking you so long?" West exclaimed at the same time Nesha said, "Go? Go where?"

Her step shortened because of her twisted foot, Nesha backed away. "Larkin, what's going on? Who are those people?"

"We're here to rescue you." Larkin picked up a chest. "Pack up whatever you can carry. Hurry."

Nesha bounced her fussy baby. "Larkin, I'm not sure... I mean, I know what Garrot has done—he told me everything. I just... I love him. He's a good man."

Was serving Larkin up to a mob to be burned at the stake good? What about killing their grandfather and all his councillors? Joining forces with the wraiths? Offering Larkin up like a sacrifice? Refusing to listen to her warnings and starting a war with the pipers that nearly got them all killed? But the worst of it...

Larkin opened the armoire and started shoving clothes in the chest. "He killed Bane. And he made me watch."

Nesha held her baby close. "You didn't see him after the battle. Didn't see him racked with torment by what he'd done." She bit her lip. "Maybe he does have a cruel streak. Maybe all leaders and warriors do. All I know is that he loves me and our son. He would do anything to protect us."

"Then why did he allow you and your baby"—she refused to think of him as Garrot's son— "to risk the Forbidden Forest?"

"I didn't give him much of a choice."

This surprised Larkin. Nesha had always been the cautious, reasonable one, while Larkin had inherited a wild streak from their father. But then, Nesha was also silently stubborn when she wanted something. She might not go head on against Garrot, but she would hide herself in a supply wagon until it was too late to send her back.

"Why would you—" Larkin began.

"To see my family again!" Nesha cried.

"Nesha—" Larkin began.

"Garrot needs me. You have no idea how much."

Mama needed her. And Sela. And Brenna. And Larkin. But Nesha would choose this horrible human over all of them. A fine mist of rage filled Larkin's lungs with all the hateful things she wanted to say. Her sigils ached with raw power. Larkin couldn't even look at Nesha for fear of setting that rage free.

"Fine. Stay with him, then." Larkin stormed toward the doorpane.

Nesha hurried after her. "Please, Larkin. Don't make me chose. I can have you both."

Larkin rounded on her. "Is posting a guard outside your door love? What about hiding the letters Mama wrote?"

With all the shouting, Soren started to cry again. Nesha pulled down her dress to nurse him. "The guard is for my protection! And the letters… Wait, what letters?"

Larkin shook her head. "You're a fool."

A shout sounded. Garrot darted into the room. West stepped in front of him, his sword at the other man's throat.

"Drop it," West said.

Garrot dropped the sword he'd taken off the ardent. Atara hurried to Larkin and helped her strap her armor back on—it looked ridiculous over the fancy dress. Where was Farwin? Why hadn't the boy warned them?

Garrot's throat bobbed. "Nesha…"

Nesha looked at him with big eyes. "Is it true? Has Mama written me?"

He gritted his teeth. "If you went to them, they would never let you return to me. They would have kept you prisoner."

A little sob escaped Nesha's throat. She forced it back. "You promised no more lies. You swore you were going to make it right."

He took a step toward her. West flicked his sword, slapping the flat side against Garrot's cheek and leaving a vivid welt. Atara jerked the strap around Larkin's waist too tight, but she didn't complain.

Mouth in a hard line, Garrot backed up. "Love, listen—"

"What did you do with the letters I wrote?" Nesha cried over her baby's wails.

So Nesha had tried to contact them. The forest take him.

Garrot's shoulders fell. "I still have them."

She shook her head in disbelief. "You know how much I miss my mama. How much I want Soren to know my family. You let me think they hated me!"

"I couldn't risk losing you." Garrot's voice shook. "I can't. Not you too."

"I'm not Magalia!" Nesha shoved the baby into Larkin's arms.

So Nesha knew about Garrot being engaged to Magalia—an engagement broken by the pipers stealing her in the night. Atara finished the last two straps.

Nesha stormed around the room, shoving dresses and jewelry into the chest. "You don't make my choices for me!"

Tears filled Garrot's eyes. "Please, Nesha. Don't take my son from me. Please."

"He's not your son!" Larkin shouted, the baby in her arms startled and cried even louder. Bouncing Soren, Larkin softened her volume but not her fury. "He's Bane's son."

Garrot's hard gaze shifted to Larkin. "You can't take them."

"You're not married to her, Garrot," Larkin said. "You have no rights."

Garrot took a step back. He was going to run; she could see it in his eyes. He'd gather his men. Stop Nesha from escaping. If the enchantresses interfered, there would be another battle today.

Denan had said no incidents.

"Stop him," Larkin said.

Garrot turned and ran through the doorpane.

CHAPTER 18

CAELIA

Before West and Atara could barrel after Garrot, he stumbled back inside the room. Caelia stepped in after him, her sword pointed at his chest.

"Ancestors!" Nesha grabbed her sobbing baby from Larkin and backed to the edge of the room.

"Do you know who I am?" Caelia asked.

Garrot searched for escape, but Atara, West, and Larkin all had their swords out.

Seeing he was surrounded, Garrot lifted his hands. "No."

Had Caelia lied to Larkin to get close to Garrot? Was this her plan all along? Or had she become worried about Larkin and come looking? "Caelia, what are you doing?"

"Bane was my brother." Caelia's voice shook. Garrot remained silent. "Nothing to say?"

"He killed four of my men," Garrot said.

Caelia's eyes narrowed. "Who were trying to kill an innocent woman and the man who'd come to rescue her!"

Garrot shook his head. "Nothing I say will change what happened. Or bring your brother back. So do what you have to do."

"Caelia," Larkin said sternly. "I know how you feel. Light, I nearly killed him at the embedding ceremony, but you can't do this."

Nesha crept closer, her eyes pleading as she held her baby tight. "He thought he was protecting his people from evil, same as you're doing now."

Caelia's gaze flicked to her. "My brother deserves justice."

Garrot held his hands out to his sides. "Then take it."

Nesha rushed forward, but Larkin blocked her. She couldn't let Soren anywhere near a sword fight.

"Larkin," Atara asked. "What do you want us to do?"

What we must. "Caelia, if you do this, I swear I will see you exiled."

Caelia gritted her teeth. "I know you hate him as much as I do. He deserves to rot in the ground. Not my brother."

"Yes," Larkin admitted. "But not like this." Not after she'd promised Denan.

Tears welled in Caelia's eyes. "I wasn't there to protect him."

Larkin was there and still didn't protect him. A wave of sorrow crashed over Larkin. She steadied herself until it passed. "Bane always had the same regret about not protecting you."

Caelia stared into Larkin's eyes for a long moment, then lunged forward. Larkin braced for Garrot's death, but Caelia only hit him in the head with the pommel of her sword. He crumpled bonelessly to the floor.

Baby pressed to her chest, Nesha gave a little cry and ran to kneel beside him, her hand over his mouth to check for breath. "He's alive."

West looked at the baby with distaste. "Can you get it to stop?"

Atara shot him a flat look. "Don't ever have children."

Caelia wiped her eyes with the back of her hand. "Let's go."

Farwin stumbled into the room. A bruise swelled on the side of his head, and his eyes were dazed. "Sorry, Majesty. He sneaked up on me."

"Go!" Larkin grabbed Nesha's arm and hauled her to her feet. The baby wailed, his face red.

"But Garrot's hurt," Nesha cried.

"He'll be fine," Larkin said.

Atara and West led the way. Larkin herded Nesha and Soren out, leaving the chest of clothes behind. They leaped over the darted guard. Larkin stayed close to Nesha, who was having a hard time keeping up with her limp. Dagger in hand, Farwin brought up the rear.

"Are the wounded out?" Larkin asked.

Caelia's gaze flicked to Nesha and her baby. "Yes, and we've finished the testing. Everyone's out but the dozen enchantresses I left in the Hall of Thorns."

They hustled down the colonnade to the stairs that wound into the training room. The enchantresses waiting below glanced up at them in surprise.

"Let's go!" Larkin cried. "Now!"

"Half in front and half in back," Caelia cried. "We're about to be attacked."

The enchantresses hustled into position. Soren had finally stopped crying. Atara and West crowded Larkin so close she wanted to shove them. Farwin still held his dagger like he might get a chance to use it.

"Put that away," Larkin snapped at him.

He grumbled but obeyed. Close on the heels of six enchantresses flaring shields, they ran out of the training room and onto the colonnade.

From above, Garrot cried, "Stop those enchantresses." He stood on the second level and pointed at Larkin. "They're kidnapping Nesha!"

In the dining room and along the opposite colonnade, druids dropped what they were doing to sprint for the Hall of Ivy. It was a race now. If the druids beat them to the rotunda, they'd be trapped.

"We have to reach the atrium first," Larkin cried.

"Run!" Caelia cried.

Larkin took Soren from Nesha, but still her sister couldn't keep up. They reached the halfway mark when druids pounded up the colonnade behind them, blocking off any chance of retreat. Nesha looked back, her eyes wide with fear.

Larkin gripped her arm and didn't let go. "Keep moving."

They entered the rotunda, but the clutch of soldiers had beaten them there.

"Halt!" Caelia stuttered to a stop.

The enchantresses skidded to a stop. Those in the back ran into them. Larkin bumped into Atara, who nearly went down. West hauled them both back by their backplates. The baby squalled in protest. Larkin pushed him back into Nesha's arms and flared her sword.

The rotunda filled with dozens of druids. The men must have already been inside the Hall of Ivy. Larkin and her group had never stood a chance. Before they could even consider retreating, the druids who'd been chasing them arrived. A dozen of them, more coming by the second.

They were trapped.

"Shield wall!" Caelia shouted. The enchantresses circled the group, shields flared. Atara and West squished Larkin and Nesha between them. No one moved to attack; they just eyed each other.

Caelia gestured to the hazy barrier, which meant it was passable. "My entire unit is waiting on the other side."

The enchantresses could fight their way to Caelia's group, but the fallout could cost them the war. Larkin had to find a peaceful way out of this. "Don't attack unless they do."

"Nesha!" From behind, Garrot pushed through his men. He stumbled and nearly fell over. One of his men shored him up. Arm around the man's shoulder, Garrot staggered to the shield wall and held out his hand to Nesha. "I know you're angry," he panted, "but we can work this out. Just come back."

Larkin pushed her sister behind her. "Nesha knows what you are now, Garrot. Let us go."

Garrot ignored her. "Nesha, have I ever been anything but kind to you?"

Tears streaked down Nesha's cheeks. "How can I trust anything you say?"

"Don't respond to him," Larkin said over her shoulder.

Garrot's expression was all loving tenderness. "It won't happen again. I swear it."

The baby started crying again. Nesha bounced and shushed him. "Like you swore you were doing Bane a favor?"

Garrot's hand fell to his side. "That's what this is about. You still love him."

"No," Nesha said. "This is about your lies. Your cruelty."

"Bane abandoned you, love. For *her*." His accusing gaze fell on Larkin.

Caelia looked between the two, her eyes wide with disbelief. And then her gaze zeroed in on Soren, who looked so much like his father. And judging by her wondrous expression, she recognized her brother in the boy.

Garrot was never going to let them go without a fight. *The forest take him.* "Caelia, get us out of here."

"Pulse!" Caelia cried.

All the enchantresses pulsed in unison. Some druids were smart enough to drop. The rest were blown back, slamming into each other or the rotunda's support walls. Some went straight through the openings, a distant splash confirming that they'd hit the lake. All in all, three dozen men went down. But a dozen still blocked the exit.

"With me!" Caelia charged, her enchantresses moving with her.

They surged forward, Atara and West sticking so close to Larkin and Nesha that she could barely breathe. As they came upon the remaining druids between them and the exit, Caelia cried again, "Pulse."

They blasted a hole through the druids and ran out onto the bridge. The surprised enchantresses waiting there parted to let them through.

"Seal them in!" Caelia said.

The enchantresses guarding the exit flared their shields over the doorpane, trapping the druids inside.

Garrot pounded on the shields. "Nesha!"

Larkin pointed to two random enchantresses. "You and you, get my sister and her baby to my hometree and guard her there."

The two bowed and stood shoulder to shoulder with Nesha. Her sister wiped the tears from her cheeks. "Larkin, don't start a war over me."

Is that what she'd just done? Denan was going to kill her. Larkin glanced over her shoulder to see more and more druids lining up behind Garrot. A couple dozen were armed with swords taken from the ardents. But they had to know they couldn't fight their way out of this—not in the middle of the Alamant.

"Garrot knows I've won," Larkin said. "Feed Soren and wait for me at the back of the enchantresses."

Larkin shot Nesha's new guards a sharp look, silently ordering them to make sure her sister obeyed. They bowed and herded Nesha away.

Larkin looked around for Farwin, but the boy was already gone. He probably had orders to report to Denan immediately if a fight broke out. Light, Denan was going to be furious.

Atara and West stuck beside Larkin as she stepped toward Garrot. She was glad to have at least some friends during all this.

"Order your men to stand down," Larkin said. "Hand over those weapons, and the treaty will remain."

"You broke the treaty when you took her." Garrot braced himself against the shields as if they were the only things holding him up.

"She left of her own free will," Larkin said. "You want to prove you've changed? Let her go."

He ground his teeth. Larkin had no doubt that he would fight through her enchantresses to reach Nesha if there was any chance he'd win. But he was also no fool.

"She's more a prisoner with you than she ever was with me," Garrot said.

A lie. "If she wants to return to you, I'll escort her here myself." Larkin would argue and delay, but she would let her sister go.

Garrot's eyes narrowed. "Prove it."

If that's what it took to keep the peace, fine. "I'll arrange a meeting with her after the embedding." If he lived that long. The man looked like death on his feet.

"I don't believe you."

Larkin stepped closer and lowered her voice. "You don't have a choice, Garrot. Anything you have is because I allow you to have it. Cross me, and I'll have you removed from the Alamant. The forest will decide if you live or die. Don't think for a moment that your men won't betray you, that one of them isn't waiting in the wings to take your place." After all, they'd already staged a coup once.

Garrot ground his teeth. Finally, he said, "In two days' time, we will have our thorns and I will speak with Nesha. Break this, and we will leave." He leaned closer. "Because I would rather the Idelmarch be dead than slaves to the Alamant."

Shoulders slumped, he turned, gestured to his men, and stormed off.

Larkin turned to go, but Caelia was waiting for her. She drew Larkin to the railing, away from listening ears. "I don't understand. Soren is Bane's child. But Bane risked the forest and the Alamant because he was in love with you."

Larkin hung her head. "He thought he could have us both."

Caelia's head came up in understanding. "And Garrot was there, ready and willing to take care of Nesha."

Larkin nodded. "Did you plan to attack Garrot?"

"You were taking too long. And then he was just... there." Her eyes slipped closed, and she leaned against the railing. "Did Bane— Did he know? About the baby?"

"Yes. But I didn't. Not until after he took me back to Hamel."

Caelia rubbed her forehead. "She was pregnant, and he left her." She finally looked up at Larkin. "I'm sorry."

Larkin blinked back tears. "Me too." She turned and left without another word.

CHAPTER 19

TRUCE

The wind picked up, thunderclouds visible on the horizon. Larkin stepped through the archway that led to her hometree. Nesha trailed behind, her limp more pronounced from overuse. She couldn't stop gaping at the White Tree.

Larkin glanced up at her chambers. Lampents sent the shadows of pages running back and forth. Which probably meant Denan was sending and receiving letters. Probably from the council. Most of them angry.

She'd broken her promise to him. Denan was going to be so furious. Harben's fury had been followed by fists and feet. Dread felt sharp and cold inside her. *Denan is not my father.* She brushed her clammy hands on her legs and glanced at her friends.

Whatever happened, she didn't want them to witness it.

"Take the rest of the evening off," Larkin said to West before turning to Atara. "Check on Alorica and see your children."

West blew out his mustache. "I didn't know you had children."

"Three." Atara backed away from them.

"Who's taking care of them?" West asked in surprise.

Atara shot him a glare. "Their father." Her gaze settled on Larkin. "I'll see you in the morning."

West nodded a tired good night—he hadn't slept at all.

"And take the night off," Larkin called to him.

He waved without turning. Larkin wasn't sure if that wave was an agreement or simply an appeasement. Sighing, she motioned for Nesha to follow her. They descended two levels to where Mama sang a lullaby in the common room.

Nesha paused outside the doorpane. "Are you sure she wants to see me?"

"It's all she wants," Larkin said simply.

Bracing herself, Nesha stepped through, Larkin a beat behind. The room smelled of dinner—amala bird, larger birds that lived in the branches. Larkin's mouth watered. Her lunch had been smashed on the floor.

Mama sat in the rocking chair. Brenna lay asleep in her arms. Lying on a new chaise below the window, Sela stared at the White Tree. Its missing boughs sent a bolt of unease down Larkin's spine.

"It's not safe to have the pane down." Larkin hurried to close it, cutting off the delicious breeze.

Mama groaned. "But the heat is making us sick, and the guards won't let us swim."

"Mama?" Nesha asked tentatively.

Mama's head snapped up, shock plain on her face. "Nesha." She let out a cry and rushed forward to envelop Nesha in a hug. The babies between them let out simultaneous squawks of protest.

Mama pulled back and let out a little laugh. "Oh, Nesha! Your baby. My grandchild."

Nesha reached out to stroke Brenna's head. "She's gotten so big."

"Trade?" Mama said, laughter mixing with her tears.

They switched babies. Brenna immediately wailed and reached for Mama.

Nesha laughed. "I'm your sister, and this is your nephew, Soren."

Brenna whimpered.

Mama stroked Soren's cheek. "Oh, little one. You look like your father." Mama cast Nesha a chagrined look, as if she'd just realized that Nesha might not want to be reminded of that fact.

Nesha only smiled. "It's all right, Mama. We've all made mistakes. I've forgiven Bane for his."

Mama breathed out in relief and pressed her forehead against Nesha's. "I never thought you'd have the chance to be a mother."

Mama looked over her shoulder to Larkin. Her brow furrowed as she took in the green dress Larkin wore. "What happened?"

Larkin didn't have time to relay the entire story or the energy to reassure her. Denan was still waiting for her. Her body suddenly felt heavy and cumbersome, as if it were made of stone instead of flesh and blood.

She pulled off her helmet and ran her hands over her unruly hair. "Nesha will tell you all about it. How's Sela?"

"As long as we keep her drinking feverfew tea," Mama answered, "she does all right."

Her expression concerned, Nesha crossed to sit beside Sela on the chaise. "Hello, sunshine."

"Hello, sister," Sela said. Sela's skin was pale, her cheeks hollow. Dark circles lined her eyes.

Nesha's brows rose. "She's not lisping anymore?"

Mama could fill Nesha in on that too.

"Does the White Tree know what's wrong with you?" Larkin asked.

Sela gave a tiny shake of her head.

"The tree?" Nesha asked in bewilderment.

Mama came to stand to the side of Nesha. "There's so much that has happened. So much you don't know." Her expression became guarded. "How long are you staying?"

Nesha stared at the floor. "I-I'm not sure."

After everything Garrot had done—after everything Larkin had risked rescuing her—Nesha was still considering going back to him. Anger surged through Larkin.

Mama tried to smile away her worry, but the fear in her eyes didn't lie. "I'm just glad you're here. All my girls together again." She wrapped her arms around Nesha and Sela and looked up expectantly at Larkin.

Larkin didn't want to embrace anyone. She wanted to shout and rage at Nesha. But looking at the joy in Mama's eyes... Larkin refused to take this moment from her. She bent down and wrapped her arms around them both.

She held the embrace for as long as she could stand before pulling back. "I have to report to Denan."

Again, Mama failed to hide her disappointment. A pang of guilt shot through Larkin—Mama had suffered so much already. But Larkin couldn't stay another minute. Not if she didn't want to lose her temper.

"We're leaving at dawn for the White Tree." Larkin turned toward the door.

"I can't leave Sela." Mama pushed to her feet.

Arguments rose in Larkin's throat—the new butler could tend Sela for a bit—but Mama didn't really need to go. "All right."

"I'll go," Nesha said.

Larkin raised an eyebrow. "You want to attend a funeral?"

Nesha bit her lip. "I've hardly seen any of the Alamant." Not since Garrot had locked her up. "I want to see the White Tree."

"Oh, that would be wonderful." Mama's hopeful eyes pleaded with Larkin.

Did Mama think the beauty of the Alamant might convince Nesha to stay? Or was she just trying to make the two of them spend time together? Either way, Larkin couldn't think of a good reason to deny either of them.

Larkin sighed. "Fine. I'll see something suitable brought to you to wear." Denan had given Larkin enough dresses, and the two of them were of a similar size.

Larkin took the stairs to her own chambers. Every step felt heavier than the last. Just how angry was he? Steeling herself, she stepped into their room. A page beside him, Denan lay in bed, a portable desk over his legs. He looked as bad as Garrot and Sela, his golden skin ashen, dark circles under his eyes, and his cheeks bright with fever.

If he heard her come in, he didn't show it. He finished writing something, folded it into a letter, and handed it to the page. The boy took off at an easy jog, bowing as he passed Larkin.

Denan studied Larkin from head to toe. "Are you hurt?" She shook her head. He sighed in relief. "I've sent for Viscott to bring your supper—my pages tell me you didn't get lunch."

That wasn't all the pages would have told him.

Larkin unbuckled her armor; her shoulders were sore from the straps.

"Gendrin and Aaryn have searched most of the Alamant. Twelve ardents were killed. We didn't lose any of our people. The rest of the hometrees have been cordoned off and will be searched tomorrow."

"During the king's funeral?"

"The chief constable offered to oversee it—he and his men."

Larkin nodded, and a heavy silence descended. When she couldn't bear it anymore, she said, "Did Farwin tell you everything?" She couldn't help but feel a little betrayed by the boy.

"Pretty much. But I'd like to hear your side."

She set about cleaning the ardent blood from her armor with a brush, rag, and some oil. As she worked, she told him the story, from when she'd arrived at the academy to when she'd left. By the time she was done, her armor was polished and put in its chest and she had finished the meal Viscott had brought. Rain had started on the panes, thunder grumbling across the sky.

Grateful for any relief from the heat, she sat in the chair, elbows on her knees, her hands hanging limply in between.

"What do you think you did well?" Denan asked.

She glanced up at him in surprise. "What do you mean?"

"Well, you didn't kill Garrot—though if there was any justice in the world, he would either be dead or at the bottom of a deep, filthy hole. You found the ardents hidden among the druids and ended them without losing a single enchantress. You got your sister out. You avoided a battle with the druids."

She supposed she had done all that.

"What could you have done better?"

Larkin let out a long breath. "I should have insisted on a shield wall when we tested the ardents."

"Wouldn't have prevented the attack," Denan said. "And from what my father reported, you had to give Garrot something."

She considered for a moment. "I should have insisted that anyone who entered that room be tested, including the cooks and Met."

Denan nodded. "What else?"

"We should have pulled soldiers at random instead of letting them line themselves up—that way we wouldn't have had a cluster of ardents attacking at once."

He nodded and sifted through the letters littering his lap. "My mother reports that none of her enchantresses have died."

The relief that washed through Larkin was so powerful that she rested her head in her hands.

"None of the druids have either, though they demanded our guards leave the entrance. Mother conceded to move them halfway onto the bridge and plans to keep a rotating company of enchantresses in the area."

Denan handed her one of the letters. She hesitated before taking it, scanning the short letter, and then dropping it onto the table in disgust. Garrot offered to step down as Master Druid if they returned Nesha.

"You can't be considering it," Larkin said.

"What would you do?"

"Tell him to go home."

Denan grinned. "I already did."

Larkin's whole body sagged in relief. "You're not upset?"

He chuckled. "Upset? Larkin, I'm proud of you."

Tears smarted her eyes. "You are?"

He motioned for her to join him on the bed. He ran the back of his knuckles down her cheek. "You are a wonderful queen— as I always knew you would be. A little more experience under your belt, and you'll be unstoppable."

She curled around him in the bed.

Sitting at the vanity in her bathroom, Larkin turned the mirror to catch the early morning light. Instead of a fine Idelmarchian dress, which she'd sworn she'd never wear again, she wore her enchantress uniform of sapphire blue, as well as her ceremonial armor, the metal bits polished to a high shine. Aside from a swipe of berry lipstick, she wore no makeup.

She leaned forward in her chair to toggle her mantle in place over her shoulders. Peaked in the front and shoulders, a knotted, three-headed serpent proclaimed her a member of Denan's house. She traced a finger along the painted, embossed tooling. Jewels hung from the four corners as well as the peaked front and back. The emerald at her right shoulder mirrored the one Denan wore and proclaimed her royalty. The sapphire on her left was for her part in defeating the wraiths at Druids' Folly. The turquoise hanging before her breasts was for her marriage.

So many memories. Not all of them good.

In the mirror's reflection, Larkin saw Nesha step into the bathing room wearing the same dress she'd worn yesterday. Larkin didn't know how to cross the bridge between Nesha and herself. She wasn't even sure she had the strength to try.

"You look different than you used to," Nesha said.

Larkin tried to see herself as her sister would. This time, she hadn't bothered trying to hide her scars and freckles or contain her wild curls. She was through taming herself for others.

She didn't look beautiful. She looked free. Powerful. And that was far more becoming than beauty.

Larkin crossed to her armoire. "Did you not like the clothes I sent to you? You can pick something else."

Nesha shifted awkwardly. "What's wrong with what I'm wearing?"

"You'll be the only one dressed like an Idelmarchian. Do you really want all the attention that will bring?" Nesha hated to be the center of attention. Larkin pulled out a tunic, trousers, and a long, embroidered vest. "Here, Aaryn, my mother-in-law, made me this."

"Do you have anything with long sleeves?" Nesha asked softly.

Larkin arched an eyebrow. "In this heat? Don't be silly."

She reached out, taking hold of Nesha's arm. Her sister drew in a sharp breath—a pained breath—and tried to pull free.

Larkin held on tighter and drew up her sleeve, revealing perfect handprints on her forearms.

Anger was a living, breathing thing inside her.

Nesha drew her hands back, her expression full of shame.

Larkin choked back the rage and said in a soft voice, "What happened?"

Nesha rubbed her wrists. "It wasn't Garrot—we never fought. He never got angry. Until the blight." She swiped tears from her cheeks. "The pain was so intense. He didn't eat. Didn't sleep. Sometimes he heard their voices. There were times when he thought I was a mulgar. There were times Met had to pull him off me."

Met. Met the ardent. Which meant the wraiths had protected Nesha. Why?

Nesha blew her nose in a handkerchief. "He was always so heartbroken afterward. How could I be angry with him? It wasn't his fault."

It was his fault. He was the one who'd made a deal with the wraiths. And Denan suffered from the same blight. He'd never hurt Larkin. She thought of a thousand different things she might say—from condemning Garrot and chiding Nesha to demanding her sister stop being a fool—but all of that would only drive Nesha further away.

So Larkin took a deep breath, forced all her fury into the chest, and dropped it into the lake in her mind. "I'm glad you told me."

Nesha looked at her in surprise. "You're not going to threaten to kill him."

Larkin spread her hands. "I can't kill him—or rather, won't. Not when we need the druids. And anyway, I'm not a murderer." She sighed. "Maybe when this is all over, when the curse has ended, Garrot will be free of the blight. And then you can decide if you want to stay with him."

Nesha's gaze finally met Larkin's, a cautious hope filling her eyes. She seemed to mull over Larkin's words, then nodded.

Larkin glanced at the sky. Lighter by the moment. "We need to go. Denan will be waiting." She pulled out a long-sleeved tunic.

Nesha hurriedly dressed. "Is it like the men said? Do colors dance beneath the bark?"

"Yes." Larkin took hold of Nesha's hand, laying it across the open sigils at her wrist.

Nesha jerked back, her mouth open with fear. "Is it really... awake?"

"Yes." Larkin took her sister's hand. Together, they circled down the stairs to the common room. Denan was waiting for them inside. He looked even worse than yesterday, pale and drawn. Worry clenched Larkin's throat.

He rose shakily to his feet and bowed to Nesha. "You are welcome in my home, Nesha."

She bit her bottom lip. "I, uh— Thank you." She did a hasty curtsy. "Your Majesty, I don't mean to question you, but are you sure we're safe, what with all the ardents?"

Denan nodded. "The sentinels were all pricked this morning before doing a thorough search of the tree. The part of the Alamant still to be searched is cordoned off. We're as safe as we can be."

Nesha nodded in relief, but Larkin noted the tension in his shoulders. He was worried—probably for their safety and for the outcry that would happen if the king's funeral turned into a bloodbath.

Frowning, Larkin stepped closer and whispered in his ear, "Don't worry. I'll protect you." He grunted. "Just promise you won't exert yourself." He nodded. She pressed a hand to his cheek. He was still fevering. "You should be in bed," she whispered.

"Really, Larkin, this isn't the time for your womanly wiles."

189

She tipped back her head and laughed.
He grinned, clearly pleased with himself.

CHAPTER 20

FUNERAL

Larkin, Denan, Nesha, West, and Atara rowed toward the White Tree. It was raining gently, which felt wonderfully refreshing. The gray day only served to highlight the colors dancing beneath the White Tree's bark. But there were obvious gaps in the tree now—places where great boughs had been cut away. And more than half the leaves had fallen onto the surface of the lake. The boat plowed them under, where they sank, never to be seen again.

Larkin looked over to gauge Nesha's reaction.

Her sister's eyes were wide with wonder. "I wasn't prepared for how beautiful it would be. And how... alive."

Larkin knew what she meant. There was a presence about the tree. A feeling of being marked by something strange and wondrous. But all Larkin's wonder had been replaced by dread. They only had nine months before all of this was gone forever.

Nesha reached over the side and pulled one of the teardrop-shaped leaves in. It was large enough to cover her from neck to midthigh. But the normal silvery green had been replaced by a pale gold that had encroached on the leaves until only a thin tracery of green veins remained.

"Are they always this color?" Nesha asked.

Squinting as if the brightness hurt his eyes, Denan tugged his hood farther over his face; he was the only one wearing a cloak. "Even dying, the White Tree is beautiful."

Nesha whirled to face him. "Dying?"

"The druids didn't tell you." Atara rolled her eyes. "Shocking."

Garrot didn't tell her, Larkin thought.

West shot Atara a disapproving look, which she ignored.

Nesha looked between them. "But isn't the tree the source of your magic?"

"The origin of most sigils," Denan corrected. "Which is why we have to defeat the wraiths before it dies."

"Larkin said they can't be killed," Nesha said.

Denan met her gaze. "Which is also why we're building an army of Idelmarchians and Alamantians to take down the Black Tree."

Nesha leaned into Larkin and whispered, "You can't jeopardize that for me."

Larkin's hands fisted around her oar. "I'm not jeopardizing anything for you. Garrot is."

The first strains of music reached them, a somber melody that spread a hush through Larkin even with her dampener amulet. Ahead, hundreds of boats crowded the White Tree's docks, all of them hooked together to leave an opening down the center that led to the base of the White Tree's steps. That line continued with White Tree Sentinels clearing the way to the wide steps leading into the tree.

Most of the inhabitants wore their dress uniforms—the sapphire of the enchantresses, the deep green of the military, the dusty blue of the healers, the silver and white of the White Tree

Sentinels. On the older generation, those uniforms were faded or ill-fitting, but the armor had been polished to a mirror shine.

Unlike Larkin's homeland, in the Alamant there were no poor. Hunger didn't carve gouges in their faces. No tattered clothing had been patched and repatched until it fell away in tatters. But there were other signs of hardship. The missing limbs of soldiers who'd been faced with amputation to avoid becoming a monster. The gaps in families, a father or brother or husband missing.

The five of them rowed straight through the opening. People on every side watched Larkin. Some glared—the ones who blamed her for the men who had died at Druids' Folly. The enchantresses bowed with respect. Even the infants were somber and silent.

Larkin kept her gaze straight ahead, her shoulders back and her chin up. In her dress uniform and armor, with the light rain taming her frizz into gorgeous curls, she felt beautiful. Powerful. This was the kind of queen she was. A warrior queen. Not a simpering one in a glittering dress.

She was done bearing the blame for something the wraiths had done, something Garrot and his ilk had done.

Nesha wiped the tears from her cheeks. "Why am I crying?"

"It's the music," Denan said. "It's enchanted."

"You and Larkin aren't crying," Nesha pointed out.

Larkin pulled out her leaf amulet and showed it to her sister. "This amulet blunts the music, and the pipers' magic makes them less susceptible. Atara has one too."

"I want one," Nesha said.

Larkin tucked the amulet back in her tunic. "They're very rare." At least for the Alamantians.

Nesha hummed in disappointment.

At the docks, the White Tree Sentinels in their shining white-and-gold uniforms tied up their boat and helped them out. The sentinels lined up four abreast in front and behind Larkin's group, slapped their hands to their shields, and stomped their right feet. Nesha startled at the noise and stepped closer to Larkin.

Atara and West took flanking positions, effectively boxing the three of them in.

His shoulders back and his chin out, Denan leaned toward Larkin and Nesha. "There isn't much expected out of you two for this. Just stand where I tell you and keep quiet. Nesha, stay behind us."

That's all that is ever required of me. Larkin bit back her words and nodded. Nesha swallowed hard and moved behind them. Larkin put her arm through Denan's. The heat from his skin wasn't as bad as before—probably the copious amounts of tea she'd made him drink.

"Lead Sentinel." Denan nodded his permission.

Into the silence, the sentinel on the far right barked, "Honor march!"

The eight sentinels stepped out in unison. Every fourth step, they slapped the flat of their shields. Larkin matched her steps to the inexorable beat of the music, the slap of the shields like a drumbeat. They left the dock and climbed the gentle slope to the base of the stairs.

The sentinels, who operated under Arbor Mytin, all lined the way to the archway at the base of the stairs. Behind them, the crowd of Alamantian elite—mostly military leaders and their spouses—stood on either side.

Larkin couldn't help but search their faces. Any of them could be an assassin just waiting to attack. Was it the woman with the gray stripe in her hair who watched Larkin a little too long? The man with the hooded eyes who looked away too quickly? The dead-eyed child who stared into nothing?

At the base of the wide sweep of steps, the lead sentinel barked a command. His men split to the right and left, spreading out at the base of the steps.

As Larkin and Denan climbed, she glanced back to see the other four guards split as well. West and Atara prowled the empty space between the sentinels and the people, their eyes never ceasing to search for trouble. Nesha kept her shoulders back and her chin up, but her eyes were wide and darting.

We're prepared, Larkin reminded herself. But then, they'd thought themselves prepared the last time they'd had a ceremony at the tree.

Nerves made her even more sweaty in the heat; her armor prevented the breeze from reaching her skin. Sweat trailed lines down her body before hitting her clothing. She longed for a drink of water, but she refused to show weakness in front of her detractors.

At the top, Mytin waited beneath the archway. Down a step and to his right was Aaryn. They both nodded a greeting. Denan directed Larkin to stand on the last step, Nesha just below her. "Whatever you do, don't step before myself or Mytin."

Another tradition that needed changing. Later. She gave a curt nod. Nesha inclined her head.

At the head of the gathered boats, King Netrish's body sailed with at least fifty members of his family. Jaslin, Gendrin, and Caelia were all there. Jaslin wore a long gray mourning cape that trailed behind her. All wore their family mantle of a six-pointed leaf. The rain had stopped, but the clouds above were heavy and dark, promising that they weren't done with the Alamant yet.

They docked. Gendrin and his brothers lifted the king's body from the boat—his body had spent its last night at his home—laid him on a litter, and took their place behind Jaslin. The music changed to a marching dirge that sounded more like a haunted wail. Jaslin must have given the command, for the White Tree Sentinels performed the same march.

People knelt in a steady wave as the king's body passed, soft murmurs breaking the silence. At the base of the steps, Jaslin lifted her long, simple dress, the hem damp, and climbed.

Behind her, Gendrin and the others brought the king's body, which was totally covered in the sewn-together leaves of his hometree. Even with the ice he'd been packed in, a faint stench of rotting meat wafted on the breeze.

On the last step before the arch, Jaslin paused.

"Who comes to the White Tree?" Mytin intoned.

Jaslin took a deep breath. "I have come to bury my husband, king of the Alamant."

Mytin paused so long that Larkin thought he meant not to answer. Then he began listing the king's accomplishments. The battles he'd won as prince. His marriage to Jaslin. How he'd become king himself at forty-two. How he'd had four strong sons and twelve grandsons. The laws he'd enacted and changed.

"King Netrish was a good king and a good man," Mytin finished. "Light grant that the White Tree accepts him."

Mytin and Denan parted to let Netrish's family pass. When the body drew even with Larkin, the smell was strong enough to make her gag. She held her breath to keep from retching. Just behind, Caelia stared at Nesha. Her brother had been executed by Nesha's lover. As hard as that was for Larkin, it must be so much harder for Caelia.

Caelia turned away, her jaw hard. A beat of guilt and sorrow pulsed through Larkin. She counted Caelia as one of her allies, maybe even a friend. She'd hate to lose that because of Nesha.

When all of Netrish's family had passed—his parents, siblings, aunts, uncles, cousins—Denan motioned for Larkin and Nesha to join him. She looped her hand through his too-hot arm. He should be in bed, but even she had to concede that he could not miss this funeral—not when so many of the Alamantians were upset with his inability to stop the assassins.

They left the guards and sentinels behind. Up the tree they wound. Until Nesha was breathing hard—she wasn't used to climbing in and out of trees all day. Denan had gone pale, his pace slow enough that they fell behind. Larkin bore as much of his weight as she dared, his every heavy step making her more and more worried.

Finally, they crossed the main platform with its glittering font of thorns and took the first branch to the left. Twenty steps up was a platform surrounded by a shroud of vines. Here, the trunk sloped, and the bark split apart like a curtain to reveal bare wood. The portal.

Larkin, Nesha, and Denan stood to the right. Opposite them, Jaslin stood with Netrish's children, parents, and siblings. Caelia's baby babbled and waved his arm, his eyes on the leaves. One son held her skirt, the other her hand. Larkin tried to catch Caelia's eye, but the woman didn't look her way.

Gendrin and his brothers paraded past with the litter bearing Netrish's body, the rest of his family filling in the space behind. They set the body down on the portal. The scaffolding came apart. For a moment, nothing happened. And then rustling vines grew over the king's body.

Nesha gasped. Larkin had known it was coming—she'd seen it all before—and still she felt uneasy. Denan released her hand to wrap a comforting arm around her waist and pull her closer. His fevering body made her even hotter, but she didn't pull away. The vines grew until they completely covered the king; only the shape of him remained.

Then he began to sink, his body being taken into the tree. Alamantians felt it a great honor to be laid to rest like this—to have their memories become part of the White Tree, to never be forgotten. Larkin found the whole thing rather unsettling—like the tree was eating people.

Within minutes, the old king was gone. After a proper amount of time had passed, Denan tugged on Larkin's hand. Just as she turned, a shape flitted beneath her feet. The king's soul? His body? She didn't know.

Shivering, they left the platform.

"What just happened?" Nesha whispered.

The two of them walked beside Denan as Larkin explained everything as best she could. Leaning on her, Denan remained quiet, the circles under his eyes darker than ever.

Nesha glanced around before whispering, "Don't ever let them put me in there."

Larkin snorted and then covered it with a cough. "Noted."

She paused under the archway with its wide steps leading to the docks. This was where she'd been forcibly married. But that memory no longer hurt. She glanced over to see if Denan was remembering as well, but he rubbed his eyes as if they pained him.

"Go stand with West and Atara," Larkin said to Nesha. "Don't leave their side." The pipers would know she was the Master Druid's mistress and Larkin's sister. That made her a target.

Nesha obeyed while Larkin crossed to her husband. Desperate to lift his burden, even for a moment, she teased, "I'd like to see you try to force me again." She flared the sigil on her hand and raised her eyebrows in a dare.

He bit back a smile. "I wouldn't have to force you. You'd come willingly."

That she would. Not that she'd ever admit it. She leaned into him and whispered, "Only if you catch me."

He pulled her into his arms, holding her close. "I know what you're trying to do."

"Is it working?"

He sighed. "A little. I just... I can't help but feel responsible."

Because, despite all the measures they'd taken to secure the embedding ceremony, the king had still died. And despite all their efforts, they had yet to finish searching all the Alamant.

Denan's parents approached them.

"Ready for this?" Mytin asked.

Ready to face the woman who'd accused Larkin and Denan of killing her husband? The woman who'd written a scathing letter of Larkin's handling of the druids the day before? No. But custom dictated that they offer their condolences.

Aaryn must have seen some of this on Larkin's expression. "You took her queenship from her. Of course she hates you." She shot Denan a look. "Why did your wife stand beneath you at the ceremony?"

Larkin felt a rush of vindication.

His mouth fell open. "It's tradition."

"Traditions change," Aaryn said.

Denan sighed. He looked so very tired. "I already have enough opposition, Mother. I can't change everything at once."

"He's right." Larkin found herself agreeing with Denan, though she'd had the same thoughts not long ago. "The people who don't support me now definitely won't tolerate me with more power."

Mytin stepped between them. "This is not the time or place for this discussion."

He was right. The line of those wishing to express their condolences watched them, waiting for the king to go first.

"Let's just get it over with," Larkin said through clenched teeth.

With a sigh, Denan wove her arm through his. His parents fell in behind them as they approached Jaslin.

Denan bowed to the former queen. "Netrish was a great man and a great king." He cleared the emotion from his throat. "I will miss him dearly."

Jaslin's sharp gaze pierced Larkin. "What were you thinking?"

"This is not the time for this," Denan said through clenched teeth, echoing his father.

Jaslin's glare shifted to Denan. "You refused to convene a council meeting. So we will discuss it now."

"I've been ill, Jaslin," Denan said.

Jaslin ignored his statement. "So you sent *her* to deal with the druids." She pointed a finger at Larkin. "After her abysmal failings at the embedding ceremony? After her background with them?"

"My job at the ceremony was to guard against the druids," Larkin said. "Which I did." Even as she said it, Iniya's words echoed through her. *You will never make it as queen.* She tried to force them back.

Jaslin's nostrils flared. "The two of you insisted that the Alamant would not survive without the aid of the druids, and then you nearly start a war with them? Over that girl!" Now Jaslin's pointing finger fixated on Nesha, who stood stoically with Atara and West at the base of the steps.

"Jaslin." Denan's persona had shifted from patient statesman to authoritarian general in an instant. Jaslin would do very well to stop talking.

Jaslin's raised voice drew a crowd—the most powerful people in the kingdom watching the king and his council fight over the actions of his queen.

Gendrin strode through them. "Mother, that is enough!"

Jaslin held her palm out to him, her gaze boring into Larkin. "I will not follow a queen who thinks herself above the safety of our entire kingdom!"

Denan took a deep breath for a retort, but Larkin's sigils were already alight.

"I bow before no man," Larkin said in a voice trembling with fury. "Especially not a murderous Black Druid who demands the life of a woman in exchange for the survival of his own people!"

"We are not our fathers' daughters," Aaryn said.

"We are not our brothers' sisters," Larkin said back to her.

"We are not our husbands' wives," Atara shouted from the base of the steps.

And then from all over, enchantresses—women—finished, "We are our own. Warriors who fight for what's ours."

Larkin turned back to the old queen. "Women will never again be used as a bargaining chip."

Jaslin turned back to Denan. "The freedom of one doesn't outweigh—"

"Silence!" Denan said, his voice low and sharp as a scythe felling wheat.

Jaslin's mouth snapped shut.

"Denan, she's grieving," Gendrin said pleadingly. "She's not herself."

Denan dragged in a heavy breath, calling upon whatever shred of patience he had left and faced Gendrin. "I am sorry, my friend, for your loss."

He took Larkin's hand. Together, they marched down the stairs. Below them, Nesha looked mortified. Atara nodded in approval. Those queued up behind them whispered. Many in the crowd watched.

Larkin's head came up. *Let them see the kind of queen I am.* She opened her sigils, the buzzing filling her with power.

CHAPTER 21

HARBEN

As Larkin and Denan left the steps and headed toward the docks, the sentinels shifted into the same formation as before, with four in front and four in the back. West and Atara moved to the flank position. The group started through the crowd. The gusting wind picked up, and a line of rain moved toward them. It would soak everyone when it came.

Nesha fell in beside Larkin. "Larkin..."

She knew what her sister was thinking. That her relationship with Garrot wasn't that bad—certainly not bad enough to warrant losing a war. Lightning crackled across the clouds.

"It's not over yet," Larkin said just loud enough to be heard over the wind.

Denan tugged his hood back on and shivered. "Let's just see how it plays out."

Nesha pressed her lips into a thin line. "It's my decision, Larkin, whether to stay or go. And if my returning to him will save anyone, it would be worth it."

Larkin glanced around to make sure no one had overheard and motioned for her sister to lower her voice. "If it comes to that, we'll have that discussion. I promise."

Nesha held her gaze and then nodded. Larkin glanced over at Denan. He was practically swaying on his feet. She threaded her arm through his. He leaned on her a lot, which told her just how sick he was.

"We need to get home," she murmured.

He shivered. "I've overdone it," he admitted.

Light, he was hot. "You need some tea." She'd stored some on their boat.

They'd just crossed over from the White Tree to the docks when one of the pages came at a run. Larkin took the letter from the boy. "It's from the constables." She snapped the seal, scanned the letter, and stopped in her tracks.

"What is it?" Denan asked.

"A woman was found murdered early this morning," she whispered. "They don't know who she was." The letter went on to detail what she looked like. Blonde, brown-eyed, voluptuous. Larkin cringed at the last—what kind of man wrote that a dead woman was voluptuous?

"Murdered?" Nesha gasped in disbelief. Obviously, Garrot had kept the numerous murders in the Alamant from her too.

"That's how the king died," Larkin said.

"What?" Nesha cried.

Beside Larkin, Denan stiffened.

Had he seen an assassin? "What is it?" She followed his gaze and saw Harben nearly upon them. The sentinels snapped their shields together, their swords sliding out of their decorative sheaths.

Larkin's first reaction was to order the guards to let him through. But there was no reason for her father to be here.

"Show us your blood," Denan said, clearly thinking along the same lines as Larkin.

Harben jerked out a knife and cut far too deep. He lifted his arm to show the red blood running down his elbow.

"Let him through," Larkin said before they impaled him—or he impaled himself.

They immediately shifted to the side. His face pale, her father sidestepped between them. She felt Nesha ducking out of sight behind her.

"What is it?" Larkin asked.

"It's Raeneth." Her father's new wife. "She's missing."

"Missing?" Denan asked, his fatigue disappearing. "What do you mean, missing?"

Harben pulled his hands through his thinning copper curls. "She didn't come home from the market last night."

The storm broke, soaking them all through in seconds, rain smearing the ink of the letter Larkin held. *Blonde, brown eyes, voluptuous.* The letter was suddenly too heavy to hold. It slipped from her fingers, landing with a shush on the dock beneath her feet.

As much as Larkin disliked the woman, her father stopped being a monster after he met her. She was a good mother to her son, and she'd been kind to Larkin. Losing her would destroy Harben.

Larkin and Denan exchanged a horrified glance. Silent communication passed between them. Did they tell her father? Larkin shook her head. Not until they were certain the dead woman was Raeneth.

Harben took Larkin's hand. "Please, you have to help me." She resisted the impulse to jerk free. "Kyden needs his mother." Harben looked lost and smaller somehow. Not the domineering villain who'd lorded over her as a child.

"I'll take care of Kyden." Wiping rain from her face, Nesha stepped out from behind Larkin. "I've plenty of milk."

Harben's eyes widened as he noticed her for the first time. "Nesha…"

"I'm not doing it for you," Nesha hollered to be heard over the storm, her jaw tight. "I'm doing it for my brother."

Harben's gaze fell, and he nodded.

"I'll come with you," Denan said to Larkin.

Larkin rounded on him. "No."

"Larkin—"

She stepped closer and dropped her voice. "You're swaying on your feet."

He breathed out in frustration. "I want to help."

"I know you worry about me," Larkin said. "But you need to trust that I can handle this."

Denan's head came up. "I know you can." He ordered one of his pages to find Kyden and bring him to their hometree. Then he pointed to Atara and West. "Requisition a boat and stay with Larkin. I'll get these sentinels to see me home."

"We can take my boat." Harben pointed to a craft about fifty yards. It had a single mast with the sail tied incorrectly. "It's small. Fast."

"I'll ready it." Atara took off at a jog, Harben right behind her.

"Wait!" came a cry from behind them.

Larkin turned to see Caelia hustling toward them. The guards stepped before her, blocking her way.

"What does she want?" Denan asked.

"I don't know," Larkin said.

"I want to go with Nesha!" Caelia said breathlessly. "I want to meet my nephew."

Those closest to the woman stopped talking to watch.

Nesha whirled on Larkin. "No."

Inwardly, Larkin groaned. She didn't need anything more to deal with right now.

"Please, Nesha," Caelia begged. "He's all I have left of Bane."

Nesha frowned at the woman before finally nodding. Denan motioned for the guard to let her pass. Caelia rushed toward them. Atara and West graciously moved out of earshot and motioned for the sentinels to do the same.

Panting, Caelia stopped before them, her gaze on Nesha. "Please, I just want to be part of his life."

Nesha studied the woman. "I'll think about it." With a glare at Larkin, Nesha stormed toward their boat.

"If she goes back to him," Caelia said under her breath, "I want that boy."

Larkin shot her a disbelieving look.

"Soren belongs with his mother," Denan said.

Caelia folded her arms across her chest. "I won't have him raised by his father's murderer."

What could Larkin possibly say to that?

Caelia shot her a fierce look. "I want your word."

Larkin couldn't take the child from his mother. And despite everything Garrot was, he'd been an excellent father to the boy.

Denan saved her. "We'll deal with that if and when it comes." He gave Larkin a gentle push down the pier. "Go."

He shot West and Atara a look. "See she's safe."

West puffed out his chest. "With my life, Majesty."

Larkin fought the urge to roll her eyes. Fighting the instinct to stay with her husband, she strode toward the boat Atara and Harben were readying. West kept close beside her.

Caelia trailed after her. "I've heard the stories of what Garrot did to you. The deal he made with the wraiths. You can't possibly want such a man around your nephew."

Rain had soaked Larkin through. It felt wonderfully refreshing after the oppressive heat. "Of course I don't." She jumped inside the boat.

West blocked Caelia from climbing in after her.

"Larkin?" Caelia said, frustration in her voice.

"That's not the right knot." Atara took the rigging from Harben and retied it.

Harben huffed in frustration and turned to Larkin. "What took you so long?"

"You?" Caelia gasped. Her gaze locked on Harben, her chest rising and falling too fast.

Gaping at the woman, Harben took a step back, tripped over a rope, and fell onto his backside. Larkin had seen that horrified look on her father's face before. When the constables had come to take him to the stocks. When he'd been summoned to court. It was the look of a man who'd done something wrong. A man who knew he was caught.

Dread seeped into Larkin's body. "What did you do?"

"I didn't... I can't... Please," Harben stammered.

"Murderer." Caelia's voice was choked with emotion.

CHAPTER 22

MURDER

The rain came down harder, bouncing as it hit the lake, the sound drowning out the low murmur of the funeral goers beyond the dock. Larkin wiped water off her face. She wanted to deny Caelia's accusation. To defend her father. But she'd seen the violence in her father's eyes before. Knew what he was capable of.

She stared at the man who raised her, the dread overwhelming her. Her father looked desperately about, but there was nowhere to go. Atara stepped closer to him. The boat drifted, bumping against the boat next to it.

Caelia's sigils came to life.

West drew his sword. "Don't."

Larkin looked down at her father. "Harben?"

Harben's mouth opened and closed, but no words came out.

Caelia pointed at Harben. "Murderer!" She pulsed, knocking West back, and leaped into the boat. Harben scrambled away from her.

"Stop!" Larkin cried.

Jumping in after her, West grabbed Caelia around the waist and held her. Harben tried to jump in the lake, but Atara snatched his collar and hauled him back. Caelia fought and screamed. Larkin tried to grab her hands and slipped on the damp dock, landing on her backside.

"You pulse again, I'll knock you flat," West shouted.

Pounding footsteps. Denan and the sentinels charged down the dock. The sentinels outran him. West managed to drag Caelia to the edge of the boat. She fought to get free, and they both fell in the lake with a splash. Larkin gave a shout of alarm and tried to reach them, but the boat was rocking hard.

Two of the sentinels hauled them up and pinned Caelia down. Denan stood over them, panting, his face ashen.

"He's a murderer!" Caelia pulsed again, throwing the sentinels off her.

Sopping wet, West stood over her, his sword at her throat. "I will kill you."

Panting, she glared at him, but she must have believed him, for she made no move. Larkin stepped up to the edge of the boat and flared her shield just in case. Two sentinels grabbed Caelia's arms and hauled her to her feet.

Atara pushed Harben next to Larkin, who didn't release her shield. Nor did she look at her father. Blood soaked West's upper lip and mustache—he must have taken a hit to the nose. He spat blood into the lake.

Denan pointed to his pages. "Find Gendrin. Now!" All four of them took off at a run toward the White Tree. He rounded on Caelia. "Murdered who?"

"He murdered Joy," Caelia said.

Larkin remembered the woman—curly dark hair, like her daughter, Larkin's friend Venna. The woman had been Bane's family servant when he was younger; he'd loved her like a mother. Larkin had the sudden taste of jam on her tongue, and the softest, butteriest bread melting in her mouth—a skill Joy had passed on to her daughter.

Joy had been found in the middle of the night, her head split open from where she'd struck it on a rock. To think that Larkin's papa might have caused it... she thought she might be sick.

"Larkin?" Atara asked, clearly concerned.

Larkin had a sudden memory. When she'd asked her papa why he had gone from a loving, caring man to a monster, he'd buried his head in his hands and said, "I did something awful." He had refused to say what that awful thing was.

Now she knew. "The forest take you," she said to her papa. "How could you?"

He turned away, as if he couldn't bear for her to look at him.

"Answer her," Denan demanded.

Harben flinched. "Larkin, I..." He trailed off.

Larkin's gaze locked with Caelia's. "What happened?" She already knew the answer, but fool that she was, hope still wavered in her heart. And she needed Caelia to douse that hope if she was ever to accept this.

Caelia pulled damp hair away from her face. "She refused to forgive his debt. He shoved her."

Denan motioned for West to lower his sword. Looking uneasy, he obeyed.

Her father squeezed his eyes shut tight. "I-I didn't mean to hurt her. I was angry. She demanded money I didn't have. I—"

"You meant to shove her!" Caelia tried to surge out of the sentinels' grasp, but they held her tight. West's sword snapped back into place. "She died in my arms. And when I threatened to tell everyone, you chased me into the Forbidden Forest! You would have killed me too if I hadn't gotten away."

Harben hadn't gone to Joy's funeral. He'd disappeared for two weeks. When he'd returned, the first thing he'd done was throw Larkin in the river in a fit of rage. Only she couldn't swim.

Bane had dragged her out and, over that long, hot summer, had taught her how to swim.

That was the first time her father had been violent with her and the first time Bane had saved her life.

And now, she knew her papa was the reason for Bane and his father's grief.

Light. Oh, light. Larkin's arms were suddenly too heavy. They dangled at her sides. Her magic stuttered and snuffed out.

Larkin had always thought her father's rage was because Mama had revealed she was pregnant with another worthless, unwanted girl. But really, he'd been racked with guilt over what he'd done. And he'd taken that guilt out on his family. For years.

A small, helpless sound escaped Larkin's throat.

"It's going to be all right," Atara murmured.

A lie.

Gendrin jogged down the dock, which shook under his bulk.

"What's going on?" Nesha called from inside Larkin and Denan's boat. The sentinels were blocking her in. She smacked their chests. "Let me go. Larkin!"

Denan groaned and motioned to the sentinels. "Let her go!"

She lifted her skirts and ran toward them.

Gendrin took in the situation in a glance. "Caelia?" He glared at the sentinels holding her. At a look from Denan, they let her go.

Caelia went boneless, all the fight going out of her. She collapsed in her husband's arms. "Gendrin, it's him. He killed her. He killed Joy."

Gendrin stared at Harben, violence hardening his expression.

"What?" Nesha had reached them in time to hear the last bit. She pushed her damp hair out of her sweaty face. "No."

Gendrin gave Harben a look that promised death and pain. West and Atara tensed to stop him if he tried anything. Larkin wanted to slap her father, scream at him. But beneath her anger, a profound loss churned. The Alamant had no tolerance for the murderers of women. He would die for this.

"Denan," Gendrin said through clenched teeth. "Do something with this man or I will."

Denan wouldn't look at her.

"Papa," Nesha pleaded. "Please tell me you didn't do this."

Larkin had no hope of that. No hope of anything, where it concerned her father.

Tears streamed down Harben's face. "Every day, I've tried to forget. I've killed myself trying to forget. I'm sorry, Caelia. Sorry for what I've done."

Nesha's hands flew to her mouth.

Caelia took a ragged breath, clearly trying to bring herself under control. "Tell that to Venna. Only, Venna is lost to the mulgars."

Nesha began to cry, tears mixing with the rain on her face.

Why did Larkin feel like all this was her fault? Why was her family such a mess? Harben's head hung low. His shoulders stooped. Denan stared at the man, his fists clenched. Harben had confessed. Denan had to decide the fate of his father-in-law. And he couldn't show mercy. Not with how divided the Alamant already was.

"Normally, you would be sentenced to death," Denan's voice rasped. "But in these perilous times, we need soldiers to fight against the wraiths. And so I condemn you to serve the rest of your days in Ryttan. May your death spare one of our soldier's lives."

Larkin felt a beat of relief—her father wasn't going to die—followed immediately by a beat of dread.

"What does that mean?" Nesha asked.

"What's Ryttan?" West asked.

"A city in the Forbidden Forest," Atara murmured. "The Alamant often sends criminals there."

Nesha held her hands over her mouth as if to keep the sobs contained within.

Ryttan had fallen centuries ago when the wraiths had destroyed the kingdoms. The pipers had rebuilt the curtain wall. The ruined city now served as a way station between the Alamant and the Idelmarch. It was a dangerous place—constantly under attack.

Denan turned to Caelia. "His life will be spent saving the lives of others, which serves more good than outright killing him. If you disagree with my ruling, you may appeal in one week's time."

Caelia nodded.

Denan frowned at Gendrin. Silent communication passed between the two—communication that Larkin couldn't read. Denan looked away first and motioned to a pair of the sentinels. "Take him to the constables. Have him transferred to Ryttan. Tonight."

Larkin stepped in front of Denan. "Not until we know for sure."

Denan's head came up, and he slowly nodded. "Hold him until I give the order for him to be sent."

"Know what for sure?" Harben asked, his eyes narrowed with suspicion.

"Where Raeneth is," Larkin said smoothly.

Harben knew she was hiding something—he was her father, after all. But he didn't protest as the sentinels stepped into the boat, took Harben over from Atara, and bound his hands. He only paused when he drew even with Nesha. "I'm not the man I once was."

She reached out and wiped the tears from his cheeks. "I know."

Larkin ground her teeth. How could Nesha forgive him so easily? But then, she always seemed to forgive even the most horrible people.

He turned back to Larkin. "Promise you'll find my Raeneth."

She reluctantly nodded. The sentinels prodded Harben. He walked past Caelia and Gendrin, who watched him with righteous indignation. He kept his head down as the sentinels led him to another boat. Caelia leaned against Gendrin, who murmured and stroked her hair.

Nesha sidled up to Larkin. "There has to be something you can do."

"He's guilty, Nesha. If Caelia wants, she can have him hanged."

Nesha shot a pleading look heavenward. "Do you— Do you think she'd drop the charges if I let her spend time with Soren?"

Larkin hadn't thought of that. "Caelia can only make this worse for Harben. Not better."

Nesha wrung her hands. "Why don't you call him Papa anymore?"

Larkin wasn't having this conversation. She had other things to deal with. She motioned Nesha toward the sentinels. "We'll talk about this later."

Larkin felt the disapproving glances of the sentinels. Their queen, the daughter of a murderer.

Denan rubbed his forehead. "Larkin, I'm sorry. I—" He listed to the side.

One of the sentinels steadied him. Larkin launched out of the boat and was at his side in an instant. West ducked under one of Denan's arms, Gendrin the other. An instant later, Denan's legs went slack, his head falling back.

"Take him to our boat," Larkin said. Someone else would have to deal with identifying Raeneth.

West and Gendrin started in that direction.

"Ready my boat," Larkin called to Atara. "We're taking him to the healing tree."

"No," Denan managed. "Take me home."

"Denan—" Larkin began.

Rain ran down his face. "I'll rest better in my own bed."

Larkin pursed her lips. But their hometree was closer. "All right, but I'm going with you and sending a page for Magalia." And this time, the healer would come.

They reached their boat. Larkin and Atara jumped in and helped Denan down. "You promised your father," Denan panted. "A little rest, and I'll feel much better."

"Someone else can identify her body," Larkin said.

West and Gendrin hopped in and stood ready in case he fell again. He collapsed on bottom, wincing at the puddles of water that had accumulated. Larkin grabbed a wool blanket and wrapped him up tight.

Nesha knelt beside Denan. "I'll take care of him. You go."

A page ran up to Gendrin and handed him a letter. He scanned it and looked up at them. "Another enchantress has been murdered. The constables saw a man running away. They've cornered him in the tree."

The ardent who'd most likely murdered Raeneth? To get to Larkin. That's what this was all about. Had the ardents known that her father had murdered Joy? That if they kidnapped and killed his wife, it would send him running to Larkin on the one day Caelia was sure to be present, the one day her father would be condemned? They were ripping her family apart. Would they keep going until she had nothing left?

She didn't need to see Raeneth's body. She knew, deep down, that the woman was dead.

Denan must have seen this in her eyes. "Go, my warrior queen."

"He's strong," Nesha said gently. "He'll be all right."

"All right," Larkin finally relented. She kissed his damp forehead. "I love you."

"You two, go with the queen," Denan said to his pages, one of whom was Farwin. "Atara, West, keep her safe."

"Her life for mine," West said.

Talox had said something similar to Denan once. He'd died that same night. A beat of dread pulsed through Larkin.

Atara rolled her eyes at West. "Must you always be so dramatic?"

"I'll keep an eye on her as best I can as well," Gendrin said to Denan. He motioned for Caelia. The two of them took off toward their own boat, probably to join the search.

Larkin, Atara, and West climbed onto the dock. Four sentinels piled into the boat with Denan, unmoored, and took the oars. One of them let down the sail. The boat pulled away from the dock.

"Make Magalia come if you have to," Larkin called to her sister. "And see Viscott sends a steady supply of tea. If he gets any worse, send one of the pages to me right away. About Sela too."

Nesha nodded. Denan lifted a hand in farewell as the boat picked up speed.

West touched Larkin's arm. "We need to go." Reluctantly, she followed him. "Fetch his mother," she told the page who was not Farwin. If Larkin couldn't be there, then Aaryn should.

"Aaryn will be leading the enchantresses in the search," Atara said.

Larkin pursed her lips. "Fetch his father, then. Requisition a boat if you have to."

The boy ran toward a pair of sentinels.

Feeling like she'd made a major mistake, Larkin dropped into the boat Denan had gifted her father. In the distance, Harben watched her from inside a constable boat. She had an aching, sinking feeling that she would never see him again. An impulse to call goodbye, at the very least to wave, cut through her. Then shame heated her cheeks, and she turned away.

HUNT

The storm eventually passed. Night fell quickly, and the moon rose, leaving the world in various shades of gray, except for the fish that glimmered a rainbow of colors in the inky waters, as well as the violet glow of the tiny creatures disturbed by the wake of the boat containing Larkin, West, Atara, and Farwin.

A pair of swaying lampent lanterns hung like curling antennae from the bow. Insects rammed over and over into the glass, making a gentle tinkling sound. Below, fish churned the waters, wet mouths appearing as they made a feast of the insects. Some jumped, their scales a quick shimmer that ended with a splash. Each time, Larkin tensed for the feel of damp fingers latching onto her and dragging her down.

Working together, the enchantresses and enchanters had cornered the ardent twice. He had escaped both times. Once, by jumping from the high boughs, a fall that would have killed a human, and escaping along the bridges. The second time, they'd surrounded the hometree, but he dove into the water and hadn't come up again.

Turns out ardents could hold their breath for a really long time—maybe they didn't need to breathe at all? Neither time had Larkin been able to spot the thing's face. Only the black cloak and deep cowl.

Sword in hand, Larkin searched the dark water for something that didn't belong. The flash of bony fingers. The glint of human eyes. The undulation of hair or clothing.

Sweat trickled down the back of Larkin's neck and into her damp collar. She shifted her rain-damp clothes, hating how uncomfortable they were. She longed to take her armor off, to let the breeze touch her skin. She couldn't remember the last time she'd eaten or slept.

An enormous mandrill swam toward Larkin's boat. The last time she'd seen one, it had swum under Larkin's boat, seemingly carrying her to her wedding to Denan. The creature's twisted horn disappeared beneath them, the flapping wings fanned out to the sides. Awed, Larkin stood to get a better look. The boat shifted in the creature's wake.

"What is that?" West asked as he adjusted his grip on his sword.

"Mandrill," Farwin said matter-of-factly.

West backed away from the edge, his expression caught between terror and determination.

"Maybe we can use your mustache to weave a net," Atara mused.

Larkin shot West and Atara a chiding look. "They're gentle creatures." She reached into the waters, her fingers trailing across the creature's slippery scales, arcs of rainbow lights emanating from her touch.

The creature bumped the bottom of the boat, jarring them enough that Larkin gripped the gunwale and sat back to keep her balance.

West crouched. "I thought you said it was gentle."

"It is—" Atara began.

Something splashed behind them, spraying them with water. Blinking the moisture out of her eyes, Larkin glanced back. The mandrill moaned, a mournful sound, its gleaming scales caught up in tentacles of the deepest red. The lethan. The two creatures thrashed. The mandrill swung its tail, the barb disappearing. Blood seeped into the water. Then they were both gone, as the lethan pulled the mandrill—a creature twice as wide as their boat—down to the depths.

A large wave rocked the craft again. Larkin's chest constricted. Unexpected tears clogged her throat. She'd been taken by the lethan once. She could still feel the tentacles wrapping tight around her ribs, forcing the air from her lungs. And suddenly, it wasn't the lethan's embrace, but the wraith's. The smell of rot and the grave strong enough to make her gag. His vile arms like a vise around her. The shadows drawing her deeper and deeper into the cold nothingness.

"The forest take me!" West cried as he stared at the waves rippling outward from where the creatures had disappeared. "Don't tell me that thing won't attack!"

Larkin gasped in a breath. "Never swim after dark, West. Has anyone told you that?"

He swallowed hard and shook his head.

She felt Atara and Farwin watching her. Clearly, they'd heard the story.

Larkin wiped the sweat from her brow. "The lethan hunts at night."

"It won't attack the boat," Atara repeated.

West shot her a disbelieving look. "Just because it hasn't happened since you've lived here doesn't mean it's *never* happened."

Shouts came from the boat ahead and to their right, but Larkin couldn't make out the words.

219

"Quiet, you two." Braced against the gunwale, Larkin strained to hear what they were saying. The lap of waves against the boat drowned their words out. But the ships shifted toward a dark, textured shape rising out of the waters.

"They must have found the ardent," Atara said. "Get down."

Larkin, Farwin, and West obeyed, ducking as the boom passed overhead. Atara put all her weight on the rudder. The boat slowed a bit before picking up speed.

In the dark, land was distinguishable by its flat texture against the liquid gleam of the water. Larkin knew this island. It was surrounded by marshy water full of reeds harvested to make rope and baskets. The interior held a vast fruit orchard, the trees tiny compared to the hometrees of the Alamant but large by Idelmarchian standards.

It was also the island she'd been held captive on after she'd tried to escape with Bane the first time.

Ahead, lampents hanging from the boughs shifted from rhythmic bobbing to jerky movements, which signaled that the boats had clearly beached and the soldiers now carried the lanterns. Within minutes, a ring of lampents surrounded the island. As they came closer, Larkin could make out the backlit forms of constables and soldiers spacing out along the shore to prevent the ardent from escaping.

From within the island came the ghostly gleams of shield walls as groups searched for the ardent. They were close enough now that Larkin could hear murmurs and shouts and even a few shrill whistles.

"He can't escape into the lake now," West said.

Larkin wanted to growl in frustration. They were one of the last boats to arrive. The island wasn't that large. The search would be over before they even beached.

"Take the sail down," Atara said.

Larkin and West unwound the rigging. The boat slowed. They scraped through reeds and shuddered to a stop, throwing

Larkin off-balance. West gripped her trousers and the mast to keep her from slamming into the bench in front of her. Farwin lay sprawled on the bottom of the boat.

"Sorry," Atara said. "That came on faster than I thought."

The four of them jumped out, the cool water a relief against the heat. Then Larkin started sinking, mud sucking her down. She tried to hurry, but she couldn't free one foot before the other stuck fast. She ended up swimming and then crawling through the thick tangle of reeds to the shore.

"You're so queenly." Atara laughed and gripped her arm, the two helping each other out of the muck.

"You have a bit of mud"—Larkin motioned to Atara's entire body—"just there."

West staked down the boat. "Women are strange creatures," he muttered. But as he passed them, he suddenly flailed, grabbing Atara. They both went down, West somehow ending up on top of Atara.

"Get your mustache out of my face!" she cried.

"Sorry." He pushed himself off her and hauled her up.

All three of them were dripping mud. Larkin snorted. They really shouldn't be laughing and teasing. Not with Raeneth dead and them hunting for the killer. But there had been so much death. So much worry. Laughter and teasing was as good a way to deal with it as any.

Farwin led the way up the bank. A constable swung a lantern over them before reaching down to give them a hand. Larkin assessed herself in the lantern light. She was a disaster. She pulled handfuls of grass and used it to scrape mud from her face and clothes.

"Queen Larkin?" the constable asked.

Was she that much of a mess that he couldn't even recognize her? "Yes."

The man straightened, offered a hasty bow, and waved toward the bluff. "General Gendrin has been looking for you."

She was immediately suspicious. His mother had made her opinion of Larkin clear. And with what Larkin's father had done to his wife... But Gendrin had also promised Denan he'd keep her safe. "Where?"

The man pointed inland. Larkin looked around for an extra lantern, but they'd left theirs back at their boat, and she certainly wasn't going back for it. The constable offered her his. "Thank you."

"You should send your page to let Gendrin know you're here," the constable said.

It was a good idea. Larkin handed Farwin the lantern. "Go."

The constable found them another lantern.

Atara took it from him. "Have they found the ardent?"

The constable shook his head. "But we have him trapped and on the run."

Larkin passed under trees. The shed, unripe fruit was hard and cumbersome underfoot and lent to the smell of sweet rot. The broad canopy shut out what little light was available, leaving them to the mercy of the lampent Atara carried—a lampent that seemed to throw more shadows than light.

This was the very place Larkin had been held captive with Bane. She wondered where the cellarlike cages were.

"Where is everyone?" Atara asked.

"They've must have already searched this area." Dried mud caked the ends of West's mustache.

They trekked silently through the watchful orchard until Larkin made out a smudge of light ringing a tree. Two figures broke away from the main group. As they came closer, Larkin could make out Farwin carrying a lantern, Gendrin behind him. The general's armor was every bit as muddy as hers, she noted with relief.

Gendrin waved them on. "Larkin, we need you."

"Did you find him?" she blurted as she caught up to him.

Gendrin walked beside her. "The ardent has taken an enchantress hostage."

"Why haven't you killed him?" she asked.

He shook his head. "We can't put an arrow in him for fear of hitting the enchantress, and he won't let her go. Just keeps telling us that he will only speak with the queen."

A wave of foreboding crashed over Larkin. "Who's the ardent?"

Gendrin's lips pursed. "He's kept his cowl up."

Larkin tripped over something in her path and would have fallen had Atara not grabbed her arm and steadied her. She didn't immediately let go. Larkin was grateful; she needed the comfort of another's touch.

"And the hostage?" Atara asked.

"An enchantress from unit six."

Which meant she wasn't one of the leaders. Just an unfortunate woman. "What do you think I can do?"

Gendrin frowned. "We'll keep you safe, Majesty."

Atara and West shared a concerned glance.

They were close enough now Larkin could make out disembodied pieces of the enchantresses and enchanters ringing the tree—a flash of an arm, a cheek, a breastplate. Never the whole person, so the whole group seemed a many-limbed creature instead of a collection of men and women.

Dread skittered up Larkin's spine.

"Aaryn," Gendrin called out when they were a couple dozen paces away.

A shadowy figure broke away from the rest. Aaryn's face appeared in the light from one of the dozens of lampents. Did she know how sick Denan was? Well, if she didn't, Larkin wasn't going to tell her. The woman had enough to worry about.

Larkin hurried to her mother-in-law's side.

"Have your guards wait here." Aaryn motioned to a group of enchantresses. "My women will see us safe."

Larkin nodded for West, Atara, and Farwin to step back. None of them seemed happy, but they didn't protest. The enchantresses surrounded them.

Gendrin stepped up beside them. "I'm going as well."

Aaryn shook her head. "One of us needs to remain in charge."

Gendrin seemed about to argue before nodding. He left them without a backward glance.

"Who is the hostage?" Larkin asked.

Aaryn frowned. "Natyla. She's a mother of four."

Larkin had never heard of the woman. She felt guilty for the relief cascading down her body. "As soon as this ardent has delivered his message to me, he will kill the woman. You know that."

Aaryn handed Larkin a lantern and took another for herself. "We've men in the trees. Just get the ardent to reveal enough of himself to give them a shot."

Larkin nodded grimly.

CHAPTER 24

HOSTAGE

The enchantresses surrounding them, Larkin and Aaryn
stepped through the collection of soldiers. Beyond the
men, a group of enchantresses had created a ring of
shields to trap the ardent inside. Beyond them was an open
space, a large tree in the center. At its base, an enchantress with
too-wide eyes watched them, pleading in her gaze.

A shock of recognition burned through Larkin, which
shouldn't be surprising, considering there were only a thousand
or so enchantresses. But it was more than that. This was something important. Larkin just couldn't figure out why.

Aaryn motioned to four enchantresses, who spread out before them, their shields overlapping. Larkin waited for the signal
to move forward before realizing she was the ranking member
here. Aaryn was waiting for her. It should be Denan. He'd been
training for this for years. Larkin hadn't even known the Alamant existed a year ago.

Steeling herself, she stepped forward. The ring of enchantresses parted, letting her and Aaryn through before closing behind them. Five steps in, Larkin could make out the dark blood soaking Natyla's chest. One of the ardent's arms encircled her shoulder; the other held a knife to her throat.

Larkin didn't like Natyla's chances of surviving this.

"That's close enough," said a deep, rasping voice. A voice that didn't sound human. Whoever this ardent was, he was only a puppet for the Wraith King.

The ardent pressed the knife in, and fresh blood trickled down Natyla's neck. The woman gasped, but she didn't beg. There wasn't a point to it. Ardents didn't know mercy. He wouldn't bargain with them. He only knew the will of his master.

And right now, the Wraith King wanted Larkin.

"I will speak with your queen," the ardent said.

"I'm here," Larkin said.

The ardent peeked out, his face still shadowed by the cowl. A hand reached up, pulling it back and revealing a sliver of his face. But a sliver was enough to recognize the round cheeks, thick blonde hair, and one brown eye.

Raeneth.

"Light," Larkin gasped. Everything was too big and too small, and she was hot and then cold. Raeneth had been in the Alamant for over three months. She'd nursed Kyden. What would that milk to do a baby? Her father. Light, they'd shared a bed.

This will kill Papa. He'd throw himself down the bottom of a bottle and never come out again. She knew it as she knew that the wraiths had chosen Raeneth on purpose. They must have gotten to her when they'd fled through the forest. Poisoned her with their corrupted blades.

She was suddenly aware that Aaryn was speaking to her. She turned to the enchantresses around her. "We're going back."

Larkin straightened her spine, her eyes narrowing into a hate-filled glare. "No. I will speak with the Wraith King."

"Larkin, Queen of the Alamant, Princess of the Idelmarch," Ramass said.

How dare he be here. How dare he steal another life. How dare he invade the one place that was supposed to be free of him. How dare he hurt another person she cared about. Because in that instant, she realized she did care about Raeneth.

"Come to the forest, Larkin," Ramass said. "And I will give you back Venna and Talox and Raeneth. I will give them all back."

His words were poison.

She studied Raeneth's gentle, rosy face, then the terrified face of the hostage. "Let the enchantress go, and I will consider it."

Ramass chuckled, a terrible sound. "Then the archers you've hidden in the trees will destroy my vessel."

Light, how had he even seen the archers in the dark?

Aaryn swore under her breath. Natyla blinked hard, her jaw tight. When she opened her eyes, they had gone from hopeful to resigned. She knew that her usefulness to the wraith was nearing an end. That she was about to die.

Her mouth moved, her lips forming the words, "Tell them I love them."

Larkin had to draw Raeneth out so the archers could kill her.

Denan's words echoed through her. *We do what we must.*

"You have until sunset tomorrow, Larkin. And then I will take what's most precious to you." Raeneth's arm tensed.

"Kill her, and I swear I will kill myself!" The forest take her, what had she just said? But the wraiths had proved one thing repeatedly: they wanted her. She was no good to them dead.

Through Raeneth, Ramass considered her suspiciously.

"What are you doing?" Aaryn whispered.

"I'm the only bargaining chip we have," Larkin whispered back. She could practically feel West and Atara's eyes boring holes into the back of her head. Larkin had to draw him out. A plan came to her. A stupid plan. But she couldn't think of anything else.

"Let the shields down," she called to the enchantresses guarding her.

Aaryn gaped at her. "You can't mean—"

"Let them down!"

"Larkin," Gendrin hissed.

Aaryn shot a look back at the crowd, her gaze locking with Gendrin's. But Larkin was the queen here. Not them. She stared Aaryn down until the woman made an unhappy sound and nodded to her enchantresses. The shields shrunk down to normal size.

Larkin crossed the space slowly, carefully. She held out her hand. "Take me. I'll go willingly. Just let Natyla go."

Ramass chuckled, low and harsh. "Mortals will make impossible sacrifices for those they love."

Did that mean he would free Natyla? She held her breath.

He shook his head. "But you do not love *her.*"

In one quick motion, Ramass drew the knife across Natyla's throat. Blood gushed, and her mouth opened and closed soundlessly.

"No!" Larkin took a step forward.

Aaryn snatched her arm from behind and threw them both to the ground. The enchantress guard piled on top of them, their shields over their heads.

"Loose!" Gendrin roared.

From beneath three bodies, Larkin watched as Natyla's eyes went unfocused. She slumped to the ground. A dozen arrows impaled Raeneth, pinning her to the tree. Raeneth didn't react; ardents were oblivious to pain. Her gaze never wavered from Larkin's.

"Remember, child," Ramass panted, black blood running from Raeneth's lips. "You brought this upon yourself."

Half a dozen pipers darted forward.

"No!" Larkin cried. Raeneth was already dying. Larkin didn't want her body maimed worse than it already was. She deserved better than that.

But West reached Raeneth first and decapitated her. Larkin pinched her eyes shut and turned away, but the memory had branded her mind. Like the deaths of Venna, Bane, Talox, and so many others, nightmares of it would haunt her for the rest of her life.

Atara helped the enchantresses off Larkin. Farwin peered down at her worriedly.

West came back, blood dripping from his sword, and pulled Larkin to her feet. "I'm sorry, Larkin."

She couldn't look at him.

Aaryn gripped Larkin's forearm. "Raeneth was dead the moment the wraith's blade touched her. As for Natyla, she never had much of a chance, and she knew it. You did what you could."

Gendrin came up behind them. "You know who the ardent was?"

"She was my stepmother," Larkin admitted.

He stepped back. "What?"

"The ardent." Larkin forced her gaze up. "She was my stepmother. She escaped the Idelmarch through the Forbidden Forest months ago."

Enchanters and enchantresses stopped to listen. Larkin could imagine the whispers. Her father, a murderer. Her stepmother, an ardent. Her own sister, the unwed lover of the Master Druid.

West and Atara shared a look and pushed the others back, giving Larkin space. She loved them for it.

"What did the wraith mean? 'You have until sunset tomorrow, Larkin. And then I will take what's most precious to you,'" Aaryn asked.

"Denan." Larkin knew it instantly. "They're coming for him next."

Aaryn's gaze hardened. "No ardent will come anywhere near him."

And Denan was too sick to go anywhere near the Forbidden Forest.

"The wraiths have proven they have capabilities beyond what we've ever guessed," Gendrin said.

Larkin rubbed her sleeve roughly across her face, took a fortifying breath, and faced Gendrin. "All the Alamant has been searched?"

Gendrin watched her with pity in his gaze. "It has."

The way he said it told her there was more to his silence. "What is it?"

He sighed. "There are more people who've gone missing."

More people like Raeneth. Ardents who'd fled before being caught. They could be hiding at the bottom of the lake, for all they knew. "How many?"

"Fifteen."

Fifteen reserved for one last dastardly plot?

Aaryn seemed to be thinking along the same lines. "I'll post boats of enchantresses all around our hometree. They won't get anywhere near him."

"Make sure each of them is retested for ardent blood," Gendrin said.

Light, Larkin was so tired, inside and out. Tired of fighting and running and worrying and always being one step behind the thrice-cursed wraiths.

Some of this must have shown on her face, for Gendrin rested a heavy hand on her shoulder. "We know their names. What they look like. My men won't stop searching."

He wouldn't find them. Not at the bottom of the lake.

Aaryn rested a hand on Larkin's back. "Go home and rest. Be with Denan. You can write to your father about Raeneth in the morning."

Larkin found one of her pages. She motioned the boy over. "Send word that Raeneth is dead to my mother. Have her tell Nesha. She can tell my father. Repeat it back to me."

The boy did before taking off at a run.

Larkin closed her eyes and considered taking Aaryn's advice. Eating something hearty and then collapsing onto her bed. Letting Denan play her into a deep sleep while he stroked her hair. But her husband was too sick to play. Her sleep would be plagued by nightmares. There would be no rest for her.

And she'd had enough dealing with the wraiths to distrust everything she thought she knew. Fifteen hidden ardents was too easy. Too obvious. Ramass had something else in mind. She just had to figure out what before he sprung his trap.

One of the men milling about Raeneth's pinned body curled his lip and spit on her before turning to leave.

Rage flooded Larkin. She sprinted forward, flared her shield, and pulsed, pinning the man against the tree. He squirmed, but he couldn't break free.

Larkin wasn't even aware she could do such a thing. But then, she was a queen. As such, her magic was stronger than the rest. "Gendrin, what is the punishment for insubordination and desecration of a body?"

"It was an ardent," the man panted, "who murdered—"

"These women are both victims of the wraiths!" She pushed harder. "You want to spit on something, spit on Ramass from Ryttan's walls!"

The man's face turned red, his lips ringed in blue.

Gendrin stepped up beside her and pointed to a unit leader. "See this man has twelve barbed lashes and put him on night duty for the rest of the year."

"Yes, sir," an enchanter said as he headed toward Larkin's captive.

Aaryn lightly touched Larkin's arm. Larkin reluctantly let the piper drop. He gasped in a breath, his hand spread across his chest. He shot her a furious look tinged with fear. The unit leader hauled him to his feet.

The enchanters watched her with something like fear. She'd rather they respected her, but she'd take what she could get. She flared her sigils. "Back to your duties."

Gendrin barked out commands. Aaryn motioned for her enchantresses to disperse.

Just as he passed Larkin, Gendrin paused. "That was well done."

She looked up at him in surprise. Maybe he didn't resent her, after all. Her gaze strayed to Raeneth's body. "I'll take her back with me." Hauling the body back to their boat would probably take the rest of the night. Exhaustion crashed down on her. But someone had to see the woman properly buried. In the Alamantian or Idelmarchian tradition? What would Raeneth want?

Light, Larkin was so tired.

"I'll take care of it." Aaryn began organizing a dozen enchantresses to make a stretcher and take the bodies to the White Tree. "You'll have to put her through the portal tomorrow."

She didn't have to say why. In this heat, a body wouldn't last long. Larkin nodded in gratitude.

"You want me to report to King Denan?" Farwin bounced from one foot to the other. How could the boy have so much energy?

Larkin motioned for him to go. He bounded off.

"Why don't we go check on Denan?" Atara said.

Larkin barely heard her. She couldn't tear her gaze away from Natyla's face. Mindful of the blood, she crouched beside the dead enchantress. She was even more certain than before. She knew the woman from somewhere.

But where?

She turned south, toward Valynthia. Something about this girl was familiar. It was important. Larkin closed her dead eyes and pushed to her feet. "The enchantress who was assassinated earlier today, the one we thought was Raeneth. Take me to her body."

"What?" West asked. "Why?"

Larkin didn't know why. "Something about Natyla... I'm not sure what, but maybe if I see the other body, I'll understand."

Without looking to see if they would follow, Larkin headed back toward their boat.

CHAPTER 25

REVEAL

Atara shook Larkin awake. She blinked away the residue of her nightmare and leaned against the gunwale. It was early morning—the light from the tops of the waves making her eyes water. Her mouth tasted awful, and she really needed to bathe.

West and the four enchantresses Aaryn had loaned them were still asleep in the bottom of the boat.

Larkin rubbed her gritty eyes. She hadn't thought it possible to feel more tired than last night, but the dreams wouldn't leave her be. Dreams about reweaving the barrier. Dreams about working in her father's fields, her scythe cutting through thick wheat, which fell with a deafening crash. Then came the nightmares about Venna, Bane, Talox, Raeneth, and Natyla. Dreams about her father being dragged away.

"How long did I sleep?" Larkin asked.

"Couple hours." Atara took down the sail. "We've had to tack into the wind. Made terrible time."

"Then why are you taking down the sail?"

Atara motioned to a boat speeding toward them, eight rowers on each side. Tam stood at the prow. When they were close enough, he jumped from his boat to theirs. They pulled away. Tam retied the sail, and their boat picked up speed again.

Tam sat beside her. "Alorica threw me out again."

"Does that mean she's doing better?" Larkin held her breath, waiting for the answer.

Tears welled in his eyes, and Larkin's heart dropped.

"Her fever broke," he managed, his voice wavering.

Larkin was so relieved that she grabbed Tam and held tight.

"There's something else," he said. "They've found two more dead enchantresses, Mavy and Qarlot."

Light, whatever the wraiths had planned, they were accelerating their plot. Larkin dropped her head into her hands. "I can't get her face out of my head." Tam looked at her like she'd lost her mind. "The enchantress who died last night. She's important. I'm just not sure how."

Tam peered ahead of her. "So you're going to the market?"

As Atara filled him in on everything that had happened last night, Larkin followed his gaze. Two hundred yards away was the market. Dozens of wooden stalls had been lashed to a floating dock to create a kind of island. Color spilled from baskets and tables—spices, fresh fruit, bolts of cloth, cuts of meat, and breads. The morning shopping was in full swing, with dozens of people picking through the wares to find the best for the day's meals.

When the boat finally pulled into the dock, Tam took the rope, tied the boat off, and gave her a hand up. They stepped off the docks and onto the floating boardwalk, which rolled gently beneath her feet.

"This way." Tam turned left as if he knew exactly where he was going.

West positioned himself beside Larkin, glaring at the boats they passed as if expecting an assassin to leap out of each one. She doubted he'd let her out of his sight after last night. Atara and the other enchantresses flared their shields in a solid circle around her.

Light, she would be glad when all the ardents were caught and she could go back to not having guards follow her everywhere she went.

The morning crowd parted for them, most of the people bowing.

"Did you know Niveena?" Larkin asked. How else would he know where to go?

Tam didn't look back at her. "She was one of the eleven single women in the Alamant. Every man knew her."

She supposed that made sense.

Most of the Alamant was nature refined. But not here. Instead, elegantly carved bits broken off from hometrees had been slapped together with driftwood. The roofs were nothing but slanted boards that would keep off most of the rain.

They passed the spice stalls, the smells at once overpowering and alluring. Food vendors sold spun sugar and candied berries. Bread shaped like elongated bowls for scooping up a chopped assortment of citrus, fish, and fruit. Meat and vegetables on skewers fried over coals.

On another day, Larkin and Denan would have wandered, sampled the food, and bought presents for her family. He always found something for her. Last time, it had been her own flute, the sides carved with snakes and birds, jewels in their eyes. It was beautiful and a little strange. She loved it.

Larkin surreptitiously wiped her cheeks and picked up her pace, pausing only to buy a breakfast of meat rolls and lilac tea for herself and her guards. They drank the tea in one go and ate the rolls as they walked.

"Tell me more about this Niveena," Larkin said.

Tam took a drink from his waterskin. "She was a widow. Her husband died in a mulgar battle a couple years ago. They had no children, but her husband's family loved her like a daughter. They're holding a vigil for her until tonight when she'll be taken to the White Tree."

Larkin wiped at the juice running down her chin—the meat was a perfect blend of savory, sweet, and salty. Denan would have loved it. "Why live here instead of her hometree?"

Tam licked his fingers. "They own one of the orchards where Natyla and Raeneth died. They split their time between the two. The community is very tight-knit. Niveena loved it here—more than anywhere else."

They came upon the back of a solemn crowd. Many were crying. They stepped aside, bowing as they let Larkin and her group pass. This must be Niveena's vigil. It ended at a fruit vendor.

An old man sitting in a chair pushed up in surprise and bowed low to Larkin. "My queen. We're honored that you have come."

They thought her here to pay her respects. She would let them think it. She smiled gently.

He led them inside, past rows of colorful hobs berries and early nala drops. The smell reminded her of the orchard from last night—overripe fruit and sweet rot. An image of Raeneth's headless body flashed in her mind. She shook her head and forced it back.

The man pulled back a loosely woven black curtain and stepped aside. The guards went first. Larkin had to duck to go inside and couldn't straighten all the way or risk hitting her head on the low ceiling.

Beyond was a comfortable room with rugs and pillows. The back doors had been thrown open, revealing rows of drying fruit laid out on stained sheets. A man, woman, and three boys sat facing a figure laid out on the floor. They all had the same black hair and eyes and were of the same wiry build. Across their legs were the thick, glossy leaves from a hometree, which they were sewing into the enchantress's shroud.

The family already kneeling by the body hurried to their feet and backed away.

Larkin was interrupting their mourning under false pretenses, but Denan's life might depend on what she found. She would use her privilege.

A sheet had been draped over Niveena, leaving only her form visible. She was obviously much taller than any member of this family. Probably taller than her husband had been. What had she thought of that? Of the small, dark-featured man who'd stolen her from her family and taken her to an impossible place?

Only to die shortly thereafter.

Larkin already knew the answer. Niveena had loved him, and he had loved her back. Judging by the swollen, reddened faces of his family, they had all loved her. And yet the family who had raised her didn't even know she was dead. If the Idelmarch and the Alamant didn't find a better way to communicate, they would never know.

Her family rose ponderously to their feet and bowed to her.

Fighting the urge to rip off the sheet, Larkin bowed back. "I've come to pay my respects to your daughter-in-law."

"You honor us with your presence, Majesty," the mother said. "Niveena spoke of you often."

Larkin tried not to let her surprise show. "She did?" Who was this woman?

The father smiled, tears welling in his eyes. "Oh, yes. The speech you gave before Druids' Folly. The way you manipulated the magic with your hands. The lives you saved."

That made sense. Every enchantress they'd been able to round up had been there that day. The day the wraiths had nearly destroyed them all.

Larkin knelt beside the corpse, reached for the sheet, and then hesitated. She didn't want to offend them. "May I?"

The woman knelt across from Larkin and gently folded back the sheet.

Larkin stared at the girl. Her swollen skin was shiny and mottled, with an unhealthy purple hue. In contrast, her shining blonde hair settled in loose waves over her shoulders. Perhaps it was the changes death had wrought upon her, but Larkin didn't recognize her.

The mother took Niveena's hand. "It's hard, seeing something that should be there but isn't."

She'd misunderstood Larkin's confusion. It was probably better that way.

A page burst into the room and held out a sealed missive.

"This isn't the time," Larkin murmured.

"Please, Majesty," he said. "It's urgent."

Shooting an apologetic look at the dead woman's family, Larkin broke the seal.

Sela and Denan are worse. I can't wake them. Something is wrong with Denan's weir. Come quick.

Mama

Light. Not Denan. Not Sela. Larkin's heart pounded in her chest. A sudden memory reared in Larkin's head—the day Larkin had made his weir. The smell of dirt and rot coming off the wraith. The look of Denan's wound, the tined lines spreading.

In the periphery of her vision, she'd caught sight of a woman's concerned brown eyes. The same color as the scarf the woman had tied over her head. Her hair would have been braided to keep it out of the way during the battle.

No.

Not braided. Loose about her shoulders. It was the blonde hair that Larkin remembered. Long and thick and wild as it shifted across her shoulder on the breeze. And suddenly, Larkin knew exactly what the wraiths had done.

She was suddenly dizzy. She began to tip over, only just catching herself.

The mother startled and reached for her. "Majesty? Are you—"

West was at Larkin's side in an instant, steadying her.

She let him pull her to her feet. "I'm sorry. We must go."

Larkin ran back the way they'd come.

Tam dodged a boy, jumped over a cart, and came up beside her. "What? What did you see?"

It wasn't what she'd seen. It was what she'd remembered. She'd used the magic of six women to weave Denan's weir. "The assassins are killing the women whose magic created Denan's weir," she panted. Light, if the weir failed, the blight would consume him. He would become a mulgar. "Niveena, Natyla, Varcie, Mavy, Qarlot…"

Tam's eyes widened. "And Alorica."

Alorica was all that stood between Denan and a fate worse than death. The forest take her, it all made sense. Denan's fever—his body wasn't fighting off an illness, but the blight. And with each assassination, the weir had grown weaker and the blight stronger.

All the sick were probably the men and women Larkin had formed weirs on.

Tam paled. "But she's safe now. The Alamant has been searched."

She shook her head. "There are fifteen missing ardents."

They weren't attacking Denan. They were no doubt skulking beneath the water as they headed toward their final target in the healing tree.

Tam turned and nearly plowed into a man coming out of a stall. "Out of the way!" he roared.

People jumped aside as Larkin, West, Tam, Atara, and the four enchantresses raced along the boardwalk and down the dock, Tam hollering at anyone in their way. At their boat, a page waited for them. Larkin and her guards jumped inside their boat, the craft shuddering.

"Majesty," the boy said.

Tam took the rudder and sail. The rest of them grabbed an oar.

West unwound the mooring rope. "The healing tree or Denan?"

"Healing tree!" Tam said.

She held her hand out for him to be silent.

Tam wasn't the queen here. Larkin was. She dug her oar in. If she went to Denan, she could rework his weir. Alorica would likely die. But if she went to Alorica first and secured her, his weir would hold long enough for Larkin to reach him. She could save them both.

"The healing tree," she agreed.

"I don't understand," West said. "Why can't the other enchantresses fix his weir?"

"It's men's magic," Atara answered. "Larkin's the only one who can wield it."

And then only because she could manipulate the magic with her hands. The enchanters had been trying for months to create a melody that would form a weir. So far, they'd failed.

West took his place beside her and furiously paddled. "Why bother removing his weir? Why not just kill him?"

"Because they know that if Denan is a mulgar," Larkin said, "I'll do whatever the wraiths want to save him."

MERCY

The boat carrying Larkin, Atara, Tam, West, and the four enchantresses cut through the water, the wind steady at their backs. Behind them trailed more than a dozen boats—at Larkin's call, soldiers and enchantresses had left their hometrees to pile into boats or run along the bridges.

There had to be over a hundred now.

The wraiths clearly meant to use Denan to get to Larkin. But then, why was Sela sick as well? She'd never been cut with a cursed blade. Never borne a weir. Perhaps her sister really was sick, but Larkin couldn't afford to believe that. But whatever the wraiths had done to her, it didn't have anything to do with weirs or Alorica. That much Larkin was fairly certain of.

The healing tree came into view. The only movement Larkin caught sight of was the gentle bob of the boats tied to the dock.

"Where is everyone?" Atara asked from beside her.

Grabbing the gunwales for support, Larkin stood to get a better look and saw what, at first glance, appeared to be piles of discarded clothes along the docks and on the stairs. But Larkin had seen enough battles to know what a crumpled body looked like. They lay in pools of blood, the dappled light reflecting off the damp bark, where the ardents would have emerged. In this heat, any water on the bark would have dried in minutes.

"What do you see?" Tam asked.

"Bodies. The roots are still damp. We might not be too late." She turned to look behind them. She couldn't see any of the runners. The boats she could see were too far back. "We're on our own."

Tam bared his teeth, his expression fierce.

"Larkin," West whispered. "You and I will stay back."

"The forest take you," Larkin shot back.

He glared at her. "Eight of us against fifteen ardents. We don't stand a chance. And I will not let you die."

She glared right back. "Try and stop me."

He couldn't, and they both knew it. He growled in frustration.

Atara reached out and gave a hard tug of his mustache. "She's not a child. Stop treating her like one."

He pointed a shaking finger in Atara's direction. "Don't ever touch my mustache again."

"I'll pulse you and your mustache right out of this boat," she shot back.

"Stop it, both of you." Larkin sigils flared hot and bright. "I know you're exhausted and stressed beyond reason. But you will hold it together until we have finished our task. Are we clear?"

"Yes, ma'am," came the chorused reply.

She sat back on the bench. The docks loomed before them, but Tam had yet to lower the sail.

"We're coming in fast," Tam said. "When I tell you, back-paddle. Just before we hit, drop to the bottom of the boat."

This is a bad idea. The dock grew closer and closer still. Larkin gripped the gunwale and her seat, her fingers bloodless.

"Tam," she said warningly. It wouldn't do them any good to arrive fast if they were all dead or injured.

"Trust me," Tam said. "I grew up on boats."

They were close enough now that Larkin could count the splinters in the boards. Sweat ran down her temple. She held her oar at the ready.

"Pull the sail!" West dug his oar in.

"Not yet," Tam said, his eyes narrowed.

Light. He was going to kill them.

"Not yet," Tam murmured. "Not yet. Now!"

Everyone dug their oars in, water sloshing, the boat slowing. They frantically backpaddled.

"Down!" Tam shouted.

Larkin hit the bottom of the boat and covered her head. The boat shuddered violently as they slammed into the dock before sliding partly on top of it. Their wake sloshed over the boards and poured into another boat. The water receded, dragging them back.

With a running leap, Tam landed on the dock without a pause in his stride. Larkin grabbed a piling and held on as the boat slid out from under her. She pulled herself up, lost her balance in the rushing water, and went down to one knee. The boat slammed down, one of the enchantresses falling overboard, another reaching to fish her out.

Tam was getting too far ahead. Fighting a sudden wave of dizziness, Larkin sloshed after him.

"Come on!" She finally cleared the wave and took off at a run. Two dozen paces in, she found the first body. It was Karaken, the cleric who was blind to anything beyond arm's length. She never would have seen the mulgars coming. Her blood was still glistening, so she hadn't been dead long.

Atara and two other enchantresses caught up to Larkin on the sloping roots. Tam was already in the carriage, his hand on the lever.

"Wait!" She was too out of breath to say more. He needed them if he had any hope of fighting off the ardents.

"Curse you, Tam!" Atara cried.

West sprinted past Larkin. "If you want her to live, wait!"

Tam bared his teeth, but he held off. Larkin and the others piled into the carriage. She didn't miss that the floorboards were soaked with water, just like the dock and tree roots had been. The ardents had come this way.

Tam pulled the lever, and they ascended far too slowly. But Larkin welcomed the chance to catch their breath—no point in starting a fight already winded. She watched the main branch come closer. The silence above was near deafening.

And then a woman screamed. Closer, and the sounds of battle reached them—the ring of clashing blades, the hack of sword to shield, and the grunts and shouts of soldiers. A beat later came cries of panic—the patients?

Larkin flared her magic, the comforting pain buzzing through her body. The weight of her blade and her shield was a relief.

Below, the first of the following boats slid into the docks. No sign of the runners on the bridges. Either they'd make it in time to help, or they wouldn't.

"Larkin," West pleaded, clearly wanting her to stay behind.

"This is for Denan." Larkin would do anything—risk anything—to protect her husband.

The carriage crested the intersection between branches and tree. Larkin jumped back from the frenzied eyes of healer.

Her eyes locked on them. "Help me."

Her bowels lay in a puddle beside her along with far too much blood. There was no saving her. They couldn't spare anyone to stay with her. Larkin reached through the bars and stroked her hair. "I'll send someone back for you."

Fifty yards away, a pitched battle was taking place on the pathway before Alorica's room. Five men held off fifteen ardents, but only because there was only room for one or two fighters on the pathways. And the men... they were druids.

"What are they doing here?" Atara said, her eyes narrowed.

"Whatever the reason," West said, "they're the only thing keeping Alorica alive."

Anticipation of the coming fight thrilled through Larkin's veins. She ached for it. Ached to make something pay.

The guards repositioned their weapons and shields. Before the carriage had stopped its ascent, Tam shoved the doors open and shot out. Larkin ran after him, West and the others on her heels. Along the way, she caught sight of an orderly crouched on a side corridor.

"There's a woman by the carriage." Larkin pointed back the way they'd come. "Help her."

Tam reached the rear of the ardents first. He cut down two in quick succession. The third turned and met him blow by blow. Larkin tried to push forward, to assist. But the way he was fighting, there was only room for one fighter at a time, and West firmly inserted himself between her and Tam.

One of the druids went down with a cry. This close, she could see the exhaustion in their movements. They wouldn't hold long. The magic panes to Alorica's room had all been turned impassible, but the supports were vulnerable.

Larkin had to find another way to the room. Had to save Alorica. Save Denan. Maybe Sela too.

"Larkin!" someone called from above.

Larkin leaned over the railing.

On the third level, right above Alorica's room, Magalia waved at them. "Help me!" The healer had a rope already tied to the railing. It dangled at the back of Alorica's room. Magalia clearly intended to haul Alorica to safety.

"West, with me," Larkin said. "The rest of you break through." She pivoted and took off at a run.

"Larkin!" Tam cried. She glanced over her shoulder. He tried to disengage from the ardent he was fighting. The thing nearly sliced his head off.

"I'll get her, Tam," Larkin said.

He turned back to the fight with a roar. Larkin took the walkway back and climbed the stairs two at a time, until she reached the third level. She sprinted toward Magalia, who knelt next to a man and held a bloody cloth to his chest.

When Larkin was two running steps away, he turned his face toward her. Through the blight clawing its way up his cheeks and spidering across his forehead, she recognized his face.

It was Garrot.

In an instant, the night Denan was cut by the wraiths came back to her in perfect detail. She had taken the magic of six enchantresses and woven Denan's weir. Then Garrot had come up behind her, black corruption starting up his neck. And for her kingdom—for the alliance they had to make—she had saved him. She'd taken the enchantresses' magic for the second time, using it to weave a weir for Garrot.

If Garrot's weir was failing, so was Denan's.

Her legs gave out from under her. She went down without a sound, falling heavily. Pain rushed from her knees, but it was nothing compared to the ravaging blackness threatening to tear her apart.

"Larkin?" West crouched beside her.

"I was wrong." Magalia shook her head over and over, her unflappable calm lost. "It wasn't sickness. The corruption leaked through the weirs and made them ill."

I am a fool. In her hubris, Larkin had thought she could save Alorica and Denan both. She should have split her group in half. Let Tam save his wife, as she saved her husband.

But Alorica was already dead. And now something far worse than death was coming for Denan.

"The weir is still slowing the spread." Tears ran down Magalia's face. "I can still save him."

Magalia had saved Garrot's life as a child. They'd grown up knowing each other. Had been engaged at one time. And then Magalia had been stolen by the pipers of the Forbidden Forest, and Garrot had set his sights on the Black Druids.

And then Magalia's words penetrated Larkin's grief. If the weir was still intact, Alorica wasn't dead.

"Help me," Magalia begged.

With the curse already touching his eyes, Garrot was too far gone to help. But Denan... his blight wasn't nearly as advanced as Garrot's. There was still time. Larkin gasped in a breath, her strength returning with her purpose.

Garrot's fever-bright eyes met hers. She'd seen the afflicted writhing in agony, but he only seized rhythmically, his eyes strangely calm.

"Tell her I'm sorry," Garrot said in a voice choked with pain.

He clearly meant her sister. He knew there was no coming back from this. All the times Larkin had wanted him dead, and now all she could feel was pity. She nodded. West helped her to her feet. Only two druids left below. Larkin needed to hurry.

"Kill him," she whispered to West. Guilt twisted inside her, but death was a kindness compared to what was coming for him. She pushed her feelings aside and grabbed the rope.

"I'll go instead," West said at the same time Magalia said, "Larkin, you have to save him."

"We need your muscle to haul Alorica up," Larkin said to West, ignoring Magalia altogether. She swung her leg over the rail.

"Larkin—" West reached for her.

Directly beneath her, two dripping ardents—a male and a female—pulled themselves up the branch that led to the back of Alorica's room. They each took an ax from inside their cloaks and hacked at the supports between magic panes.

There wasn't time to argue.

Larkin flared her shield, placed it under her feet, and dropped. She slammed into the male first. Bones crunched. She fell forward and rolled, her shoulder wrenching. She bit off a cry of pain.

The male ardent's arm hung at an impossible angle. Still, he pushed sloppily to his feet and grabbed her legs. The cloaked female battered through the supports—not nearly as thick as the ones at Larkin's hometree—and ducked inside. Alorica was waiting for her and pulsed the ardent across the room and hobbled toward her, sword raised.

"Larkin!" West made to jump over the rail. "Behind you!"

"Stay there!" Larkin turned to find the ardent right behind her. She kicked him. He staggered back. She charged and lopped off his head. Turning, she rushed into Alorica's room. The female ardent stood with her back to Larkin. Alorica was against the wall, her sword pinned to the pane. The ardent drew back her blade. Larkin had no choice. She pulsed, slamming Alorica and her assailant into the wall.

Larkin charged, driving her sword toward the ardent, who reared up, sword blocking. Larkin's blade slammed into the pane. The ardent looked at her. Tangled black hair and brilliant blue eyes framed her pale face.

Maisy.

It all made a twisted kind of sense. Maisy had always been in the periphery of Larkin's life. Manipulating and twisting and prodding and hinting. She was the final assassin. The reason Denan's weir had failed.

Larkin could have killed Maisy at Druids' Folly. Instead, she'd let her go. Out of a sense of friendship. Or maybe pity. But mostly because she'd believed Maisy was still in there, buried deep beneath the shadows that tainted her blood.

Because of that mercy, Denan's life was now at risk.

From the floor, Alorica dragged herself away.

"Maisy," Larkin breathed, an accusation and a plea both. She had known Maisy was a part of this. She had tried to pretend otherwise, but deep down, she had known. She blinked back stinging tears of betrayal. "Why?"

"You never listen." Maisy twisted to the side and drove her shoulder into Larkin, catching her off guard. Larkin stumbled back. Maisy darted toward the door. Larkin lunged, her sword aimed for Maisy's middle. She dodged at the last second. The blade sank into her shoulder. Black blood sheeted. And then she slipped out of the room.

Larkin longed to chase her, but her priority had to be getting Alorica out. Then she could go back for Denan. Rework his weir.

"Come on." Larkin motioned for Alorica to follow as best she could. Her shield flared, Larkin peeked between broken supports. Maisy was nowhere to be seen. Larkin edged out and peered over the branches in time to see large ripples in the lake.

Maisy had jumped. She didn't resurface. Not that Larkin expected her to.

She turned, but Alorica was nowhere in sight.

West dropped down from the rope. If he was angry with Larkin before, he was furious now. "I told you to wait!"

Larkin's four enchantresses and the druids spilled through Alorica's room and out the ruined side, their eyes scanning for any other ardents. Alorica must have opened the doorpane.

"You all right?" Atara asked.

Not bothering to answer, Larkin pushed back inside. Tam gently settled Alorica onto the bed. Her teeth were locked, her face a grimace, but she didn't appear to be bleeding.

"You were late," Alorica said.

Larkin grunted. If Alorica could throw out insults, she'd live.

Larkin rushed outside and paused to gauge the wind. It blew in the wrong direction. The bridges would be faster. She took off at a run.

"Let's go!" West motioned for the enchantresses to follow him.

Atara and the other enchantresses hurried to catch up as Larkin leaped over bodies of druids and ardents, then slowed her pace to a ground-eating jog.

At the archway, the woman whose bowels had been cut was gone. Instead, two druids carried a stretcher. On it, Garrot was bound and gagged. He strained against his bonds, the tendons at his neck standing out in stark relief, his eyes solid black. The men were obviously taking him back to their barracks. Fools.

Where was Magalia?

He deserved this and so much worse. And yet, as she passed them, she felt such a burst of pity. "Killing him would be a mercy."

Not-Garrot stilled, his gaze following her. Through those eyes, the wraiths watched her. She shuddered.

"He's the Master Druid," one of the men said.

"Not anymore." She pushed past them and ran.

CHAPTER 27

DENAN

Through the web of bridges, Larkin, Atara, West, and the two remaining enchantresses ran. Larkin's head pounded, and nausea crowded her throat.

West's long legs quickly outpaced her, his mustache streaming behind him. He motioned at anyone in their path to make way. Larkin formed a knife in her hand and cut her armor free. She threw the dead weight aside, her gaze fixed on her hometree. The sound of enchanter music floated from the within.

She ignored the scream of protest from her legs. The taste of blood in her mouth. She raced death, both closing in on Denan.

And she had to get there first.

The guards at the archway waved her on. "Hurry, Majesty!"

"They can't get the music right," the other cried.

Larkin burst through the archway, jumped the railing, and landed on the branch beneath. Ignoring the sharp pain in her ankles and feet, she sprinted to her chambers and pushed through the barrier.

Nearly a dozen enchanters stood around her husband, all of them trying to form the weir. The weave fell apart. The men weren't strong enough. Not like a queen was.

"Get out." She pushed through them.

Denan lay in the bed in nothing but his trousers. The blight had grown from the size of her palm to covering most of his torso, the tendrils disappearing beneath his trousers. His back arched; the muscles and tendons of his body stood out grotesquely. He locked his teeth as if to keep the scream trapped inside him.

Looking at her husband, all she could see was Garrot. Garrot, who had been a loving husband until the blight grew beyond his ability to control it. Garrot, who heard the wraiths' voices. Garrot, whose eyes were now solid black.

She wanted to weep, call out to Denan, collapse on his chest. She couldn't let herself.

Gasping for breath, her head throbbing and spinning, Larkin drew from her sigils and wove her enchantment. Her fingers formed triangles for strength, circles for flexibility, and points of light for longevity. Her legs lost strength partway, and she collapsed to her knees. She managed to keep hold of the weave. Her fingers smoothed ruffled ends and wobbly lines. She was vaguely conscious of West ushering the enchanters out of the room.

When the weave was as good as she could make it, she threw her enchantment around that darkness like a fisherman casting a net. As it settled beneath Denan's skin, Larkin shuddered at the feel of the evil, clawing darkness and the suffering that echoed through her magic.

Once the enchantment had slipped past the blight, she drew the ends toward her like she was drawing in a net. It fit around the corruption like the sheen of oil over poisoned water. She wove again, seaming the ends together until the enchantment was one.

She'd nearly lost him. The wraiths had nearly won. And even now, she could feel echoes of Denan's agony through her magic.

Again, she looked at Denan and saw Garrot. His skeletal body. The black circles under his eyes. The way three months had aged him a decade. Denan would survive, but only just.

She couldn't bear it. Couldn't bear the thought of her undauntable husband reduced to a caricature of himself. Staggering, she forced herself to her feet. Denan was insensible with pain.

"I have to try." Larkin pushed her hand in the center of his blight. He groaned, his whole body curling around the pain, but she didn't let go. She flared her sigils until they burned white, an avalanche of magic pouring through her. She fisted her magic around the edges of the weir she'd just woven and pulled.

Denan screamed, an inhuman sound that tore her soul in two. But the blight receded, leaving wicked scars. Tears burned in her eyes, none falling. She was too dehydrated for them to fall.

Denan writhed.

"I'm sorry," she cried.

Someone stepped past Larkin and leaned over Denan. It was Mama. She pressed her hand to his chest. "Larkin, stop!"

She didn't understand. Didn't know what this blight would do to him. Didn't know that it was Larkin's decisions that had led them to this moment.

"Larkin!"

"I can't, Mama!"

Mama shoved her. Larkin stumbled back, the weave slipping from her fingers to rebound back into place. Denan collapsed as if he were a puppet and his strings had been cut.

Good. If he's unconscious, it won't hurt anymore. Larkin came at him again, but Mama blocked her.

Larkin had the sudden urge to hit her. "He can't live like this, Mama." Her voice came out small, broken. "It will break him." She couldn't bear watching him become a shadow of his former self.

"You're killing him!" Mama pressed her ear to Denan's chest. She didn't move. Didn't move. Didn't... Larkin rested her fingertips against Denan's throat. Nothing.

Light, had she already killed him? Every fear she'd harbored in the secret folds of her heart had come to pass. And she had caused it.

A pulse fluttered beneath her fingertips. She cried out and tied off the weave.

Mama instantly went to her bag and pulled out a powder. "Someone bring me a plate and a cup of water. Now!"

West shoved half a cup of tea in Larkin's hand—she had forgotten he was even here. Mama measured in the powder with a steady hand, mixing it to a paste with her fingers. She spread it across Denan's chest. It smelled sharp and metallic.

"That will wake him up a bit." Mama pulled out another vial. "Get him up on your knees."

Larkin tried to lift him, but his body was heavy with muscle. Her arms shook so hard she couldn't manage it. West bent down and helped her. Larkin slid under him, and West laid Denan's head on her chest. Larkin curved around her husband, desperately wishing that she could share her strength with him. That he could absorb it through her skin.

"Denan!" Mama said firmly. "I need you to wake enough to swallow this medicine."

Denan didn't stir.

"Denan!" Mama commanded.

Still nothing.

Larkin leaned next to his ear. "You'll always come for me, remember? Come for me now, love. Please."

He shifted ever so slightly. Mama pushed the vial between his lips. His mouth didn't work, but his throat did. One tiny swallow after another.

Mama checked his pulse and began to relax.

Arms encircling him, Larkin felt each expansion and contraction of his chest. "Is he going to be all right?"

"He's young and he's strong. The medicine I gave him will speed his heart back up."

Larkin rocked her husband. "I'm sorry, Denan. I'm so sorry." Light, she'd saved him only to nearly kill him. Her eyes and head ached with the tears she could not shed.

"Ancestors, why didn't I see it?" Larkin cried. She should have recognized the symptoms. After all, she'd seen them before. The night Venna had been cut by a wraith blade. Larkin had held her friend as her body burned with fever, as the pain engulfed her until she was mad with it. Had watched the blight marks reach her eyes. Watched those eyes turn black, their bright compassion replaced with animal hatred.

"How could you?" West said. "The ardents didn't just attack enchantresses. They killed the king. And Denan wasn't the only one sick."

"Light," Mama said, her hands over her mouth.

"The wraiths know Denan is the way to get to me. As for the king..." Larkin shuddered. She glanced toward the door. She suddenly remembered her sister. "Is Sela all right? There's still no sign of the blight on her?"

"No, but I can't wake her." Tears filled Mama's eyes. "She's still sick. That's why I wasn't here when you came."

Larkin's eyes fluttered closed. "The wraiths did something to her. I'm sure of it." The assassins got to her. But how? Simple poison, perhaps? And how could Larkin counter it? "Did you send for Magalia?"

"Magalia's already tried everything she knows for both of them."

"I'll send someone to fetch her." West stepped out.

Larkin's nausea sharpened suddenly. She was going to vomit all over her husband. She slid out from under Denan and tried to stand, but her legs buckled, and she went down. She dry heaved, her head throbbing.

Mama knelt beside her. "Larkin?"

Her legs were stiff, locked into position. Getting up felt impossible. She collapsed on her side and tried to offer Mama a reassuring smile. "Too much running, I think. And I didn't sleep much last night." Or any night.

Mama's face was drawn with worry. She pinched Larkin's skin. It peaked and remained that way. She hustled to the table. "When was the last time you drank anything? Ate?"

"This morning?"

"You're heat sick." Mama went to the table and poured a pitcher of water. She brought it back to Larkin and helped her sit up. "Drink it slowly—you don't want to vomit it all back up."

Unable to be parted from Denan for even a moment, Larkin leaned against the bed and threaded her hand through his as she sipped the tepid water.

Mama opened the doorpane. West and Atara were gone. Probably in search of something to eat, as they should.

Mama motioned to one of the pages, who stepped into the room. "Inform Magalia that Larkin is convinced the ardents have done something to Sela."

The boy started off.

"And I want an update on Alorica!" Larkin hollered, which made her throat throb even harder.

Still running, the page performed a little bow before passing out of sight.

Thinking of Alorica made Larkin think of the events that had happened at the healing tree—events involving Garrot.

Mama pointed to someone out of sight. "Have the butler bring a meal and lilac tea for the queen." She closed the barrier.

Larkin pressed her cheek against Denan's arm, drawing comfort in the warmth of his flesh, the pulse at his wrist beating against her own. He was alive. He was not a monster. If nothing else, she had that.

It was hard to think with the throbbing in her head, like her skull was a door and someone was pounding on it from the inside. All she wanted to do was close her eyes, but there were still things she needed to do.

"I need to speak with Nesha." Her sister needed to know what had happened to Garrot. Better to hear it from Larkin than anyone else.

Mama mixed some pain powder and handed it to Larkin. "She isn't here."

Larkin drank the bitter draft. "Where is she?"

"Some druids came not long before you. They said Garrot was sick, dying. She went with them."

Larkin didn't blame Mama; Nesha would have gone one way or another. Her sister still loved Garrot. Maybe a part of her always would. What would Nesha do when she learned that Larkin could have halted his blight's spread? That she was glad she'd never have to see him again?

He was too far gone. Still, a flash of guilt tore through her. And even stronger was pity for the monster waiting for her sister. Larkin shoved it in the chest with all the rest. Another thing to deal with it later. When there was time for such things.

"Did she take some guards?" Ardents were stronger than men; it was possible Garrot could break his bonds.

Mama nodded. "How's your stomach?"

"Perfect," she lied.

"How does your head feel?"

"Happy as a bee in springtime."

Her mother's disapproving frown said she didn't believe her. Viscott came in with a bowl of cold soup, nala grains, ripe red berries with thick cream across the top, and a pitcher of cold lilac tea. Larkin's gaze locked on the food, and she found she couldn't look away.

She was reluctant to leave Denan's side, but she'd pushed herself too far today. She needed food and sleep. Mama and Viscott helped her to her feet. Stiff, sore, and weak, she hobbled to the table and eased into a chair. The cook poured the tea. Larkin drank the whole cup in one go.

"Slowly," Mama admonished.

Larkin poured the thin soup over the grains and ate them one measured bite at a time. She hummed at how delicious it was, creamy and sweet and sour all at once.

Viscott grunted in satisfaction as he refilled the cup. "Anything else, Majesty?"

Her mouth too full to answer, Larkin shook her head. The man turned on his heel and left. In the quiet that followed, Larkin could hear a baby cry.

She eyed Mama. "Brenna or Soren?"

Mama's shoulder's fell. "That's Kyden."

Larkin's spoon froze halfway to her mouth. Ancestors, with Nesha gone, that meant Mama was caring for Harben's love child.

"Caelia brought him this morning," Mama said. "She told me his mother is dead. Harben had been informed and sent to Ryttan."

Light, her poor father. Was there any alcohol in Ryttan? What if he couldn't bear it and tried to kill himself? Light, she couldn't deal with another family member in crisis. She laid her head on the table, too weary to lift it.

Mama gave a bitter laugh. "It all makes sense now. It was after Joy's death that your father started trying to drown himself in drink."

The baby's crying rose in pitch. What would happen to Kyden now? "Light, Mama. You can't be expected to raise him." He'd been nursed by an ardent. Was he corrupted too?

The clatter of a spoon stirring a cup. "We're the only family he has now."

The crying stopped.

"You found a wet nurse?"

Mama set another cup of pain powder next to Larkin's face. "I can't care for three babies by myself." Mama smoothed her hair away from her face. "But I need to get back to them, to Sela."

Mama gestured for a hug. Larkin downed the bitter stuff and then embraced her. She smelled of her childhood—of sun-warmed skin and hair... and sour milk. The last made Larkin smile. "I love you, Mama."

"Love you too." She pulled back. "Get some sleep. You're no good to anyone dead on your feet."

With the food heavy and filling inside her, she felt sleepier than ever. "Send a page to the druids, advising them to kill Garrot. Another to Mytin. Tell him to embed as many druids as possible." Whatever the wraiths had planned, they were trying to weaken the Alamant first. They needed all the help they could get to deal with what was coming.

Mama nodded. "I'll take care of it."

That done, she climbed into bed beside Denan. She wanted to curl up beside him, her head on his chest. But she didn't dare, for fear he was still hurting. She settled for taking his hand and rubbing the back of it with her thumb.

She should have realized what was happening. Should have woven a new weir days ago. "I'm sorry. I'm so sorry."

CHAPTER

CURSE

For once not worried about assassins, Larkin stood at the windowpane, watching the storm rage. Thunder rumbled, lightning speared, and the lake heaved. The wind shredded the leaves, bits of gold falling like snow in a blizzard. The breeze pushed her clothes against her body, the rain skidding down the pane.

Her dreams hadn't been as bad as usual. Just one that she could remember. Valynthian women weaving the enchantment around the wall. She didn't understand why the tree was showing her Valynthian barrier magic. It wasn't like she could use it with her warrior magic. But then, why did the White Tree do anything?

She rubbed her eyes, wondering what catastrophe had occurred while she slept on, oblivious. She decided she didn't care. Someone else could deal with it for once.

Denan still slept. His lips were cracked, his skin ashen, but his forehead was cool. Once he had some food and water in him, he'd be back to his old self. She'd let him sleep a bit longer though.

Hissing at the soreness of her muscles, she shambled toward the bathroom. She longed for a hot bath but didn't want to bother anyone with hauling hot water, and none of them would allow her to do it. She settled for a quick shower.

Rubbing oils into her damp hair, she tiptoed across the room and stepped out to the guards, surprised to find West and Tam.

"How's Alorica?" she asked.

Tam pulled her into his arms, squeezing so hard she could barely breathe. "She's coming home tomorrow." Larkin sagged in relief. "Thank you. For saving her. Again."

Would Tam hug and thank her if he knew that she regretted saving his wife at Denan's expense? Feeling tainted, she stepped back from his embrace and looked for something, anything, to change the subject. A rotation of pages waited just out of ear-shot, Farwin among them.

"Have Viscott bring up breakfast," she told Farwin.

The boy took off.

West handed her a stack of letters. "We've been collecting missives for you."

She took them. "Not working the night shift anymore?"

West puffed out his mustache. "Someone has to save you from yourself." The words were dressed in a joke, but beneath them was the meat and bone of truth with a measure of chiding.

Two could play at that game. She smacked him with the missives. "And who's going to save you from me?"

He didn't look chastised. He needed to learn she was in charge. Not him. A lesson that was growing closer and closer every day. They were both instinctively circling it, avoiding the confrontation their friendship might not survive.

"Magalia just went in with Sela," Tam said.

She pointed to one of the pages. "Don't let her leave without reporting to me."

The boy nodded and hurried away.

She stepped back inside, leaving the doorway hazy but passable for Viscott to bring their breakfast. Denan still slept soundly; she'd let him rest until breakfast came. She sat at the table and scanned the missives while she waited.

Gendrin and Aaryn both wrote that they hadn't found Maisy, but they were following a trail of black blood. Mytin conveyed that a hundred druids had been embedded this morning, though they still refused to kill Garrot and imprisoned him instead.

What were they planning to do with a mulgar? Keep it in the pit beneath their palace like they had Larkin? That would be ironic.

Magalia's hasty note relayed that she'd stopped in last evening. She didn't know what to do for Sela any more than Mama had, nor whether Sela's illness was natural or cursed. She would stop by midmorning.

Farwin called from outside, "Majesty, I've your breakfast."

"Come in," she said. Farwin settled the tray on the table. "Where's Viscott?"

"Busy serving Lady Pennice, Majesty."

Larkin made a note to check on Mama and the babies after breakfast, sat on the bed beside Denan, and rested a hand on his chest. "Denan. Denan, love, you need to wake up."

His eyes came open, his pupils swallowing his iris. She drew a startled breath. His fist slammed into her jaw. Everything went black. Her ears rang. She crumpled to the floor; the sound of a porcelain cup shattering sounded far away. Then Denan was on top of her.

"No!" Farwin cried.

Denan shifted above her. A struggle. The sound of a fist connecting. Someone falling. Larkin reached for her magic. But her mental grip was slipping, the buzzing in her sigils flickering to life before dying again. Denan's crushing weight was suddenly gone.

"Larkin?" Tam's voice came from right beside her.

Light flashed like dying fireflies. Someone laid a gentle hand on her shoulder. Tam? She tried to answer, but what came out of her mouth was gibberish.

"Get Magalia!" Tam shouted. "She's with Sela!"

Scrambling steps. Farwin? One of the other pages?

"Just lie still," Tam said.

Larkin closed her eyes—her inability to see was less disturbing if it was her choice. She concentrated on her breaths. Not the fact that her husband—her heartsong—had just brutally attacked her.

It isn't him. It's the wraith inside him, corrupting his mind.

Light. The wraiths were slowly taking everything from her. Again, she could only see Garrot.

Lock it up. Like he taught me.

She breathed in, slowly filling her lungs. Breathed out the hurt. She took that hurt, locked it in a chest, and threw it in a lake. That lake iced over, trapping her emotions behind a thick pane. As the chest sunk out of sight, a cold numbness spread through her body.

More steps sounded on her right.

"Drink this," Magalia said.

Larkin opened her eyes and was relieved to find her vision back. Tam and Magalia knelt on either side of her. On the floor, West had Denan in a headlock, the corruption a jagged, evil thing on his torso. Denan's expression was blank, his body limp. What did that mean?

The pages crowded at the doorpane with their mouths hanging open. Farwin's eye was rapidly swelling shut. Farwin must have jumped on Denan right after he'd attacked her. Denan had hit the boy.

The chest deep in the frozen lake rattled, desperate to break free.

Magalia helped Larkin sit up. She swayed a bit. Magalia steadied her and handed her a cup. Larkin brought it to her lips and drank the bitter draft. Magalia gave her a damp compress that smelled of herbs. Larkin pressed it to her cheek, wincing as the pain sharpened.

"Anything broken?" Magalia asked, her voice brisk.

Just my head. Magalia wouldn't meet her gaze. "I'm sorry," Larkin whispered, too ashamed to say the words out loud. "But Garrot was too far gone to save."

Magalia swallowed hard three times before she spoke, her voice shaking. "You could have tried."

"We would have lost Alorica and Denan," Larkin said.

"I know." Magalia stood. "But I don't think I can forgive you."

Larkin understood. Sometimes anger wasn't rational.

Tam scooped Larkin up and laid her on the bed. The compress leaked water that ran around her ear and into her hair.

Magalia handed another compress and some pain powder to Farwin. She motioned to all the boys. "Out."

"You will keep this to yourselves," Tam said sternly.

Each boy nodded profusely. But no secret remained for long. What would happen when news spread that the king had hit his queen and one of his pages? The fact that he'd done it because of his blight would only make it worse. Make him seem out of control. Corrupted.

Magalia knelt before Denan. "Denan. Denan, look at me."

He blinked a few times and shook his head. "Magalia?"

She looked up at West. "Let him go but be ready."

Tam shifted so he was between Larkin and Denan, his weight on the balls of his feet and his arms up. West eased his hold a little at a time.

Denan sat up on his own. "Light, the nightmares." He breathed in through his teeth. "Hurts." He put his hand to his side.

"He's himself again," Magalia said.

Clearly confused by the healer's words, Denan looked about the room, his eyes catching on Larkin. He swore and tried to stand, fell back, and groaned in pain. "Larkin, what happened?"

"You happened," Magalia spat.

Denan blinked at her in confusion.

"Magalia," Tam said warningly.

She stormed to her kit, pulled out different vials, and began pouring them into a glass bottle.

Hand on his side, Denan struggled to stand and shuffled across the room. He dropped to his knees before Larkin and reached out as if to touch her before pulling back. "I— I did this?"

He'd hit her. It wasn't him, but still... The safety she'd always found in his presence had been turned against her. A trust had been broken. The thought tugged tears from her eyes.

She tried to blink them back. "It wasn't your fault."

"No, I would never..." He shot another pleading look at Tam.

"Look at your hand," Magalia snapped.

Denan held up his fist, his right knuckle red and swollen. His eyes widened. He sank to his haunches and leaned against her nightstand. "No."

Larkin hated the tears spilling from her eyes. "It wasn't you."

Magalia handed him the bottle. "One swallow."

Denan took the bottle with shaking hands and downed a mouthful, wincing at the taste. The smell of it wafted through the room. It was the same medicine Garrot had been sipping from a flask. Magalia must have given it to him.

The healer stomped back to the table.

"The cursed have a hard time grasping reality right after waking," Tam said. "None of us blame you."

"I blame him," West muttered.

"West, stop being so overprotective," Larkin barked.

"It's my job!" He rounded on Denan, one hand on his sword hilt. "I won't stand by and let anyone hurt her. Even if that someone is you. Understand?"

"I'm glad of it," Denan said with a shaking voice.

"How dare you," Larkin seethed at West.

Tam beat her to it. He squared off in front of the other man. "Out."

West clenched his jaw and seemed to consider arguing. But Tam was his commanding officer. Muttering, West departed.

"You too," Magalia ordered Tam.

Tam paused beside Denan and rested a hand on his shoulder. "I'm just glad you're awake. You had us all worried." Tam hurried for the doorpane before either man had to watch the other tear up.

"Call for my council," Denan called after him, his voice thick.

Nodding, Tam left.

Magalia rounded on them. "First, you should know that Sela's condition hasn't changed, though we got her to drink some water. It may be something the ardents caused; it may not. I don't know, and I'm sorry."

"It was the ardents," Larkin said. The helplessness of not being able to help her sister ate at her.

"I searched her everywhere—there's no sign of blight," Magalia said. "I've tried everything I can think of."

Larkin nodded. "Thank you for that."

Magalia nodded once and turned to Denan. "I've been treating Garrot since he came to the Alamant."

Denan didn't seem surprised, but then, he had spies watching the academy day and night.

Magalia softened. "It's going to be much worse than before—the nightmares, the pain... you might start to hear the wraiths in your head."

Oh, light, Larkin thought. *Oh, ancestors. Please. Denan is the best person I know. He doesn't deserve this.*

Magalia's lips tightened, and she shook her head. "The concoction I gave you will make it bearable. But it will also dull your senses, and eventually, it will kill you. I'm sorry." She quietly left.

Larkin's fists clenched at her sides. "We're going to have to move up the timetable for the invasion into Valynthia."

Denan sat heavily beside her on the bed. He studied her bruised cheek. "Light, I swore I'd never hurt you."

Larkin huffed a laugh, ignoring the pulse of pain. "You've hurt me plenty of times during sparring."

He didn't even try to laugh at her joke. "Tam's rubbing off on you."

"Garrot lasted at least three months, and his blight was more advanced than yours. If we move up the invasion a couple months, we can have the Black Tree down in three."

Denan braced both hands on either side of her head. "Larkin, we both knew that this moment might come."

She finally met his gaze. "You can't give up."

"I will fight to the end," he said. "But we also have to prepare for other options. I'm going to grow weaker. You're going to have to take my place."

She'd never felt more overwhelmed than in that moment. "I'm not ready."

"When the time comes, you will be."

He pushed to his feet, picked up his chest, and stuffed clothing inside.

She pushed up on her elbows. "What are you doing?"

"I'm moving into one of the other rooms."

"What? No." She pushed herself out of the bed, wavering woozily for a moment before finding her balance.

Denan hefted the chest and started toward the doorpane. She blocked him. His arms were already shaking—his sickness had clearly sapped much of his strength.

He set the chest down. "I'm not safe to be with."

The chest felt like a wall between them. She circled it and came to stand at his side. "Only at night. Sleep in the nursery. We'll raise the barrier."

"I won't risk you."

She took his face gently between her palms and stepped flush against him. He froze, his body thrumming with tension.

"I am a woman; I'm not so easily broken. And neither are you. We're going to get through this."

He closed his eyes. A tear tracked down his cheek. He looked so defeated. So weak. This man, whose strength was as unbreakable as a mountain... was breaking. It tore her in two. Desperate to comfort him—to connect with him—she lifted and pressed her mouth against his. He hesitated a moment, as if frozen with indecision.

"Denan," she whispered against his lips.

He crushed her to him, his grip so tight it hurt. His mouth claimed hers. She kissed him back just as hard. Held on just as tightly. He hauled her shift over her head and pulled her against him, skin to skin. An unnatural cold seeped into her from his blight. A wrongness.

She didn't care. This was Denan. Her heartsong. And she would take every bit of him, good and bad, for as long as she could.

CHAPTER

COUNCIL

Larkin slipped into Mama's room. Mama and the babies were nowhere to be found. Sela lay on the bed with a thin blanket pulled up to her chest. Her hands rested at her sides, her hair splayed over the pillow. She looked so still and pale that Larkin rushed to her side and placed a hand before her mouth, relieved to feel a puff of breath against her fingertips.

Larkin collapsed on the bed and held her head in her hands. "I wish you would wake up." Open her green eyes and smile. Larkin took her sister's hand. She didn't so much as stir. "What did the wraiths do to you, sunshine?"

Magalia and Mama had both searched for any signs of the blight. They hadn't found anything. But they didn't have Larkin's magic. She flared her sigils and wove the weir enchantment—strands of liquid gold in a gossamer net. Larkin pressed them into her sister, spread the magic wider and wider. Sigils rooted through Sela's body, magic like Larkin had never felt be-

270

fore humming in them. But she found no trace of shadow. No darkness.

She shook her head in frustration and released her sigils, letting the magic fade to nothing.

"You didn't find anything?" Nesha stood by the table.

Larkin hadn't heard her come in. Her sister's eyes were red-rimmed and swollen from crying. No matter what Garrot had done, Nesha had loved him. Now that he was gone, Larkin found that she could see past her hurt and anger to the compassion that resided beneath.

"No," Larkin admitted.

Nesha's fists tightened. "You couldn't save Raeneth or Papa. You refused to help Garrot. You can't help Sela. What can you do?"

No matter what Larkin said, it wouldn't be good enough. "If you want to blame someone, fine. Blame me." She bent and kissed Sela's forehead and then started for the door.

Nesha caught her arm, a beat of remorse crossing her face. "I'm sorry. Denan... Magalia told me."

Garrot's fate will not be Denan's. "I can't." Larkin pulled free and stepped, gasping, outside. Denan leaned against a rail, his arms folded over his chest. The guards and pages stood a respectful distance away.

Denan crossed the distance to her. "What's wrong?"

Larkin braced herself against the rail and breathed deep, concentrating on keeping everything locked away. It was a beautiful day. The lake was a patchwork of shadows pooling beneath trees and vibrant blue water. But in the distance, the White Tree was missing more branches—emptiness where before there had been color and light.

"I'm fine."

He reached for her. "Larkin—"

She pushed past him and changed the subject. "I thought the council was waiting for us. What's this meeting about?"

Denan considered her before letting it go with a sigh. He started toward the common room. "We've always planned on making you a true queen."

You will never make it as queen echoed in her head. Larkin stiffened in dread. Was the Alamant ready to accept her for the queen she would be? She wasn't sure. "Are you sure this is the right time?"

"I'm sure."

Together, they stepped through the doorpane. Gendrin, Aaryn, and Mytin waited on the other side, all of them dripping sweat in the cloistered room. Larkin was relieved Jaslin wasn't there.

Aaryn pushed back from the table and hurried over to Denan. "You look like you haven't eaten in a week!" She fussed with his tunic, tugging out wrinkles and straightening the shoulders of the garment she'd made for him.

Denan bore her ministrations patiently. "Any more citizens unaccounted for?" He directed his question to the entire room.

"No," Gendrin said. "I've lent the constables as many men as I can spare for patrols."

Viscott came in with the butler, both bearing trays of cold fish and salad greens. The three of them joined Gendrin at the table. Across from her, Mytin poured Denan a cup of cold lilac tea. Already sweltering, Larkin fanned herself.

"Are you all right, dear?" Aaryn murmured, eyeing the bruise on Larkin's face.

Larkin gave a tight smile. "All part of being an enchantress."

Aaryn hummed unhappily.

"The populace has been instructed to seal off all panes," Gendrin said. "No one is swimming anymore." He wiped the sweat from his brow. "Which is why we've had an increase in heat sickness."

Mytin heaped a fillet of fish and salad greens onto Denan's plate. "You need to regain your strength." He cooked the meals in their family. He was good too. He eyed Larkin's bruised face. "You too, dear. Greens are good for healing."

Keeping her gaze down, Larkin dutifully ate a mouthful of leaves drizzled with a reduction of gobby and vinegar. At her first bite, she realized how hungry she was. Mytin grunted in approval as she ate in earnest.

"Farwin," Denan called.

The boy came in and handed Denan an official-looking document sealed with Denan's crest of the three-headed snake—the decree naming her queen. Denan nodded at the boy, who shot Larkin a smile and took his leave.

Mytin and Aaryn exchanged a loaded glance. The four of them had discussed this at length, so they had probably guessed the document's contents.

Denan passed it down to Gendrin. Fancy gold filigree flashed as he broke the seal and unfolded it. Larkin's stomach tightened, and she found it hard to swallow. She set down her utensils. Gendrin looked up, both his eyebrows raised.

Denan laced his hands together and sat back in his chair. "I have named Larkin my equal. In the event of my death or incapacity, she will rule in my stead."

Mytin and Aaryn exchanged another loaded glance.

Aaryn reached into the bag she always carried with her and began knitting. "I thought you meant to wait until things settled down before bringing this up."

Denan sipped his tea. "We live in dangerous times, Mother."

Clearly, her husband had no intention of telling his parents that his blight had spread, which wasn't fair to them. But they were his parents. Larkin wouldn't interfere in their relationship.

Gendrin braced his elbows on the table and leaned into his steepled hands. "Denan, you have always valued my honesty. So

I'm going to be honest with you now. I have nothing against Larkin. I even believe she'd be a fine queen, but I can't support her. At least, not yet."

And here she'd thought Gendrin might be growing to respect her.

"Why?" Denan asked evenly.

"The people won't accept her," Gendrin said.

The words hurt, but he wasn't wrong.

Mytin leaned forward. "You seem to have forgotten that Larkin has the monarch sigil. The White Tree has already chosen her as queen."

"The enchantresses adore her," Aaryn added.

Gendrin nodded. "Yet another reason the men won't follow her. A king ruling lends balance. A queen further tips the scales toward the enchantresses. The imbalance of power makes them uneasy." At Denan's hard look, he held out his hands. "I'm not saying no. I'm saying not yet."

Funny thing was, Larkin agreed with Gendrin. She wasn't ready. Nor were the people. They needed Denan to lead them.

Denan leaned forward. "The tree is dying. There isn't time for dissension." He rose to his feet and braced his hands on the table. His gaze locked on each member of the council. "The people will follow you. You will follow her."

Gendrin stared at the decree for a long time. "Very well." He reached down and signed it. "You need to be very careful how you proceed, Denan. Take your time."

Denan winced, his hand going to his side. "I don't have more time."

Aaryn's needles stopped clacking. "What do you mean?"

Denan's questioning gaze locked with Larkin's. Should he tell them?

"They have a right to know," she said gently.

Denan hesitated before hauling his shirt over his head, revealing his chest, darkened with black tined lines. Larkin had seen his blight before, but still, she winced. Aaryn shot to her feet, her ball of yarn unraveling as it rolled across the floor. Mytin's throat bobbed up and down.

"The weir failed," Gendrin stated the obvious.

"It's holding for now." Larkin fought the tears rising in her eyes.

"That's why you pushed this decree," Mytin said.

Denan eyed Larkin with an unfathomable sadness in his eyes. "It's just a precaution."

"But the pain..." Aaryn said.

Denan gave her a small smile. "I have something to make it bearable." He didn't mention that Magalia had said it would eventually kill him. "Now, the next group of Idelmarchians are due to replace the first this week, with one group arriving every week afterward."

Larkin would be relieved to see the druids go back to the Alamant, though she felt sorry for the pipers who would have to go with them to train them on how to use their new sigils.

"Now that the ardents have been taken care of," Denan went on, "we need to shift our focus to training the Idelmarchians to use their sigils. Sela has indicated that we have nine or so months before the White Tree dies. I believe we can be ready to invade Valynthia in five. All our energies must be directed toward this endeavor."

No more was said about Denan's weir. Instead, they went over the logistics of stationing and training an army of thousands of druids. Then moving both armies across mulgar-infested territory.

Their last-ditch effort to save mankind before the wraiths destroyed them all.

CHAPTER

NIGHTMARE

Sometime in the darkest part of night, Larkin woke drenched in sweat. Without the breeze coming through the panes, it was unbearably hot. She bent over her drawn knees and pushed her hair out of her sticky face, trying to banish the last vestiges of the dream. But the darkness, the taste of rot, lingered on her tongue. She couldn't shake the feeling that something was terribly, horribly wrong.

As if to echo the feeling resonating inside her, a low, mournful horn sounded. The magic panels shivered like the lake in a hailstorm. Larkin swore she felt that vibration deep in her bones.

"Queen Larkin! King Denan!" West called from outside the doorpane. "The warning horn is sounding!"

That must have been what had woken her. "What's going on?"

"We don't know yet," Maylah answered.

"Give me a moment." Larkin stood and made her way to the nursery to wake Denan, but the panel was already down. Denan panted and writhed in the bed, as if he, too, were trapped in a nightmare. She shifted her gaze to the panes around her—all the milky color of impassibility. The only way this pane could possibly be down was if someone in the main room had taken it down.

She spun, her sigils flaring to life and driving back a bit of the darkness. From the shadows at the edge of the room, Maisy's face came into view, her right shoulder crusted with black blood—a wound Larkin had given her.

"You." Larkin spread her shield before her. "West! The ardent is here!"

Pounding on the doorpane. "You have to let us in!" West cried.

To do that, Larkin would have to leave Denan undefended. "Break in!"

West and Maylah called for reinforcements and hacked at the supports with their swords.

Behind her, Denan moaned.

"Denan?" Larkin called, not daring to take her gaze from Maisy.

"You stopped my task." Maisy inched toward her. "I'm glad of it, and yet it must be done."

"What have you done to my husband?" Larkin cried.

"You're not listening! I'm trying to save you, save him, save everyone!"

"By turning him into a mulgar? How does that save anyone?" Larkin asked.

Maisy had the gall to look wounded. "Because then you will finally be willing to do what you must."

"What does that mean?"

Beyond the panels, light revealed dozens of shadows. They'd found an ax and had managed to cut through one of the supports.

"I was the reason you went into the Forbidden Forest after your sister," Maisy said. "The reason you received magic and a piper. I was the one who convinced Bane to go after you. I was the one who made you a queen!"

By killing the king. Light, could it all be true? The sinking sensation in Larkin's gut said it was. How many other strings had the woman pulled to maneuver Larkin into this position? Did Maisy really think she was helping Larkin? Judging by the fanatical gleam in her eyes, she did. Larkin's lips twisted in disgust— at Maisy for the monster she was and at herself for ever believing she could be anything different.

The guards' hands appeared, wrenching at the wood.

"Why has the alarm horn sounded?" A couple more steps, and Maisy would be within reach.

"They're distracted," Maisy whispered.

Just like Maisy to layer riddles within riddles. "What are you talking about?"

Maisy lifted a dagger. "You're still not listening!"

Larkin never should have let Maisy escape that that night. "I should have killed you when I had the chance."

Larkin pulsed, sending Maisy careening into the opposite pane. Both hands above her head, Larkin swung down hard. Maisy moved, faster than humanly possible. Her knife deflected Larkin's blow, so it sailed harmlessly to the side. Braced behind her shield, Larkin rammed into her, sword jabbing from below. Maisy rolled sideways, their blades locking, tips scratching the floor.

Larkin strained, trying to gain the advantage. Maisy was too strong. Larkin twisted, her sword slicing Maisy's calf. Unaffected, Maisy finished her rotation, coming up behind Larkin and shoving her.

Completely unguarded, Larkin staggered forward. Maisy's next blow would come from above or below. Knowing she was as good as dead if she didn't do something, Larkin thrust her sword behind her. It sank into flesh and then bone. Before Maisy could retaliate, Larkin rolled forward onto her shoulder, wrenching her sword from Maisy's gut, and bounded to her feet, shield back in place.

And instantly realized her mistake.

She'd left her husband unguarded. Moving preternaturally fast, Maisy darted inside. Larkin ran after her and stopped short in the doorway. Maisy had one hand behind Denan's head; the other held a knife to his throat, her glittering eyes locked on Larkin.

The ardents, the wraiths, the curse—all of it had taken too much. Larkin would not let it have Denan. Never him. She gathered her magic, preparing to flare.

Maisy's hand tensed. "Don't! I don't want to kill him!"

Larkin's magic buzzed painfully under her skin, a river of light begging to be released. She drew her magic slowly, painfully, back into her sigils. Maisy didn't seem to notice the black blood soaking the middle of her tunic.

A dozen guards finally rushed into the room, coming up behind Larkin. She motioned for them to stop. West realized what was happening first and physically blocked the others.

Larkin dared not move. Barely dared to breathe. "Not him, Maisy. Please."

Maisy held perfectly still. "You have to save him, Larkin."

That's what she'd been trying to do for months! The very thing Maisy and her cursed wraiths were trying to prevent! Larkin swallowed her angry words and held out her hands, palms up in supplication. "Tell me what to do."

Maisy's eyes widened, and her head swiveled to the south. "I'm out of time," she muttered to herself. She shot Larkin an exasperated expression. "Haven't you figured it out yet? You are the light."

Nearly the same thing Sela had said. *How can that be?* Larkin thought.

Maisy licked her lips. "Trust me, Larkin. Just one last time."

If Larkin hadn't trusted Maisy in the first place, Denan would have never been corrupted. "You swear you're telling the truth?"

Maisy nodded.

Larkin sighed and reached out a hand. "Then I'm sorry for ever doubting you."

"Larkin," West hissed.

She ignored him.

Maisy smiled then, the brilliance cutting through the madness like light breaking through dark clouds. She eased Denan back onto the bed, crossed the room, and reached for Larkin's hand.

Instead of taking it, Larkin flared her sword and thrust it into Maisy's chest. Maisy looked down at the gleaming, magical blade disappearing in her ribs. Her expression was devastated—betrayed.

Larkin fought a twin knife of guilt that pierced her center, just as her blade pierced Maisy's. This moment would cost her dearly, but she had no choice. "Can you hear me, Ramass? I'm not falling for any more of your tricks."

Larkin pulled back her sword. Maisy jerked and coughed, blood spewing from her lips. The ardent looked down at Denan—still close enough she could throw her knife.

Instead, she opened her hand, the knife clattering to the floor. "I've always been your friend, Larkin. Always. And when the time comes, you'll remember that."

"I'm sorry," Larkin choked. She drew her sword back, twisted her hips, and swung her sword through Maisy's neck. The woman's head hit the floor. Black blood pooled toward Larkin's feet. She staggered back. Not fast enough. The sticky warmth seeped between her toes before cooling on her skin.

West gripped her arms. Called her name. She couldn't answer. Because Maisy was dead. And Larkin had killed her.

No.

Not killed.

Executed.

Wearing his nightclothes, Tam knelt beside Denan—he must have been one of the guards to rush into the room. She was suddenly glad he'd decided to move into her tree. Except then maybe Alorica wouldn't have been stabbed and her baby wouldn't have died. But that wasn't right. Alorica was stabbed because the wraiths wanted to destroy Denan's weir. Larkin laughed at how silly she was.

The guards kept sneaking surreptitious glances at Larkin.

Tam was suddenly in front of her. "Larkin."

Her laughter switched to broken sobs. "I killed her, Tam."

Denan started shouting.

Tam leaned toward West. "Get her out of sight and cleaned up." He hurried to help the guards restrain Denan.

West swore and hauled her toward the bathroom. He pushed her fully clothed into the shower and turned on the water.

She gasped at the shock of cold and turned her face to the stream. Leaning against the wall, she sagged to the floor. She gulped in one breath. Then another. Her head began to clear. "The warning horn?"

West took a washcloth and wiped her arms, heedless of the water soaking him. "We still don't know."

She closed her eyes and tried to still her dark thoughts. "Is Denan all right?"

"Does it matter?" West said through gritted teeth.

Shivering though she wasn't cold, she shot him a glare. "He didn't do anything."

"Exactly! He lay on his bed while an ardent tried to kill you!"

Maisy had never tried to kill her. "This isn't about Denan. It never has been. This is about your guilt for keeping me prisoner." West went an alarming shade of white and leaned against the bathroom wall. She gentled her voice. "That wasn't your fault. You didn't know what the druids were doing."

"I knew," he whispered. "I swore I wouldn't let anyone or anything else hurt you ever again. I mean to keep that promise."

Something crashed in the other room. Grunts and moans. Denan was awake and fighting the guards. West moved to leave.

"You're hurting me now," she called after him.

He froze in place.

"You're undermining my orders. Undermining my husband."

West's fists clenched. "I'll do what I have to."

How could the man not see he was making the very mistake he was trying to atone for? "Then I'm going to have to reassign you."

He whirled on her in surprise. "You can't mean—"

She pushed to her feet. "I do."

He strode toward her and gripped her arms. "Larkin, don't do this."

She knew he cared about her, but the very fact that he was fighting her now—squeezing her arms so much they hurt—was confirmation she was making the right choice.

She flared her sigils in warning. "Go to Gendrin. Ask him to reassign you."

West's face went rigid. He took one step back and then another. "Larkin..." He shook his head, as if he couldn't find the words. He turned and left.

For half a breath, she felt as if a weight had been lifted.

"He's awake," Tam called from outside the doorpane.

The tight, clipped way he said it told her all she needed to know. "He's fighting them?"

"He'll come out of it." A pause. "What happened with West?"

"What had to happen." She took the soap and scrubbed between her toes. "Have one of my enchantresses bring my clothes."

"Right."

She pulled off her sopping nightgown and kicked it in a corner. She scrubbed her shaking hands over her skin to remove any lingering blood—no time for more soap. The water ran out before she was completely done. It would have to do.

She stepped out and toweled herself off. Moments later, Atara came into the room with Larkin's clothes.

"You missed your shoulder buckle." Larkin slipped the undertunic on, the quilted gambeson over it.

Atara fixed her shoulder strap, while Larkin settled the tasset over her hips.

Atara watched Larkin solemnly. "The mulgar army has been spotted on the shore."

A sick, wrenching feeling tore through Larkin. She buried her head in her hands. They were supposed to take the fight to the Black Tree. They were supposed to have more time. She was supposed to face this with Denan beside her.

"We're not ready," she murmured. *I am not ready.*

Atara settled Larkin's breast and back armor over her shoulders and tied the side straps. "You're not alone, whatever you may feel."

Aaryn, Mytin, Gendrin, Atara, Tam... Atara was right. Whatever happened, she wasn't alone. She reached out and squeezed the woman's hand in thanks.

"Speaking of alone," Atara said. "Why isn't West hovering?"

Larkin cleared the emotion from her throat. "I'm having him reassigned."

Atara look surprised and then frowned. "Oh. Well. I suppose that's for the best."

"I thought you'd be happier about it." The two of them clearly hated each other.

Atara shrugged.

Larkin didn't have the time or energy to deal with Atara's emotions. Outside the room, she found Denan sitting on the edge of their bed and tying his boots with shaking hands. Tam stood over him, and he wasn't watching for outside danger. He was watching Denan. The other guards were gone, probably banished by Tam once Denan was himself again.

The pale, hunched man before her seemed like a stranger. A swell of pity knocked her off-balance—pity quickly followed by guilt. Powerful, unshakeable Denan had been the foundation upon which she'd built her new life. But now… that man was gone. She felt adrift. Lost. And betrayed. She couldn't trust Denan anymore. Wasn't sure how much of her husband was even left. A good wife wouldn't have such thoughts.

Had Maisy been ordered to kill Denan, but whatever humanity lurked inside her hadn't allowed it?

No. The wraiths wanted Denan a mulgar, not dead.

So why had Maisy come?

Larkin didn't know. And right now, there were bigger concerns. The wraiths might not be able to cross water, but the mulgars and ardents could. If they broke through the city's defenses, it would be a slaughter.

With a heavy sigh, Denan lumbered to his feet. "Why attack now? Why not wait until the White Tree dies?"

He didn't seem to expect an answer, and in any case, no one offered one.

Farwin stepped into the room. "The ardents are launching boats."

Ancestors. It isn't supposed to happen this way. We are supposed to bring the fight to them. If anything, they were worse off than they had been before. Larkin pushed her helmet onto her head and hurried toward the door, Atara and Tam on her heels.

"I'm coming with you," Denan called after her.

She halted and turned to study him. He was back from whatever nightmare had held him captive. She could see it in his eyes. "You're not well," she said gently.

"I don't plan on fighting," Denan said. "But I will be there."

Larkin pursed her lips. He was the king. She couldn't stop him. And even if she could, she wouldn't do that to him. She gave a curt nod.

Denan motioned to Farwin. "Take my armor to General Aaryn's tower. I'll put it on there." Because he didn't want to waste his diminished strength carrying the extra weight.

Farwin shot Larkin a questioning look. She didn't miss the humiliation that flashed across Denan's face at the boy's dismissal. Larkin wanted to sharply reprimand Farwin, but that would only humiliate Denan further. She locked her jaw around her tongue and nodded.

Oblivious, Farwin stepped out long enough to bring one of the other pages in. They each took one of the chest's handles and waited for her.

Larkin motioned for Denan to join her, but he stayed where he was. "Are you coming?"

"You go on ahead," he said. "I'll catch up."

She didn't want to leave him. But she was needed at the wall and fussing over her husband would only embarrass him. So she gave a curt nod and left, Tam falling in behind her.

"Tam, if you would stay," Denan said.

His back to Denan, Tam winced. Before he turned, he had his customary grin in place. "Wanting to keep the best guard for yourself, eh?"

Tam waited a beat. Waited for Denan to step into the opening he'd left. To say, *If I wanted the best guard, I'd have kept Atara*—or something like it.

Denan missed his cue entirely. A nervous uncertainty shivered throughout the room—uncertainty highlighted by another wail of the warning horn.

Tam nodded to Larkin, his expression telling her he would look after her husband. She nodded back. She and Atara left the room at a jog, half the pages and guards falling in behind them.

CHAPTER 31

DYING LIGHT

The night was still and hot. With Atara and Maylah leading the way, Larkin jogged along the bridges that connected the trees, sweat soaking her tunic. Behind her came two more guards and two pages, one of them Farwin.

Judging by the moonrise, it had to be sometime around midnight, but nearly every hometree in the Alamant was lit up. Children, obviously woken by the warning horn, wailed as their parents left them in the care of their elders and joined the procession of enchantresses and enchanters streaming toward the wall.

Those soldiers before her stepped aside to let her pass. More than one had a face streaked with tears. As Larkin met their gazes, she felt an overwhelming sense that she had to protect as many as possible. Send as many as possible home to those crying children.

Out of breath, Larkin crossed the last bridge into the dead space between the city and the wall. Before Larkin stood the steel-reinforced main gate—the only part of the wall not made by living trees. It rose out of the water, an intricate pulley system for each side. All along the wall, catapults crouched, ready to loose the payload stacked to the side of them.

A high tower on each side of her, Larkin stepped under the leafy, arched colonnade, complete with arrow slits. Enchanters and enchantresses lined the walkway. Young men bustled about, setting up bundles of arrows, piles of rocks, and buckets of water with ladles for drinking.

Larkin sidestepped a running squad of enchantresses and spared a glance back the way she'd come. Denan and his guards weren't in sight yet. A week ago, he would have outrun her by double. Now he couldn't come close to keeping up.

"Larkin." Atara motioned for her to hurry from where she waited at the entrance to the eastern tower.

Pushing her worry away, Larkin hustled to catch up.

"Watch the entrance," Atara said to the two trailing guards. She led the way up the winding steps, with the pages bringing up the rear.

They stepped through the trapdoor to the top of the tower, a handful of guards and a dozen pages eyeing them. Aaryn stood on the far crenellation, which jutted out thirty feet from the main wall. Leaving Aaryn a respectful bubble of space, two dozen archers ringed the exterior, bundles of arrows at their feet.

With a goodbye nod, Atara directed Farwin and the other page to set the chest down out of the way at the back of the tower and then join the other pages. She took her place with the other guards. Larkin stepped up beside Aaryn. Her mother-in-law took one look at Larkin and handed her a waterskin. She drank greedily.

The lake was still—so still it reflected the starlight and moonlight, leaving the night unnaturally bright. About a hundred yards away, an enormous, ugly raft with a battering ram bobbed in the water. Behind it, a dark line of mulgars marred the shore.

Thousands of them. They stood eerily still, not a sound, not a movement. That eerie silence sent a shiver down Larkin's back.

"They can't really believe that ram is a match for the barrier," Aaryn said.

All the dreams the White Tree had sent Larkin—about how to make the barrier that encased the wall—sent a nervous jolt through her. She flared her magic and examined the faintly different filaments of light woven in a complex pattern—a pattern familiar to her because of the dreams. Geometric shapes, mostly triangles, overlaid in a locking pattern, every strand in perfect order. It somehow reminded her of an impassable mountain range of craggy cliffs and sharp peaks. It fit over the wall like a second skin.

She sank onto her heels in relief. The barrier was impervious to everything but magic. And magic was something ardents and mulgars couldn't bear. With the wraiths unable to cross water, the only way for the enemy to get into the city was over the wall. To do that, they'd have to go through the Alamantian army.

"We'll hold them." Aaryn shot a look at the sister tower. Larkin could make out Gendrin ordering about his aides and advisors. Denan should be the one giving those orders.

"Ready to kill some mulgars?" a familiar voice said breathlessly.

Larkin turned to see Tam muss Farwin's hair and tweak the other page's nose. Only then did Larkin notice the fear in the boys' eyes. She'd been so wrapped up in other things that she hadn't noticed. Tam had. He was good at calming everyone.

He nodded to the other guards and came to lean against the crenellation. He had always been an adviser as well as a guard. Larkin felt better with him by her side.

"Where's Denan?" she asked.

"Sent me ahead." He sniffed. "Said my expertise was best served guiding you womenfolk."

She drove her shoulder into his arm, knocking him off-balance.

"Hey!" Tam said in mock anger.

She almost smiled. The pages weren't the only ones Tam was good at calming.

"Here." Atara handed Larkin a telescope.

Larkin peered through the concave glass. Ardents prowled in front of their army and watched their former homes with the kind of voracity reserved for wild beasts driven mad by hunger. Some had even lit a fire, which threw terrifying shadows across the eerily silent army.

Behind them, the faces of dozens of mulgars jumped into view. The vast majority looked tattered, spent. Like corpses whose bodies hadn't been allowed to decay. Some wore rudimentary armor. Some were naked—as if their clothes had rotted from their bodies. Others were missing arms or legs. One woman was missing her left breast, the scars thick and twisted. But each had the telltale tined black marks and the all-black eyes.

Perhaps even more disturbing were the couple hundred whose armor still shone with polish. They weren't even dirty. Where had they come from?

"There's a whole bunch of Black Druids to the east," Aaryn said.

Larkin swung her telescope, catching sight of a knot of three hundred or so druids amid the mulgar army. The second company from the Idelmarch wasn't coming. Not anymore.

"What are the wraiths waiting for?" Larkin paced. "What do they know that we don't?" Because the wraiths had spent nearly three centuries plotting for this moment. They had a plan. And Larkin needed to know what it was if she hoped to counter it.

Tam studied the mulgars through one of the telescopes. "Maybe they're as desperate as we are. Maybe their tree is dying as well, and this is their last chance at destroying us."

Tam always had been too hopeful. Aaryn wore the same tight expression Larkin did. Then Tam growled low in his throat.

"What is it?" Larkin whispered.

Mouth tight, he moved her telescope and pointed down the length. It took her a moment to find what he'd seen. Shadows tore apart and writhed like snakes in their death throes. Slowly, they stilled. Coalesced.

Ramass lifted his head. The Wraith King's sickly yellow eyes stared at her, as if he knew exactly where she was.

How could he possibly know?

The Wraith King motioned. A mulgar shambled up behind him. Unlike the other mulgars, Venna was clean and wearing a ridiculous pink dress. If not for the black tined marks and soulless eyes, she would be beautiful. Next came Talox. His clothes were threadbare and stained black. His bottom lip had been rent in two, one piece hanging limply. But it was his eyes that tore at her—eyes full of hate where before there had been only gentleness.

He'd become this to save her life. He'd paid too high a price.

The Wraith King reached toward her, his fingers curling, beckoning her to him. His words through Raeneth's mouth sent a tendril of ice down her neck. *Come to the forest, Larkin,* Ramass had said. *And I will give you back Venna and Talox. I will give them all back.*

He was a liar. She shot him a very rude gesture. Let his army come. Let them bash themselves to pieces against the wall and its barrier.

As if he'd seen her refusal, he again motioned. Another mulgar came forward. One of the men with armor that shone in the moonlight. One arm hung limply, as if the shoulder had been broken. And the face was badly bruised and swollen. But still, Larkin recognized Harben.

Her father was an mulgar.

Her father.

So many memories.

His fist slamming into her cheek. She cowered in the mud. Spit flew from his mouth. Veins stood out in his reddened face.

But there had been a before. A before of horsey rides and teaching her to plant a field and bringing her home a blue hair ribbon even though they couldn't afford it.

And there had been an after. An after of heavy sorrow and the beginnings of forgiveness.

And now there was an end. Because her father was gone.

Larkin's legs sagged. Tam caught her.

"Ryttan," she managed. "Ryttan has fallen?"

Tam and Aaryn exchanged a look. "She doesn't know?" Aaryn asked.

Mouth in a thin line, Tam shook his head.

Frowning in disapproval, Aaryn pointed to the west. Larkin didn't see anything at first. But then... a faint red-orange glow gleamed, like the last traces of a dying sun. But no. The sky was too dark, morning too far off. That was fire.

Ryttan was burning.

All those new mulgars... they were all that was left.

Ancestors save her, they'd sent her father to Ryttan. Sent him to this death.

"It's why the warning horn sounded," Tam admitted.

If Tam knew, then so did Denan. Someone must have told him while she'd been washing away Maisy's blood. *Light, I've lost so many of them.* Larkin squeezed her hands into fists to keep the anger from erupting and jerked away from Tam. "Why didn't either of you tell me?"

Tam's jaw tightened. "Because he knows the danger of fighting distracted."

Is that why Denan had asked Tam to stay behind—to convince him to spare her the horror she was feeling now?

Aaryn wrapped an arm around Larkin's waist. "Denan knows that there is no time for grief in a battle."

At that, her anger softened. In Denan's place, she might have done the same. She had to accept that her father was as good as dead. His body a puppet for the Wraith King, who would kill them all. She needed her focus on the lives she still had to save, not the ones she had already lost.

So Larkin took her father's not-death and buried it deep in her imaginary lake. She wiped the tears from her cheeks and faced the Wraith King. She didn't know how, but he could hear her.

"I'll die before I let you take me."

Ramass didn't react, but the ardents and mulgars tipped back their heads and screamed, their cries rending the night.

CHAPTER 32

BATTLE

Mulgars swarmed into the lake, kicked up purple algae, and disappeared beneath the water. Wave after wave of them dove out of sight, until the shore was bare of everything except four wraiths standing just far enough back that the water wouldn't touch them.

The lake grew still again, as if nothing had happened. But beneath the surface, her father and her friends were coming to kill them.

"Where's the lethan when you need it?" Tam muttered.

Larkin shivered at the mention of the creature with its sucking tentacles and sharp beak.

Using poles and oars, the ardents pushed the massive raft forward. To think of the creatures breaking into the city, launching unseen out of the lake to attack each hometree in turn... It would be chaos. It would be a slaughter.

We must hold the wall.

"Enchantresses," Aaryn called. "Prepare to shield." The command rang up and down the line. Enchantresses stepped forward, sigils flaring to life.

"Ready the catapults!" Gendrin called from the other tower. A command that should have been given by the king.

"Where is Denan?" Larkin asked. He should have joined them by now.

Tam motioned to a random page. "Find the king. Report back."

The boy left at a run.

Larkin was glad Tam hadn't sent Farwin. High and heavily guarded as this tower was, this was the safest point along the wall. She wanted the boy near her in case things went wrong. She lifted the telescope but found no sign of mulgars beneath the still water.

"Release!" Gendrin called, so loud that it made Larkin jump.

There was a heavy thud like the beat of an enormous drum as the catapults launched. Rocks and gravel sailed overhead, arced downward, and slammed into the lake. Purple water rocketed upward.

Larkin waited for any sign that Gendrin had hit his mark—blood or bodies. There was only the gradual fade of the algae to black.

"He's firing blind," Tam said through gritted teeth.

"The mulgars are probably too deep," Aaryn said.

If only they could see what they were hitting! A sudden idea struck Larkin. She turned back to the pages. "Bring me all the extra lampent blossoms you can find. Hurry, before they attack."

About ten of them took off.

"Two of you stay back," Aaryn said.

The rest left at a run, and this time Farwin went with them. Larkin had to stop herself from calling him back. Light, she was growing as overprotective of the boy as West was of her.

The catapults groaned as they shifted and twanged as they launched, closer this time. More water surged. Before the water had even settled, the catapults twanged again. Again, the shot hit another location. Gendrin was searching for a target.

Farwin returned, his tunic loaded with lampent blossoms. Larkin took one and smashed it into a ball, the juices making her palms glow faintly. She hurled it out into the water, where it sunk just beneath the surface. The juices illuminated the water around it.

"Ancestors, you're brilliant." Tam took one of the flowers and copied her. Other soldiers caught on. Lampents were picked from where they grew wild in the canopy and along the parapet. Crumpled flowers sailed over the wall, landing in the still water. Some sank, some floated, and some hovered in between.

A shout. A soldier leaned over the parapet and pointed. At first, Larkin saw nothing. But then, in the stillness, a ghostly figure slid beneath the water. They weren't blind anymore. And the creatures were much closer than Larkin had anticipated—almost as if some had been waiting in the lake all along. Waiting and watching her. That's how the wraiths knew where she was and what she had said. A shiver of unease coursed through her.

"Catapults reconfigure and fire at will!" Gendrin cried.

The catapults groaned as their captains shifted them into position. The first one twanged. Rocks slammed into the water, and between the gleam of lampents, black blood plumed. The first body, broken into pieces, floated to the surface. Then another. And another. Then a dozen. The pipers cheered, their fists raised to the sky.

Larkin didn't join them. Was Harben among those bodies? Talox? Venna? The idea horrified her, even as the logical part of her knew it would be better for her friends to die than be slaves to the wraiths.

Soldiers kept throwing lampents. Round after round came from the catapults. But fewer bodies floated to the surface.

"They've gone deeper," Aaryn said.

The catapults adjusted and began striking closer and closer to the walls. The raft with the battering ram slid ever closer. Then the first of the mulgars came too close for the catapults to hit. Close enough that Larkin could make out the flash of a beaked nose, a bald head, a smooth calf ending in a mangled stump. Could smell the stench of death that surrounded the mulgars like a miasma.

The cheers fell silent. An air of anticipation grew, for the assault that would begin any moment.

"How many are there?" Larkin whispered, as if afraid to break the hush.

"Perhaps ten thousand," Tam said.

Ten thousand mulgars against three thousand Alamantians. *Light save us.*

"Archers at the ready!" echoed along the wall. Archers, including those in the tower with Larkin, drew their bows.

"Arrows won't kill them," Larkin said.

"But they will slow them," Aaryn said.

"Makes them easier to kill," Tam added.

Up and down the wall, dozens of mulgars churned just below the surface like fish writhing in full nets. Crossbows floating on small rafts suddenly emerged—how they'd sunk them and managed to move them through the water, Larkin didn't know. Mulgars swarmed onto the small rafts and loaded the cross bolts with grappling hooks.

"Light!" Tam swore.

"Enchantresses, shield!" Aaryn cried.

Behind her, one of the enchanters played notes on his pipes. Enchantresses flared their shields wide, spreading them over the parapet and the colonnade.

Larkin flared her own sigils. "Will those hooks reach the tower?"

Tam studied the crossbows. "We're too high."

Larkin wanted to believe him, but she'd learned long ago to never underestimate the wraiths. So she kept her sigils lit, and she didn't miss that Aaryn did the same.

Below, hundreds of crossbows released with a discordant snap. Larkin flared her shield—whether she needed it or not, she felt better with it in her hand. Hooks shot up and over the enchantresses' shield walls and the woven colonnades, catching on the woven branches.

Larkin had an instant to feel relief that none of the hooks came anywhere close to the towers. Then the ardents hauled back, and the hooks caught, dark ropes going taut. Mulgars exploded from the water and scurried up like spiders. If they made it over the wall... Cold fear clenched Larkin's stomach. She swallowed at the bile rising in her throat.

"Cut them down!" Aaryn shouted.

Enchantresses flared their weapons and hacked at ropes as thick as their thighs. Their magical blades should have cut through as easily as a hand through cobwebs, but the cursed things didn't even fray.

"How is that possible?" Larkin asked.

"Archers!" Gendrin called before anyone could answer her.

The archers drew their bows and sighted their targets.

The enchantress units lowered their shield wall. The archers released. A hundred twangs sounded. A flock of arrows illuminated by the lampents sliced into the mulgars. The creatures bristled with them, but there were no screams of pain. No grimaces or hunching over wounds as black blood spread through the purple-tinted water like ink. If a mulgar died, three more rose to take its place.

The first wave of them breached the wall to Larkin's right, driving the Alamantians back.

"Aim for those ardents holding the crossbows!" Gendrin roared from the other tower.

More arrows soared through the night. A rope finally snapped, mulgars falling back into the lake with a purple splash.

Aaryn cupped her mouth and shouted to her enchantresses, "Pulse when you see a hook sailing over you! Knock it back!" The orders were relayed up and down the line.

Seconds later, a unit of enchantresses flared their shields, knocking a hook wobbly, though it still caught in the end. Another unit flared, and this time, the hook ricocheted back into the lake. This was repeated all up and down the line, the flashes of light leaving a faint shadow in Larkin's aftervision.

Every time a hook was flared off course or a rope was cut down, another two took its place. And then the first mulgar climbed over the wall. An enchanter instantly beheaded him. A second later, the rope snapped, mulgars free-falling in silence.

But in their place, a handful of mulgars crested the wall. Then a dozen. Then two. More and more mulgars reached the wall. More and more and more. And yet still they came on.

And the Alamantians met them. The enchantresses and enchanters worked together. Enchantresses hacked at the ropes, flared to deflect hooks, and created shield walls. Enchanters cut down the mulgars as they came over and tossed their twitching bodies back over the side. All their training, all their drilling, was paying off as they worked together in perfect concert.

Not a single mulgar survived the climb long enough to do any real damage. The wraiths were throwing their army away. Vast though it was, they couldn't keep this up forever.

Except.

The battering ram came close enough that Larkin could make out the uneven, molten metal that had been poured over the shaft, the end tipped to a wicked point. The mulgars cranked the ponderous thing back.

"What are they doing?" Tam asked.

Larkin flared her magic and studied the weave over the gate. She couldn't find a single weakness.

"Aim for those ardents!" Gendrin pointed to the raft.

Within moments, their bodies were riddled to the point they couldn't move for the arrows in their joints. More ardents and mulgars rose from the deep, dragged their fellows into the water, and took their place.

Larkin couldn't just stand here, useless and safe in a high tower, while her countrymen died defending their home. "The forest take them," Larkin cried. "Farwin, get me a bow!"

Farwin turned to run toward the stairs when Tam shouted, "Look!"

Larkin whipped around. A line of ardents drew on ropes that disappeared over the edge of the raft.

"What are they doing?" Aaryn asked.

Something was emerging from the water. Larkin leaned over the parapet. A hinged platform rose. Four contraptions that looked like enormous crossbows had been bolted to it. Nestled inside the pocket were sharp hooks—hooks aimed directly at Larkin's tower.

The wraiths were doing what they'd been trying to do all along. Come after her.

From the other tower, Gendrin shouted something Larkin couldn't understand for the rushing in her ears.

"We have to go!" Tam dragged her toward the stairs, where Atara was already waiting.

"What?" Larkin cried. "No." She wasn't some untrained girl. She was a warrior!

"It's not safe for you here anymore," Tam said.

"It's too late to run!" Aaryn flared, knocking a hook back. "Atara, Larkin, help me!"

Tam released Larkin, and she and Atara lined up beside Aaryn. The other three hooks fired.

"Wait," Aaryn said as the hooks shot toward them. "Pulse!"

Larkin, Atara, and Aaryn pulsed, managing to knock two of them off course. The third came right at them. Tam wrapped Larkin up and rolled her under him.

ROPE

Larkin hit hard enough that the breath was knocked from her lungs. From between Tam's arms, she saw that Atara had done the same to Aaryn.

And beyond her friends, blood and chaos. The hooks had hit the archers, knocking down half a dozen of them. As she watched, their bodies were dragged, knocking more men down. Then the hooks caught on the edge of the parapet, cutting through the men and catching fast. Larkin looked away from blood and gore and screaming, twitching bodies.

Tam grabbed the back of Larkin's breastplate and hauled her toward the stairs, Atara leading the way.

"No!" Larkin tried to pull free, but she was having a hard time keeping her feet under her. "I'll fight." The other pages ran to her side.

"They're after you!" Tam came to a sudden stop as mulgars exploded up from the trapdoor. He shoved her behind him.

To the right, a hundred ropes clustered; thousands of mulgars had overrun the area around her tower. Hers. Not Gendrin's. Not anywhere else either.

"Of course they're after me," she ground out. "They're always after me."

The other guards meet the mulgars swarming into the tower. Larkin shoved the four pages behind her and moved to join the guards. Atara blocked her.

Tam jerked her back. "They won't fight you. They'll swarm you and drag you off. Stay back."

Light, he was right.

Gendrin's shouts finally reached her. "Get the queen to safety!"

"But the boys!" And the others. Tam, Atara, Aaryn. She couldn't leave them.

Tam remained planted firmly before her. "Curse you, Larkin!"

This attack couldn't possibly be about bringing her in. The wraiths wanted her, but they wanted to overthrow the Alamant more. And yet, the mulgars and ardents had overwhelmed the center of the wall and weren't even attempting to raise the gate.

Whatever the wraiths wanted with her, it was worse than anything she could imagine. Fear like she'd never known flooded her. She flared her sword as sharp as it would go. It would be nothing to drive the tip into her heart. Stop it beating. The wraiths couldn't use her then. It might destroy her friends and family, but maybe it would save them too.

Atara gripped her arm, squeezing her sword sigil so hard it hurt. "Don't." The woman looked straight into her eyes. "Not unless they take you."

Larkin gave a grim nod. Tam backed Larkin toward the edge of the parapet. She let him. Aaryn flared her weapons and hacked at the fat ropes alongside half the archers—the other half were busy firing at the mulgars halfway up the rope—but they weren't making much headway.

This, at least, Larkin could do. She sharpened her blade to a razor point and joined Aaryn. Their weapons were sharp enough to cut through a falling leaf, but they were barely managing to fray the rope. Black rope with a strange shimmer.

Aaryn's expression turned grim. "It's made of the Black Tree."

The pages took out their daggers and helped. Tam shot a look at the guards barely managing to hold off the mulgars swarming through the trapdoor, then at those mulgars three-quarters of the way into the tower.

They were going to be overrun.

Tam leaned over the parapet and gauged the distance to Gendrin's tower. "Rope! I need rope!"

"There's some in the bottom of Denan's chest." The chest they'd left on the other side of the tower.

"I'll get it!" Before Larkin could stop him, Farwin took off.

"No!" Larkin lunged at him, her fingers barely managing to brush the back of his tunic.

Tam held her back as the boy darted between two pairs of fighting men, dove between a mulgar's legs, and crawled between more battling men. He grabbed the chest, unlatched the lid, and hauled out bits of armor and an extra pair of boots before reaching the rope at the bottom. He swung the coils over his shoulder.

Larkin wanted to shout at him not to risk it, but he couldn't stay there. Not without a mulgar taking a shot at him.

His dagger in his hand, Farwin set his teeth and dove back into the fray. A mulgar pivoted and lifted a crude weapon to kill him. At the last moment, a guard deflected the blow; he received a spear through his chest for his trouble and fell, coughing blood.

Farwin was already up and running. He wasn't going to make it. Not without help. Larkin dodged Tam and rushed toward the boy. She drove her sword into the neck of a mulgar one of the guards was fighting and hamstrung another. Tam and Atara took up posts on either side and fought with her.

Farwin was a mere step away. She shifted so he could dart past her. He smiled up at her in relief. Then jerked. His smile disappearing. He stared down at the sword point sticking from his chest. Behind him, the mulgar Larkin had hamstrung had reared up and stabbed him.

"No!" she screamed. Not this sweet, eager, adventurous boy.

The pages screamed Farwin's name, as she swept the boy out of the way with one arm and beheaded the mulgar with the other. Farwin fell backward against her. His blood pulsed against her forearm as she dragged him to safety. Atara and Tam closed ranks to fill the gap she'd left behind.

He sagged, and she couldn't hold him. They both went down, Larkin's back to the parapet and Farwin on her lap. She tore off the boy's sleeve and shoved it into the gushing wound, pushing hard enough that he cried out.

The three other pages gaped at Farwin in disbelief. A boy with the barest whiff of a mustache held utterly still. His expression went from terrified to furious in a heartbeat. He yelled a fierce battle cry, snatched a sword from a fallen guard, and motioned for the other boys to follow him.

"No!" Larkin cried.

They were children. No match for the speed and ruthlessness of the mulgars. If they joined that fight, they would die. But the boys didn't listen to her pleas. With fierce expressions, they pulled out their daggers and leaped into the fray.

She couldn't go after them, not with Farwin bleeding so badly.

One jumped on a mulgar's back and thrust his blade into the joint between neck and shoulder, jerking it free in a spray of blood. Another page fell, a mulgar tearing him to pieces. The third boy screamed an animal scream as his friend died. He jumped onto the back of a mulgar and stabbed over and over with a savagery Larkin had never seen.

Ancestors. They were children. They weren't supposed to fight, let alone so brutally. But then, there was no place for children in war. If any of these boys survived, they wouldn't be children anymore.

Tam took the rope off Farwin's shoulder, wound it around a fat arrow, and stood next to Aaryn, who was now firing arrows with the archers. Larkin was soaked in Farwin's blood.

I must get him to Magalia. "Help me bind his chest," she cried to anyone who would listen.

But the guards were nearly staggering in exhaustion. Four of them lay dying on the ground. Atara fought off any mulgars who managed to break through. The archers had given up hacking at the rope to concentrate on maiming the mulgars climbing the ropes. And still, the mulgars were nearly upon them.

Larkin pushed her free hand through the parapet, gathered every ounce of her power, and pulsed at those on the ropes. Light flashed. Hundreds of mulgars went flying, slamming into the water below hard enough to shatter bones.

That massive pulse had cost her dearly, her monarch sigil was nearly drained. She could perhaps manage another three pulses. That was enough to hold this half of the mulgars off. For a little while, at least.

Tam fired the arrow, rope trailing. They could find a way to tie Farwin to it, and the other tower could pull him in. Surely, Gendrin had a healer present. She just had to buy a little more time.

Farwin's breaths gurgled. The blood gushing against her arm slowed. Light, he was so pale. She couldn't deny it anymore. Couldn't pretend Magalia could save him. No one survived a sword through the chest. The page who'd led the others went down screaming and writhing in agony.

"I want my mother," Farwin gasped, his breaths crackling with blood as his lungs filled. His eyes were wide with terror.

Larkin brushed Farwin's hair out of his eyes, as she imagined his mother had done a hundred times, and kissed his cheek. "I'll send for her, all right?" She wouldn't. Couldn't. But it wouldn't matter in a moment.

She held him as if he were her own son. "I'm here, Farwin. I'm right here."

Tam tied the other end of the rope into a loop. "Stand up. They'll pull you up on the other side."

He wanted her to leave them. To leave them all to die. She met Aaryn's gaze. The woman nodded.

"I can't." She couldn't just abandon her friends to die. Abandon Denan's mother to die. But what came out was, "I can't leave Farwin."

Tam tested the knot, his expression haggard. "He's already gone."

She shifted to see Farwin's face. His head had tipped forward, blood staining his chin and tunic. But it was his utter stillness that confirmed Tam's words.

"No!" she cried.

Tam hauled her up. Farwin slipped from her arms to land in a heap on his side like discarded trash. A breeze hit the boy's warm blood soaking her and made it cool. Even with the oppressive heat, she shivered so hard she had to clench her teeth to keep them from clacking.

At the far tower, Gendrin had tied the rope fast to the parapet. Tam slipped the loop over Larkin's head and tightened it around her waist.

"Larkin!" Aaryn pointed to the mulgars on the ropes, now a mere ten yards away. Larkin pulsed twice. At least a hundred mulgars were sent spinning into the abyss. One pulse left.

Tam grabbed Larkin's shoulders and tried to push her over the edge.

She gripped the banister. "I'm not leaving you!"

Tam grabbed her face. "Go to the other tower, and the mulgars will shift focus. We might survive."

No. The mulgars would kill him and Aaryn. They were too important for the wraiths to let live. She searched for help—for some kind of miracle—and saw a defensive line of enchantresses nearly to the base of her tower. They pulsed and retreated, allowing another rotation of enchantresses to march forward and pulse. Then they repeated the same maneuver. Behind them, three hundred Black Druids decimated the mulgars that the enchantresses had felled.

And Denan led them.

"Look!" She pointed.

Tam ground his teeth. "He won't reach us fast enough."

Above the sounds of battle, a great moaning sounded. A sound Larkin had heard before. A sound that came from everywhere at once.

"What was that?" Aaryn asked.

It was coming from beneath them. From the lake.

Something dark shot up from the water. In the faint light, it looked like a thousand snakes, some the size of a boat. They writhed and slammed and crushed mulgars. The ropes snapped, mulgars falling. Then the thing turned, and Larkin had her first glimpse of the monster that had nearly killed her months ago.

The lethan.

An enormous squidlike creature in deepest, wine red. It tore through the raft in a rage, breaking it like tinder. The ropes snapped. The mulgars fell into the dark water and were crushed. The lethan rolled, dragging a hundred more into the depths.

Now they just had to fight those mulgars in the tower.

"Larkin—" Tam began to protest.

In answer, she cut the rope from around her and glared defiantly up at him. "Denan is coming for me." And if he didn't...

Not unless they take you, Atara had said. She would die fighting with her friends rather than abandon them.

"So be it." He turned a deadly gaze upon the mulgars who'd nearly overwhelmed what remained of the guards, pages, and archers and charged forward. Aaryn, Atara, and Larkin followed a step behind.

Larkin beheaded a child mulgar. She dodged a swing from a naked, dripping mulgar, swept aside the thing's arms with her shield, and cut deep into its side. The mulgar canted to one side, swinging at her crookedly. Larkin drew back and stabbed through its neck.

She turned as another swung a cudgel at her legs. She tripped over a body and managed to slam the edge of her shield into its head, the hit reverberating through her arm.

"Bring her to me," every mulgar in the place said at once.

Larkin beheaded the one before her, silencing it mid-sentence. She'd nearly reached the trapdoor. Unable to avoid the piles of bodies, she stepped on them and flared, knocking half a dozen creatures down the stairs. Tam and Atara rolled bodies off the trapdoor, slammed it shut, and slid the bolt home.

If she flared again, she wouldn't have enough magic for her sword and shield. At least not until her sigils had time to recuperate.

"Larkin!" Atara warned.

A crack sounded as the mulgars hacked at the trapdoor. It wouldn't hold them long. But it would hold long enough for Denan to reach them.

The remaining handful of guards, pages, and archers cornered a group of the creatures. Atara and Aaryn flared and sent them careening into the air above the walkway. Enchantresses scattered as the mulgars slammed into the canopy. On the other side of the tower, Tam and a page fought the last three mulgars side by side.

The floor slippery with blood and uneven with bodies, Larkin made her way over to help Tam and the pages, but they finished the creatures before she arrived. One boy was bleeding badly. The other seemed all right. Larkin tore the sleeve from her tunic and tied it around the boy's bleeding leg.

Ancestors, if the boys hadn't fought, the tower would have surely fallen. But the cost was too high.

She made eye contact with both boys. "All right?"

They nodded. She finished her knot over the boy's leg and wiped her bloody hands on her tunic. "Stay off it or the bleeding will start again." It was a foolish thing to say. When that trapdoor broke, the boy would have to fight. And with that injury slowing him down, he would likely die. But what else could she say?

Two pages, three guards—Maylah was not among them—a single archer, Tam, Atara, Aaryn, and Larkin were all that were left standing. Another handful of Alamantians were too injured to do much.

"Tend to your wounds," Tam told them. "The rest of you, pile the bodies onto the trapdoor." He and one of the pages took hold of a mulgar's arms and legs and tossed him onto the door. Some of the others moved more bodies. Others tended to wounds.

Unable to watch, Larkin found herself standing over Farwin. Trying hard to keep her mind blank, she turned him over and straightened his limbs. She folded his hands over each other and closed his eyes. If not for the stillness, he might only be sleeping.

He still had acne on his cheeks and was in desperate need of a haircut. He'd probably never kissed a girl or even left the Alamant. And now he never would.

"Light, Farwin." How could she ever tell his mother and father?

A crack sounded, and some of the bodies sank toward the stairway.

Maybe I won't live to tell Farwin's parents anything. She was beyond feeling horror or even sorrow by the idea. Just grim acceptance.

"Larkin!" Aaryn barked as she flared her shield and stood guard over the entrance.

Larkin and Atara took their places beside her.

"I don't have another pulse in me," Atara said.

"Nor I," Aaryn said.

Larkin hauled out her amulet and gripped it between her shield and her hand. The branch slipped into her skin. "I don't know how many this will create."

The three of them formed a shield wall. The remaining enchanters took their place behind them, the longest weapons they could find in hand.

"We just have to hold out until Denan and the druids reach us," Aaryn said. "Brace us."

The men set their feet and planted their hips and thighs in the enchantresses' backsides.

"He'll come soon." Larkin felt strangely calm about that.

With another crack, the trapdoor split in two. Mulgar bodies fell into the gap and were immediately wrenched out of the way. The first mulgar emerged and threw himself at Larkin's shield; she could feel the grime on his skin through the magic.

With Tam bracing her, Larkin easily held back the mulgar. Together, they held the next five. But when an ardent began coordinating their heaves, Larkin felt her feet sliding back.

"Pulse," Aaryn said.

Larkin flared, sending the masses of mulgars careening into each other, the bodies beneath breaking their fall. A dozen scrambled up the stairs in a coordinated effort and hit Larkin's shield, driving it upward, and knocking her amulet free. A hand clamped down on her ankle and jerked. She fell hard on her

backside and sucked in a breath, her shield held uselessly overhead.

Having gained a foothold, mulgars poured into the gap,
grabbed her arms and legs, and hauled her toward the crenellations.

CHAPTER

34

THE THREAD

Larkin kicked and screamed, but the crush of mulgars overpowered her. Tam and Atara fought madly to reach her, but a wall of mulgars blocked the way. Atara managed to break through and came close enough to kill two of the mulgars holding Larkin, but more surged in to take their place and forced Atara back.

Larkin dangled over the twenty-story drop. Below, mulgars waited with a sleek-looking boat—where had that come from? The ones holding her slipped ropes over her ankles and arms, tightened them, and braced to throw her over. She couldn't let the wraiths have her. She'd drown herself first.

She bucked, managing to kick one leg free. She shoved her foot through the woven crenellations, hooking it around one of the vines. The mulgars tossed her over backward. She swung, foot wrenching hard, and banged into the crenellations. Pain shot up and down her leg.

Her amulet dangled to the side of her head. She gripped it, the sharp branch piercing her palm. She drew its magic for another pulse, sending the mulgars above her careening. The crenellations protected the ones scrabbling at her foot. She shifted her aim to pulse again when a mulgar dislodged her foot.

She fell. The rope caught, stopping her with a jerk, before sliding out fast between mulgar hands. Those in the boat strained toward her, hundreds of reaching, stretching arms. She flared her sword and swiped at them. They reached for her with stumps. She couldn't overpower them all. When they caught her, they would drag her kicking and screaming toward shore. And then... black, sucking shadows and the smell of death.

I can't let them take me. She managed to pull herself up and grab the rope, climbing hard and fast. Three mulgars suddenly blasted over the edge and fell, one of them banging into her. The rope jerked. She barely held on. Blinking through the stars in her vision, she looked up, expecting to see mulgars throwing themselves at her to knock her off.

Instead, she searched her husband's frantic face. She let out a sob of relief.

"Larkin!" Denan cried. He was covered in blood and gore, same as she.

Someone out of sight yanked her up fast. As soon as she was in reach, Denan grabbed her wrist, hauled her into his arms, and crushed her to him.

She held on just as tightly as her head swam and her heart pounded. "You came. I knew you would come."

"Always," he murmured against her. "I thought I was going to have to dive in after you."

The fall would have likely killed him. "That would have been a colossally idiotic move."

"I would have done it anyway."

For a moment, all else fell away, and it was just Denan. The solid strength of his body and the gentleness of his soul. And then reality crashed down. Farwin was dead. She'd come within a hair's breadth of being captured. Her left ankle swelled tight in her boot. She let out a single sob.

"Lock it away," he whispered. "To be dealt with later."

He was right. She couldn't fall apart. Not yet. But when it came... She imagined her iced-over lake. Imagined her shoving the fear and the pain and the dread deep inside an iced-over chest. And then she threw that chest into the blackness, forced it to ice over again.

From the deep, a rumble sounded, the ice shuddering. But it held.

"Better?" he asked.

She nodded and made herself pull back. Take in her surroundings. Denan reluctantly released her. The tower was flooded with druids, who beat back the mulgars with vicious precision. As she watched, the last mulgar died.

One of the men turned to her.

It was West, wearing druid black, one side of his trailing mustache red with blood. She blinked at him, not understanding. He took a step toward her before coming to an abrupt halt. His expression clouded over, shuddered.

He turned and ordered the druids, "Throw the bodies over."

The druids moved to obey, taking hold of the mulgars by ankles and wrists and tossing them over the side.

"How?" she murmured to Denan with a significant look at her former guard.

"I figured we might need the druids' help," Denan answered. "Found West there, already trying to convince them to join in the fighting. I put him in charge, and the druids accepted him."

"He's the new Master Druid?" she asked in disbelief.

Denan nodded.

It was too much to wrap her head around. And there were more important things, like securing the tower.

Aaryn leaned over the crenellation and shouted orders to her enchantresses. Atara glared at the trapdoor as if daring any other mulgars to come through. The archers were all dead, as was another page—the injured one—but two guards were still alive. There was only one person missing.

"Where's Tam?" she asked.

"Here." Eyes closed, he leaned against the crenellations behind her, a wicked knot on the side of his head. "Next time, Larkin stays in the hometree. Agreed?"

"Agreed," Atara said.

Denan made a sound that was half growl, half grunt of agreement.

"Is it over?" Larkin asked.

"Not until the sun rises," Denan said.

The sky was still dark with stars. Mulgars still scaled the ropes. The Alamant had rallied—thanks to the druids—but that charge had weakened them.

"What are we going to do?"

No one answered.

She turned to find Denan crouched beside Farwin's body. His gaze went to the other dead pages, a profound grief etched in his face. He closed his eyes and breathed deep. She knew what he was doing. Deep beneath her own frozen lake, a tremor shook Larkin's foundations. When her grief came, it would shred her in pieces.

Denan wavered under the anguish that passed over him before he caught himself. He stood. "Get her out of here."

Tam pushed to his feet. Atara marched over. Larkin didn't bother to argue—she was a liability to all of them. She'd limped half a dozen steps toward the trapdoor when her sigils suddenly opened of their own accord. There was something empty beneath the warm buzzing of magic. Some yawning nothingness that brought tears to her eyes.

She looked up from the lines on her skin to find every single enchantress and enchanter lit up, all of them staring in bewilderment at their sigils.

"What is this?" Atara asked.

A sudden, sharp pain lanced Larkin's back. With a cry, she dropped to her knees. Her monarch sigil was on fire, burning into her skin. Magic rushed into it, so much magic she thought it might kill her.

She was conscious of Atara kneeling beside her, taking her hand. "Larkin, what is it?"

Larkin couldn't answer. Not just because of the pain. Because with a sudden snap, her monarch sigil split. Panting, she turned wide eyes to Denan, who lay flat on his back, his jaw locked and the sinews of his neck standing. Yet none of the other enchanters or enchantresses seemed racked with pain.

The burning in Larkin's back eased a little at a time. Enough that she dragged herself over to Denan and grabbed his hand.

"The White Tree?" He directed the question at Tam, a desperate undercurrent in his voice.

Tam understood what Denan was asking before the rest of them. He grabbed a telescope, crossed to the opposite side of the tower, and lifted it.

A breathless, heavy moment passed, and then he lowered it. "The White Tree... it's gone dark."

"That's not possible." Aaryn snapped the telescope from him and peered into the Alamant. The telescope dropped from her limp fingers. "Sela said we had a year! It's only been a week!"

The druids exchanged blank looks, clearly not understanding.

Larkin was tempted to fight the truth with the rest of them. But she could feel it in her monarch sigil. It was still alive, but...

cut off, no longer an unending flood of magic but a winding stream.

Still. She had to see for herself. She left Denan, picked up the telescope, and scanned. She found nothing. No moon-bright White Tree peeking between the branches of the hometrees. Because it no longer gleamed.

The White Tree was dead.

"The wraiths knew it would happen tonight," she said in despair. "How could they know?"

"The mulgars are breaking through!" Atara cried.

Larkin hurried to her friend's side. Mulgars by the thousands used handheld hooks to chop through the wall as if the barrier didn't exist. In minutes, they would overrun the city's defenses.

"But we still have our magic," Atara said. "How can the barrier fail?"

"Sela said this would happen." Said the barrier would fail when the White Tree died. It had sent so many visions, but Larkin had been so tired she hadn't paid attention. She wasn't sure she could fix this.

"Lower the boats!" Gendrin cried from the other tower. "We have to stop them as they break through!" If they didn't, the mulgars would slip into the lake and be impossible to find until they reared up. It would be a massacre.

Larkin flared her magic. The geometric pattern of the barrier came into focus, strands of light woven into mostly triangles, but larger circles and some squares added for strength. But unlike before, there were obvious gaps. The weave itself wavered, the edges dissipating like smoke on the wind.

"You have to fix it," Aaryn said to the men.

Tam shook his head. "We don't know how. Not anymore."

"You can do it." His teeth still locked around the pain, Denan forced himself to his haunches and met Larkin's gaze. "I know you can."

I thought I had more time, she thought.

With Tam's help, Denan managed to reach his feet. He gave her a solemn nod. Knowing she would need all the magic she possessed and more, Larkin hauled the amulet out from her dress and squeezed, the point slipping into her skin. "Flare your shields."

Eyes never leaving her husband's, Larkin hummed the melody. He pulled out his panpipes and motioned for Tam and the other two men to play with him. With her sigils lit, she could see a fine mist of color about them.

Tam leaned over the parapet and motioned to the pipers along the wall and in the other tower. Was it enough? She wasn't sure, but it was the best they could do. She took hold of the edge of the barrier and tossed it toward the night sky. It expanded, the missing threads glaringly obvious now. Aaryn gasped.

"I didn't even know that was possible," Atara said.

Larkin gathered the men's and women's magic and compressed it into a fine ribbon. She studied the barrier, filling in the missing threads in the existing pattern of geometric shapes within shapes. A maze of different strands of light. If she missed just one, the entire thing would fail. The unraveling barrier stilled. The weave stopped fading. She forced her fingers to be sure, her eyes shifting frantically in search of any missing pieces.

Suddenly, the city's warning horn sounded so close Larkin could feel its low tones resonate through her body.

"They're breaking through!" someone cried.

The horn sounded again and again, warning those in the city that the wall had been breached. The only people left in the city were those who were too old, too young, or too maimed to fight. They would huddle in their hometrees behind their panes. The mulgars would chop through the supports. The strongest would face them. They might end some of the mulgars, but eventually they would be overrun.

The piper music cut off as every spare man joined the fight. Larkin reached for another strand of magic. Her hands grasped at nothing.

The enchanters were too busy fighting to play. Beneath her feet, a fine vibration spoke of axes biting into the wood. Sweat streamed down the sides of her face and soaked her tunic. She longed to wipe the moisture away and drink to quench her thirst.

Was it over before they'd even begun?

But then she heard more music coming from behind. The enchanters in the city must have heard the music and guessed the need. She reached out and pulled the music toward her, it came in streams that broadened to rivers.

And she wove. Even as the sounds of battle grew louder, more frantic, she filled in the remaining pieces. Would any of them bear any magic after this or would it all be trapped in the wall? She wasn't sure. But at least they'd be alive.

A shattering sound. She startled and looked back as mulgars charged into the tower. Denan and the druids met them. As did Aaryn, Atara, Tam, and the rest.

Denan's movements were slow; he had yet to recover from his long illness. A mulgar slipped through his guard, his blade slicing across Denan's thigh. Denan growled in frustration and anger. He grabbed the mulgar by the wrist, hauled it forward, and headbutted it. The creature reeled back. Denan lunged forward, his sword cleaving head from shoulders.

Then Denan staggered back, his teeth locked, his head tipped back as if he were holding in a scream. Larkin saw it then. The tined lines on his neck. The same as Garrot.

And she understood.

When the tree died, more than the barrier failed. So had her monarch signal and, as a result, his weir. Denan had known and chosen not to say anything so she could repair the wall. Known he was going to turn.

No. No. No. No.

She ran toward him, her fingers already beginning the weir.

Denan pointed behind her. "Larkin!"

She turned back in time to see everything she'd been working on unraveling. She grabbed the end of the thread, holding it tight, and looked back at the man she loved. For a moment, their eyes locked.

She would have to choose between saving the barrier or saving Denan. Saving their kingdom or her husband.

"We put our people first," Denan said.

She shook her head. She couldn't do it. Couldn't lose him.

Anger flashed across his features. "Save my parents and my brother and my people. Save your sisters and mother. The babies."

Everyone she loved. Or the one she could least afford to live without.

"Denan," she cried in utter anguish.

"We do what we must, Larkin. Always." Without looking back, he dove into the fray. Into the men and women dying to keep her safe long enough for her to repair the barrier. Repair it before all was lost.

Heart breaking, she turned back to her work, weaving and spinning. Hooking and bending, until the wall weave looked just like it had in her dreams.

It was finished.

She shifted it back into place over the wall. The barrier pulsed, cutting the mulgars inside the wall in half and sending thousands of others free-falling. In her hand, the amulet broke into dust that stained her hands with ashes. She spared a glance to make sure the enchantment held.

It did.

She turned. All but a handful of the mulgars that had invaded the tower were dead. The druids lay among them. Denan wasn't one of those standing. She found his mother first. Aaryn knelt beside her son, his hand in hers, Tam on the other side.

Pale, cold terror sliced through Larkin. *There's still time. There must be.* She ran to him, slipped in red and black blood, and fell hard to one knee. She scrambled up and shoved Tam aside.

She drew magic from the women, her bloody fingers forming the pattern. Denan grabbed one of her hands. The weave fell to tatters. She tried to jerk free, but his grip was like iron. She opened her mouth to yell at him. But then she saw his face. Saw the corruption clawing up his cheeks.

"It's too late," he said, his voice choked with pain.

Every part of her threatened to break. Holding herself together with every shred of hope she possessed, she tried to wrench free. "It hasn't reached your eyes. We can still—"

"I can't live like this!" he said in fits and starts, his body spasming.

She froze, her breath half in and half out. She shook her head, over and over and over again.

He reached up, running the back of his knuckles down her cheek. "I swore I'd keep you safe. Did you doubt me?"

She pressed his hand to her heart. "Never."

He smiled. "You are a warrior queen. The queen our people need."

No. The White Tree was dead. She'd seen the sheer number of mulgars. Thousands and thousands and thousands. The barrier might hold, but eventually, the mulgars would make it over the wall. And when they did, the Alamant was finished. Humankind was finished. She hadn't saved anyone. She'd only delayed the inevitable.

She didn't say any of this. Denan was dying. She would not let him die thinking it had been for nothing.

His gaze shifted to his mother. "I don't want you to see this. Take the others and go."

Tears streaming down her face, Aaryn held his hand tight. "I was there when you came into this world. I will not leave when you depart it."

He seemed about to argue and then pressed his lips into a thin line. He turned to the others. "Everyone else but Tam, out."

The druids left first. Atara hesitated, shooting Larkin a look so full of sorrow that Larkin's hard-won composure threatened to break. Then she, too, left.

Denan took his mother's hand. "I'm sorry for the hurt you will suffer."

Tears slipped down her cheeks. "I'm proud of you, my son. So proud to be your mother."

Denan panted in pain. The marks ringed his eye sockets. The tremors shook his hand now. But he fought them. Fought the betrayal of his body.

He reached out, his hand cupping Larkin's neck. "My heart-song, my little bird. When it's your time, I will come for you. As I always have."

"Always." She bent down and pressed a soft kiss to his lips.

His pleading gaze shifted to Tam. "We made a promise, long ago."

Tam's expression shattered. Pale as death, he took out his sword. He meant to kill Denan. To end his life before the corruption turned him into a monster. Just like Maisy had said would happen. *Ancestors, I cannot watch the light leave his eyes.*

And suddenly, Larkin's conversation with Maisy came back to her just as jumbled as all her conversations with Maisy had ever been.

"I've always been your friend, Larkin. Always. And when the time comes, you'll remember that."

"What have you done to my husband?" Larkin had cried.

"You're not listening! I'm trying to save you, save him, save everyone!"

"By turning him into a mulgar? How does that save him?" Larkin had asked.

"Because then you will finally be willing to do what you must."

But what must I do, Maisy? Larkin thought.

"Haven't you figured it out yet, Larkin? You are the light."

She didn't know what that meant!

"Trust me, Larkin. Just one last time."

As if in response to the memory, Larkin's sigils gleamed. She looked at them in shock; she hadn't opened them.

Where light is, shadow cannot go, Sela had said. *Remember.*

Larkin found her gaze drawn to the south. In the direction of Valynthia. A city of shadows.

And Larkin suddenly understood what they had been trying to tell her all along. How to destroy the wraiths. And in return for that knowledge, Larkin had killed Maisy.

Larkin panted—the horror of what she had done and what she had yet to do driving the breath from her body. But there would be time for guilt later. And grief. And loss.

"I'm the light," she murmured. She held out her free hand between Tam and her husband. "No."

Tam shot her a pleading look. "I have to."

"Larkin." Denan fought for each word as the black siphoned into his eyes like wisps of smoke. "Let me die cleanly. As myself."

Denan's eyes rolled up. His body convulsed. Tam gripped her shoulder.

She surged up, Tam's tunic in her fists. This man who'd become as dear to her as a brother. This man she had to make understand. "The mulgars will keep coming, Tam. By the thousands. And one day very soon, maybe even tomorrow, they will make it over the wall."

He shook his head. "What does that—"

She gritted her teeth. "There's only one way this ends. I have to kill the wraiths." The monsters who dared to steal her husband from her. Well, she would steal him back. And she'd kill them for it.

"They cannot die," Aaryn said.

Larkin faced the woman. "Maisy said the wraiths are weak during the day. If I go with them, I can find a way to kill them."

"Go with them," Aaryn said, aghast.

"It's what they've wanted all along, isn't it?" Larkin said. "Me for all the mulgars. And in return, the Alamant will be safe. Denan will be safe." At least for a time.

"Not if they turn you into a mulgar," Aaryn said.

"They can't," Larkin said. "They tried already, and it didn't work, remember? Maybe... Maybe I can even end the curse." Eiryss had said someone in her line would break the curse. Sela had broken half of it. Maybe Larkin was meant to break the other half, and to do it, she had to go to Valynthia and kill the wraiths.

"Larkin—" Tam began.

"They'll be back tomorrow night," she cried. "And the night after that. And the night after that. How long do you think we'll last?"

Neither Aaryn nor Tam answered. Because they both knew that within a few days, a week at most, it would all be over.

"We don't have anything else," Larkin whispered.

"He'll never forgive you," Tam said softly.

No. He won't. But he'll be alive, and that's all that matters.

Aaryn gasped and reared back from Denan. Larkin was already moving. She pinned her blade against Denan's throat. But he was not Denan anymore. His eyes were fully black, his skin pale as death. He was a mulgar now.

Even as she watched, that black imploded into his pupil, the forked lines disappearing from his skin as if they'd never been. Save for his eyes, he looked perfectly human again. Longing drove a spike through her chest.

"I will give him back." The words were from Denan's lips, but her husband hadn't said them. Instead, the wraith watched her through her beloved's eyes.

"I will meet with you." She gritted her teeth. "But I need everyone to think my husband is still Denan. Do you understand?"

Not-Denan nodded. She eased back, her body tense for the ardent to attack. He did not. The ardent lay docilely on the ground, watching her with a predatory hunger that made a chill crawl up her spine.

She couldn't afford to think of the thing before her as her husband, as the man she loved.

"Light," Tam said. "He's obeying you."

For now. Larkin didn't dare wipe the tears from her cheeks. "Tie his hands."

Denan lifted his wrists. Tam looked about, but it was Aaryn who found the rope Larkin had cut from around her waist earlier. Wincing at the blood, his mother cried as she tied Denan's wrists.

The rings and grunts and shouts of battle suddenly stilled. Larkin peered over the edge of the crenellations to see the mulgars jumping from the wall, slipping back into the water. The Alamantians looked about in bewilderment.

The hairs on the back of Larkin's neck rose. She was going to the wraiths. Terror seized her middle, and she wasn't sure whether she was going to vomit or cry. Not wanting any of them to see, she turned her back to them and tried to calm her frantic breathing. To focus on the world around her.

The horizon had lightened to gray, the pitch dark of the dead of night giving way to a hazy charcoal. In a few hours, the sun would rise. Below, the water was littered with bodies, thousands of them. But thousands more climbed out of the water to disappear into the forest beyond. And in the center, she could make out a darker patch of shadows.

The wraiths were waiting.

CHAPTER

BECOMING WRAITH

Shielded from view by the tower to her left, Larkin watched as the boat swung over the crenellation and lowered so that it was even with the wall. Not-Denan stepped over the parapet and into the little boat. Larkin and Tam followed him. Tam did his best to shield them from view as Larkin bound Denan's ankles to his hands, just in case. He bore it without the slightest protest. Larkin started to turn away but became ensnared in the shine reflecting off Denan's soulless eyes—eyes that followed her every move.

"Larkin," Aaryn said.

Larkin saw the question in her mother-in-law's eyes. Was Larkin sure she wanted to do this? She gave a curt nod and pulled her dampener amulet over her head. "Give it to Nesha." She grieved the loss, but she didn't want this getting into the wraiths' hands.

Aaryn tucked it in her pocket. "Lower it."

The enchantresses manning the pulleys hesitated. Lowering anyone into the lake—especially their king and queen—was surely sending them on a suicide mission.

"Do it!" Aaryn barked.

The enchantresses lowered the boat. Larkin flared her shield, took hold of her magic, and molded it into a modified dome that encircled them. The craft rocked gently as it lowered down the side of the wall and settled in the lake.

Larkin and Tam unhooked the ropes. The lampent flower in its woven cage bobbed up and down, casting soft light over the rippling water. But there were no colorful fish leaping at the bugs attracted to the light. Instead, it illuminated bits and pieces of the dead as they churned together—an arm, a leg, a sightless head...

Shuddering, she sat on her bench. Her paddle found purchase between the bodies and turned them toward shore. Bodies bumped into the bow and slid along the hull. They were dead. They couldn't hurt her.

So why did they disturb her so? Because they were empty? Or because someday, her body would turn cold and sightless and then molder? Generations would pass, until one day no one alive would ever have known her. She would be utterly forgotten.

And then what? Memories lived on in the sacred trees—provided you were entombed in one—but even sacred trees died. Not that it was an honor she would have. Not now. Which left what?

She didn't know, and the not knowing terrified her. *I don't want to die.* Would she ever see her family again? See Denan again? She glanced back at him, sitting unnaturally still just behind her.

Light. It hurt to have him seem so alive—so *him*—when he wasn't.

Shouting from the soldiers lining the wall. Larkin looked up, up, up to see Gendrin and Atara leaning over the wall to look down at them. Atara had gone to fetch the general as soon as she realized what they planned to do.

Gendrin cupped his hands around his mouth. "Come back now! I order you to come back!"

Larkin technically outranked him. That wouldn't stop him from killing Denan. Involving the council.

It was better—cleaner—this way.

Ignoring him, Aaryn lifted her hand in farewell. The stillness of the woman's expression—grief on hold—burned into Larkin's memory like a brand. Larkin knew the question in her eyes: would her son still be lost to her after this? Or would she lose all three of them?

Larkin felt a stab of resentment. Had Aaryn been so willing to let Larkin go because it meant her son would return to her? Larkin turned away from the useless emotion.

A cloud passed over the moon. She was grateful she could no longer see the horrors all around her. Her head ached from lack of sleep. She was bruised and battered, her muscles stiff and achy. The cold from the frozen lake inside her seeped into her body, making her shiver despite the heat. She drove her paddle in harder, her teeth clenched to hold herself together.

It wasn't long before they reached the shoreline stacked with bodies like driftwood. The sky was black overhead, and a dusky turquoise along the rim. Dawn was coming. She wondered if she'd ever see a sunrise again.

Tam stopped paddling first. "We can still go back."

"I couldn't be the kind of queen my people needed, couldn't be the queen my king needed. I made so many mistakes. But I can do this. I can save him."

For the first time in months, she was right where she was supposed to be.

Frowning, Tam threw anchor. They fell back to uneasy silence. They drifted as she searched the shoreline, but it was impossible to distinguish shadow from shadow.

"I know you're there." She was surprised at how calm she sounded. She certainly didn't feel calm. "Show yourself."

For a time, nothing happened. She became hyperaware of Denan's gaze. She could not live in a world where he was a monster. Nor could she let anyone kill him. But if her plan worked, she was forcing him to live that exact scenario in her place. She could think of no greater cruelty.

"I have a bargain to make," she said.

Silence stretched so long she despaired that it was too late. That the wraiths no longer needed her bargain. Then she felt a sudden wrongness—the taste of death in her mouth, the dirt of an old grave crumbling beneath her fingertips. Even the lampent's dim light seemed weaker.

Directly before her, the darkness became a living thing—a thing that sucked away all light and joy, leaving hatred and corruption. She couldn't make out the telling features of the individual wraiths, but she knew it was Ramass. It was always Ramass.

Tam drew his sword.

Larkin leaned forward, one hand braced on the gunwale, the other gripping her sword. "Break the curse, restore the mulgars, and I will come with you."

A horrible sound, like the grinding of broken glass. It couldn't be... Had the wraith actually laughed? "That was not our bargain."

She lifted her chin. "It is now."

More wraiths materialized from the shadows, their conversation the sound of a dark spell being cast.

"My king," Vicil said. "She can't hold the dome forever. Let us take her through the shadows."

"We already tried that," Hagath's more feminine voice responded.

"She has to come willingly," Rature agreed.

Larkin hadn't known the wraiths were at odds about this. Their discord gave her hope that she really might pull this off.

Vicil stepped toward the shore. "If we can't force her through the shadows, let our mulgars transport her over land. Kill the man."

"Not if I kill you first," Tam growled.

"I can hold this dome until dawn." She was almost certain that she could.

"You think we cannot take you another way?" Vicil asked. "Eventually, our mulgars will sweep over the wall and—"

"I'll kill myself before you ever touch me!" she cried. Even the torn shadows of the wraiths' cloaks went still, and she knew she'd found her leverage. Because this time, they believed her. "Break the curse. It's the only way you'll ever have me."

"My king—" Hagath began.

"Enough!" Ramass shouted at the other wraiths. Thoroughly cowed, they stepped back. Ramass faced her. "Yourself for the mulgars. That is my only bargain. Reject it and my army will overpower your city within the week and mankind will no longer exist."

She could see it. Mulgars swarming the wall and out of the water. Men, women, children, dying. Like Valynthia, the Alamant would become a city of the dead. Dread seeped like poison from the top of her head all the way to her feet. But still, she couldn't move. And then she realized why.

I don't want to die.

The wraiths would use her for some evil purpose. And she could not allow herself to be used. Which meant she would take her own life, one way or another.

I don't want to die.

"You don't have to do this," Tam whispered. He glared at the wraiths. "How did you know the White Tree would die today?"

"Because Maisy poisoned her with my blood, and through her, your sister," Ramass said. "The same day she killed your king."

It had been poison, after all. Larkin's heart dropped, and she thought she might vomit. "The forest take you." Had her sister survived the tree's death or had they lost her as well?

Larkin sensed rather than saw movement. Faint light appeared from within the folds of Ramass's robes, revealing a crushed lampent, one that emitted a poisonous green light between mailed fingers—light that gleamed off the points of Ramass's crown. Three figures stepped up beside him, their faces cast in shadow.

"Will you not save them, Larkin?" Ramass moved to rest the lampent beneath one of their faces.

Venna. Tined black lines etched eyes that were all back. The girl had been soft in all the right ways. Unsure. Lonely. Now she was a monster. Something inside Larkin broke all over again. Something she'd thought had been healed. Ramass moved, the light leaving Venna's face.

Now Ramass lit up Talox's chin.

"Talox." The word slipped from Tam's lips, a plea and prayer both.

An ardent, Talox's skin was free of the black marks. But he'd added fresh injuries to the old ones. His shoulder hitched unnaturally, likely disjointed in the battle. An injury that would cause even the strongest to weep with pain. And yet he hadn't even bothered to put it back in place. Instead, he stared at her with such indifference that she wanted to weep.

Ramass moved on, returning Talox to the shadows. The third face opened a fresh wound in Larkin's heart. A wound that pulsed hot and hard. She gasped at the sight of her father. At the unnatural markings and black eyes. Whatever sins he'd committed, Harben paid for them tenfold. And at his end, instead of the natural death that came for them all, he'd become something far worse.

The clouds passed beyond the moon; the light illuminated thousands and thousands of faces. Marred skin and black eyes filled with a predatory watchfulness. Larkin's body screamed at her to retreat from the enormity of the corruption—the wrongness—before her. A wrongness made so much worse by the expectation in their eyes. She would take their hatred—Ancestors, give her their hatred—rather than their expectation.

And her own husband. The king their people needed. She thought of her family—Mama, her sisters, her nephew, her half brother. Atara, Tam, Magalia, Alorica. And she knew her decision was made.

Larkin's heart hammered in her chest, sweat running down her cheeks as her body fought to live. She licked her dry lips, her voice coming out warbling. "What proof do I have that you'll keep your word?"

The wraith's dark gaze bore into her. "Cut your hand, lay it against Denan's wound, and you will see."

"Larkin," Tam murmured. "This is a bad idea."

It had always been a bad idea. She formed a thin knife and sliced her palm, hissing at the sting. Ignoring Denan's unnerving gaze, she peeled back the sticky bandage on his side to reveal the stinking wound beneath. She gagged and steadied herself, waiting for the nausea to pass.

Steeling herself, she rested her open hand against Denan's wound. Between the folds of her parted skin, a darkness niggled like a maggot nudging for rot. Her magic rebelled, shoving the rot away. And she understood. The wraiths didn't want her to simply go with them. They wanted to infect her like all the other mulgars.

"You have to let it inside you," Ramass crooned. "Let it take hold."

"Larkin…" Tam warned.

Ancestors, dying is one thing, but this…

"I can do this," she snapped at Tam.

Maybe… Maybe there's a way around it.

She wove a weir at her forearm—Magalia could remove her hand if needed—and pulled in the dark shadows, so cold they burned as they spread through her hand. Those same shadows receded from Denan, enough that she could see hints of the whites of his eyes again. Like a parasite, tiny claws gained purchase, scrabbling and tearing their way toward her wrist.

It was agony.

Until it was done. All of Denan's blight throbbed in her hand and wrist in the familiar tined lines of the curse. Light, he'd endured this pain for months without complaint. Suddenly dizzy, she clutched her hand to her chest and tried to swallow back the bile climbing her throat.

Tam shot her a questioning look and knelt on the other side of her husband. "Denan?"

Denan took a deep breath, as if coming awake. "Water?"

Tam handed him a waterskin.

Denan drank deep, and then his eyes met hers. "Larkin."

A rush of joy flared in Larkin's chest. Denan was back. She leaned forward and kissed his forehead, his cheeks. She laughed. She'd done it.

"Larkin—" Before her name was even fully out of his mouth, his head tipped to the side as he lost consciousness.

"Denan?" She held her hand under his nose, relieved to feel the reassuring puff of his breath. Tam pried his eyes open. The black was gone.

"He's passed out," Tam said.

His body had been through too much. "Let him rest." It was enough that he would be all right. She kissed his mouth for the last time. "We do what we must to protect our people, Denan. You taught me that."

Steadying herself, Larkin faced the horde.

"You see?" Ramass crooned. "I keep my promises."

Ancestors, she hated him.

It was light enough now that she could make out individual faces. And through the shadows infecting her hand, she was now connected to all the shadows—the thousands of souls trapped by the curse. She could cleanse every mulgar. But to do it, she'd have to take their blight into herself.

What would become of her then?

She met Tam's gaze and whispered, "There is a chance I can trap the blight with a weir, but if not... will you do for me as you swore to do for Denan?"

He reeled back. She knew what she was asking him—to kill her before she turned. But he was the only one.

His gaze shuttered, and he turned away. "Please, Larkin."

"Will you?"

He choked, unable to look at her, and nodded.

She crossed to the bow of the boat as the four wraiths watched her, their cloaks streaming in the gentle breeze.

Through the shadows that connected her to the horde, Larkin felt her father's despair at knowing his parents would rather have him dead than a failure. His impotence at farming and the hungry eyes of his children. The knowledge that he would never, ever be enough. His unending shame at Joy's death and Caelia's disappearance.

All his fault.

This was how the corruption worked. It fed off hurt and anger, trapping them in a vortex of shame. That shame left room for the darkness to take hold. Take over. But she could take all the shadows away. She stretched out her hand to her father, calling to the shadows just as she had the enchantment. Those shadows came to her in a stream of darkness.

In the moonlight, she watched as the black shifted from her father's eyes, draining through the tined lines and flowing into dark ribbons of magic. She opened herself to the corruption. Felt it pierce her, cold and calculating. What had been a scrabbling parasite turned into a multilegged millipede. Her fingers turned black as death.

She bit back a whimper.

Her father staggered. "Larkin? What— Where am I?" His eyes rolled back, and he fell as if he were a puppet and his strings had been cut. She watched his chest rise and fall. Passed out. Same as Denan. He would be all right.

"Soon, you will welcome the pain," Ramass said. "For it will make you strong."

Soon, she was going to kill him.

Her gaze shifted to Talox. The darkness churned inside her, throbbing like the beat of a black heart. How long before it took over and there was nothing left of herself?

But then, Talox had willingly made the same sacrifice for her. Reluctantly, she opened herself to his shadows. Talox had witnessed his uncle touching his older brother in twisted, disgusting ways. The uncle had caught Talox and threatened to kill him and his brother if he ever told. He had been too terrified to tell his parents. To tell anyone. And so he stood by, knowing it was happening and doing nothing to stop it. Nothing to protect the older brother he adored.

That brother had killed himself five years later.

The last of the shadows left Talox. He dropped to the ground. Like her father, his chest rose and fell.

"Not the hero you've always believed him to be, is he?" Ramass asked.

Hero? Yes. Perfect? No.

The churning shadows roiled inside her, pushing against the weir, fighting to break free. Most of her hand was black now. Sweat broke out on her brow. She panted against the pain. Every part of Larkin rebelled against taking more shadows—it was poisoning her soul as surely as nightshade would poison her body.

Eventually, it would kill her.

"Larkin?" Tam asked.

"Two hands seem redundant, don't you think?" she tried to joke.

He didn't laugh. Didn't even crack smile. Which wasn't fair—he was the one who taught her to make light of the impossible in order to bear it. She turned and drew from Venna before she could change her mind.

Overwhelming loneliness assaulted her. So wide and so deep it had carved a canyon through Venna. The girl's mother worked from sunup to sundown for Lord Daydon; there wasn't time left over for her daughter. Her grandfather was a quiet man. He never really spoke to her. To anyone, really. She longed for them to say they loved her. To hold her tight.

And then her mother had died, and Venna had taken her place in the manor house. She had watched Larkin and Nesha with a jealous eye. Wished she had a sister to defend her from the village bullies as voraciously as they did each other. Wished desperately for a friend.

Larkin collapsed, her vision white with pain and her ears ringing.

"Larkin!" Tam gripped her shoulders.

The weir had shattered. The blight climbed up to her elbow, the ache sharp as a blade carving all the way to the bone. With one trembling hand, she wove another weir across her upper arm.

Tam shook his head. "Larkin, that was only three mulgars. You can't take on the horde."

Not and survive. She met his gaze. "I'll carry that burden, if you'll carry yours."

His whole body sagged under the weight of her charge. But despite it, he nodded. She leaned forward and kissed his cheek. "Tell them I love them. And I'm sorry. Tell him." She threw a glance to her sleeping husband and then quickly away again. It hurt to know that after this moment he would hate her for trading her life for his.

Not waiting for Tam's answer, she stood and threw out her hand, drawing all the shadows to her at once. Like a living, breathing thing, those shadows dove into her hand, shattering her weir as if it had never been. They clawed up her arm, her shoulder. Stabbed into her heart. She tipped back her head to scream, and they tore down her throat. She gagged. Could not breathe. She dropped to her knees and grabbed her neck, choking on the river of darkness that ripped and tore and shredded, razing her from the inside out.

Choking out the light.

Ancestors, she hadn't even known how full of light she was until the last of it was snuffed out. And then she couldn't remember why she'd cared. Shadows spilled out of her pores, twisting and shifting like a dark cloak. Ramass had been right. The shadows still tore and rent, but she welcomed the pain. Because the dark made her powerful. Immortal. What was a little pain in comparison to that?

She straightened up to find Tam swinging a blade at her, tears streaming down his cheeks. She pulsed, sending him careening through the air. He screamed in despair before landing with a splash.

The boat pulled hard for shore. Rature had tossed a rope, the hook catching on the gunwales as he pulled her in. The mulgar horde had collapsed—she'd taken all their darkness. But it was nothing to give that darkness back. She lifted her sword—now wreathed in black shadows that would reinfect all of the horde—and prepared to leap onto shore.

"Wraith!"

She whipped around as Denan drove Tam's sword into her guts. Her eyes widened with shock, mouth falling open.

"What have you done with my wife?"

The pain would have consumed her, had she not been consumed already. She gripped the sword and dragged it out of herself. "I am your wife."

All the color leached from Denan's haggard face. "No. No. She wouldn't."

Larkin took advantage of his horror, striking his sword from his hands and stepping into his guard. She held her sword to his throat. But before she could reinfect him, Tam surged out of the lake, grabbed her belt, and wrenched her back.

The boat tipped, dumping all three of them into the water. Through the pain searing her middle, she stroked for the surface. Among all the bodies, she struggled, barely managing to keep her head above water. Denan appeared a moment later. He shook the water from his hair as he whirled. His eyes fixed on her, and he kicked forward, his sword drawn back. She bashed aside the blade with her own, and then he was on top of her.

They both went under. A gulp of water seared her throat on the way down. Another flair of pain, the point of his sword bright and sharp in her chest. She tried to escape. Tried to writhe free. Another stab to her chest. Searing, burning light. She broke apart.

CHAPTER

THE CHILD AND THE MONSTER

Knowing her name and nothing else, Larkin found herself completely disoriented, shivering, and wet in the forest. She didn't know who she was or where she was, but she knew she had to move. The night was dangerous—full of tearing and black blood. The fear planted deep in her breast compelled her to slip silently through the woods in search of shelter from whatever hunted her in the dark.

Between the trees, she caught sight of light softly filtered through the windows of a little cottage on the edge of a field. Safety. She picked up the pace, nearly running now. A tortured cry arose. She stopped cold in her tracks. Before she could decide if the house was safe, a sudden movement made her jump.

A crouched figure slid along the hedge and stepped straight through Larkin. She cried out and stumbled back. The woman showed no signs of hearing her. Of having felt herself going through her.

How is this possible?

The middle-aged woman had curly hair, a fine wool coat, and a fat ring on her delicate hand. Though Larkin couldn't make out any color, she could tell her eyes were blue simply by their paleness. Somehow, Larkin knew that she was a fine lady.

Why was she here, watching this house in the dark rain?

Not for any good purpose.

Another guttural cry came from the house, and this time, she recognized it. Mama had been a midwife, so Larkin had often heard a woman laboring to bring a child into the world.

"What is this?" Larkin asked.

The woman showed no signs of hearing Larkin. A baby's indignant cries cut through the night. As if this were the signal she'd been waiting for, the lady unhooked a long reed pipe of sacred wood from her belt. It had a wide horn and finger holes all along the length, glints of gems flashing in the moonlight. She played a song that brought an image to Larkin's mind of a lord with a close-cropped beard, silver running through his dark hair.

The lady shimmered like moonlight over rippling water. Slowly, she began to change, growing larger, her hair disappearing, her clothes shifting. After a few minutes, she had taken on the appearance of the man Larkin had envisioned. Just as elegant. Just as refined. And as she knew that the woman was a lady, she also knew that she'd donned the visage of her husband, the lord.

Larkin gaped in shock.

The lady slipped her flute in her pocket and stepped past the hedge into the tiny cottage. An astonishingly beautiful girl lay on the only bed. In her arms, she held a baby with milk-white skin and a shock of dark hair. Between her legs, a midwife waited for the afterbirth.

"He's not who you think he is," Larkin cried in warning.

But the girl only beamed at the false lord. "You came!" She held up the baby. "Look, our son, just like I said."

The girl's joy vanished as the lord glowered at her. She drew her baby close, a confused look on her face. Larkin tried to flare her blade, but it was as if her magic didn't exist. The lady drew a sword from inside the fold of her cloak. Larkin tried to shove her, but she went through her.

The midwife jumped to her feet, only to receive the flat of the blade to the side of her head. She went down without a sound, a knot already forming, and lay unconscious. The only testament that she lived was the rise and fall of her chest.

The girl scrambled back in her bed, her teeth bared, her eyes knowing. "You're not him."

Even as she said it, the illusion faded away, leaving the lady, her chin tipped at a haughty angle. "Die knowing he'll soon join you."

"Please," the girl begged.

The lady shifted her weight, and Larkin placed herself between the lady and the girl. "Don't!"

The lady lunged, sword sinking into the girl's neck. A hack with the length of the blade, and the baby died instantly. Blood gushing, the mother gasped for breath that wouldn't come. She held her dead child tight, her gaze accusing the lady, who waited calmly until the girl's eyes went wide, unseeing.

Larkin dropped to her knees, her head in her hands, hair pulled tight. "Light, what have you done? Oh, light!"

The lady looked down at the unconscious midwife, gaze assessing. When her chest continued to rise and fall, the lady gave a tight nod of approval and left the cottage. Larkin didn't want to follow her, but it was as if her body was tethered, and she had no choice.

Larkin felt her soul trying to leave her body—a feeling as natural as an exhale. But something... held her. Bound her. Refused to let her go. She came to, crumpled on her side. She gasped for breath, desperate for air. All around her was black, but with each breath, the darkness dissipated, and she steadied. A gray world came into focus.

The midwife had lived just long enough to give a damning testimony. Larkin had been surrounded by a mob screaming for the lord's death, been with them as they found him. Hung him. All the while, the lady watched. Pretending concern. Pretending devastation. What she really felt was superiority. Righteousness. Vengeance.

A predator who'd convinced her prey she was one of them.

But Larkin knew. Light, she knew.

She would find that monster. She would kill her. Slowly.

But first, she had to figure out where she was. Who she was beyond just a name. The color came back to her vision, allowing her to see farther away. This was not the forest around the cottage.

Where was she?

She turned slowly. She was in a bowl-shaped depression surrounded by enormous branches that stretched high overhead. Glittering black branches. Beneath her was white moss. To her right was a font on a dais, the wicked thorns shimmering in the soft morning light. To one side of it was a small building made of rough-cut lumber, weathered gray.

A sacred tree. But not one of light and color and a sense of something infinite and wise. This was all sucking darkness and murder and never-ending hate.

How had she come to be here? She searched her memories... water and blood and pain. She shied away from those memories—she'd had enough of helplessness and suffering.

Beneath the tree's bark, shadowy claws scrabbled at her, as if trying to break free. She shoved away, landing on a patch of damp white moss, her back fetching up against the gritty bark.

She panted, trying to catch her breath, trying to orient herself. Next to her, a flower gleamed a bright, pale green, its petals breathing in and out delicately. Even as she watched, a moth landed on those petals, which instantly snapped shut. It was no flower at all, but the jaws of some strange lizard that blinked at her with discordant eyes, the moth caught in its mouth.

Larkin gave a cry of alarm and darted to her feet.

"Hello, Larkin."

She whipped around. A man warily approached. He had bright copper curls, thick freckles, gray eyes, and a trim build. He wore strange, simple clothes that fit loose around his broad shoulders. He was young, handsome, and familiar in a way that raised her hackles.

Larkin slipped into a defensive stance. "You can see me." No one had seen her in the forest. Not when she screamed at the townspeople that the lord hadn't killed his mistress, even as the poor man wept over the girl's grave. Not as Larkin watched his legs twitch as he dangled from a tree. Not when Larkin whispered the horrible things she would do in that monster's ear.

Her attention snapped back to the man. He'd come closer. Too close. Magic surged, and she flicked her blade into place between them. "How do you know my name? Who are you?" *Who am I?*

The red-haired man paused, studying her with infinite sadness instead of fear. "You know who I am."

She didn't. His accent was strange and rolling in a way she was certain she'd heard before. But for all her thinking, she couldn't place it. "Where is that woman? The lady?"

"Larkin, there isn't much time."

She lunged, her sword tip at his throat. "Where is she?" *I have to kill her.*

He backed slowly away. "Whoever she is, she's long dead. As is anyone who ever knew her."

This man thought to trick her. She advanced on him, sword at the ready. "Where is she?"

"Look at your chest, Larkin."

She felt it then. The pain. The stickiness. He was at a safe distance. She risked glancing down. Her front was saturated with... ink? It couldn't be blood. Blood wasn't black. She checked to make sure he was still a safe distance away, pulled out her collar, and gasped in horror.

The wound was black and deep. Deep enough that she could see ashen organs beneath bone. Even as she watched, the blood slowed. Stopped. Bone and flesh knit together, leaving an angry dark line that faded to white before disappearing as if it had never been.

And then she remembered.

Denan—her beloved, her husband—had stabbed her. "But that was days ago." Long before the monster who called herself a lady. And besides, Denan would never hurt her. Except he had. It was like he hadn't recognized her.

"It was last night," the man said.

"That's not possible."

Shadows. So many shadows. Tearing and cold and empty.

Wraith.

She couldn't breathe.

Denan had killed her because he thought her a wraith.

She hauled up her sleeves, staring at her pale, freckled skin. The sigils were still beautiful, opalescent. She was not a wraith. She looked up to find the man had moved closer. Close enough to touch her.

She danced out of range, keeping her sword between them. "Stay back!"

"Larkin, it's nearly sunset. The shadows are coming. You have to listen to me."

Sunset? But it was morning.

Jangled visions.

Shadows and blood and snot and piss.

She didn't know what was real anymore. Her magic slipped from her grasp, sword flickering out. She rocked back and forth. Hit the heel of her palm against her head. "What's happening to me?"

The man gripped her arms. "You became a wraith last night. Denan killed you. The Black Tree brought you through the shadows, showed you a memory. Something horrible. Forgive the people in those memories. Find the good in them, and you will find yourself. Only then can you fight back."

Forgive? She searched the man's face.

"Ramass," she gasped. Her enemy. "But this can't be. You're a man."

"I am always a man. But at night, the shadows take me."

He was a monster. A monster like the lady. She shoved him hard. "You killed Venna and Talox and my father." So many others. Thousands and thousands. "You did this to me!"

Stumbling, he closed his eyes, his jaw hard. "Not willingly."

He deserved death and worse. She'd forgotten her purpose, but now she remembered. She'd come here to kill the wraiths. To kill him. Maisy had been right. The wraiths were weak during the day. Because they were human. Which meant Larkin could finally kill him.

Her sword and shield flared to life. They were wreathed in shadows. She hadn't noticed before. But she was certain they would still cut. She took an offensive stance.

Ramass sighed. "If you must." Instead of moving to defend himself, he pulled off his long shirt—he wasn't wearing pants—and stood before her completely naked. He was covered in red-gold hair and even more freckles. And black blood, though she saw no wounds.

He tossed his shirt to the side and tapped just to the left of his sternum, where his heart was. "Here." He gripped his wrists behind his back and gritted his teeth, waiting for her.

Traps. Always traps. She circled him. "You want to die?"

"Rather than become a mindless monster each night..." He closed his eyes and breathed out, "Yes."

Lies and traps and poison. Watching for tricks, she adjusted her grip and eased forward.

Shadows and blood and snot and piss.

Monsters must die.

She struck, burying the blade in so deep that a hand's breadth stuck out his back. Ramass hunched over her sword. His face darkened; the veins in his neck stood out. Black blood seeped down his chest. He coughed, blood spraying onto her armor, and dropped to his knees.

She felt a thrill of excitement. A bone-deep satisfaction. The monster she'd originally hungered for wasn't here. Now. But this one was. And she'd killed him.

She let her magic fade and stepped back. Without her blade to stanch it, blood gushed. Ramass collapsed onto his side. But then the bleeding slowed. The gaping wound seamed together. The black line faded to white and then disappeared like it had never been.

Just like it had for her.

CHAPTER 37

MONSTERS

Ramass wiped blood from his lips and grimaced at his black-soaked torso. Watching her warily, he rose to his feet, his hands held out at his sides.

Larkin gaped at him, her chest rising and falling hard and fast. She had given up everything—her husband, her family, her life—to kill this monster. She'd put her sword through his chest, straight into his heart.

Yet he hadn't died.

Her ears rang, her vision going fuzzy around the edges.

"Slow your breathing," Ramass said reasonably.

"Don't tell me what to do! You're a monster. You made me a monster! You tricked me!" She cut into his side.

Grimacing, he danced back and hunched around the bloody slash. "I didn't make you a wraith, Larkin."

Shadows and blood and snot and piss.

"Liar!" She stabbed him again.

He fell to his knees, his face pale. But even as she watched, the slash was healing. "Ancestors, Larkin, do you think I would still be alive if someone could kill me?"

He must be like the mulgars. A sword to the chest wouldn't kill him, but beheading would. She took a running step and drew her sword over her right shoulder. He closed his eyes and turned away. Her sword cut through flesh and bone and sinew. His body collapsed. Blood geysered from what was left of his neck and part of his jaw, where muscles were torn like shredded rope and chunks of white bone poked through.

His head rolled a few paces away and came to a stop.

She felt a burst of satisfaction. Until she noticed Ramass's gaze fixed on her.

Like he was still alive.

Horrified, she watched as sinew wormed forward, latched onto the severed ends of the neck, and twisted the head into place. The gaping wound sealed. In moments, only the blood and urine pooling around Ramass's body remained as a testament to what she'd done.

She leaned over and retched, spitting bitter bile.

Ramass pushed himself onto his back, his eyes screwed shut with pain. "Do you believe me now?" His voice was raspy with damage.

She didn't bother answering. "You're a monster."

"The monster I was made to be."

Too many emotions swirled inside Larkin for any of them to take a firm hold—like she was empty and yet overfilled. "I don't understand."

Ramass took a deep breath and said as if by rote, "The sacred trees have no ears with which to hear nor eyes with which to see. So they borrowed them. No. Not borrowed. Traded. The trees grew thorns, which mankind slipped into their skin. Bits of living, thinking magic that took root and grew, giving men and women access to the trees' enchantment. In exchange, the trees took the memories of the dead and the companionship of the living.

"It had always seemed to the sacred trees a fair trade. More than fair. For though their minds could not understand the strange thoughts and ways of mankind, for the first time, they experienced color and light, patterns and music, and the glory of purpose and movement."

Larkin had never considered what life must be like for a sacred tree. "It sounds like they were lonely."

"Lonely?" He considered her words. "They didn't used to be."

"I still don't understand."

"Have you never thought about what lies beyond the three kingdoms of Valynthia, the Alamant, and the Idelmarch?"

What a strange question. "There isn't anything beyond the forests. The world ends where the sun sinks beneath the ground."

He huffed. "No, Larkin. The world is far larger than that. And it was covered in sacred trees, kings and queens of their forests. Their roots intermingled, memories and music and emotions flowing from one to another in a steady stream."

"What happened to them?" she asked in a small voice.

He frowned and said heavily, "We did." At her confused look, he motioned to the font. "Look into the font. See for yourself."

The font crouched at the top of the dais, its wicked black thorns glittering in the dying light.

Fear took root inside her, its roots digging deep. Breathless and dizzy, she let her sword fill her hand. It probably wouldn't do any good, but its presence made her feel a bit more in control.

She eased up the steps. Careful of the sharp thorns, she peered into the font. Beneath the amber sap, there was a blackness, deep and consuming. A blackness that sucked her in, pulled her down, ripped her in two. She couldn't escape. She would never escape. She deserved to die. She and every other human.

To rot in a grave. Even now, she could smell it. Her own grave as her body rotted around her.

A hand latched around her arm and pulled her back, breaking her gaze. She stumbled back. Ramass stood by her. She didn't shy away. As much as she loathed him, he had pulled her from that emptiness. And the touch of another human grounded her in a way she couldn't pull back from.

"I know that black, sucking feeling." It was what evil *felt* like. Like looking into the wraiths' eyes. But Ramass's eyes weren't black and sucking but full of pity and sorrow. So different from the feeling beating down on her like a freezing sun. Hatred. Hatred for all mankind.

Hatred that emanated from the Black Tree.

Beneath Larkin, shadows scrabbled at her again.

Shadows.

She let out a short gasp. "The wraiths aren't the source of the curse."

"The Black Tree is," Ramass said softly. "The Silver Tree realized people were using its powers for evil. It first despaired. Then grew angry. Then vengeful. It decided all men needed to die."

People using its powers for evil—like the lady murdering the girl and her child. Light. All these centuries, everyone had believed the wraiths had created the curse. Had twisted the once glorious Silver Tree into something wicked and dark. But it had been the other way around.

"The Silver Tree created the curse," she echoed, trying to make her mind believe.

"And became the Black."

She knew it was true. Knew it as surely as she knew that the Black Tree would take her soul and warp it as surely as it had warped its own. She finally understood. The wraiths had never been monsters. It was the sacred tree—the Black Tree. And she was now its slave.

She looked up at him. "But if you didn't bring me here, what did?" Even a sacred tree didn't have such powers.

He gestured to the formless shadows beneath her. They'd given up clawing at her and now shifted back and forth like a hunter trapped in a cage.

"What are they?" she whispered.

Ramass watched the sun cut in half by the horizon, a look of dread on his face. "Shadows, the souls of the dead, twisted by the Black Tree just like the rest of us. Eiryss's countercurse bound them to the night and the Mulgar Forest, though they can travel beneath the trees of the Forbidden Forest."

That explained why no spies ever came back from the Mulgar Forest. "So the vision I saw of the lady and the girl and the lord, it was a memory from one of the shadows?"

He nodded.

She closed her eyes against the horror of it. "And when night comes?"

Ramass glanced to the west, at the sun slipping beneath the horizon. "You let him in; you can force him out."

What? She felt it then—a cold slithering around her feet, a cold that sank its teeth into her over and over again. Frozen with fear, she looked down at the shadows seeping from the tree in the shape of thorned vines that snaked around her ankles, each thorn drawing black blood. They stung like a thousand poisoned barbs.

Those same vines wrapped around Ramass. He closed his eyes as if he couldn't bear to see what came next. "Don't fight the shadows. It will only make the Black Tree angry."

"Please." This couldn't happen. Not to her.

His eyes were ancient and filled with grief. "If I could spare you this, I would."

What would the Black Tree make her do? But she already knew the answer. She'd seen it often enough. She would turn her people into a mindless army and kill anyone who tried to stop her.

Including Denan.

Where the emptiness inside her had been, now there was only venom from the vines that crept up her calves, poisoning her blood with seething madness and hatred and murder.

Memories of monsters.

Already, she was losing herself.

She flared her knife and cut at the vines. They dissipated like smoke. More vines lashed out, wrapping her up. She kicked free and staggered back.

Ramass didn't try to stop her, only watched her with an infinite pity. "Remember what I told you."

Light, I'm going to become one of them. A monster.

Shadows and blood and snot and piss.

She ran. The shadow vines clung to her, tearing her flesh. Her thighs. She was half in the here and now, and half in the memory of the beautiful girl. The way she'd clutched her dead baby tight, though she herself was dying. Later, the lord had been so racked with grief he hadn't even fought the mob. His legs had kicked and his bladder had loosed as he hung from a graveyard tree.

No.

She couldn't face this again.

She'd go mad.

A hundred yards across the platform was an ornate, rusted carriage. If she could reach it, she could make her way down to the lake. Wraiths couldn't cross water. So maybe the shadows wouldn't reach her. She sprinted.

She was nearly there when a vine caught her leg and wrenched hard. She heard a snap, felt a pop. She pushed up on her elbows. Through the shadows, she made out her foot turned the wrong way. Her leg was broken.

The thorns pinned her shoulders, clawed up her face. She struggled free, clothes tearing, blood soaking her. In her mind was the beautiful girl's eyes and the lord sobbing. Begging.

She crawled to the carriage and hauled herself up on the metal curled in the shapes of flowers and vines cankered with rot. Maneuvered to the side. Hanging over the long drop, she had an impression of wildness—untamed hometrees rife with birds and crawling creatures.

But instead of a beautiful turquoise water gleaming with fish, there was a fen filled with patches of deep water, swamp, and swatches of land. Huge glowing mushrooms and flowers grew among short grasses. A dracknel with wide, sharp antlers looked up at her and bared its pointed teeth.

The thorns lashed up her neck, her cheeks, blood dripping. Pulling her down. She looked down the long drop, wondering what the fall would do to her.

Can't be worse than becoming a wraith, she thought. She tensed to throw herself headfirst into the water.

"Don't," said a voice with the same strange, rolling accent as Ramass.

The vines stark against her pale skin and freckles, a woman panted behind her. The thorns clawed over her skull and wrenched her head viciously to the side. Beneath their cruel grip, her curly red hair flared, the breeze tugging it to and fro. She looked so much like Ramass that this could only be his sister.

Hagath, the only female wraith.

Inexplicably, the woman was stark naked. "The water repels wraiths, and the fall will break every bone in your body."

Larkin shuddered. "I'd rather endure anything than become a monster."

"Nothing will stop you from becoming a monster," Hagath said. "It'll just hurt so much you might lose your mind for the next decade or so."

Ancestors.

Shadows grew over Hagath's eyes. "The Black Tree controls us, but it doesn't understand us. Use that to your advantage. Like Maisy used the rhymes. Trick him."

Maisy was dead! "What are you talking about?"

Even as she said it, the sun went out. Larkin didn't have to see it. She could feel its lack inside her. Feel its absence like someone had snatched away her soul.

Why had the Black Tree hunted her for so long? "Why give up his army to get me?" Larkin cried.

"Because you're far more dangerous than all his mulgars combined," Hagath whispered.

The vines surged, pinning Larkin painfully against the bark. She gasped, and the shadows dove into her mouth, tore down her throat, rooted into her lungs, her guts.

Pain.

Pain and screaming.

Roots grew from the shadows and pierced her brain, their thorns biting deep. The Black Tree invaded her soul. She witnessed a young bride thrown into a dark cellar because she'd burned the bread. An infant, filthy and starving but not bothering to cry because it knew no one would come. A grandmother being beaten by her grandson—a boy who was barely more than a child.

By the time it was over, all of them were dead.

Then dawned the inescapable truth. Humanity was pain. Humanity was depravity. Humanity was the true monster. The Black Tree had seen it all in the memories of the dead. Memories that had poisoned his mind until he realized there was only one thing that would save mankind.

Death.

The Black Tree would end humanity. And Larkin would help him.

She spread her arms, welcoming the soul of the Black Tree, reveling in the pain. She recognized the sharp shadows of the dead that had torn down her throat—the bride, the infant, and the grandmother. Now, they caressed her, cloaked her skin, hardened into breastplates, greaves, shin guards. Her sword formed in her hand. She became one with the Black Tree.

She knew what she had to do.

Larkin crossed to the glittering font. One thorn flashed bloodred. She broke it off with a snap and pushed it into her right forearm. It throbbed in time to the beat of her heart.

A vision flashed across her mind of a tender sapling pushing through the ashes of a burnt forest. Before she could guess what it meant, the shadows turned her inside out and jerked her back.

No. Not back.

In.

She had the sensation of being torn apart and traveling at great speed through the roots of the Mulgar Forest until she reached the Forbidden Forest. Then the shadows took her deeper—deep beneath the rich loam and network of interconnecting roots—before shoving her upward.

The shadows lashed her back together slowly. Woven throughout her soul were barbed thorns, shadows that connected her to the Black Tree and the other wraiths. Those same shadows also allowed her to see clearly in even the darkest nooks.

She was in the White Tree's forest, not far from the border that separated the two forests. Men had trod the ground here. Recently. She could smell them.

Those men had gone south.

Cloaked in the shadows of the dead, Larkin followed the scent. Her fellow wraiths—separate and yet not—were to the right and left, moving as silently as she. And then the trail was gone. Keeping herself hidden, her gaze searched the canopy above—trees loyal to the White Tree.

They were up there somewhere. Hidden. The forest protected the men. Hiding them from her.

An echo of loss and longing tore through the Black Tree. He showed her what he wished her to do. Larkin slashed one of the trees and her arm, pressing the wounds together.

As the sap mingled with her corrupted blood, the Black Tree sent visions into Larkin's mind, and from her into the Forbidden Forest. She saw the way things used to be. When the Silver Tree and White Tree had been connected by a vast network of intertwined roots, memories and music flowing freely back and forth. One tree added to the melody before sending it along to the next, until the whole forest sang with the sweetest music.

The White and Silver Trees were two separate minds bound as one.

Mates.

The last of their kind.

And then the Silver Tree had turned black. Blood had soaked the roots. Instead of memories, the shadows had spread through the forest. To save herself, the White Tree had severed their twining roots and killed the connection.

But still the Black Tree remained loyal. The White Tree was not his enemy. Even when she protected those he'd sworn to destroy. Even when her forest fought back against his presence.

The vision shifted to the White Tree as her light had died, a pulse of overwhelming grief flaring with it. Grief and longing to gain back a piece of what was lost. For the two forests to become one once more.

As they were meant to be.

Another vision niggled inside her, this time from the Forbidden Forest. A vision of mulgars setting the trees on fire. The music was a long, discordant note. Larkin remembered that night. The night the wraiths used fire in an attempt to destroy Gendrin's army. That was the night Talox had been turned.

The Forbidden Forest was furious about the murder of their fellows.

The Black Tree tried to force his consciousness into the Forbidden Forest, but the trees blocked him.

"Show me my prey!" the Black Tree screamed from Larkin's lips.

Bright white light and a cacophonous shriek screamed in Larkin's head. Light that stabbed into her center and flailed the thorns back. It tore into her very soul as the Forbidden Forest drove her mind back and severed the connection.

A horrible screeching filled her ears—the sound of her own ragged screams. She staggered back, her body echoing with terrible pain.

The Black Tree had his answer. Even with the White Tree dead, her forest would fight him. Protect mankind in their canopy.

She growled in frustration.

And then, through the shadows that connected her with the other wraiths, a call came. The humans had been found. She surged forward, her passage not even stirring the foliage. She met up with three other wraiths. Moving as one entity, they climbed an embankment, where Ramass waited for them.

She peered through thick brush to a shallow bend of river. Two men stood in water up to their waists.

Denan and Tam.

The White Tree was dead. There would never be another king. Never another human with Denan's daunting magic. Kill the king, and all the Alamant would weaken.

Forever.

"Beware the trees," Ramass rasped, soft enough not to be heard over the rushing river.

Larkin looked up and caught sight of movement. Archers in the boughs.

"I know you're there," Denan called. "I can smell you."

The smell of the dead.

"Draw them from the water," Ramass said to Larkin. "The rest of us will flank them."

She left cover and flowed down the embankment to the edge of the water. She shifted her voice to panicked, desperate. "Denan. Light, Denan. You must help me. I'm trapped." He watched her, his dark eyes reflecting the moonlight glancing off the water.

"Why did you do it, Larkin?" His voice wavered. "You knew I would rather be dead than see you like this."

Something deep within Larkin trembled. A thought came unbidden. *You let him in; you can force him out.* What did that mean?

The shadows of the dead dug their thorns in deeper, angry at the intrusive thought. They swirled around her, their fear and pain and fury biting deep. She needed Denan to understand how unredeemable mankind was. How broken and cruel and petty.

She eased forward another step and reached for him. "I know how to break the curse. Come with me, and we'll break it together." By killing every human in existence.

Denan stepped closer. So close. Almost within striking distance. She thrilled at the thought of turning him. Of depriving mankind of one of their strongest weapons.

"Denan," Tam said behind him.

"I have to know, Tam," Denan said.

He paused just out of her reach. His clothes clung to his taut body—so beautiful. He shivered, gooseflesh rising across his skin. "Why didn't you kill the wraiths, Larkin?"

"There are four of them and only one of me. I need your help."

He took his last step. She stretched out. He took her hand. Through the shadows, she could feel the warmth of his flesh. She gripped hard, jerking him forward.

No. This is wrong. But the blade had already formed in her hand.

Force him out. The thought echoed. She grasped for something, anything. Too late. She thrust. The Black Tree screamed with joy, but she felt only bitter cold.

Instead of hunching over, instead of blood, a faint light rippled over Denan's skin like water struck by a pebble. He looked sad. "I had to know."

He was armored. A magic that hadn't existed since the old days. Until now.

"Sela," Larkin hissed.

Denan's sacred sword sailed through the air, cutting through the shadows to bite into her flesh. She hunched over at the searing heat. The shadows screamed. Sacred arrows flashed in the night, her fellow wraiths moving to avoid them.

She was trapped, pinned by the sword and Denan's hand. An arrow shattered her shoulder blade. Searing agony burned through her.

Denan pulled her close. "If any part of you is left, know that I will always come for you. I will not let you stay this way."

He wrenched his sword free. She tried to block. Would have. But a part of her was screaming, fighting. His sword cut through her again. Then she was falling. Back through shadow. Back through the murderous memories.

CHAPTER

HAGATH

The Black Tree tortured Larkin for what seemed like days. Showed her depravity after depravity. The shadows left her slowly, from a scene so soaked in the blood of murdered Valynthians, she could taste it. She dropped to her knees, dry heaving. The wounds in her side and neck felt like fire scouring her from the inside out.

Just when she thought the pain would consume her, it began to fade. The blood gushing between her fingers slowed. Her vision gradually returned. She knelt at the edge of the docklike roots of the Black Tree. Just beyond reach, water lapped gently.

The last of the shadow's thorns seeped from Larkin's skin, soaking into the tree. She crawled forward, washing blood from her shaking hands and arms. One look at her soaked, shredded clothes, and she gave up, falling onto her back. Above, branches glittered like frost in the moonlight. Beyond them, the stars faded. Dawn was coming.

The memories of the bride, infant, and grandmother tormented her. So much death. And before that—she'd tried to kill her own husband. And come nightfall, she would try again. She would kill all her friends if given the chance.

If they weren't dead already.

All she'd sacrificed to save them, to save him—the fighting, the council, the murders. *Maisy*. Light. Larkin had been so convinced that Maisy and Sela had been trying to tell her something. That by coming here, Larkin could actually destroy the wraiths with her light.

She was a fool.

I executed her. Her hands clenched into fists as she fought the memory. The guilt. Worse was what she'd done to Denan. The agony he must have faced when he'd realized what she'd done, that she'd willingly become a wraith. He'd felt betrayed. Rightfully so. Because she *had* betrayed him. She had chosen to wound him as deeply as a person could.

From deep within, the ice buckled. All the emotions she'd spent weeks drowning suddenly broke the surface, clawing their way into being.

A broken sob tore from her body, followed fast by another. And another. Until she was crying so hard that she could barely breathe, tears and snot making a mess of her face. She cried until she was exhausted, her stomach muscles sore and her eyes puffy. Yet she couldn't seem to stop.

The horizon had brightened to marigold when, not ten steps to her right, shadow vines clawed their way into being. What new torture was this? She jumped up, staggered dizzily, and backed away. Her sword formed in her hand.

A wraith was returning.

Wraiths. The monsters of her nightmares. Larkin's fear was so real she could taste it. But it wasn't a rational fear. The wraiths weren't a danger to her. Not anymore. And even if they were, Ramass had already shown her they couldn't be killed.

I can't be killed.

The real danger was the Black Tree—the very thing she stood upon.

The shadows dragged a figure from nothing and deposited Hagath onto the roots. Letting her magic fade, Larkin rushed to her side. The woman was naked save a jewel-encrusted flute hanging from a chain around her neck. Blood seeped from numerous puncture wounds in her body—wounds that slowly healed from the inside out. Hagath gasped and sat up. She coughed up copious amounts of blood and then lay back, her face pale and sweaty. She was covered in sigils, though the blood obscured them.

Hagath blinked, her hands reaching blindly for Larkin. "Are the others back yet?"

"No."

Just as she said it, more swirling shadows came into being, revealing a naked man wrapped in thorns. They released him suddenly. He dropped to his knees and slumped over. He had a blade sigil on one hand and a shield sigil on the other. He was lean and muscular, his hair the palest gold. His face was too pretty to belong to a man.

Hagath turned, unseeing, toward the sound, her body tense. "Is he clean or filthy?"

Larkin looked him over, blushing at all that exposed skin. "Besides the blood?" Hagath nodded. "Clean."

Hagath sagged in obvious relief. "That's Rature, my husband. We call him Ture."

Two of the wraiths were married. They had nicknames for each other. That was so... human. Larkin supposed she shouldn't be surprised. After all, Ramass and Hagath had both seemed normal enough.

Larkin wiped the tears and snot off her face with her bloody tunic and hoped the dimness hid her blotchy skin and swollen eyes. "The other one, Vicil?"

"Help me sit up," Hagath said as she took Larkin's hand and pulled herself upright with a grimace. "Vicil doesn't have anyone to keep him sane." She opened her mouth to say more but then seemed to think better of it. "He's dangerous. Stay away from him."

So even in this forsaken place, Larkin was in danger of being attacked day and night. Lovely.

The color was coming back to Hagath's face. She looked over at her husband, who was beginning to stir, and then up at the sky. She crossed to Rature—Ture—and helped him sit up. He grunted, one hand wrapped around his middle.

They didn't even seem to notice their nakedness. Growing more uncomfortable by the minute, Larkin kept her eyes averted.

"The others?" Ture asked with the same accent as the other two.

"Larkin is here," Hagath said.

Mouth tight, he nodded.

The other wraiths were still out there, trying to turn her friends into monsters. Perhaps they already had. As she would have done. Suddenly cold, she wrapped her arms tight around herself, wincing as the movement shifted her clammy clothes.

"Denan? Tam?" she asked in a small voice.

"They're shielded," Hagath answered.

"There's nothing that can break the shield?" Larkin asked.

"Not since the curse fell."

Larkin sagged in relief. Denan and her friends were all right. That relief was quickly followed by dread. The White Tree was dead. Whatever Sela's magic had been, it was forever diminished. Larkin was surprised she'd even managed to armor Denan and Tam.

Ture slipped into the water. Minnow that flashed like silver coins swarmed him, feasting on the blood. Using the moss, he scrubbed the blood from his skin.

"Why can we touch the water now but not last night?" Larkin asked.

"The water doesn't repel *us*." Hagath placed emphasis on the last. "It repels the shadows of the dead that possess us. It's part of the countercurse, you see. The shadows can't cross water or bear sunlight. Nor can they enter the Forbidden Forest without a host."

Hagath bent to pull her own tufts of moss free. She had to have been nearly three hundred years old, but her body was lithe, her skin tight, and her breasts firm. She was beautiful—the kind of woman men ogled and women hated.

Cheeks hot, Larkin averted her gaze. Her blood-soaked garments stuck to her skin, making her itch. She desperately needed a bath, but not with a man present.

"We're making Larkin uncomfortable," Hagath said.

Ture clenched his jaw. "She'll get used to it."

The man hadn't looked at her once since she'd arrived, and whenever she spoke, he clenched his teeth. "Why are you angry with me?" Larkin asked.

His face flushed red. "Perhaps because your coming here has doomed all of humanity."

Larkin flinched as if he'd hit her.

Hagath shot him a look sharp enough to pierce iron. "Eiryss always said one of her heirs would have the ability to break the curse."

"If not for Eiryss, the world wouldn't have suffered for centuries." He tossed the moss and stormed out of the water and onto a grassy pathway leading away from the tree and deeper into the fen.

It was hard to glare at someone while blushing at their perfect backside.

"He was forced to kill a pair of druids last night," Hagath said sadly. "Otherwise he'd be a little better mannered."

Light, these people have suffered more than anyone, she thought. And then she realized what Hagath had said. There were druids with Denan last night? But then, she supposed they'd fought at the wall too.

"Is Ture right? Have I doomed us all?" She hung her head in shame.

"No," Hagath said firmly. "Eiryss had an amulet from the White Tree. It gave her visions sometimes. She said someday there would be a girl who the curse couldn't touch. That girl would free us."

Hope lightened Larkin's heart. Maybe it wasn't all for nothing. "How?"

"She kept that knowledge a secret," Hagath admitted.

That hope guttered out like a spent candle. "I could never find her grave or her amulet."

Hagath looked at Larkin strangely and then quickly away. "Ramass made me promise to let him take care of that part."

Before Larkin could ask what that meant, Hagath gestured to Larkin's bloody armor and ruined clothes. "You learn to strip before the shadows take you. That or all your clothing ends up ruined. We've all seen each other naked enough that we don't really notice anymore."

Larkin supposed that made sense, though she wasn't sure she would ever share the sentiment.

Motioning for Larkin to follow, Hagath walked to the opposite side of the roots and lifted her flute to her lips. The blood-soaked sigils all over her darkened as she played a brisk tune full of abrupt starts and stops. She wove a complex pattern of geometric shapes—a pattern Larkin had seen a dozen times in her dreams.

Hagath's song changed, the weave warping and stretching until it covered them both in a smoky half circle. "There, now we have privacy."

"Men's magic," Larkin breathed. But then, why had she been able to use it before? Sela had said she couldn't. Had her sister been lying?

"It's the reverse for a Valynthian, as our tree is male. I have barrier magic. The men have warrior magic."

Had someone told Larkin that before? She couldn't remember. She touched the dome in awe—it was so much more intricate than the one she'd managed. It rippled, the shapes gleaming into view around the pressure of her fingertips. And then they warped.

Hagath jerked Larkin's hand away. "Ancestors! You're a weaver!"

Cracks spread from where her fingertips had touched. "I broke it?"

"If you broke it, you can fix it." Hagath took Larkin's hand and gently maneuvered her fingers. With Hagath guiding her, she tugged the threads in the weave back into place.

"See?" Hagath said. "A weaver."

Larkin glanced at her fingertips and then back at Hagath. "I thought it was just because, as queen, I'm stronger than the other enchantresses."

Hagath shook her head. "Very few enchantresses can do what you did. But then, I shouldn't be surprised. The trait runs in families."

That could only mean... "Eiryss?"

Hagath nodded, slipped into the water past her chest, and scrubbed the blood from her body, revealing her gorgeous sigils in lovely floral patterns—lovely but for the darkness emanating from them. They seemed to come in pairs: two on her forearms, two on her thighs, two on her calves.

But that beauty was marred by the thick, horrible scars. Slipping off her boots, Larkin stepped into the water, hardly noticing the cool wetness against her sticky skin. The silver-scaled fish swarmed them both, cleaning Larkin's armor as they went. They tickled where they touched her bare skin.

Larkin gently took hold of Hagath's arm. The woman tensed and then allowed Larkin a closer look. The scars were even worse than she'd originally thought. As if someone had tried tearing her sigils out.

That's exactly what happened, Larkin realized. Horror rippled through her. To rip the sigils from her own body... The pain and loss would have been unbearable. Who would have done such a thing?

Hagath pulled her arm back, her expression rigid.

"Why didn't the Black Tree heal the scars?" Larkin asked gently.

Hagath wouldn't meet her eyes. "Because he wanted me to suffer."

"He's punishing you." Larkin's hands reflexively covered her own sigils, glad they were of the White Tree. "Why?"

"Because we tried to stop him."

Larkin had seen Eiryss and her husband, King Dray, fight back the shadows.

Hagath's gaze narrowed on Larkin's wrist. "You have a new thorn."

Larkin resisted the urge to cover the red, swollen mark. "We can cut it out." It wouldn't hurt as much as Hagath's, as it hadn't rooted.

Hagath seemed not to have heard her. "He made me take all new sigils, yet he only gave you one. Why?"

Larkin formed a dagger, took a deep breath, and pressed the point to her skin.

Hagath laid a hand on her wrist. "Wait until Ramass says you should."

Larkin hesitated; she didn't want anything from the Black Tree inside her. But Hagath knew more about these things than she did.

Hagath swam to the edge and climbed out. "I'll be back."

While she was gone, Larkin pulled up her own tuft of moss—the texture was rough and firm—and scrubbed the blood from her armor before spreading it on the roots to dry.

She stripped off her now-ripped clothing and eagerly scrubbed the black blood from her pale, freckled skin. Skin nearly identical in color and freckles to Hagath's. The woman could easily be mistaken for one of her sisters.

The fish swarmed her, their tickling nearly driving her mad until she pulsed gently, which scattered them.

Fully dressed, her hair simply braided, Hagath returned with some simple, cream-colored garments neatly folded. Stepping out, Larkin dried herself with a bit of cloth Hagath gave her and dressed in a loose-fitting, knee-length tunic. Hagath handed her a belt made of gilgad skin, which gave the garment a little shape. The fabric was soft, breathable, and easy to move in.

Hagath wrung her hands as she looked Larkin over. "It's not much, but the weave is tight. I wish I could have dyed the fabric deep green. That's my favorite color on you."

Larkin looked up in surprise. "You made this for me?"

Hagath bit her lip and nodded.

Even Hagath figured the Black Tree would catch me eventually, Larkin thought dejectedly. "Clearly woven by an expert. Thank you."

Hagath suddenly hugged her. "I'm sorry. I'm so sorry, but it's been so long since I've spoken to another woman. You don't realize how much you need women in your life until they're gone."

Larkin wrapped her arms around Hagath and held her as she cried.

Finally, Hagath pulled back and wiped her face. "I apologize."

"Don't." Not for being lonely.

"I shouldn't complain. I have Ture, after all."

Larkin's brows furrowed. "Not Ramass?" Hagath's own brother.

Hagath hesitated. "After Ramass lost Eiryss... it was like he wasn't there anymore. A ghost rather than a man." She met Larkin's gaze. "All that changed after we found you. You gave him hope. You gave us all hope."

Except for Ture, apparently. Larkin still couldn't get over the fact that the wraiths were people every bit as broken by the curse as everyone else. Perhaps even more so. And they were desperate for Larkin to save them. She didn't even know how to begin.

Hagath played a tune that reminded Larkin of a clear stream tinkling down round rocks, with a bit of waterfall thrown in. The dome dissipated like mist melting before the morning sun.

Outside was moments from dawn. A clutch of gilgads ten feet long were aimed right for them. Heart catching in her throat, Larkin took a step back.

"Our blood attracted them." Hagath lifted her pipes to her lips and played a tune that had the lizards ducking out of sight beneath the water.

From one of the hometrees, an enormous bird with a purple shimmer to its black wings dove beakfirst into the water and came up with a four-foot-long gilgad speared through the side. It writhed but didn't break free. The bird landed in a tree, pinned it with the talons of one clawed foot, and started eating.

Swallowing hard, Larkin looked around at the fen. While it was beautiful in its own way, it seemed a violent, dangerous place.

"It used to look like the Alamant, but things changed after," Hagath said. "He needed a pathway for his shadows to leave the city, so he built a fen." Hagath's gaze went distant, as if she were seeing another time and place. "I wish you could have seen it before. The magic and the beauty." The light faded from her eyes. "But for all the beauty, there was equal ugliness."

Valynthia, the fallen city. It was every bit as beautiful as the Alamant. It shouldn't be. The trees should be twisted, dead things. The waters polluted and stinking. A silent, empty place.

Nothing was how it should be.

"How am I more dangerous than all the Black Tree's mulgars?"

"Doesn't matter how." Behind them, Ture wore the same shapeless tunic. "What matters is he's going to use you to destroy mankind."

Twin beats of dread and guilt drummed through her. He was right, she knew he was.

"There's still hope," Hagath insisted.

"She should have stayed in the Alamant," Ture said.

A fat tear skimmed Larkin's cheek. She quickly wiped it away.

Hagath shot Ture another glare.

He ignored her. "The little one—the new Arbor—she shielded them?"

"Sela," Hagath confirmed.

Light! The realization hit Larkin all at once: her five-year-old sister was in the Forbidden Forest. She must have been in the trees when Denan had lured Larkin to the edge of the water. Had Sela seen Larkin try to kill her own husband? She would have succeeded if Sela hadn't shielded him. And if Larkin's wraith-self got a chance, she'd kill Sela too. *Light help me.*

Ture huffed in disbelief. "The fools took their strongest weapons straight into danger. What could they possibly be thinking?"

Denan's words echoed in Larkin's head. *I will always come for you.* The phrase that had felt like a threat at first had turned into an endearment. Now, it was a mixture of both. "They're coming here. To the Black Tree. To kill us."

"But we can't die!" Hagath said.

"They don't know that," Larkin said. "How many were there?"

"Less than twelve, more than eight," Ture said.

Who would be fool enough to risk the wraiths in Valynthia? But then she remembered something Denan had told her. The men who had died protecting her hadn't done so because she deserved it. They'd done it because they'd loved her.

They were risking the forest because of love. Tam would be among them. West too. Alorica, if she were able. Atara. Gendrin. Mytin and Aaryn were too important to abandon their posts. Mama and Nesha weren't fighters. She couldn't think of anyone else willing to risk death or worse for her.

"But the source of Sela's magic is dead," Larkin lamented.

"And at night, the shadows will attack," Hagath said. "The Mulgar Forest won't protect them like the Forbidden Forest did."

"That little girl made an orb that burned a fist-sized hole in Vicil," Ture said. "If she can do that, she can keep the shadows off them tonight."

"And can she keep us off them?" Larkin asked, dread making her stomach churn.

Ture didn't answer, which she supposed was answer enough.

Larkin held her head in her hands. Tam, Denan, Sela, and the rest were all walking into a trap. Had the Black Tree known they would? "All of it—all I sacrificed—was for nothing." Her life, her freedom, her humanity.

Hagath rested her hand on Larkin's arm. "No. Not nothing. The mulgars and ardents are whole. Denan is whole."

For now.

"Did the Black Tree know they would come for me?" Larkin asked. "Was that why it brought me here?"

"All we know for certain," Hagath said, "was that Eiryss claimed one of her line would break the curse. Sela already broke half of it." The part that took the magic and the memories. "You must be meant to break the other half."

Larkin didn't know how to break anything. "My friends are coming here. They're going to die."

On the horizon, the sun broke the last holds of night. In that same instant came a tearing sound. Suddenly chilled, Larkin shivered and glanced down. Creeping over her feet, the shadows gathered into a knotted mass not ten feet from Larkin. Shadows that rolled and boiled and twisted.

Thorns dragged a naked Ramass from within, dumping him in a heap. He was split from shoulder to hip, the wound raw and pulsing black blood that pooled around his body.

Larkin swore and hurried to his side. Hagath beat her there, pushing his shoulder back into place. Larkin leaned over and retched again, managing to get up nothing but bile. She hadn't eaten in what? Two days? Yet she didn't feel hungry or thirsty.

Wiping her lips, she staggered back, coming to a stop beside Ture. How many times had they died horribly, only to be brought back to life? How many times had the voices in their heads forced him to kill—were any of those their friends? How must it feel to have every person within the last three hundred years think you a monster?

The endless hopelessness carved a hole through her. "How do you not go mad?" She felt on the precipice of it herself.

Ture's eyes clouded with so many memories. "We have, at times." His gaze rested on his wife with a tenderness that shook Larkin.

Ramass reared up and sucked in a desperate breath. His hand wrapped around his shoulder. He rolled over, coughing and convulsing. The wicked scar faded to white and then nothing at all.

"They survived the night," Ramass panted.

Larkin sagged in relief.

Hagath bent over him. "The Black Tree gave her one thorn. Should she try to remove it?"

Ramass swore.

"The last thing she needs is more magic to murder all humanity," Ture muttered.

Larkin choked back tears and flared her knife. "I'll cut it out."

Ramass got to his feet. "Not yet."

CHAPTER

39

EIRYSS

The sun sneaked up the horizon like an egg yolk on a crooked pan. Larkin knelt on the roots and scrubbed her trousers, boots, and tattered shirt; the blood stains would never fully come out. She'd just laid them out to dry with her armor when Ramass appeared behind her.

Freshly bathed and dressed in the same simple smock as the rest of them, he looked none the worse for wear. In fact, with his muscular build, angular features, and full lips, he was devilishly handsome.

"Come with me."

Larkin pulled on her boots and hurried after him. He led her beyond the roots and up the sweeping steps. At the top was another small building of rough lumber. Through the glassless window, Larkin made out beds, woven baskets filled with clothing, and a loom. That must be where Hagath made their clothing.

At the carriage, Ramass shut the door behind them and pulled the lever. A clever system of gears and counterweights churned into action. They eased up the side of the tree, the lake growing smaller and the boughs larger.

Without the Alamant's regular structure of platforms and their magical panes, Valynthia looked wilder. The way it would have looked before the first man and woman discovered the font and its magic. Before it had been forced to know evil. To commit it.

Such a beautiful, terrible place.

The carriage reached its apex. Ramass unlatched the gate and stepped out onto a level branch. She didn't follow him. She couldn't. Because after all he'd been through, she'd been his hope. A false hope. "I can't break the curse, Ramass."

"The song—"

"Eiryss's tomb was empty. Wherever they buried her is lost to time, and the amulet lost with it."

His eyes grew distant. "I attended the funeral of a man dearer to me than my own father. We all swore he would never be forgotten. Now, anyone who remembers anyone who knew him is dead. He has been forgotten. We are all forgotten."

He let out a long breath. "So much is lost to the ravages of time. People have a way of warping history. Of forgetting the most important things. But the curse has given us one advantage: I remember everything."

He turned without seeing if she would follow. She hesitated. Did he mean that he remembered where Eiryss was buried? Then why didn't he fetch the amulet himself? Eventually, the thought of Sela, Denan, and Tam drove her forward.

Muttering curses, she scrambled to catch up. Inside the main platform, they started up one of the side branches. Within minutes, sweat streaked down Larkin's body, soaking her tunic.

Five minutes later, Ramass left the branch, leaping to another. Larkin looked down at the long drop, her heart clogging her throat. *It's not as if I can die.* But she suspected it would hurt bad enough she'd wish she were dead.

She backed up and took a running jump. She hit the other side, arms windmilling. She made the mistake of looking down, so far down she couldn't see the waves on the water. *This is going to hurt.*

A hand grabbed her arm and righted her.

"Sorry," Ramass said. "I didn't think about how much shorter you are."

The insult she wanted to shout came second to gasping for breath.

"It's gotten harder since the bridges rotted." Ramass glanced at the sun and frowned. "We'll go the longer way." He hustled off.

She was breathing hard when she caught sight of something between the boughs above them. Flashes of a bright, honey gold. A sudden, sharp pain shot through her foot. She yelped and jumped back.

A thorn had gone straight through the sole of her boot and broken off inside. Wincing, she yanked it out, sidestepped, and nearly impaled herself on another. She swore. From here on out, thorns grew thick. Some short and needle thin. Others curved and long as her thumb.

"What is that?" she asked.

"The tree's attempts at keeping me out."

She divided her attention between the thorns and the bit of gold visible between thorny vines. Then they stepped between an archway carved of wood. Lying on a natural platform was a casket made of amber. Inside lay a woman, a pearl-encrusted blanket tucked under her clasped hands.

Larkin had seen this before in a vision. She hurried forward and peered down. "No," she gasped. It couldn't be.

She polished the surface of the casket with her sleeve. She recognized the delicate features, the full lips—the top lip rounded and bigger than the bottom—and the pale hair—gold shot through with silver.

This was Eiryss. And judging by the slight rise and fall of her chest, she was very much alive. "She— She can't be..." She needed someone else to say it. Someone to confirm that she wasn't going mad.

"She is."

"She lived to be an old woman. I saw it in a vision." And it had been well documented that Eiryss had ruled the Idelmarch well into old age. She'd had several children as well—one of them Larkin's ancestor. Yet this Eiryss was young, no older than Larkin.

"Passage through the shadows healed her aging body just as it healed our injuries."

Larkin gaped at him. "You captured her like you captured me?"

"She came to me." At her incredulous look, he continued, "By then, she knew if she had any chance of defeating the curse, it was here."

Eiryss had willingly gone with the wraiths. Traveled the memories of murders and worse. Just like Larkin had. She stared at the woman in disbelief. She'd never thought to find the legendary Curse Queen, let alone see her alive. "How long has she been like this?"

Ramass laid a hand on her coffin. "Too long."

"How did she end up in here?"

He swallowed hard. "The amber grew around her in her sleep. Every morning, it became harder and harder for her magic to break her free. Until she knew it would be her last day. She dressed in her old finery—the stuff from before the curse. We spent the day together, dancing and laughing and holding each other. And when I returned in the morning, I found her like this."

The grief and longing on his face tore at Larkin's heart. *A cursed queen, her lover lost.* "You're in love with her."

"We were engaged." His thumb stroked the smooth surface. "And then I became this."

"But the curse came the day she was to marry the Alamantian king. I saw it." The White Tree had shown her that vision enough times that Larkin had it memorized. She'd seen the fear on Eiryss's face. The loss, the treachery. "You betrayed her."

"Not everything is as it seems." He glanced at the midmorning sun. "That's a story for another day."

His sword flared in his hands—a sword swathed in shadows that curled around it like drifts of smoke. He lifted it above his head and sliced down diagonally. And the sword suddenly stopped as if gripped by an unseen hand.

Ramass tried to push through, his teeth gritted and the veins at his temples standing out. He gasped and released it. "I can't hurt the tree. But I think you can."

"Me? How?"

"Your sigils aren't corrupted."

She flared her sword and did an experimental swing. Her sword bit into the bark at the side of the coffin. She blinked at the damage she'd done, the black sap welling. The hatred around her sharpened. She swore she could taste the Black Tree's bitter anger.

She waited for the tree to retaliate, but nothing happened. "What about the shadows?"

"Eiryss's countercurse created boundaries the shadows cannot cross—like the water and sunlight." Ramass let out a long breath.

Where light is, shadow cannot go, Sela had said.

But how do I defeat those shadows? Larkin screamed on the inside.

There was no answer.

"Hit it again." His voice trembled with emotion.

She swung again, harder this time. The blade chopped off a corner of the coffin, a chunk of amber spinning. Larkin reversed her swing, breaking off an equal piece on the other side.

"Press the tip of your blade into it, here." Ramass pointed to the largest blank space, which sat between Eiryss's neck and the edge of the coffin. He'd clearly put a lot of thought into placement where it had the least chance of causing damage.

Still.

"Can she heal like you?" Larkin asked.

"The tree won't let her die. He's too eager to torture her."

Larkin positioned the tip of the blade, making sure it was level, and pushed. Her blade, which was sharp enough to cut a falling leaf, didn't so much as make a scratch. She pushed harder. Then harder still. Then she pushed as hard as she could.

There was a sharp crack, like the ice breaking over a river. A fissure appeared. And then another. Another. They spiderwebbed. A single bead of viscous liquid rolled out. Larkin's sword sank in, embedding just to the right of Eiryss's face.

Larkin let her sword fade; sap gushed. Eiryss's hair shifted, flaring as if she were underwater. Ramass cried out. Larkin held out her arm to hold him back. She flared her shield and slammed the bottom point into the seam. The coffin shattered.

Ramass dropped to his knees, scooped Eiryss out, and pulled her into his lap. Sobbing with joy, he tugged her hair out of her face.

"Eiryss, love, can you hear me?"

Larkin held her breath, waiting for the woman to make the slightest movement. Ramass's eyes darted all around her face. "Eiryss, please. I can't lose you again. I just can't."

She still didn't move. Larkin held a hand to her mouth. She couldn't have come this far and lost so much and then have it be for nothing. She couldn't watch a man who had borne so much bear even more.

Ramass pulled Eiryss against his chest. "I remember when we were little and we spun, our hands locked together, until we fell in the grass. And when we were older, I held you in my arms as we spun to the music. And then later still... you fit against me, Eiryss, like you were meant to be in my arms. And then you spun out of my life and into the arms of another. But I held space for you. And you came back. Come back now, love." He bent down and kissed her lips.

She opened her brown eyes, and their gazes locked. "I remember," she whispered.

Ramass broke down sobbing and rocked her in his arms like an infant. Larkin wasn't meant to see this tender moment. She backed away, turning to go back the way they'd come.

"Wait," Eiryss cried.

Larkin hesitated before glancing over her shoulder. Her gaze locked with Eiryss's. A connection snapped into place between them—a belonging and warmth that felt like coming home. It was such a powerful feeling that tears welled in Larkin's eyes.

"Larkin," Eiryss breathed.

"How do you know?" Larkin asked.

A shadow passed over Eiryss's face. "I saw many things the Black Tree didn't mean to share." She shook away her frown and smiled up at Ramass. "She looks like our daughter."

Our. Larkin stared at Ramass, who met her gaze steadily. A man with familiar red curls and freckles. A man who reminded her of her father. Of herself.

"But," she protested weakly, "King Dray is my ancestor." King Dray who Eiryss had been marrying the day the curse fell.

Eiryss shook her head. "Ramass is your grandfather."

Larkin's first instinct was revulsion, but a beat later, she relaxed. Ramass was not a monster. He never had been. Ramass made a sniffling sound. Larkin looked up at him, at the love shining in his eyes.

"My grandfather," she said, wonder in her voice.

He nodded. It was impossible. And yet, so many things that she'd believed impossible... weren't.

Eiryss struggled to stand. Ramass helped her up. She leaned against him, one arm over his shoulder. The other she held out to Larkin. A little unsure, Larkin stepped toward the woman.

Eiryss pulled Larkin into her damp embrace. Though this was the first time Larkin had ever met her, she knew this woman. Knew her down to her marrow. Ramass hugged her too, every bit as tightly.

They were part of her family.

"Blood of my heart, marrow my bone," Eiryss said.

A line from the song she had written. One that the Alamantians had sung for generations. Sung to the tune of one of the pipers' songs. Larkin's mind automatically skipped to the next few lines. *Consumed by evil, agents of night, Seek the nestling, barred from flight.*

"Your song was about me," Larkin said. "I'm the nestling. You knew the wraiths would convince me to come."

Eiryss trailed a hand down Larkin's cheek. "Fear not the shadows, for you are mine."

The truth about the shadows was there all along.

"But I am afraid," Larkin whispered. "Afraid my coming here has destroyed everything I ever loved."

"In my arms, the answer lie: a light that endures so evil may die." Eiryss slipped the chain off her neck, revealing a silver ahlea amulet that sparked with inner light.

Larkin held it reverently in her hand. "The amulet is how I defeat the Black Tree?"

Eiryss eased it over Larkin's head. "The amulet. And you, Larkin. You and your sister."

CHAPTER

THORNS

Standing to one side of the docks, Larkin swung her magical ax with all her pent-up anger. The thwack echoed through the empty city, sending raucous birds flying. A sliver struck her in the cheek, sending a bead of blood running down her face.

She jerked it free and pressed on the sting. Sharp as her ax was, it hadn't bit deep. The tree had probably done more damage to her.

It would not win. Not again.

Thinking of Ramass, she gritted her teeth and swung again. And again for Eiryss. And again for Hagath and Ture. One for every broken city and rotted skeleton she'd come across in the Forbidden Forest. And then she swung for herself. For Ramass and the rest of her family—the torment she'd put them through.

Chips tumbled into the water, sending the colorful fish darting for cover. Silver sap wept, spraying her with each impact. Surprisingly, it smelled sweet and earthy instead of like blood and rot. She worked until well after midday, when she could barely lift her arms and sweat soaked her tunic. Sap clung to her skin, the stickiness at the crease in her elbow driving her mad with each swing.

Gasping for breath, she let her magic fade; the constant sigil use had left her arms numb and buzzing. She surveyed the arm's-length crease she'd carved from the side of the tree. Half a day's work, and she'd barely managed to hurt him. It was like trying to take down a mountain with a hammer.

She tipped back her head back and looked up, up, up. She'd need a dozen armies of enchantresses and weeks of time to chop the Black Tree down. Not for the first time, she wished she could simply burn him to the ground, but sacred trees were more mineral than wood. They couldn't get the fire hot enough to burn.

She turned at the sound of steps approaching. Hagath. Larkin's however-many-greats aunt and Ramass's twin sister. She'd lived in another world completely—one filled with glittering prestige and unimaginable power. Now, she wore a homemade smock and ate fish raw from the lake. Even the power had turned against her.

The words of Iniya's curse came rushing back to her. *All your happy memories will turn to bitterness. Your own magic will turn against you. And everyone you love will come to hate you.*

Light, every bit of it had come true. Had the old woman somehow used magic? Or just gotten lucky? Larkin's sword cut out, and she slumped to the bark.

Hagath came over and held out a cup of water. "What does it feel like? To hurt him?"

Larkin shook out her arms before taking the cup and drained the cup, wishing for another. "Better." She studied the small dent she'd made. "And worse."

Hagath nodded as if she understood.

"Any sign of Vicil?"

Hagath frowned. "He's hunting."

Probably hunting me. "Ancestors," Larkin muttered.

Hagath tipped back her head and laughed.

Larkin shot her a questioning look.

"It's just that Eiryss actually made 'Ancestors, help me' the official Idelmarchian prayer, hoping it would help her people look to her for help someday."

How many clues had the woman buried in their culture that Larkin didn't even know about? The thought made her feel even more exhausted. She made the mistake of rubbing her eyes. The sap sent them stinging and watering.

Muttering curses at the tree, she descended the steps that crossed the length of the root, slipped into the delightfully cool water, and washed. But no matter how hard she scrubbed, the stickiness remained.

Hagath led her over to a fire at the end of the dock where Ture cooked fish in dark leaves.

The smell made Larkin's mouth water. "I'm hungry." For the first time in two days. "I was starting to think we didn't need to eat."

"The tree won't let us starve to death." The darkness in Ture's voice made Larkin think they'd tried it. "Then he couldn't torture us anymore."

"Will you tell me the story of what really happened?" Larkin asked.

The two of them sighed, shoulders falling.

Hagath's hands were clenched, her eyes shut tight. "Do you know what it's like to watch everyone around you, everyone you love, die? To watch your entire kingdom destroyed— forgotten, as if it never existed at all? No one to mourn the dead—no one but you?"

Was that the future that awaited Larkin?

Ture pulled Hagath in close. "Nothing good comes from talking about it."

Beneath Larkin, the dead scrabbled at her. All people trapped for centuries in the darkness of the Black Tree. She curled her fist around the scar in her hand from her embedding ceremony. Would mankind have been better off had they never taken that first thorn? There would be no wraiths. No curses.

No magic.

Was the price of magic too high?

From above came a creak and grinding sound. The carriage descended, Ramass and Eiryss inside.

"I suppose that means they're done with their *alone time*," Ture said with a suggestive wiggle of his brows.

Hagath elbowed him and tried not to smile. "Stop that." She scraped the coals back together. "After all that, I'm sure they're starving."

Ture burst out laughing.

"That's not what I meant!" Hagath said with a roll of her eyes.

Eiryss and Ramass came out of the carriage, holding hands. Eiryss had changed into the same long tunic the rest of them wore. The two couldn't stop looking at each other. Eiryss had a wide smile on her face, revealing crooked teeth. Had Larkin and Denan been as bad? That one misty morning at a hot spring... She blushed.

"Gah," Ture said under his breath. "It's like they're newly-weds again."

Hagath bumped him with her shoulder. "Hush. They deserve this happiness."

Ture made a face. "But must we watch?"

She grinned at him, and there were so many stories, so much history, in that one look. Once again, Larkin was out of place. Light, she missed her husband. How much more would her longing be if she'd had to watch him marry another, as Ramass had? Would she ever hear his laugh again? Ever hold him tight?

Eiryss reached them and hugged Ture. Larkin couldn't help comparing Eiryss to her other grandmothers. Iniya had been an old woman embittered by the loss of her family and her title. Fawna had been lost and hopeless. Yet after all Eiryss had gone through, she still smiled. Still loved. What had been the difference?

"Light, woman, you've already hugged me into paste." Ture's smile belied his words.

Ramass stayed a few paces back, a dazzled expression on his face.

From a distance, Larkin watched the two pairs—siblings who had married siblings. One pair with copper curls, the other with straight, silver-and-gold hair. Had any of them borne children since becoming wraiths? If they had, there was no evidence. Larkin suspected that if the Black Tree could heal a scar, he could prevent or remove a baby. Larkin shuddered at the thought of another injustice heaped upon them.

Had any of them ever deserved any measure of it? After all, they'd been involved in starting the curse, though Larkin wasn't convinced they meant to. She was beginning to feel even more out of place when Eiryss's eyes landed on her.

"I've waited long enough for answers," Larkin said.

Eiryss frowned and then nodded. "The Black Tree's mulgars have been bringing my descendants here for generations. They force a thorn on them. And they become... like Maisy."

Maisy was also a descendant of Eiryss and Ramass? That meant she was family. A wave of torment washed over Larkin.

Eiryss's eyes were sad. "She managed to retain so much of her humanity after the thorn turned her. She was able to fight him off. Hide from him, more than any of the others." Her gaze met Larkin's. "Help to bring you here."

I'm your friend, Larkin. I've always been your friend. And Larkin had executed her for it. She staggered to the edge of the roots, dropped to her knees, and screamed until her voice was raw. Punched the tree until her knuckles were broken.

After an immeasurable length of time passed, she picked herself up and sat back around the fire, where Eiryss was quietly waiting. The rest of the Valynthians were nowhere to be seen.

"She understood, Larkin. She didn't hate you for it."

That didn't make it right. "Will I become like Maisy too?" Light, Larkin's hands hurt. She welcomed the pain. She deserved that and so much more.

"The curse can't touch you." Eiryss sighed. "The amulet gave me visions sometimes. Visions of you, Larkin. And your sister Sela. Both of you breaking the curse." She reached into Larkin's tunic and pulled out the ahlea amulet dangling from a thick gold chain. "And you used this to do it."

The ahlea was of the White Tree—that much was obvious by the gold sheen and colors that danced beneath. This amulet was alive, just as the tree had been. "What am I to do with it?"

Eiryss pushed to her feet. "We have to give you barrier magic."

An hour later, the wind had picked up, storm clouds blotting the horizon.

"She already has a thorn." Hagath paced before the glittering black font. "I was going to cut it out."

Eiryss made a calming gesture. "Larkin has to have barrier and warrior magic to break the curse."

Ramass sat on the steps, his arms folded. "You still haven't explained how she's going to do that."

Eiryss rubbed her forehead as if she had a headache. "I told you, the visions are in images, feelings, music. It's hard to piece it all together."

Ture threw his hands in the air. "Then how do you know you're right about the thorns?"

Eiryss shot him a flat look. "I spent decades in that coffin. I was able to suss a bit of it out."

"*If* you're right," Ture emphasized.

"I was shielded from the curse within that dome," Eiryss said. "Same as my unborn child. And her children after her."

That meant she was pregnant with Ramass's daughter on her wedding day to King Dray. Had he known about the child? Had Ramass? And exactly what kind of woman was her grandmother?

"If she was safe from the curse," Hagath asked, "why was he able to make her a wraith?"

"She willingly took in the shadows," Eiryss said. "And she can reject them—*if she has enough magic*." She put extra emphasis on the last bit.

Ture speared Larkin with a look. "And when he nearly forced you to kill your husband?"

Memories swarmed Larkin. Her sword slamming into Denan's side. His broken voice. *I had to know for certain.* Light, if not for Sela, Larkin would have killed him.

"That was unkind," Hagath murmured to her husband.

"She needs to understand what she's getting herself into," Ture said defensively.

"And if you're wrong?" Ramass asked Eiryss. "And the sigils only bind Larkin tighter to the Black Tree?"

Eiryss turned to Hagath, who watched them with a haunted expression. "What's the first thing the Black Tree made you do?"

"Take sigils," Hagath said in a small voice.

"Yet he only forced one on Larkin," Eiryss said. "Which means he knows the damage she can do with them."

Hagath took a deep breath. "She's right."

"You cannot be on her side," Ture huffed.

"Sela, Denan, and the others will be here in two days," Hagath said. "If the Alamant loses their Arbor and their king, they don't stand a chance."

"They never did," Ture responded.

Larkin flared her sword. "I've put up with a lot from you out of pity, Ture. But my pity just ran out."

He stared at her before turning to Hagath. "I can see why you like her."

"Apologize," Ramass demanded.

Ture lifted his hands in surrender. "All right. I'm sorry."

Larkin glared at him long enough to be sure he meant it before letting her sword fade.

"The Black Tree will have a plan," Hagath said. "He always does."

"This is just another one of Eiryss's mad schemes," Ture growled. "As likely to get us all in trouble as not."

Ramass smiled crookedly. "But the times we didn't get in trouble were fun indeed."

Ture chuckled despite himself. "Fine." He crossed to Eiryss and ruffled her hair. "I really did miss you. Pranks aside."

She bumped him with her shoulder. "I missed you too."

He shook his head. "But I still think your plan is mad."

Eiryss turned to Larkin. "It's a risk we're going to have to take."

Feeling vulnerable, she gripped her new amulet; she'd missed the comfort of her old one. "What's to stop the Black Tree from removing the thorns when I become a wraith?"

"Had he been able to do that," Eiryss said, "he would have taken your White Tree thorns."

Larkin hesitated before turning to Ramass. "What do you think?"

He let out a long sigh. "If there's another way, I can't see it. But it's your decision."

The four of them waited for Larkin. She shuddered at the memory of barbed shadows forcing themselves down her throat, crawling through her lungs, her guts. She heard the sobs and cries of the girl and the grandmother and the baby and the bride.

She wiped at the sweat beading her forehead. "I don't want anything else from the Black Tree in my body."

But then she thought of her husband and little sister. Of her friends. Of all those who would die if the Alamant fell. She turned to face the font of wicked thorns, glittering in the evening light. "But a lifetime of bearing the thorns would be better than the memory of their deaths."

Eiryss patted her leg and turned to Ramass. "You know the Black Tree will try to stop us."

Ramass glanced at the sun. "We have a couple hours until sunset. Let's get started."

Eiryss looped her hand through Larkin's arm and started up the stairs to the font.

"What if I fail?" Larkin blurted. "What if I can't do what you need me to do?"

Eiryss's brow rose. "You're a queen, just like me. We do what's best for our people."

"What if I'm the wrong kind of queen?" Larkin asked.

"That's not possible," Eiryss said.

Larkin wasn't so sure.

They'd just stepped onto the dais when a man dropped from above, landing in a crouch between them and the font. His shin bone snapped and pierced his skin. He didn't even wince as it straightened itself. He was naked and filthy, covered in layers of drying blood. His hair was matted and crawling with lice. He smelled of rot and unwashed bodies. Even through all that, the resemblance to Ture and Eiryss was unmistakable.

This had to be Vicil.

His mad gaze fixed on her. "She will not touch the font."

Eiryss held out her hand in a pleading gesture. "Vicil, do you remember me? I'm your cousin, Eiryss."

"You should have stayed in your coffin." Vicil charged.

"Eiryss," Ramass cried.

Larkin stepped between him and her grandmother and pulsed, throwing Vicil into the font. Ramass and Ture shifted to flank Vicil, their magic blades and shields in place. Eiryss and Hagath pulled their pipes from inside their dresses and began playing. The weave rose before them, geometric shapes and delicate vines.

Blood dripping from his back where the thorns had torn into him, Vicil launched two knives in quick succession, hitting Ramass in the leg and Ture in the stomach. Both men staggered. Larkin charged.

Vicil dropped and swept his leg out, catching Larkin's ankles and sending her toppling down the stairs. He crossed the remaining space with frightening speed. Her training told her to shift to the side and let his momentum carry him past her. But that would put Hagath and Eiryss in danger. She had to hold.

Rising to one knee, Larkin flared the enchantment into an arch that shielded all three of them. Vicil slammed into her. She braced, every muscle in her body screaming as she held her ground. He pounded on her shield with his blade. Once. Twice.

She pulsed again, sending him careening back. Then Ramass was there, his sword thrusting. Vicil danced out of reach just in time. Ture joined in. Vicil retreated, trading blows with both Ramass and Ture. Larkin trailed after them, but she didn't want to leave Eiryss and Hagath, who were nearly done with whatever enchantment they were weaving.

"Head for the font," Hagath said to Larkin.

Ture's blade slipped past Vicil's guard and into his lower left ribs. Vicil didn't seem to feel the pain.

"Go, Larkin!" Ramass said.

Larkin ran to the font. Vicil tried to double back, but Ramass caught him in the thigh with a crippling slice. Vicil's leg buckled; he went down and did not rise again. Ramass and Ture backed away. Why hadn't they finished him? But then she saw the pity in their gazes. He was their family. And besides, what he'd become wasn't his fault.

The enchantresses stepped forward, their music bending the weave into a dome that settled over Vicil, who watched them with hatred in his eyes. For a moment, the symbols gleamed silver. And then the song changed, and they faded, leaving only a faint sheen along the edge of the dome to reveal it was there at all.

Having trapped Vicil, the four of them turned to Larkin. Taking a deep breath, she faced the conduit thorn. She didn't allow herself to hesitate. To overthink. She just pushed her hand into the thorn. The sparkles darkened to black as her blood pushed through.

Instead of warmth and lightness, the Black Tree's sap seeped inside her, cold with bitter hatred. She gasped as it clawed its way up her arm. The thorns didn't light up like they should. Ramass came to stand on one side of her, Eiryss the other. Ture and Hagath circled to the opposite side of the font.

"You're going to have to force him to give up your thorns," Ramass said.

"Larkin!" a voice cried. Denan's voice.

"Denan?" She turned toward the sound.

Ramass took hold of her shoulders.

Eiryss held her hand in place. "That's not Denan, Larkin. It's the Black Tree. Making you experience things that aren't real."

A high-pitched little girl's scream. "Larkin, oh, light, Larkin," Sela cried. "The mulgars have got me."

The sounds of a battle. Swords and grunts and curses and the pounding of feet.

"Larkin," Denan cried. "We're going to be overrun."

"It's not real," Ramass said.

But it sounded real. The panic in Larkin's body was real. Her instincts screamed that it was real.

The Black Tree's doing.

She turned away from the sound and concentrated on forcing her consciousness into the Black Tree as it had done to her. "You will give me what I want."

More screaming. The cold sap inside her seeped into her eyes, into her brain. Now she could see them. Mama. Nesha. The babies. Her friends. They were here. Dying all around her. But she did not break the connection. Did not turn away as they died agonizing deaths again and again and again.

And then she was through.

"I see one!" Hagath cried.

Then the Valynthians were all moving. One, two, three, four, five, six, seven snaps as they broke off the thorns.

"That's all of them," Eiryss said.

Larkin staggered back. The screams abruptly cut off. The visions took longer to fade. Feeling bone-deep cold, she wrapped her arms around herself.

"Hurry," Hagath said.

Ramass stood in front of her, his face hard. Behind him, the horizon had cut the sun in half.

"But we had a couple hours," Larkin said.

"Two hours in which you fought him," Ture said.

Light. Had it been that long?

Ramass held up a thorn. "Where?"

Cold gathered on her right arm, the sap instructing her where it needed to go. She tapped the spot and turned away as he slid it inside her skin.

Hagath held up one. "This one?"

Her right thigh. She tapped it. They repeated the process until all the thorns were in her body. Her shaking knees gave out from under her. Ramass caught her and eased her to the ground.

Hagath pushed back her hair. "When you come back, you'll be better."

Back from being a wraith. Already, she could feel the shadows forming like a poisonous mist around her. The others stripped out of their tunics.

Larkin had just watched her family die a dozen times in a dozen horrible ways. She couldn't endure watching more murders and then be forced to murder. Panic reared up and struck.

Larkin tried to escape, but a vine slithered over her legs. She struggled, but she was too weak. "There has to be something you can do," Larkin gasped. "Tie me up. Cut off my arms and burn them. Something."

Eiryss unbuckled Larkin's belt. "You are not bound by the curse. You can fight back. Push him out."

Larkin cut through her panic to say, "How?"

"You're stronger than he is." Eiryss gently pulled Larkin's tunic over her head.

It was too late. The sun was gone.

Vicil began laughing manically even as the thorns grew over his shoulders, breaking first his right and then his left. "You'll never escape him."

Thorns wrapped around Larkin, pinning her. Ture and Ramass's bones snapped. They screamed, the sound ringing in Larkin's ears. Beside her, Hagath was reduced to a third her height.

The only one free of the vines, Eiryss shook her fist at the tree. "Stop it! Leave them alone!"

The vines crushed Larkin, her ribs caving in. She coughed up blood. It hadn't happened this way the first time. This was the Black Tree, showing them his displeasure.

CHAPTER

WATER

A traveler, murdered in the night by an assassin wielding a magical blade. A thief, his hand removed by another magic ax. He'd died from the infection spreading from his stump. His sister had died of thirst days later, her little body wrapped around the rotting corpse of her brother.

They'd died alone. In agony. And Larkin couldn't help them. Could only feel relief when they finally drew their last breath. Then, the vision was over, and all she was left with was hollow emptiness.

That emptiness was filled with helpless rage. Mankind had done this. Mankind was a disease. And she would end it. She welcomed the rage. It filled the nothingness inside her. Battered away her hurt and confusion and pain. Pain made her weak. Hate made her strong.

She sped through the Mulgar Forest. His trees told her stories. Stories of men hiding amid their trunks. Twenty Alamantians, in fact. But they were not her quarry. The Black Tree had a different prey in mind.

Just before she reached the Forbidden Forest, the shadows took her deep beneath the trees' roots. Larkin emerged on the banks of the Alamant as a mere shadow, like that cast by a cloud slipping over the moon.

The sun had set, but only just barely. The sky was a lurid purple, the clouds blowing in on the horizon orange and gold. Far to her right, a pyre of corpses smoldered, their skulls grinning at her from beneath the flames. The lake itself still teemed with the dead, the stench thick and cloying.

The Black Tree urged her onward. But she couldn't cross water. She paced the shore, the urge to move growing stronger and stronger until she couldn't resist a moment longer. Knowing she couldn't cross water, she resisted.

And then the Black Tree offered her the memory of a voice. *You are not bound by the curse.*

Larkin suddenly understood. She turned her gaze to the city. Beyond the wall, the tops of the trees gleamed with lampent light. Even from this distance, the quiet murmur of the inhabitants echoed over the still water.

There would be no sleep this night. Only death. "I am not bound by the curse." She smiled a wicked smile and seeped over the water with its bobbing bodies. At the wall, she scuttled up its smooth side, finding handholds that only a shadow could grip. At the top, she hid in the hollows of the branches.

A young sentinel paused, his head coming up. "Do you smell that?" he called to his partner, an enchantress a dozen steps away.

Larkin gripped the branches that made up the roof of the colonnade and pulled herself up, her negligent weight shifting the branches no more than a gentle breeze.

The white-haired enchantress came to stand beside the sentinel. "What?"

"I thought I smelled a wraith," the guard answered.

She sniffed, but it was too late. They were already downwind of her. "Wraiths can't cross water."

He shifted uneasily. "I know what I smelled."

"It was probably just the dead in the water." She turned and headed back the way she'd come.

The man ground his teeth. "You think I can't tell the difference?"

She sighed. "You want to sound the alarm—wake the whole city—for nothing more than a smell?"

Larkin waited. If the sentinel sounded the alarm, their mission would become much more difficult.

When he didn't relent, the white-haired woman sighed. "Signal the others to be on high alert."

He pulled out his pipes and played a melody that might have been nothing more than the wind through chimes, if not for the undercurrent of danger.

Favoring speed over stealth now, Larkin slid down the other side of the wall and roiled across the water, fish darting away from her unnatural presence—even if the humans were too stupid to recognize danger, their prey wasn't.

How she longed for the day when the monsters were all dead.

Larkin paused before the White Tree. She was still white, still glorious, but the colors that had lived beneath her bark had stilled. For a moment, the rage was gone, leaving the Black Tree's unassailable grief howling through her.

Grief was weakness. Anger was power. She latched on to the shadows' anger—the Black Tree's anger—letting it fuel her hunt. She scaled the tree as easily as she had the wall earlier; only this time, there were no guards to avoid. She bypassed the main platform, slipping up one of the side branches until she came to the portal. The same portal the king had last disappeared inside.

From within the shadows of the dead, she drew a single thorn that glittered with malice. One quick thrust, and it had embedded in the wood. For a moment, nothing happened. And then the graft sent out spiraling roots that tunneled through the White Tree's corpse, which would soon be possessed by the shadows. They would scour the city, destroying it in a single night.

By tomorrow, the very being the Alamant worshiped would be the source of their demise.

Having accomplished her main task, Larkin left the White Tree and crossed the lake. She found a familiar hometree and slipped past the enchanters at the docks. These men were wiser. They did not question their instincts. One of them lifted his pipes and began to play. Others soon joined him. The enchantresses flared their weapons. The tree shifted as more guards woke and shifted into position.

The Black Tree did not understand language, but music he knew. And this music tried to drive her back. To make her forget why she had come. But she had the magic of a queen. The magic of the White Tree. And the enchanters' familiar magic washed over her like a gentle rain.

Larkin found the chambers she wanted and seeped through the floorboards. She tore shadows from the world for a cloak and stepped into being.

Nesha lay on the bed, her auburn hair spread across the pillow and one hand beside her face. On her wrist was a newly inserted thorn sigil; the wound was still swollen and red. On the floor beside her, Soren and Kyden nestled in a basket.

Nesha's nose wrinkled slightly in distaste, and she shifted.

A thousand memories pulsed. Two girls giggling as they splashed each other in the shallows of the river, the water shocking and delightful. Running through a field of dandelions, the seeds rising like a cloud around them. Curling together beneath the safety of a blanket and promising to always protect one another as their father raged.

Anger and hatred still pulsed from where the thorns pierced her, filling her with memories of senseless death. Of humanity's failings. She wasn't killing anyone. She was saving them from a lifetime of suffering.

Her sword filled her hand.

In the basket, one of the babies wiggled, its mouth opening and closing again. Something about the mouth was familiar, like she had seen it before. The memory came in a rush. Bane's mouth pressed to Larkin's. She had frozen, too shocked to react.

He had pulled back. "Hurry. Before I lose too much blood."

Bane. His name echoed through her. She had loved him. Loved him still. And Larkin loved her sister and her nephew and her little brother.

She would not do this. She backed away, her sword winking out.

The Black Tree's full consciousness shoved its way inside her, taking over her body. The wraith lifted her sword. He was going to kill her family!

"No!" she screamed.

Nesha's eyes snapped open, and she gaped at the wraith towering over her.

"Roll!" Larkin cried.

Nesha shoved off the bed and onto the floor just as the sword cut the bed in half.

"Run!" Larkin tried to wrest control of her body back from the Black Tree. The shadow's thorns strangled her from the inside out.

Nesha scooped up the babies—one under each arm—and ran toward the doorpane.

"Miss?" One of the guards pounded on the barrier. "You have to open the pane!"

"Go!" Larkin cried, and then the Black Tree wrested control of her mouth.

The Black Tree rushed toward Nesha as she struggled to open the pane. The Black Tree drew back Larkin's arm for a killing stroke just as Nesha fell through. Larkin wanted to sob with relief. Four guards streaked into the room. Larkin recognized all of them—men and women who'd guarded her when she'd been queen.

Kill him! she screamed, her words silent.

The Black Tree scrambled back, leaped over the bed, and pulsed at the guards, who flew back. Larkin lunged for control, trying to distract him long enough for the guards to reach him. To kill him. He merely batted her aside. He cut a triangle through the floor, which dropped out beneath him.

They broke through the branches beneath and landed on a bough before Mama's chambers. Two guards stood before it.

The city's warning horn sounded, the sound resonating inside the Black Tree.

"What's going on?" Mama called from within the chambers.

Hide! Larkin tried to cry out, but she didn't have control of her body. Didn't even have a shape. She was merely a presence within a form.

Satisfaction rolled through the Black Tree. He wanted to take something from Larkin, just as she'd taken something from him. That's why he was here, attacking her family instead of Aaryn or Gendrin. Her suffering was more important than winning the war.

The Black Tree charged the guards.

You think mankind is a monster? she cried. *Look at what you've become!*

A sudden vision swept over her. A man killing an intruder in the night. As if the Black Tree was trying to tell her that he was only protecting what was his.

That's not the same!

The Black Tree pulsed, sending the guards careening. A distant splash confirmed that they'd hit the water. With their heavy armor on, they were sure to drown.

Larkin had to gain control!

The Black Tree's sword shifted to an ax. He chopped at the wooden supports that held the barriers in place, cutting through the right side and then the top. One more hit, and the whole thing would cave in.

Bright, hot pain exploded through her back. The shadows that held them together thinned. The Black Tree reached behind him and jerked a sacred arrow from between her shoulder blades. Another arrow clattered against the windowpane, sending it rippling. Another cut through his shadow cloak.

Two archers had taken up position in the branches behind him. Another two archers were running to join them. He flared his shield, blocking another arrow. Four soldiers ran at him. He pulsed them back, two falling into the water.

Two more hits, and he would die. Blood and cold shadows gushing from the wound, he ran to the other side of the chamber, the side facing open water. They couldn't sneak behind him here, and he had plenty more pulses.

He is going to kill Mama and Brenna. Fighting against him wasn't working. Larkin had to find another way to gain control.

Three chops at the supports, and the entire pane came down. He pushed inside and followed the baby's cries to the bathroom. Mama had bolted the door. Five swings of his ax, and he wrenched the ruined thing from its hinges. Mama, a sacred dagger in her hand, stood between the Black Tree and a screaming Brenna.

Mama's eyes widened, her breath coming fast. "Larkin?"

Even with the shadows cloaking Larkin, Mama had recognized her. She would die thinking a twisted version of her own daughter had killed her.

He tipped his head back, savoring Mama's fear. Reveling in Larkin's pain. He was like Vicil, she realized. He'd seen so much killing he'd grown to enjoy it.

"Larkin," Mama said. "We've always protected each other, you and I. Protect me now."

A rush of memories. Mama making Larkin a new shirt even though her own was in tatters. Mama giving her children the larger portion. Mama telling them to hide down by the river when Papa beat her. And something strange happened. The thorns binding her loosened. As if her love for Mama had weakened their resolve.

Booted feet sounded as sentinels entered Mama's chambers. Two more hits, and the Black Tree was finished. He rushed at Mama.

Larkin surged forward, managing to regain control of her mouth. "Stab him, Mama! Quick!"

Mama gripped the dagger with both hands and lifted it above her head. Larkin lost her hold. The Black Tree took control, his grip snapped around Mama's wrists. A knife formed in his hand.

Larkin would never forget the look of terror and forgiveness in Mama's eyes. This was Larkin's body. Not his. *You let him in; you can force him out.* It was as natural as breathing, to reach for her magic. The White Tree's magic. Magic that the Black Tree could no more touch than he could control.

From deep within, she pulsed. The thorns tore free, leaving her soul wounded. But she stepped fully into herself. For a moment, the shadows pulled back just enough to reveal her true self to Mama.

"I'm sorry, Mama." She formed her blade—a blade free of shadows. Before she could thrust it into her own chest, pain exploded from her back. The Black Tree dove back in, took back control. He turned enough to see Alorica behind her, face set with determination. The woman's sword was black with blood.

"If there's any part of you left," Alorica said through clenched teeth, "know that we won't let you stay this way." She drove her sword into Larkin's middle.

The shadows that held Larkin together broke apart, and she was sucked into the dark.

CHAPTER 42

HATE

The shadows spit Larkin out. Pain robbed her of a voice, reduced her to a blind, dumb beast. Naked, she rolled on her side to reduce the pressure on her gash, waiting for the bleeding to stop. The wounds to close. The scars to fade.

Visions swirled in her head. Visions of murder and abuse. But she had been able to hold on to herself through them. To realize they were moments of long ago.

The last of the pain faded, and her senses returned. Small bits of hail drummed painfully on her bare skin. She pushed herself up on shaking arms. She was somewhere in the boughs of the Black Tree. The world had shed its black cloak for a gray one. Thunder rumbled.

And then she remembered who she was—what she was—and what she had done. She had crossed the water—something that was supposed to be impossible for wraiths. She'd shoved a graft into the White Tree's corpse. A graft that would link the trees, allowing the shadows to enter the Alamant.

The Alamantians couldn't fight the shadows like they had the wraiths and mulgars—nothing could. She'd managed to spare her family, but their reprieve would be brief. By tomorrow, every man, woman, and child in the Alamant would be dead.

She'd always wondered why the Black Tree had hunted her so hard. Why she was worth more to him than a mulgar army.

Now she knew.

The horror of it—of the fact that she was the instrument of the demise of her people... "I should never have come here."

I want to go home. To die with my family and my people. She gripped Eiryss's amulet, wishing it was the one Denan had given her. That she had some piece of him with her. "I want Denan."

Tears traced her temples and soaked into her hair. She gave in to them, biting a hank of her hair to keep from making a sound—she had a lot of practice at silent crying. Harben wouldn't tolerate any sniveling from his girls.

But then she remembered what Eiryss had said. That there was a way to defeat the Black Tree. It had to be done today. Because if not... there wouldn't be a tomorrow.

Wishing she had something to cover her nakedness, Larkin pulled her long hair over her shoulders and hurried down the bough, the hail sharp beneath her bare feet. Aside from the swollen, sore spots of her thorn insertions, she was healed. The wind cut across the blood that smeared her, making her shiver.

She reached the main platform. A larger piece of hail struck her shoulder, sending an ache down her arm. Another piece glanced off her cheek. Blood welled. She needed to find Eiryss and get out of this storm.

Arms over her head to shield her, she ran for the little building and ducked inside. It was empty. A flash of lightning revealed shelves and bedding. The hail was larger now.

"Eiryss?" she called.

A strangled, choking rasp. Another flash of lightning revealed a crumpled shape on the steps to the font. Had one of the other wraiths come back?

Larkin grabbed a blanket off the bed, held it over her head, and rushed back into the storm. Lightning skated across the sky, revealing Eiryss's long silver hair, which shone like moonlight in the dimness.

Larkin knelt beside her, blanket over them both. Eiryss's face was in stark contrast to the shadows, her skin exceedingly pale. She gasped for breath.

"Eiryss? What happened?"

She was obviously hurt, but Larkin couldn't make out any injuries. "Did you fall?"

Eiryss reached blindly for Larkin. But instead of grasping, she shoved with all her strength. "Run."

Larkin went cold all over. She heard it then, the whisper of a boot against the moss. Dropping the blanket, she shot to her feet, wet hair swinging as she whirled around. Her sword and shield formed in her hands. Hail drummed her head, shoulders, and back, leaving bruises, welts, and cuts.

Dark, hooded shapes blocked any escape to the carriage or stairs. There were at least six of them. She was painfully aware of her nakedness. Idiotic to worry about such things in a time like this, but then, the mind did idiotic things when panicked.

"Who are you?" They couldn't be Denan and the others. Her wraith-self had sensed their group nearly two days away. But then, who else could it be? "Ancestors, don't you know the danger you're in?"

The shadows could come for them at any time. But... nothing happened. She reached for the darkness inside her, reached for that connection. She had a sudden vision of the shadows filling the White Tree. Of the Alamantians crying out in terror as their beloved tree turned black.

But the White Tree must have anticipated this, for she'd left row after row of barriers that the shadows were busy fighting through. That left only the wraiths free to fight. The Black Tree had called them back. Even now, they rushed through the Mulgar Forest with inhuman speed. They would arrive within minutes.

The intruders circled closer. She was hopelessly outnumbered. They couldn't kill her, but she couldn't protect them from the wraiths if she was dying.

Her instinct screamed at her to run, but she couldn't abandon Eiryss. *We can make it up the stairs behind the font.* With room for only one fighter at a time, Larkin could hold them off.

She reached for her grandmother. Two figures stepped up behind her. Too late. They were surrounded. It was too dark to make out their faces in the shadows of their hoods. Light, if she had barrier magic, she could seal them safely inside a dome. Hoping against hope, she tried to light her new sigils, but the only answer was a throbbing ache.

"Please," she begged. "The wraiths are coming. You need me."

Instead of answering, the hooded figures charged. Knowing she needed to lead them away from Eiryss—to give her time to heal so she, too, could fight—Larkin rushed the two standing between her and the carriage. They flared enchantress shields. She pulsed, her magic overpowering them and throwing them back.

She leapt over one of the fallen intruders' bodies and sprinted for the carriage a hundred yards away, the amulet thumping rhythmically against her chest. If she could ride down, she could reach the roots far ahead of them. Hide somewhere in the fen and ambush the wraiths before they reached the Black Tree.

Hail pelted her. One slammed into her eye, blinding it. An arrow stuck into the bark in front of her. Another zipped past her head. If one hit her, she was done for. They would capture her and kill her. Ignoring it all, she focused only on the carriage.

Ten steps away, someone stepped in front of her. She skidded to a halt, already turning to the next closest escape—the archway and the stairs beyond. But she quickly calculated the angles; her pursuers would reach it first.

She backed away from the person in front of her, angling until she reached the edge of the platform, nothing but the empty space beneath her. She considered jumping, but death by sword was less painful than that fall. A fall that would take far longer to recover from, leaving the wraiths plenty of time to take these people by surprise.

"The wraiths will be coming. I can protect—" She choked. Gasped. Blood spilled from her mouth. There was no pain, but she felt the broken bones; the arrow lodged in her left ribs, shifting slightly when she choked.

She tried to suck in a breath, but her lung was already full of blood. She coughed, black blood spewing from her mouth. She could feel death coming for her, looming dark and hungry.

A second arrow in her middle. Her body lost its strength. She fell backward, nothing but open air beneath her.

Light, this is going to hurt.

Hands grasped her arms, pulling her back to the safety of a warm embrace. His face was in shadows, but Larkin knew the smell of her husband—metal and paper and resin and leather. She knew how her body fit next to his.

"I promised I would always come for you." She could hear the tears in his voice. "And now I have."

"Denan," she gasped. "Please. I can't protect you if—"

Bright, hot pain in her chest. He'd stabbed her below her sternum, the knife going up into her heart. His hand was trembling; she could feel its vibrations through the blade inside her. He pulled it back and eased her to the ground.

"Larkin." He cradled her close. "I'm sorry. Sorry I failed you. Light, please forgive me."

She wanted to tell him that she understood. That she wasn't angry. That he didn't need to grieve because she couldn't die.

"I'll be all right," she managed.

And then her body went limp.

Denan broke. He sobbed and rocked her back and forth. Each movement shifted the arrows inside her, the pain robbing her of sight. Sound. Was this what Eiryss had felt when she'd been trapped in amber?

Larkin felt someone else's presence. "I'm sorry. We had her surrounded. But she got away."

She knew that voice. Tam.

Denan's answer was a keening wail that stabbed Larkin's heart all over again.

"Be at peace now, Larkin," said another low, masculine voice that was hauntingly familiar, but her overwhelmed brain couldn't place it. Someone else wrapped her in a cloak. Denan's cloak.

Flesh grew inside her, driving out the arrowheads and knife. Like hot pokers burning through her. She couldn't scream. Couldn't move. Could only burn and burn and burn.

After what seemed ages, the pain eased. She could see again. Hear again. That was how she noticed Eiryss creeping up behind the men, her hands working, her sigils gleaming like star-light.

Eiryss threw the weave. Light flashed, blinding Larkin. Something passed over her—something that felt a lot like passing through the barrier at the Alamant's city gates. Denan and the others were suddenly ripped away.

Larkin's back hit the bark, which triggered a cough. Blood spewed from her lips. She gasped in a breath and coughed again. Gasped and coughed. But she couldn't get enough air through her ruined lungs. She groaned when the hole in her lungs sealed.

A light flashed, so bright it blinded her. Shielding her eyes, she found herself and Eiryss locked within a small dome not far from the carriage, hail slamming against it. Her friends were scrambling up from where they'd been thrown.

The small dome rippled violently. A sacred arrow clattered to the ground. Melting bits of hail ran in rivulets across its surface.

"They won't get through." Eiryss pulled ribbons of light from her sigils and wove a pattern.

"Retreat!" Denan cried.

They scrambled to their feet, running for the stairs.

Larkin wanted to call out to them, but the pain was between her and the words. *Denan. Don't run. I can't protect you if you run.* The hole in Larkin's heart closed. Her broken bones righted themselves. She sobbed at the pain of it.

Eiryss made a throwing motion, and the ball of light grew so large it overtook the group and then sped past them. The enchantment formed a second dome around the entirety of the main platform, a dome that quickly faded to transparency. Now, Denan and the others were trapped within a larger dome that encapsulated Larkin and Eiryss's smaller dome.

Clearly not realizing what the light meant, one of them ran headlong into it and fell hard on their backside. Light rippled from the impact, which revealed Tam shaking his head and scrambling to his feet.

Of course it would be Tam. He was the quickest of them.

His back to her, another man stabbed at the larger dome, his sword skittering across its surface. "It's blocked!" a big man cried.

The group in the Mulgar Forest—they'd been a ruse. Something to keep the wraiths occupied while Denan and the others had sneaked into Valynthia. How had they managed to hide themselves?

Denan turned, his gaze darting about. "Spread out! Find another way down!"

Eiryss's face was screwed up with concentration as she gestured with her hands. Larkin wasn't sure at first, but then... yes. The dome trapping her friends was shrinking.

They ran around the platform, their swords dragging along the edge of the larger dome, which sent it rippling, the weave revealing itself. Wincing as if the contact hurt, Eiryss knelt beside Larkin and tugged up the cloak that had fallen off her shoulders.

The blood pouring from Larkin slowed to a trickle. The hail under her back was hard and freezing. She glanced at the dome. "Will it hold against the wraiths?"

Eiryss hesitated. "For a while."

Light! "Help me up."

Careful to keep the cloak around her shoulders, she staggered to her feet, her head spinning.

Denan must have realized the hopelessness of finding a weakness. They'd gathered nearest the stairway, about twenty yards away. All but Denan wore the pied cloaks of the pipers; Larkin was wearing his. Two were playing their pipes, the melody like water crashing against a cliff. The enchantresses pulsed. The larger dome bulged and snapped back, before shuddering back to normal.

It was light enough that Larkin could make out the shredded leaves littering the platform. The hail eased, intermixing with a dribbling rain. She was covered in bruises and welts from the cursed stuff.

"They're not doing much damage," Eiryss whispered. "But that larger dome is going to need all the strength it can get when Hagath gets here. It would help if I could let release this smaller dome."

"Stop it!" Larkin called to them. "Denan, it's me."

"Don't listen," Denan panted. "She is just like an ardent. You can't trust a word she says."

"If I wanted to hurt you," Eiryss said dryly, "you'd already be dead."

Denan stormed toward them, his eyes black and empty in a way she'd never seen before. His face was haggard, his hair filthy and matted. He looked thinner too. And when he finally turned his attention on her, there was hatred in his gaze.

He stabbed at her, would have killed her again, had Eiryss's smaller dome not been there.

Larkin flinched and backed away.

He paced before her like a caged animal. "If you mean us no harm, then let us go!" Denan never panicked. He truly believed he'd led his friends into a trap. That they were all going to die if he didn't get them out.

"The wraiths are coming," she cried. "The big dome is protecting you. Stop trying to destroy it!"

"The wraiths are coming?" he echoed in disbelief. He laughed, a bitter, humorless sound. "You *are* a wraith!"

He thought his wife dead. That she was the monster who had killed her. His words shouldn't hurt, but they cut to the bone.

Tears welled in her eyes. "Stop it." A hurt, frustrated tear slipped down her cheek, quickly followed by another. "Listen to me."

His eyes darkened with loathing. "Don't you dare pretend to cry. Don't you dare use her to manipulate me."

How could she get through to him? She reached for her connection to the shadows again. The wraiths had just crossed into Valynthia.

Larkin dropped to her knees. "Please, you have to listen," she begged.

Eiryss stepped between Larkin and Denan. Above her hand floated a ball that looked like molten lava wrapped in lightning. Larkin had never seen one before, but she'd seen the damage wreaked by one when Sela had used it on an ardent. This had to be an orb.

Eiryss's gaze fixed on the archway. "The wraiths will come through there." She pointed. "Get behind me."

"What makes you think I'd believe a word you say?" Denan asked.

Eiryss shot him a withering look and held out the orb. "If we were wraiths, you'd be dead by now."

He bared his teeth, seemed about to say something else, and then marched to the others, who huddled into a tight formation right by the archway. They all held their weapons at the ready, as if they expected Larkin and Eiryss to yank a cloak of shadows into being and attack.

They weren't watching the archway at all.

"Will the larger dome protect them?"

"Depends on how the wraiths attack," Eiryss said, the orb casting eerie shadows on her face. "Before you ask," Eiryss said under her breath to Larkin, "I can't make an orb big enough to destroy the tree. The big ones took an entire unit of enchantresses and enchanters from my time."

"Let the smaller dome down," Larkin said. "I'll try to draw them away from the archway."

"Not a chance."

Larkin glanced into the shadowed boughs, searching for the archer hidden somewhere up above. Was Sela with them? Larkin hoped against hope she wasn't.

Denan didn't bother answering. It was light enough now that Larkin could make out the other's faces even with their cloaks up. Denan, Tam, Atara, Caelia, and—

Larkin gasped. "Talox!"

Her friend stiffened and slowly shifted to look at her, his brow furrowed. The wicked cut cleaving his bottom lip had been stitched.

She choked on a sob. "You survived." The man who had become a monster to save her life. And now he was risking it again. Who else had come back from being a mulgar? "Venna?"

He hesitated before nodding once.

Larkin had held Venna while the humanity had drained out of her. Watched as her sweet demeanor had shifted to a savage, animal hunger for the death of all mankind. Had witnessed Talox's pain and guilt at her death. And now, he had her back.

Her voice broke. "My papa?"

She hadn't called him Papa since he'd abandoned them for another family. But he really had been trying to change.

Again, Talox hesitated. Then he shook his head.

"He's dead?" She had to hear it. Had to know for certain.

Talox wet his lips. "He didn't survive his wounds."

Light. Her last words with her papa had been sharp, cold ones. She'd been too hard on him. Expected too much. She tried to shove the knowledge into her frozen lake, but the ice was still broken and jagged. Her legs cut out beneath her. She buried her head in her hands and sobbed hard, gut-wrenching sobs.

Talox walked toward her. Denan grabbed his arm.

"One of us has to," Talox said.

"Then let it be me," Denan said.

Talox rested his hand on his friend's. "I was one of them. I know how they lie."

Denan hesitated before releasing Talox.

"Denan," Tam said. "You can't."

Denan ignored him. Talox came right up to the smaller dome, crouched before her, and scrutinized her. There was a heaviness to his gaze—a heaviness that reflected in her own eyes. No words were spoken, but in that moment, the pain of being used for evil linked them together.

"I remember everything," he whispered. "I remember capturing you. Turning you over to Ramass."

She shook her head. "That wasn't you." Any more than embedding a thorn into the White Tree was Larkin, but that didn't take away the guilt.

He rose to his feet, his gaze on Eiryss as he removed his weapons. "Let me through. I won't hurt her."

"The forest take you, Talox," Tam said. "We just got you back! What about Venna? Are you going to leave her again?"

Talox ignored him. Denan watched with a fierceness that took Larkin's breath away.

Eiryss studied him. "If you're not an enemy, the magic will know and let you through."

"Denan." Tam rounded on him. "You have to stop him."

But Denan stood so still she wasn't sure he was breathing.

Talox stepped through. He waited, as if to see if Eiryss would attack him. When she only watched him blandly, he knelt beside Larkin and gathered her into his arms.

She melted into his embrace, this man who'd been like the big brother she'd never had. "I'm so glad you got her back," she wailed.

He rubbed her arm. "You saved us both."

She cried even harder, so hard she couldn't see through the tears. Moments later, arms came around her, pulling her from Talox's embrace and into his lap.

She held on tight. "Denan."

Denan pulled her hair out of her face and kissed her temple. "Shh, my love. I'm here. I'm here."

CHAPTER

ORBS

Larkin was shocked at how much Denan had changed. His cheeks were hollow, his skin ashen, his eyes bloodshot. This is what her leaving had done to him. She clutched his rain-soaked tunic; she was so desperately afraid he would leave her again. "I won't hurt you. Please believe me."

He tucked her head under his chin. "I do."

Caelia came next, though she hung back. "Is it really you?"

Caelia should not have come. She had three little children—one an infant—who depended on her. None of them should have come.

"At first light," Larkin said, "you must leave this place. Run south and never look back." Ramass had said the world was wide. Maybe they could find a place far away from here. A place so far away even the Black Tree and his shadows couldn't reach them.

Atara stepped up next to Caelia and said dryly, "Not going to happen."

Denan held her tighter; his voice turned to steel. "I'm never leaving you again."

"I'm not leaving you either," Tam said, his arms crossed.

"You don't under—" she began.

"Larkin," Eiryss said sharply.

The intensity in her gaze made Larkin sit up straight. She felt it then. The wraiths had reached the tree. "They're coming."

"Who?" Tam asked.

"The other wraiths," Eiryss said. "Call down your archer."

"I'll get him," Tam said and ran out before any of them could stop him.

Larkin hoped they had time to return before the others came.

"Follow me," Eiryss said. As she walked, she banished the smaller dome and drew the larger dome closer still. It rippled as the raindrops scattered across its surface. They ended up standing just before the font, a good eighty feet from the archway.

Talox stepped back from the edge. "What are you doing?"

"Easier to defend a smaller space than a larger one, and now I have a clear field of view." The dome was only about a dozen paces across now. "All of you, light your sigils." The Alamantians obeyed, and Eiryss siphoned some of their magic into her weave. "Light, your magic is so slight."

Atara's eyes narrowed into a glare. "Then don't use it."

"Didn't mean offense," Eiryss said with an apologetic look. She tossed the weave up where it melded with the dome, which flashed before going transparent.

"They can break through?" Denan asked.

"Ramass or Hagath can," Eiryss said.

Atara started on the straps of her chest armor. "Caelia, help me."

Caelia moved to obey.

"What?" Talox asked, his eyes wide. "Why?"

"Because I have the longest tunic," Atara said.

The women had seen Larkin's need for clothing and taken care of it without even consulting each other. Larkin felt an intense sisterhood, a love for her fellow women and their intuition.

The two enchantresses busied themselves getting Atara out of her armor. She had on a quilted gambeson. Under that was her tunic. Her back to them, Atara tugged her tunic out from under her belted skirt and tossed it to Larkin.

As Atara and Caelia replaced the gambeson and armor, Denan held the cloak while Larkin pulled Atara's tunic on. His gaze caught on her embedding sites. Judging by the fear in his gaze, he knew what they were and where she'd gotten them.

"Larkin—" Denan began.

"It's all right." Larkin wrung rainwater out of her hair.

He eventually nodded; he clearly didn't like it, but he trusted her. Besides, they didn't have time for full explanations. The tunic went down to her knees. She was so relieved to be covered, she didn't even mind that it was damp with someone else's sweat.

Tam came back, bursting into the dome and bracing against his knees. "He won't come. Says we still need an archer."

"Who is it?" Larkin asked.

"West," Talox said grimly.

The forest take him. Always determined to protect her, no matter what. "The Black Tree knows where he is, and so will the wraiths."

Denan cupped his hands. "West, get—"

Before he could finish, a wraith shot up from the stairs and streaked toward them.

Eiryss smacked Denan to get his attention. "Too late now. He's better off staying where he is."

Denan bared his teeth, his grip tightening on his sword. Larkin knew he wanted to go after the man.

"Which one?" Talox asked.

"Ture," Eiryss said grimly.

Seeing him this way, knowing what she knew, changed everything for Larkin. Instead of seeing a monster, she saw the tortured shadows cloaking him. The soul-sucking sensation she felt upon looking at his face originated from the Black Tree that controlled him. Twisting him. Instead of horror, she felt pity.

"Took them long enough," Tam growled, clearly itching for a fight.

Eiryss frowned. "The shadows can't bring them back unless they're dead."

"They had to run back?" Atara asked.

Eiryss nodded.

Ture thrust at the dome repeatedly. Each time, it rippled, and a sliver of the weave became visible. An arrow cut through his shadow cloak and embedded on the other side of him.

He raised his shield and kept on cutting.

In an instant, Denan's face became that of a commander. "How long before the barrier breaks?"

"It's called a dome," Eiryss supplied. "Depends on when Hagath arrives."

Another hit, the dome shuddering with impact.

Eiryss's quick fingers tugged at the lights from her sigils. All the times the White Tree had shown her the weave, Larkin hadn't paid attention. She paid attention now. If the Black Tree's thorns took root and she gained control of this magic of Eiryss's, she'd need to know how to use it.

Another orb spun over Eiryss's palm.

"What is that thing?" Tam edged closer and reached toward the crackling orb. "Can I have one?"

Eiryss batted his hand away. "It's an orb, and no. Larkin, distract Ture. I'll try to hit him with this." She motioned the group. "The rest of you, stay here."

"Why?" Denan demanded.

"Because we can't die," Larkin shot back.

Denan stiffened in affront. "We've been battling wraiths our entire lives."

Atara, Tam, Caelia, and Talox lined up, their gazes set.

"We don't need nearly seven people to deal with one wraith," Eiryss said.

She'd no sooner said it than Vicil reached the top of the stairs, his shield over his head, and shot toward them.

"Not anymore," Atara said.

Eiryss made an exasperated noise as the second wraith attacked the barrier opposite Ture.

"Tam and Atara, stay behind me," Larkin said. "The rest of you take Vicil. If you get in trouble, return to the dome."

Not looking convinced, Tam lined up beside her. Caelia and Talox moved into position.

Larkin turned to go. A hand pulled her back.

Denan pressed a quick kiss on her mouth. "Don't ever leave me again."

He would be the one leaving her; she'd make sure of that. She wanted him as far away from the Valynthians as he could get before night fell. But she couldn't think about that now. She pushed him toward Talox and Caelia. "Stay alive."

Atara and Tam took up position behind her as Larkin flared her weapons. The wraiths had centuries of experience and unnatural speed and strength. She would have to strike swift and sure.

She dove through the dome into the rain and flared at the same moment Ture did. A thunderous bang. His wraith pulse slammed through hers, the percussions throwing her against the dome. Something cracked in her back. She slid down, unable to breathe or move.

Tam and Atara charged Ture. They fought, driving him back. Larkin's vision darkened, and she faded into unconsciousness. She woke when something snapped into place on her back. On the ground, Atara dragged herself toward the dome; determination lined her face. Tam positioned himself between her and the wraith.

Even as Larkin watched, the wraith's sword skidded off Tam's shield and drove into his thigh. Tam cried out and staggered back. Larkin's friend was about to die because she'd underestimated the strength of the Valynthians' superior magic.

She hauled herself up, forcing her feet to move. Something else snapped into place in her back, sending a bolt of pain up and down her spine. Suddenly, she could run.

She sprinted, jumping over Tam as he fell. Ture battered away her thrust and swung the top of his shield up toward her chin. She blocked its edge with her own shield, turning to drive his momentum down, which left his middle open. She whipped her sword up and into his chest. Black blood burst from Ture's wound, wetting her knees. The move would have killed a normal man.

Instead, his shadows flickered.

Two more hits. She tried to pull back, but her blade was stuck in his ribs. He lifted his sword for a killing stroke. She released her sword and grabbed his wrist, holding him with all her strength.

Ture stepped into her guard. She jerked back, but not before he headbutted her. He missed her forehead, instead connecting with her nose. Blood gushed, filling her mouth and staining her borrowed tunic. Pain flared, but it was distant, unreachable.

She'd managed to keep her hold on his wrist, but he was slowly driving her arms down. Overpowering her. She spat blood in his eyes and kneed his groin. He turned at the last moment, and she connected with his thigh instead. But his feet skidded on the soaked bark. His hands lost their grip enough that she was able to twist away. She called for her sword just in time to block a horizontal swipe.

He tried to draw his sword inward to slice the front of her legs. She dipped the point of her sword into the bark at their feet.

He drew back for a thrust. She lifted her shield to block. Her sword was stuck. She released and flared it again. His sword slammed into her shield, his superior strength again overpowering her. He kicked her in the chest again. She fell back, ribs broken, unable to draw breath or move.

Thunder grumbled behind him as he stood victorious above her. She'd lost this fight. He would kill Tam and Atara.

He lifted his sword, and an arrow slammed into his chest. *Thank you, West.*

Ture staggered back, shadows fading. And then he regained his footing and came at her again. This time, an orb hit him square in the chest, leaving a hole the size of her fist straight through him. Lightning flickered over his body. He convulsed and dropped. The dead boiled out of him and back into the tree, leaving him naked, mortally wounded, dumb, and blind.

Larkin winced at the pain he must be in. "Sorry, Ture." Hopefully, he heard.

Eiryss stepped into sight, grabbed Larkin's nose, and yanked it back into place with a pop. Her eyes watering, Larkin let loose a string of curses.

"I'll go help the others." Eiryss turned and ran off.

Larkin turned to find that Tam and Atara had made it back to the dome. Tam held Atara, her head on his chest. Blood soaked his leg. But the lost look in his expression as he stared off into nothing…

Larkin had held Farwin just like that. *No. She's all right. She has to be.* Larkin rushed inside and knelt over Atara. But her eyes were wide and staring.

"Atara!" Larkin cried. "No!"

"He broke her back with his shield," Tam said, his voice monotone. "When I grabbed her to turn her over, she died." He lifted haunted eyes. "How am I ever going to tell Alorica?"

ARMOR

From above, thunder rumbled, shaking even the tree. The dome trembled. Tam stared into nothing, clearly in shock. "I promised Alorica I'd look after her." He passed a hand down his face. "Light, I think I killed her."

If it was anyone's fault, it was Larkin's. "She died because I miscalculated Ture's strength." Larkin couldn't think about that now. Tam was losing too much blood. She unbuckled Atara's skirt armor—she wouldn't need it anymore—and strapped it tight above Tam's injury.

Eiryss stepped inside the dome. "We took care of Vicil. They're—" Her head whipped around to face the archway. "Get the others back inside."

Larkin didn't need to ask why. Ramass had set foot on the tree. She could feel it. Eiryss set about strengthening the dome. Talox, Denan, and Caelia were tying Vicil up.

"Get back inside," Larkin cried.

There must have been something in her voice because no one questioned her. The three of them abandoned Vicil and sprinted toward the dome. Larkin breathed a little easier when they stepped inside.

"What is it?" Talox asked.

"Atara!" Caelia knelt by her side and began searching for signs of life.

When she didn't find any, she hauled the woman into her arms and wept bitterly. Atara and Caelia had grown up together. Had been taken from Hamel at the same time.

Denan and Talox didn't ask any questions. How she died didn't matter. Only that she had. And with Tam injured, they were down two soldiers. There would be time for grief later.

If Larkin was going to see the rest of her friends survive this, she would have to do the same. She forced the loss and guilt back and faced the archway.

"Caelia!" Denan barked. "See to Tam."

Caelia wiped her tears. "Atara was the healer."

"Do it," he ordered.

Swallowing back her tears, Caelia reached into a pouch tied to Atara's waist, pulled out bandages with shaking hands, and bandaged Tam's wound. Lightning flashed in the distance.

"Why are we hiding?" Talox panted.

"Hagath is on the tree," Eiryss said.

"And Ramass," Larkin added.

Talox made a slashing motion with his sword, as if to cut her words in two. "We've been dealing with Hagath and Ramass for centuries."

Eiryss wove another orb. "The Black Tree has held many things back, waiting for the right time to use them."

"Hagath can make orbs," Larkin guessed.

"An orb that will break your dome," Denan said.

Lips thin, Eiryss nodded.

"Light and ancestors," Talox swore.

Denan glanced up at the gray clouds churning above. "Sunrise isn't far off."

Eiryss pursed her lips. "Not close enough."

His wounds nearly closed, Ture dragged himself toward them. Talox rushed out and carried him back. He set him down. Suddenly, Tam was moving, screaming, driving his sword into Ture's middle.

Larkin pulsed, sending Tam flying back. He hit the inside of the dome and scrambled back to his feet. Denan stepped in front of him and grabbed his tunic. "Stop!"

"I didn't protect her," Tam cried. "I failed them both."

Denan shook him. "You also promised Alorica you'd bring Larkin back. Remember?" Tam rocked back and forth. Denan shook him again. "You can't break, Tam. Not again. We need you." Tam stopped shaking, then seemed to waver. Denan shoved him toward Talox, who caught and held him. "Fall into line. Now!"

Tam's gaze shifted again to Ture, rage flashing. Denan shoved him again. "You're a soldier, and you will obey orders!"

Tam bared his teeth, jerked out of Talox's grip, and faced the archway. He gripped his hilt, his knuckles white. Blood trickled down his leg. She wasn't sure how he was standing, let alone not limping. Except, maybe wherever he was now was a place beyond pain. And that place was better than the madness and despair of moments ago.

Talox and Denan shared a look of profound relief.

Larkin knew she'd just had a glimpse into the horrors they'd suffered together. The battles they'd won and lost. How they'd kept each other together and alive. The friends who never came home. Was that why Tam rarely slept? Why he clung to banter and jokes to keep himself from falling into despair?

Light, the horrors these good men had suffered. Were still suffering. It had to end.

Choking back tears, Caelia closed Atara's eyes and folded her hands over her middle. Except for her profound stillness, she looked like she was sleeping. The holes in his side closing, Ture rolled over and tried to stand. Fell back.

Talox set Ture on his feet, but he didn't let go of his shoulder. "I'm sorry. He doesn't understand."

Talox did. He'd been a monster too.

Ture shook his head. "I've been where he is." Tears welled in his eyes. "If it makes him feel better, he can stab me all he wants."

Nodding, Talox gave Ture his cloak and belt, which Ture used to tie the cloak around his waist.

What had Talox done while an ardent that Larkin knew nothing about? She decided she didn't want to know.

Music, eerie and dark, crept through the platform and tiptoed down Larkin's spine. Searching for the source, she turned in a slow circle. It seemed to be coming from everywhere.

And then Hagath and Ramass stepped up the stairs. Hagath played her pipes, drawing streamers of magic from Ramass's sigils as well as her own. They stopped in the center of the platform, about fifty yards away.

An arrow flashed down, narrowly missing Ramass. Hagath formed a dome over her and kept working. Ramass flowed up the stairs to his left.

Tam tried to run after him. Talox held him back. "There's nothing we can do for him."

Larkin wouldn't abandon West. "I'll go." It wasn't like the wraiths could kill her. Just take her out of the fight for a while. Larkin had only made it two steps when Ramass reappeared, blood dripping from his sword. There was only one reason Ramass would be returning this soon.

West was already dead, and he'd died alone. Everything inside Larkin stilled.

Tam beat against the dome. "No!"

428

A crackling, tearing sound. Before Hagath's upraised hands, a churning mass of black, smoking shadows bound with black lightning came into being. A dark orb that grew to the size of a small melon.

If Eiryss's orb was enough to burn a hole through a man, how much damage could one ten times that size do?

Talox forced Tam away from the edge of the dome.

"The forest take us," Caelia swore. "They get bigger?"

"They used to be the size of a house," Ture said.

"Light, that would have destroyed a city," Talox said.

"It did." Eiryss maneuvered herself between the group and the orb. "Stay behind me." Her sigils gleamed silver as she weaved an orb of her own.

She meant to shield them with her own body. Well, she wasn't the only one who couldn't die. Larkin took her place beside her grandmother. Still healing from his wounds, Ture shuffled up to stand beside them.

Sweat ran with the rain down Eiryss's face to stain her tunic. Her grandmother was terrified. But not for herself. "They never should have come," she murmured.

Fear felt fuzzy and sharp in Larkin's gut, like gripping fistfuls of thistle flowers gone to seed. "There has to be something we can do."

Eiryss hitched a shoulder and wiped at the damp on her temple. "I'll hold them off as long as I can."

It was clear Eiryss didn't believe it would be long. There had to be another way. Larkin studied Hagath and Ramass. Or rather, the Black Tree possessing their bodies. Hagath was siphoning off Ramass's magic while he stood guard over her. If Larkin could distract him—make him use his magic—it might weaken the orb. Her weapons flared, and she moved to leave the dome.

Denan grabbed her from behind. "Larkin—"

"I can't die," Larkin said.

"You might if that orb blasts you into a thousand pieces!"

Larkin opened her mouth to argue when a sound like a clap of thunder had her covering her ears and gasping in pain. Lightning arced across the dome, which reverberated, cracks appearing in the surface, the weave distorting.

Hagath had thrown the orb and was already forming another. Larkin needed to get out there.

Denan tightened his grip. "Larkin!"

Larkin searched her husband's frantic gaze. "The dome won't survive another hit."

Denan must have understood what she wasn't saying: that if they didn't do something, all the Alamantians were going to die.

Denan released her. "We'll go together."

"You're not going without me." Caelia flared her shield as large as it would go. Talox took his place beside her. Tam grinned, a wild, ferocious thing that truly frightened her.

Larkin's instinct was to argue—unlike the Valynthians, the Alamantians were vulnerable. But then, if they didn't stop those wraiths, they'd all be dead.

"Your best chance of survival is if we all work together," Ture said.

"We'll try to flank them." Judging by Denan's grim expression, he clearly didn't like their chances but knew they didn't have a choice. He looked them over as if memorizing each of their faces for recall later.

But maybe some of them will survive, Larkin thought. *And then run somewhere far, far away from all this.*

Larkin, Caelia, and Ture formed a shield wall. Denan, Tam, and Talox lined up behind them.

"The next hit will shatter the dome," Eiryss said. "After it does, charge. When you're close enough, pulse. I'll reform a dome for you to retreat to."

The Alamantians looked to Denan. He nodded in agreement.

"Remember—" Eiryss began.

An explosion swallowed up whatever she'd meant to say. Larkin managed to keep her feet through the blast. Ashes like burning paper fell around them and mixed with the slashing rain. Larkin, Ture, and Caelia raced forward, their shields before them and the men on their heels.

"Look out!" Ture shouted.

Hagath's orb flew toward them.

Larkin braced behind her shield. "Pulse!"

She and Caelia pulsed. A brilliant flash of light. The orb connected. Heat and lightning bit through Larkin's shield. Tongues of fire licked her hands. She smelled burning hair. A second later, lightning locked teeth around her body. Her jaw clenched. One of her molars cracked in two. But she couldn't utter a sound.

When it was finally over, she dropped to a puddle on the ground. Caelia and Ture lay in heaps beside her, their wet clothes steaming.

Eiryss appeared above them, the dome weave half formed. "Charge them!"

Denan, Tam, and Talox raced forward. Larkin tried to stand but only managed to brace herself on locked arms. That orb had blasted through most of her magic, but she managed a small shield.

Another orb swirled above Hagath's hand. The enchanters were only halfway across the platform. They wouldn't reach the wraiths in time.

Then the dome around the wraiths suddenly burst apart in a shower of lightning. Hagath jerked. Her shadowy sigils flickered. She stumbled, revealing a sacred arrow in her back.

West? Had he somehow survived? But no, the angle was all wrong. This arrow hadn't come from above but behind.

Backlit by the coming dawn, Sela stood in the archway, an orb forming in her hand. And, ancestors save them, Garrot stood by her side. He loosed another arrow, which struck Hagath in the throat. Her shadows grew tattered and moth-eaten.

Ramass sprinted toward them. Sela threw the orb, striking him in the chest. He tipped back his head and roared, the sound raw and grating against Larkin's ears. A moment later, the Alamantians were on him.

Always the fastest, even now, Tam slid on his knees under the wraith's guard, his sword stabbing up and into his guts. Ramass kicked his injured leg and stabbed down, but Denan blocked the blow. Talox hammered into Ramass's arm, which broke with an audible crack.

The two men drove the wraith back. Larkin tried to stand, but her body betrayed her, and she fell back into the puddle. Tam made it halfway up before his leg gave out. Hagath screeched, a terrible, insect sound. She rushed Tam.

Garrot shifted his aim to Hagath, released another arrow. And missed.

Tam tried to stand again, but his leg wouldn't bear his weight. With a rabid smile, he spread his arms wide, as if welcoming Hagath.

Larkin's cracked molar sealed together with a snap. Swallowing a scream, she pushed clumsily to her feet. She had to help him. Had to save him. Before Larkin could take a step, Hagath brought her sword down.

"No!" Larkin screamed as the wraith's sword connected.

Only the sword didn't cut Tam.

Instead, he shimmered with rippling light, the weave glittering with gold and scattered rainbows. He was armored with White Tree magic. In the next second, a sheen of armor settled against Larkin's skin.

Sela.

Sela had armored them all.

Hagath whipped around and ran half a dozen steps toward Sela. Garrot put an arrow in her thigh. The shadows ripped open, and the true Hagath spilled out. Talox rammed Ramass with his shield and knocked him off his feet.

He rolled, coming up to run away from them. The enchanters were a half step behind him.

"Let him go." Sela's voice was calm and clear—exactly the opposite of how a five-year-old should sound in this situation.

Let him go? Why would Sela say such a thing?

The men ignored her. Larkin staggered to Tam and knelt at his side. He lay, staring up at the sky with that blank look on his face again.

Ramass rushed up some side stairs and suddenly cried out. The dead sizzled in the sunlight. Flames erupted across his body. Flames that turned to burning orange embers. Those embers fell away, and the true Ramass tumbled down the steps, his body blackened and burned to the bone.

Denan reached him first, his sword drawn back.

"Don't!" Larkin shouted.

Denan stood over Ramass, his gaze fierce. As if he couldn't turn off his predator instinct. "He killed West!"

"The Black Tree killed him," Larkin cried.

Talox reached Denan and rested a hand on his friend's shoulder. Denan took one reluctant step back and then another. He let out a long breath and pulled a shaking hand through his soaked hair.

"It's all right," Ramass said through ruined lips. "I understand."

Shuddering, Denan looked away.

Caelia had managed to sit up. Her clothes were still steaming, and weeping blisters covered her hands and upper arms. "Everyone all right?"

Tam lay on the bark, his expression blank. "I guess we won." He was still bleeding.

"Hagath!" Larkin cried.

The woman was the only healer they had left.

The arrows shuddered out of her. "The font," she managed.

Eiryss was already running toward them with a cup full of sap. She pressed it to Tam's lips. "Drink it all."

He stared at her with hatred in his eyes.

Denan stood over him. "That's an order."

Tam bared his teeth at Denan.

Larkin ran her hand over his damp curls. "Do it for Alorica."

Some of the savageness left his eyes, and he drank it. Eiryss took the cup from him and poured the contents on the deep stab wound on his leg. Ture handed another cup to Caelia. "It will help with the burns."

Larkin sat down hard and looked around. Four of them had survived the night. Thanks to Sela and Garrot.

Sela.

Her baby sister was *here*.

CHAPTER 45

WHITE TREE

Larkin rushed to Sela and lifted her sister into her arms. She pressed her nose to her hair and swore she could smell sunshine and daisies and... mud. For all her sister had changed, she still smelled like the little girl Larkin remembered.

Sela remained stiff, her arms dangling as if she didn't know what to do with them. She may smell like a little girl, but she wasn't one. Not anymore. A pang echoed through Larkin's heart.

Why was she here? And with Garrot, of all people?

The Black Druid's gaze jumped from Ramass to Hagath and back to Ture. Thankfully, Vicil was nowhere to be seen. Garrot was clearly shocked to find humans instead of wraiths, but he didn't ask any questions.

Motioning for his Alamantians to hang back, Denan jogged toward Larkin. But it wasn't Larkin he was looking at. His hard gaze was fixed on Garrot. "I ordered you to return to the others." He had to be referencing the pipers in the Mulgar Forest, the ones he'd used as a diversion while he and his group had advanced. "So instead you followed us?"

Denan came toe to toe with Garrot. "Your obedience was the condition upon which you were allowed on this expedition."

They must have really needed volunteers.

"I don't take orders from you." Garrot motioned to Sela. "I take orders from her."

"How could you bring her? She's just a child."

Garrot's hands fisted at his side. "The same reason you brought her to the Mulgar Forest: because I had to."

Lightning arced across the sky. Denan shifted slightly. Larkin had sparred with her husband enough to know he was about to hit the druid. She released Sela, pushed herself between the two men, and stared Denan down. "Why did *you* risk her like that?"

"Because I'm the only one who could protect them from the shadows," Sela said to Larkin. She shifted her attention to Denan. "And as I've told you before, I have to be here."

The amulet gave me visions sometimes, Eiryss had said. *Visions of you, Larkin. And your sister Sela. Both of you breaking the curse.*

"You will take her back to the others and flee to the Alamant," Denan said. "Now."

Larkin pressed a hand to his chest. "I think— I think she has to be here."

He swung wide, disbelieving eyes to her.

Larkin crouched before her sister. "You knew? You knew all along we would all have to come here. That *I* would have to come here."

A guilty look crossed Sela's face. "She's had this plan in motion for centuries." *She* being the White Tree. "Just waiting for the right players to come along and make the right decisions."

Denan moved closer to Larkin. She recognized the gesture for what it was—his support. She pushed to her feet, and he wrapped an arm around her shoulders. Light, she'd missed him.

"All this time." She tried to banish the hurt from her voice. "You knew that I would trade my life for Denan's. That I would become a wraith... what that meant, that Denan would come after me and bring you with him. And you didn't bother to tell me?"

Sela glanced up at Garrot. "Join the others."

Garrot didn't question her. Denan glared at the druid as he stepped past. Larkin tensed—Garrot had saved their lives, but that didn't erase what he'd done. Nor did it make her trust him.

When he was out of earshot, Sela continued, "We refused to force you, Larkin. Merely gave you the opportunity to rise to the occasion."

We. Not I.

Maisy had called herself "we" once as well. It all suddenly made sense. "You're possessing my sister, just like the Black Tree possesses me." *And Maisy.* But then, why was she there during the day?

Sela folded her arms. "We're friends. We share this body."

No one has that right! Larkin was so angry she couldn't speak. Couldn't move.

"Get out of her," Denan said, his voice low, dangerous.

Sela's eyes changed—turning white with flashing colors. Her voice changed too, becoming more whispery, like wind through leaves. This wasn't her sister anymore. This was the White Tree. "How is this any different than the sigils I gave you? Or the visions?"

Larkin curled her hands into a fist to keep from trying to shake the White Tree out of her sister. "You have no right to steal her childhood!"

"Or to use her as a tool," Denan said. "You got into her, so get out!"

Sela held Larkin's gaze. "I can shift my soul, not eliminate it. There's nowhere else for me to go."

Larkin huffed as she rose to her feet. "You will go right now."

Those white eyes hardened. "Then you will all die."

"You're already dead." Larkin wiped rain from her nose.

"Part of me is," the White Tree answered.

"What does that mean?" Denan asked.

The White Tree frowned. "My soul is not like yours. It can be split, grafted onto something new. The individual trees of the forest and the monarch sigils, they are each a piece of me."

Which explained why the Black Tree could possess so many at once. And what Larkin had done last night. "The Black Tree is possessing your body."

Sorrow filled Sela's eyes. "I'm like the mulgars now."

"What?" Denan asked.

Light. Light, the suffering this one deranged tree had caused; it was simply too massive. Larkin couldn't understand the breadth of it. She couldn't repeat it over and over again. She'd wait until she'd gathered everyone.

Denan turned back to Sela. "Why didn't you just tell us all this?"

"I am not a human. My thoughts are not in words but memories. It was only after I bonded with Sela—a child—that I began to understand language and how... truly disconnected all of you are."

Sela's eyes shifted back to their familiar emerald green. "You were so happy, Larkin," she said in a small, childlike voice. "I didn't want you to be scared."

Even with the chaos, the time Larkin had with Denan and her family had been the best of her life. Sela had been trying to protect her—to give her a gift. Larkin softened a fraction. Denan's arms around her tightened. His open gaze said he was thinking the same thing.

Denan nodded, and the three of them headed toward the others. Eiryss and Ture tied up Vicil, the smoking hole in his chest indicating Eiryss had sent an orb through him—Larkin was shocked that she'd heard nothing of it. Ramass wrapped Caelia's burnt hands. Tam lay where they'd left him, Hagath stitching his wound. Garrot stood off to the side, watching them, his expression unreadable. Talox was nowhere to be found.

Denan, Larkin, and Sela crossed to stand over Tam and Hagath.

"How is he?" Larkin asked.

"I've cleaned out the chips of bone and stitched it." Hagath wore one of her tunics, which was dark in places from her own blood. Ture returned from the shelter with strips of torn cloth—clearly one of the shirts—which he handed to his wife.

Hagath set about bandaging Tam's leg. "He needs to stay off it for at least a week."

"Which one of you is waiting on me hand and foot?" Tam laughed shrilly at his own joke. Then his veneer fell away, leaving behind dark bitterness. "Just give me something so I can fight. I know you have it. Healers always do."

Hagath gave him a disapproving frown and motioned to Ture.

He went to the font, drew the dregs of sap, and poured it into four vials. He offered one to Tam. "Any more than this, and you'll be drunk with it."

Thunder cracked as Tam downed one vial and stuffed the rest in his pocket.

Movement in Larkin's periphery caught her attention. Talox descended the stairs with West in his arms. West's neck arched at a painful angle, his arms swaying unnaturally.

Unable to bear it, Larkin turned away. Caelia began to cry softly. Denan hung his head. Tam cried out and tried to stand. Hagath attempted to calm him.

Ramass went to Atara's body and picked her up as well.

"No!" Tam pushed to his feet despite Hagath. "Don't you touch her! Don't you dare touch her!"

Denan stepped in front of Talox. "It wasn't them, Tam. It was the Black Tree."

Tears streaming down his face, Tam turned toward Talox. "Stop him."

Talox finally looked up and met his friend's gaze. "I was there—at Ryttan. I killed dozens of my own people. Some were friends. I—" His voice broke. "I can't imagine bearing that burden for as long as they have."

All the fight drained out of Tam, and he sagged against Denan.

Larkin had so much to tell them. But it would have to wait. They had to bury their dead first.

CHAPTER 46

PLAN OF ATTACK

The rain had stopped, though it was still overcast. West and Atara's bodies lay side by side on lashed-together strips of driftwood, a boat grave. This was the Idelmarchian funeral custom, and the sight brought tears to Larkin's eyes.

She combed West's mustache over his top lip, the ends trailing down his chest—just the way he liked it. Caelia rebraided Atara's hair and placed a dagger in her hand. The rest gathered leaves to cover their bloody bodies—there wasn't time to sew their shrouds.

They would have hated being buried together, Larkin thought. They were not overly fond of each other to begin with.

Finished, the group looked at Larkin and Denan expectantly. Denan took his place at the head of the bodies, and Larkin slipped in beside him and held Sela's hand.

"The greatest testament of love is a man who has laid down his life for his people." Denan eyed them. "They died for us. To

441

honor that sacrifice, we must live our lives in the same manner; we must love our fellow men enough to die for them. And perhaps harder still, that we live for those we've lost. Live so that when we meet again, they will be proud to call us friends."

Tam broke down crying. Tears streaming down her face, Caelia slipped her hand into Atara's.

Denan closed his eyes. "May my life and my death be as honorable as yours."

That left Larkin. She struggled to maintain control and then leaned forward. "Wherever you are now, I hope you've found peace."

She reached out and kissed both their cheeks. Their skin was still warm. Eiryss and Hagath took out their flutes and played a funeral dirge, one that made tears stream down Larkin's face.

It was time to push the funeral boat into the water, but Caelia wouldn't let go of Atara's hand.

"Caelia," Larkin said gently.

"Even after the whole town turned against me, she stood by my side." Caelia wiped her cheeks. "I killed a wraith—or thought I did. Did you know that?"

Larkin shook her head.

Caelia sniffed. "I did it in her memory. Her honor. Imagine how thrilled I was to find my dearest friend alive after all, waiting for me in the Alamant." She bent down and pressed a kiss to Atara's cheek. "I'll do it again, Atara. For real this time."

She finally released her and stepped back. The five remaining Alamantians dug their shoulders into the raft, launching it into the lake. Larkin hoped she lived long enough to tell their families how they died. They deserved to know.

One by one, the others drifted away. Caelia reached out, taking Larkin's hand. The two of them watched the raft until it moved out of sight beyond the trees.

It was done, and Larkin would never see them again. At least not in this life.

Above, the storm broke, the clouds scattering. "Come on," Larkin said to Caelia. "We can't mourn them. Not yet."

The two of them turned toward the others. The Valynthians had prepared another meal of fish, waternips, and gobby. The Alamantians clustered to the opposite side of the fire, most sitting on or leaning against large pieces of driftwood, gorging themselves.

Garrot sat apart from both groups, Sela asleep with her head on his lap. Larkin bristled at the sight. He'd killed her best friend. Nearly killed her. He had no right to touch any member of her family.

But then, Sela had been alone with him for at least a day. *Garrot is calculating but not cruel.* Larkin decided to keep an eye on him but let her sister sleep. For now.

Denan started toward the group, but Larkin held back, dreading what she had to tell them.

"Larkin?" Denan asked.

Sighing, Larkin sat gingerly on the bark between Tam and her husband and leaned against the driftwood. She took a handful of waternips for herself and passed the rest along.

She couldn't help but notice how the Alamantians watched the Valynthians warily. She couldn't blame them. It was disorienting, having the monsters that had nearly destroyed mankind turn out not to be monsters at all.

Beside her, Denan wolfed down his fish without bothering to wait for it to cool. This was clearly the first hot meal he'd had in a while. Judging by how thin he'd grown, probably the first full meal too.

Time was running out. Larkin couldn't put it off any longer. She leaned forward, elbows on her knees. "I know why the Black Tree hunted me so ruthlessly." Everyone's gazes snapped to her. She swallowed hard. "When the curse was formed, Eiryss was safe behind a dome. She wasn't cursed, nor was the child inside her. I'm descended from that child."

She took a deep breath, gathering up her courage. "I crossed the water into the Alamant last night. I went to the White Tree and embedded it with a thorn—a thorn that will connect the two trees. Shadows were already filling it when I left. When night falls, those shadows will be released into the Alamant."

Denan stiffened. "You're saying the shadows we faced in the Mulgar Forest last night will attack our homes? Our families?"

"Without Sela to protect them," Talox said, "they won't last the night."

All my fault.

The Alamantians reacted instantly. Tam pulled at his hair, repeating Alorica's name over and over and over.

"My babies," Caelia cried, her hand over her mouth.

Talox and Denan hung their heads.

The Valynthians remained silent, varying expressions of horror on their faces.

"Was anyone hurt?" Ramass asked.

"The Black Tree tried to force me to kill my family," Larkin said. "But I was able to slow him. I even broke free a little."

"What do we do now?" Ramass asked Eiryss.

But it was Sela who answered, "We have to kill the Black Tree."

Sela pushed herself off Garrot. Her white irises danced with colors. Not Sela at all—she was probably still asleep.

Eiryss regarded her. "I know what you are." Clearly, Eiryss had recognized the preternatural light in Sela's eyes. "I saw that you would come."

Ramass looked at her questioningly.

"What's left of my consciousness resides in Sela's body," Sela said.

444

Only it wasn't really Sela. This was the White Tree speaking through Sela's lips. Larkin had to remember that, to call her that. She clenched her teeth to keep her accusatory words back.

"Are you sure your body has had enough rest?" Garrot followed the White Tree, clearly concerned.

"It will have to be enough," she said.

The way the two interacted, as if they'd confided in one another, made Larkin's blood boil.

The White Tree came to stand before Larkin. "The Black Tree isn't the only one who can penetrate a sacred tree. I'm going to bore a hole into him—into his heartwood. The rest of you will protect me until I've gone deep enough."

"How long will it take?" Ture asked, his expression filled with dread.

"I'm not sure," the White Tree said. "Long after nightfall."

The Alamantians would have to fight the wraiths again. Fight her. Looking at her exhausted friends... Some of them wouldn't survive. They might not succeed at all. Could Larkin force the Black Tree's shadows out in time to protect her friends? She would have to. She couldn't face losing any more of them.

"Then we don't have a choice," Denan said. "We have to kill the wraiths again. Turn them back into humans."

"This won't be taking on one or two wraiths at a time like last night," Larkin said. "We'll all appear at once."

"Sela can shield us," Caelia said. "Like she did before."

"I might not have enough magic as it is," the White Tree said. "I cannot spare some to protect you."

Silence hung heavy and dark over the group.

"We do what we must," Talox said.

"Can't we just tie you up?" Tam asked miserably.

"No bond exists that the shadows cannot break," Ture said. "And no matter where we run, the shadows will find us and drag us where they want us to go."

Ramass leaned forward. "Eiryss will create a dome to protect Sela while she drills into the Black Tree."

Denan nodded. "The rest of us will take down the wraiths."

"When we're human," Ramass said, "Eiryss will take as much magic as she can hold and shoot the biggest orb she can make down the hole. Over and over, until she's reached the heartwood."

"Where does that leave me?" Larkin asked, knowing there was more. After all, Eiryss has said it would take Larkin and Sela both to break the curse.

"You will use your warrior and barrier magic to finish him," the White Tree said.

"How?" Larkin asked.

The White Tree moved toward the carriage. "Come with me."

Not quite understanding the dread that filled her, Larkin started to obey but paused when Denan made to go with her. "Get some rest. You're going to need it."

He wavered, clearly exhausted, but there was also real fear in his eyes. He opened his mouth to say something and then glanced self-consciously at his friends. "You might need me."

Larkin had never seen him so unsure. And she knew why. He was afraid to let her out of his sight. Was this one of the consequences of her actions?

She gave him a gentle smile. "I can't die, remember?" He deflated and finally nodded. She kissed his cheek. "I'll be right back.

Larkin quickly caught up to the White Tree.

"The Black Tree and I searched for someone like you for a long time, Larkin. The Black Tree found many who were close—Maisy, for instance. She had the lineage."

The White Tree stepped into the carriage. "We're both lucky I found you first. Lucky that you pricked your hand on a thorn in my forest. I recognized your blood—it's all in the blood, you see. That's how I knew your lineage. Your determination. That's why I gave you a bit of my magic."

Larkin had guessed as much. "I wish you would have chosen someone else's body to inhabit."

"My presence would have driven another mad, but not Sela. She was lonely, desperate for a friend, and young enough not to break."

Larkin hadn't known Sela was lonely. Vulnerable. Another wave of guilt slammed into her. This time, it turned to anger. She stepped inside and slammed the door. "Surely you have other descendants to choose from."

The White Tree watched her as if she didn't understand.

Larkin pulled the lever. The carriage began its journey up. She gripped the bars of the carriage and stared over Valynthia. The water shimmered in the morning light. The heat was rising. It would be a beautiful day for a swim. And suddenly, she remembered Bane. How he'd taught her to swim, his hands at the small of her back and her thighs. The bright sun filtered through the leaves to spin off the top of the water. His voice was muffled from the tinkling water filling her ears.

His death had been like those the Black Tree had shown her. Wrong. Heartbreaking. Unfair. What she wouldn't do to go back in time and change things.

The carriage arrived at the main level.

Larkin wiped the tears from her cheeks. "What must I do?"

The White Tree stood on tiptoe to unlatch the carriage gate. She crossed the main platform toward the font, then diverted into the little building and came out with a cup. They climbed the steps to the dais.

The White Tree circled it slowly, dipped in the cup, and held it out for Larkin. "Drink the sap."

Larkin didn't want anything from the Black Tree inside her. "Why?"

"To dull the pain."

Light, hadn't Larkin endured enough pain for one lifetime? Taking a deep breath to steel herself, she took the cup, hesitated, and then gulped it down. She was surprised that it tasted the same as the White Tree's sap—sweet and resiny with a mineral finish.

Within minutes, her head felt tingly and light, and the world was painted with rainbows.

"Kneel down," the White Tree said.

Larkin knelt before her. The White Tree placed the heel of her palm on Larkin's forehead and closed her eyes. Warm, buzzing magic nudged into Larkin's head, her face. It spread downward, and when it met her sigils, they lit up with joy.

When Larkin's whole body was alight with it, her newly embedded thorns began to feel warm. Then they grew, tunneling beneath her skin. The pain was there, but the sap kept it bearable. When the White Tree was done, Larkin peered at her legs, arms.

Beautiful curving vines and flowers and geometric shapes covered her limbs. She flared them experimentally, and they gleamed like liquid silver beneath her skin, with none of the shadows of the Valynthians' sigils.

"You cleansed them?"

The White Tree nodded. She looked tired, as if the magic had cost her. "Never before has a human borne both warrior and barrier magic."

Larkin looked from the beautiful sigils to her sister. "What must I do with them?"

"Do you remember the dream I gave you of working in your father's fields, your scythes felling wheat?"

Larkin hadn't known that dream came from the White Tree. "Yes."

"First, you must pulse to cleanse the shadows. And then…" The White Tree pressed her hand to Larkin's forehead again, and she saw a weave full of blinding light and razor sharpness. A weave that would change her blades.

Over and over, the weave appeared in Larkin's head, until it was branded in her memory.

She collapsed on her haunches. "But if I perform this enchantment, I'll still be inside the tree when it falls."

"Yes," the White Tree said.

Larkin's eyes fluttered shut. She was going to die. But to save her family and all mankind, she wouldn't hesitate. "You can't—" Her voice broke. "You can't tell Denan." Not with how broken he was. How afraid of losing her.

When it was finished, the White Tree stepped back and held out her arms. "Pick me up and place me in the font."

This was her baby sister. "She's just a child."

"I know her better than you, Larkin. If it is within my power, I will save her."

Larkin hesitated and picked her up. "Let me speak with her—just her."

The White Tree blinked hard, and her eyes turned emerald.

Sela beamed at her. "Larkin!" She wrapped her arms around her and buried her head in the crook of her neck. "Where have you been?"

Exactly how long had the White Tree kept Sela asleep? Larkin breathed deep the smell of sunflowers and sunshine and mud.

"I miss Mama, Larkin."

Larkin squeezed Sela tighter. "I miss her too." She never wanted to let go. Never wanted this moment to end. But no matter how tightly she held on, it couldn't last forever. "I love you, sunshine."

"Love you too." Sela sighed. "The White Tree says I should go to sleep again, Larkin. She says when I wake up, it will be time to go home."

Larkin leaned down, placed Sela in the font, and kissed her forehead, her amulet slipping out of her tunic. "Sweet dreams."

Sela's green eyes were swallowed with white. The White Tree reached out, cupping the glittering amulet in her hands. "All the good that ever was in him is in this amulet." The amulet glowed a faint silver. She closed her eyes, opalescent tears flowing down her cheeks. "But it is just an echo, a memory of what he was."

How must it have felt for the White Tree to lose her mate and a good portion of her magic all in one day? And then to suffer through the Black Tree's evil while so many of her people died for so many years?

All the horrors of the curse had happened to her too. Yet she hadn't chosen darkness like the Black Tree.

"I'm so sorry for all that you have suffered."

The White Tree reached up, resting her hand on Larkin's cheek. "Of all the humans I have known, you are one of my favorites." She released the amulet, her hands tucking against her chest. "I've given everything I am to end this, but I'm tired. So very tired."

She sighed, her eyes slipping closed as if she wasn't strong enough to keep them open. Her body jerked, her back arching. Vines shot from her back and sank into the center of the font, shooting down into the depths of the Black Tree.

Her poor sister's little body. Larkin choked, her hands over her mouth. Suddenly, arms wrapped around her from behind. Denan. How long had he been there, watching? She sank into his embrace.

From all around them, a deep, eerie moan echoed, the branches swaying ominously.

CHAPTER 47

FACING THE FIRE

When Larkin turned from the font, she found all of her friends from the Alamant waiting for her at the base of the steps. She'd never thanked them for risking their lives to save her. And if she didn't do it now, she would never have another chance. Like she hadn't had a chance with Atara and West.

She bit her lip, fighting back tears. Her hand in Denan's, she descended to stand before them. "Thank you. For coming for me."

Talox picked Larkin up and hugged her so hard she thought a rib might crack. Again. "You gave me back my life and my Venna. I would face the fire for you, my queen." He set her down and stepped back. "Denan. Can Tam and I speak with you a moment?"

Denan shot Larkin a look, silently asking if she'd be all right. She nodded for him to go. The three men stepped aside, leaving Larkin alone with Caelia.

"Bane would have wanted me to come," Caelia said.

That's why the woman had left her children. For Bane. To honor him in the only way she could.

Caelia gave a small smile. "Nesha let me meet Soren. He scowls just like his daddy."

A tear fell, tracing Larkin's cheek. She quickly wiped it away. "I'm not sure I'll ever forgive myself for failing to save him."

"Oh, Larkin," Caelia said gently. "You were running from a wraith army in the Forbidden Forest. You couldn't have known."

It had been so hard since his death. If not for Denan, Larkin wasn't sure she would have survived. Her husband with his obsidian eyes, golden skin, and angular face. He moved with precision and grace. She memorized each expression and movement for recall in the afterlife. If there was one.

"Do you think he'll ever forgive me for leaving him? For putting him through my death?" Twice. Denan hadn't shown any signs of resentment toward her, but they had to be there, buried deep.

Caelia followed her gaze. "Did you know Gendrin and I aren't really heartsongs?"

Larkin shot her a disbelieving glance. "But you said you were."

"He found me in the forest. Saved my life. His selflessness, his goodness, his kindness… How could I not fall in love with him?" She gave a small smile. "Though after I discovered the truth about the pipers abducting girls, I fought him with everything I had. Even then, he never played the heartsong. He let me choose." Her gaze bored into Larkin's. "I don't need an enchantment to know he's my heartsong."

"He's still never played the song for you?" Larkin asked in disbelief.

Caelia met her gaze. "Love is a choice, Larkin. Denan will always choose you."

Larkin hoped he would move on, someday. He deserved to be happy.

Overhead, the sun had already reached its zenith. If Larkin wanted forgiveness, she had to ask before it was too late. "Thank you, Caelia."

She left the woman to splash through puddles to the three men, but the tension among them gave her pause. Denan's arms were folded across his chest, and he looked anywhere but at Tam, who only looked at the bark. Talox studied them both with an exasperated look. They'd clearly been fighting.

Larkin was afraid this would happen. That Denan would blame Tam for letting Larkin go with the wraiths. Would hate him for it. So of course Tam would have followed Denan around. Plied him with jokes, which Denan would have responded to with stony anger. She couldn't let these two lose their friendship. They needed each other.

Especially after she was gone.

"He didn't betray you, Denan," she said softly. "He only did what you taught us both: put our people first. Even if that means before you."

Denan's hands fisted.

"You're not really angry with him," Larkin said. "You're angry with me." Tam had just been a convenient target.

Denan wouldn't look at her, which only confirmed her suspicions. Not wanting to have this conversation in front of everyone, Larkin reached out, taking his hand. "Come with me."

She led him up a side branch toward Eiryss's coffin. If nothing else, he'd probably like to see it. "You were all supposed to be resting."

"The world is ending," Denan said. "How could I sleep? And I didn't like being so far away from you."

For a while, they climbed in silence. When they reached Eiryss's broken coffin, Denan bent down and picked up a piece of the amber. "You found her, in the end."

"She was never lost," Larkin said. "Nor has she ever been the monster history made her out to be, Denan. She only ever did what she had to. They all did."

She waited for Denan to say something, anything, but he remained silent. Implacable. One thing that had always worked before was sparring. "Come on."

She crossed to a place she'd noticed on her climb with Ramass. A place where one branch diverged into six, leaving a small room lined in white moss, the sides graced with mushrooms and flowers of so many vibrant colors, sizes, and shapes. It was like a little garden.

She turned to him and took a defensive stance. He stepped back and shook his head. "I don't want to spar with you."

Her hands fell to her sides. "Then talk to me."

He pulled his hand through his hair. "I'm not angry, Larkin. I just... You were gone—twisted into a monster. I grieved like you were dead. And then I became angry. And that anger made me strong enough to come here and do what I needed to do."

She knew all about channeling anger, using it to numb pain.

He dropped to the ground, his hands over his eyes. "I killed you while you begged me not to. You died at my hands for the second time."

Larkin knelt beside him and wrapped him in her arms, her chin resting on the top of his head. She was shocked again at how thin he'd grown; he was still muscular, but the skin now stretched far too thin over his body. He clearly hadn't been eating.

"I can't watch you die again," Denan said. "I can't be responsible for the deaths of more of my friends. I just can't."

Light. How could she force him to endure this twice? What could she say to make it better? She ached to tell him what was coming for her, to warn him. Be comforted by him. Say her goodbyes. But she couldn't risk him being distracted in battle any more than he had risked her.

"I understand why you didn't tell me about my father's death." She looked at him, willing him to remember this conversation later. "You were protecting me, even though it cost you." *Like I'm protecting you now.*

He met her gaze, his obsidian eyes overflowing with dread and grief. "And if we lose each other again?"

She blinked back tears. "If there is an afterlife, I will find you."

"And if there isn't?"

She cupped his face in her hands and kissed away his tears. "I have no regrets, Denan. None. If our story ends with one or both of us dead, I would still choose us."

He buried his head in her chest and wept. She held him tight, murmuring reassurances into his hair. She wished with everything she had that she could take away his pain. But that was impossible.

Or maybe it wasn't.

She tipped his face up and wiped his cheeks with the hem of her tunic. The movement exposed the length of her leg. She took one of his hands and rested it on the smooth skin. Then she tipped up his chin and pressed a feathery kiss to his mouth.

One, two, three times.

He sucked in a breath, his hungry hands tracing fire across her body, and deepened the kiss. "Larkin, we don't have any maidweed tea."

She liked that he was already breathless. She tugged him to his knees and undid his belt. His skirt armor clanked as it fell. "That's not a problem for wraiths."

He trailed hot kisses down her jaw and to her neck and then up to her ear. "Are you sure?"

In answer, she pulled her shapeless tunic over her head. "I'm sure."

CHAPTER

FIGHTING

er arms wrapped around her sleeping husband, Larkin watched him as the sky gradually lost its rich, vibrant hue, fading to a pale, smoky gray. Far above, the Black Tree's branches bit into the sky like thorns, making it bleed crimson along the horizon. Sunset was less than an hour away.

It was time.

Tonight, either mankind or the last of the sacred trees would go extinct. And if the Black Tree won, what then? His mate was gone. It wasn't like there would be any saplings after him. Perhaps the first time mankind had taken a thorn, he or she had ensured the mutual destruction of both species.

Larkin wished she could let Denan sleep longer. She wished this wasn't their last night together. She reached down, running the back of her hand along his scarred cheek.

He startled awake, his eyes wide and unseeing. He reached for his sword.

Larkin placed another hand on his shoulder. "Shh, it's just me."

He stilled and glanced toward the bloody horizon. "Light, why did you let me sleep so long?"

"Because you needed it."

"And you don't?"

She shook her head. "I haven't slept since I became a wraith." She pushed to her feet and pulled him up. Hand in hand, they returned to the main platform. Someone had built a fire and filled an ancient pot with fish soup at the base of the dais.

The Valynthians and Alamantians both sat all around the steps, guarding Sela while she fought to reach the Black Tree's heart. Larkin dished up the thin soup and handed Denan a bowl. He nodded his thanks and drank it down in one go.

Only Garrot stood alone, at the edge of the platform behind the dais. Arms folded, his eyes on the horizon, he looked lonely. Lost. Hating him was a habit as natural as breathing. But he was clearly trying to change. And even if he wasn't... Larkin didn't want to end up like Iniya—so full of bitterness that it destroyed any chance of happiness.

If this was her last night—humanity's last night—she would die at peace. Larkin fetched a bowl of soup and crossed to stand beside him. He looked at her in surprise.

"Why did you come?" she asked.

He considered her. "Becoming a mulgar made me face what I'd done." His throat bobbed. "Nothing could be worse than that. Except maybe not doing what I can to repair the damage."

Maybe Garrot could change, just like her father had.

For the first time, she didn't feel hate when she looked at him—or fear or repulsion or fury. Instead, she felt compassion. She held out the bowl of broth. When he hesitated, she motioned for him to take it. He did so, gingerly.

"I'm never going to like you," she said. "But you're clearly trying to change. That counts for something." She moved away, feeling like a heavy burden had been lifted from her shoulders.

"Larkin," Garrot called after her.

She turned back. He reached into his shirt and pulled out a lovely gold chain, which he slipped over his head and held out to her. She stared in shock at the ring dangling from it. A large ruby, the band made of twining vines. The ring Bane had given her when he'd asked her to marry him.

She took it, closed her eyes, and held it to her breast, tears threatening.

"I genuinely believed Bane a traitor," Garrot said, "same as you. When I returned to the Idelmarch, I went through his things and found this. I took it, meaning to send it to his father. But it became a reminder to be a better man. The kind of man who would give his life for someone he loved."

That was why he'd really come. Eyes shining, she nodded her thanks and strode to Caelia, who sat on the dais steps. She held out the ring and the chain. Larkin was tempted to keep them, but they were not her family's heirlooms.

Caelia's eyes widened. "Those were my mother's."

"Garrot gave it to me. For what it's worth, I think he's genuinely sorry."

Caelia slipped the ring on her own finger and held out the chain for Larkin. "I think my mama would have wanted you to have it."

Larkin would have loved it. "I'll get it from you tomorrow."

Caelia frowned at her in confusion and then shrugged and slipped it over her head.

Larkin's gaze drifted up to her sister. Sela's eyes darted beneath her closed lids as if she were sleeping. Or nightmaring. Her body was still shaking, the branches still forcing their way deeper into the tree. Creaks and groans and snaps came from beneath Larkin's feet. She imagined the White Tree rooting into the Black Tree's every weakness, expanding, and cracking.

How much was this costing the White Tree? More importantly, what was it costing Sela?

Sunset loomed before them. Mere minutes away. All of them sensing it, the Valynthians gathered around Larkin.

"Have you gone deep enough?" Ramass called up to Sela.

Sela's white eyes shot open. A single rainbow tear slid from the corner of her eye. "I need more time."

Denan ground his jaw and turned to them. "You know what to do."

Already, Larkin could feel the shadows gathering. Eiryss began to weave. Tam, Caelia, Talox, and Garrot all piled inside the dome. Ramass, Hagath, and Ture lined up outside it. Denan hung back with Larkin.

"When the sun sets," Denan asked, his voice hoarse, "the shadows will begin their attack on the Alamant?"

Ramass gave a slow, sad nod. "The Alamant and the Idelmarch both."

"Those who make it inside the magic panes will survive," Hagath said. "At least for a little while."

So many people were going to die tonight. What if Mama, her sister, or the babies were among them? What about Aaryn and Mytin? Alorica?

"We'll give you as much time as we can." Ramass shot the others a meaningful look. They gave grim nods in return and ran toward the carriage.

Denan took hold of Larkin's hand. "Be careful, my little bird."

Wincing as the shadows clawed their way up her ankles, she pressed her forehead to his. "I'm not afraid."

"Larkin," Hagath called sharply.

Blinking back hot tears, she kissed his cheek, then turned, her hands slipping from his, and ran after the Valynthians. She caught up to them standing at the edge of the tree near the carriage and looked down, down, down. Below them was a patch of deep water ringed by the soggy grass.

Hagath's words echoed in her head. *It'll just hurt so much you might lose your mind for the next decade or so.*

Hagath was shaking. Ture was pale. Ramass's hands were clenched. In the distance, the sun was halved on the horizon.

Light. This is going to hurt. Fear made Larkin's palms damp and her heart race. Unable to resist, she turned to look back at her husband. Trying to memorize the planes and ridges of his face. The way the light turned his skin golden. The way his hair stuck up on one side from his sleep.

Light, I love that man.

Her breaths heaved in and out of her throat, her vision turning dark around the edges. The shadows climbed up her chest, reaching for her shoulders.

"Now!" Ramass cried.

For Denan and Mama and Nesha and Brenna and Soren and Kyden. She stepped off. Clenching his eyes shut, Denan turned away. Faster and faster she fell, until the wind tore at her hair and clothes, the vibrations against her body painful. The thorns dug deeper, clawed their way up her shoulders. Her neck. The back of her skull and cheeks.

The water rose, the details of each little wave growing clearer. Until she could make out the scales of the darting gilgad beneath her. She opened her mouth to scream.

And then she hit.

Her legs broke first, the sharp ends of her thigh bones pushing through her hips, which shattered on impact. Her spine exploded. Her ribs broke into sharp shards that pierced her every organ.

She did not pass out.

The shadows couldn't touch the water. They had to settle for waiting for her broken body to brush up against the tree. She screamed as they latched onto the back of her head, dragged her out of the water, and deposited her on a root beside the broken bodies of her comrades.

She had just enough wherewithal to see that the sun had set. Their plan to buy more time was working. It was then that the healing began and the shadows tore down her throat.

She became pain.

Pain that exploded every time one of her bones wrenched back into place or her skin knit back together or her shredded organs healed. The healing came in waves, each one bringing a fresh burst of agony—agony compounded by each swell of water.

Memories melded with her own. Memories of a woman in her garden, who hummed as she pulled weeds and tossed snails in a pail. There was a small white house and lots of trees. On the far side of the river—so far away Larkin could cover them with an outstretched hand—two men worked a plow. Children's laughter sounded from somewhere out of sight.

The woman sat up for a moment and stretched her back, revealing her mounded belly. She turned in the direction of the bright laughter. "Five more minutes, and then it's time for supper."

They were her children. By the sounds of it, at least three. And she was pregnant with another. The woman gathered up the pail and opened the garden gate. She swung the pail as she headed toward the river. She didn't notice the older man lying in wait for her in the forest.

Larkin didn't know how she knew that the woman was a Valynthian. Only that she was. And the man was an Alamantian.

He unhooked a gem-studded reed pipe from his belt. The man played a song of a lover's gentle arms in the quiet hush of a summer morning. An enchantment so lovely that it brought a sigh of contentment from the woman's lips.

She didn't notice the discordant note. The undercurrent of lies. The bucket slipped from her fingers, rolling down the little path until it came to rest with a clang against a rock. Her expression dreamy, she followed the man deep into the forest.

So deep that no one heard her screams.

Next came a baby, beaten to death by his own mother because he wouldn't stop crying. A man enchanted to kill himself by his wife because she wanted his money and his brother.

The Black Tree was right. As long as men and women existed, they would do terrible, awful things to each other. She became a wraith. Without form or substance, she traveled the shadows.

Nearly an hour after sunset, she came into being in the middling boughs of the Black Tree. Below, four wraiths fought five Alamantians. Eiryss stood inside a dome, guarding Sela. A dozen paces from Larkin, Garrot sighted down his bow and released an arrow into the chaos beneath them.

Garrot, who had turned her sister against her. Garrot, who had driven her into the forest. Garrot, who had killed Bane. He deserved to die.

She charged the druid, who swung around and loosed an arrow at her. She flared her shield and ducked behind it. Garrot retreated even as he drew another arrow and released all in the same smooth, practiced movement, striking her in the thigh. Pain blazed. Pain she welcomed gladly.

She wrenched it out without slowing. Her shadows flickered. His expression shifting to shock, Garrot dropped the bow and arrow to draw his sword and shield. Their swords clanked. Slash, parry, stab, parry. She drove Garrot until another step would drop him to the platform, a fall which would certainly break a few bones.

Garrot braced behind his shield and shoved her with all his strength, nearly knocking her over. He pressed the advantage, ducking down to swipe at her legs. She jumped. Garrot lunged, his sword flashing as it thrust into her ribs.

One more hit, and she was done for. She roared in frustration and drove him another step back. His heel slipped, and he managed to brace his shield against a branch.

He gritted his teeth. "Larkin, you can beat him! You've done it before."

Beat the Black Tree? Beating him would leave her as just Larkin, and Larkin would never kill Garrot. "You killed Bane."

She drew in her magic for a pulse that would send him to his death. With a shout, he lunged, wrapping his arms around her. They fell to the branch. Garrot's flesh steamed where it touched her. He cried out as his skin blistered.

You fool! Larkin thought. *Don't you know not to touch me?*

But of course he didn't. He'd never fought a wraith before. She rolled, coming up on top of Garrot, her sword cocked back.

And hesitated.

Because she'd been in this exact position before. Only she'd been the one with an enemy straddling her, a blade about to come down. And the fear in Garrot's eyes... it was the same fear she'd felt.

Garrot punched her jaw, rocked his hips, and shoved hard. She fell to her side and rolled to her feet. He faced her with his knife—the only weapon he had left. Her shadows faded. If he hit her again, she was through. But what chance did he have with a single dagger against a sword and shield?

Larkin charged. With a shout of desperation and rage, so did Garrot. She swung. He managed to block with his dagger and shove up. He kicked out, his heel connecting with her crotch in a hit that would have dropped a man.

She was not a man.

She swung her shield, hitting Garrot hard in the temple. He crumpled, blood gushing from a crescent wound around the top of his ear. He tried to push up, but his body failed him. His eyes weren't quite able to focus on her.

"Nesha and Soren... tell them I love them." Then he passed out completely.

She raised her sword above his head. And hesitated a second time.

Garrot loved her sister. Loved another man's child as his own. He'd allowed his grief to turn him into a zealot. Had been tricked by the Black Tree, like so many others. But he'd never been evil. He had saved her life only yesterday. And she'd forgiven him. Felt the peace of that forgiveness.

I don't want to do this.

The Black Tree turned his full attention on her. Again, the senseless deaths of the woman, baby, and man flashed in her memory.

Mankind isn't worth saving. The thought echoed in her head.

You're wrong, Larkin thought. *My father was worth being saved. As were Talox and Venna. Even Garrot deserves a second chance.*

The Black Tree attacked, trying to wrest control of her body. She flared her sigils and pulsed, forcing him back. Forcing the dead back. The shadows split open and peeled apart. She emerged and dragged in a free breath, stepping from the shadows like a cast-off garment.

And somehow, she knew that she'd thrown off the Black Tree forever. Thrown off the wraith.

Weakness hit her a moment later, as if fighting off the Black Tree had taken all her strength. She dropped to her knees. She waited a beat for the healing to set in. Nothing happened. She was no longer a wraith, and that meant she could no longer heal.

Before her, Garrot wasn't moving. *Light, please don't let me have killed him.* She crawled to his side and turned his head toward her. He was still bleeding, which meant his heart still beat.

"Garrot?"

He moaned.

She breathed out in relief. Movement out of the corner of her vision. She spun. Hagath charged up the branch toward her. Larkin reached for her magic. Tried to stand. Her legs refused to take her weight. Hagath drew back her sword for a thrust. Larkin flared her shield, but she hadn't braced herself. Hagath kicked the shield aside.

Larkin landed on her hip. She put both hands on the shield and held it before her. Hagath kicked it to the side again and ground her heel into Larkin's arm. She cried out in pain.

Hagath bent over her and said in the Black Tree's voice, "You should not have defied me, woman."

The Black Tree drew her arm back, the shadow-wreathed sword spitting smoke. A blade that would kill her for good.

At a shout, Hagath's head jerked up. Screaming, Garrot charged. He didn't even have a weapon. Hagath didn't bother moving into a defensive stance. Simply shoved her sword into Garrot's guts.

Without pause, he wrapped his arms around the wraith and drove toward the edge of the bough. The wraith fought him, managing to grab a branch just before they toppled. His flesh smoking and his face blistering, Garrot met Larkin's gaze. He gave her a single nod and wrenched his body, taking the wraith with him off the side.

"No!" Larkin gasped. She crawled to the edge of the branch and watched them fall. Watched Garrot hit, water exploding around him. Hagath bounced off, slamming into the side of the tree with enough force to break every bone in her body. Again.

Face down, Garrot's broken body bobbed to the surface. He didn't move.

He'd died to save her.

CHAPTER 49

THE DEAD

A sound like shadows ripping in half. Larkin knew that sound. The sound of a wraith returning. Far below, the dead spit Hagath out on the tree's roots. At least, Larkin thought it was Hagath. Her limbs didn't look like limbs, but wet, bent noodles. As if every bone in her body had been pulverized. A hundred yards to the right, Garrot's body rode the gentle waves.

Horror tried to overcome Larkin. To paralyze her. She shoved it down. She couldn't save Garrot. No one could. Nor could she spare Hagath her pain. But she could help the others.

She crawled down the branch. Her body gained strength by the moment, until she was able to stand. Then jog. Then run. She reached the main platform. Caelia and Talox fought Ture in front of her. On her right, Eiryss struggled to keep ahead of Vicil. Tam crawled for the dome. On the far side, near the font, Ramass hammered Denan with his shield. Denan blocked the blow but dropped to a knee.

Her husband needed her most.

Larkin dodged Caelia and Talox and sprinted for her husband when Vicil knocked Eiryss flat. He straddled her. She pulsed, sending him sailing in front of Larkin. She caught the edge of the blast, which sent her staggering, though she managed to keep her feet.

Vicil lay sprawled a step to her left, not two steps from where Tam dragged himself. Vicil's gaze fixed on Tam. Larkin had a split second to decide. Trusting Denan's skill to hold out for a moment longer, she sidestepped and sliced through Vicil's chest. He imploded.

Leaving him for Eiryss to tie up, Larkin rushed to Denan's aid. Ramass swung from the left. Denan moved to block. It was a feint. Ramass's blade flicked out. Blood bloomed on Denan's side. With a cry, he stumbled and went down.

Ramass drew back for the killing blow. Larkin pulsed, throwing him back. She leaped over Denan. Ramass stumbled to his feet. Before he could fully recover, she bashed his shield to the side and thrust into his chest. She let her sword fade and form again in an instant. Then she thrust again.

He imploded.

She rushed to Denan. He lay on his back. His right hand held his left ribs, blood gushing through his fingers. His head was thrown back, his jaw clenched against the pain. Larkin snapped the straps of his armor with her blade and tore open his tunic. The cut was long, from just under his armpit to the top of his stomach. His ribs were visible, the white shocking against the blood and meat.

She should have come to his side instead of ending Vicil. She'd known he was flagging. Known he needed help. In her hubris, she'd thought she could save Tam and Denan both.

Larkin sprinted to Hagath's shack, grabbed a cup and bandages, and then ran to the font. Her sister's body was still shaking, the roots still digging deeper. Beating back the horror, Larkin took the sap first to Tam and then hustled to kneel back beside Denan. "Here."

He took the cup from her. "Go help the others."

That would leave him vulnerable.

As if guessing her thoughts, he glared at her. "Go!"

She pivoted, but Talox and Caelia had already defeated Ture. Two claps of thunder, one right on top of another. Vicil was already coming back to life and fighting against Eiryss. Tam staggered to his feet and hobbled to them. He stabbed Vicil through the chest, leaving his blade embedded.

"That ought to pin him—" Before Tam could finish, his sword was already being forced out. "Ah!" He stabbed Vicil repeatedly. "What does it take to kill you, you cursed cockroach!"

"He's the same way with spiders," Denan panted.

"Light's sake." Ture glared at him, his body slowly being put back together. "Just tie him up."

Caelia came to help Eiryss do just that.

Tam fell back hard on his backside. Talox picked him up and carried him to the dome around the font, where he patted Sela on the head, cupped his hand, and drank deep. Ramass and Ture lay still, their wounds slowly closing.

Larkin turned back to Denan. *Light, there is so much blood.*

Hagath suddenly pushed her out of the way. "Let me do it." She smeared a strong-smelling salve onto bandages and bound Denan's ribs. "No point in stitching it until the fighting is over—he'll just tear them."

Denan tightened up but then seemed to relax. The sap was working.

Tam giggled. He bent down and slurped more sap from the font. "Remember that time at the academy?"

Denan grinned. "You shot out of bed in the middle of the night, dancing about as if the floor was on fire."

Talox stood over them. "Stripped down to nothing and used his shirt to beat at the floor."

Tam grinned. "Our house mother came in to see what all the fuss was about. She blushed every time I winked at her after that."

Talox laughed so hard he held his ribs.

Hands shaking, Larkin gaped at him. "How can you laugh at a time like this?"

Tam threw his hands in the air. "Because we won! Against all odds, we won!"

"But our people are dying," Larkin cried.

"The sap is making them giddy," Hagath said.

Larkin wiped a tear tracing down her cheek.

Tam sobered. "He'll survive, Larkin. He's had far worse."

A sob escaped Larkin's throat. She swallowed the next one down and refused to let another surface. "Garrot didn't. He died saving me."

Silence sliced through the Valynthians and Alamantians both. None of them had even considered the druid. He deserved better than that. Better than any of them had given him.

"Sorry," Tam mumbled.

Denan reached for her hand and squeezed it. "Go check on your sister."

He must have known she was moments from a full break-down and needed a distraction. She kissed the back of his hand and hurried to the dais.

Eiryss stood between Tam and the font. "You've had enough."

"Aw, come now, you old goat." Tam wiped his lips.

Eiryss's face whitened with anger.

Larkin smacked Tam upside the head. "We haven't won yet! Go lie down!"

"Just like my wife," he muttered, but he lay down and was asleep a moment later.

"Sorry," Larkin said to Eiryss.

She shrugged. "At this point, that's the best place for him."

Larkin peered into the font. Sela was pale, her strawberry curls fanned around her head in a perfect halo. The plan was going perfectly so far. The wraiths were defeated. Sela was tunneling into the tree. And Eiryss was still at full strength for her orb.

They had more than half the night to take the tree down. "Sela? Can you hear me?"

Her eyes flashed open. "Gather the others inside the dome."

Larkin didn't understand. "But we defeated the wraiths. The danger is—"

A low, wailing moan curled through the trees. A moan that wasn't quite human. She'd heard that sound before. A sound that struck a chord deep inside her, fear resonating through her body until her instincts demanded that she run.

There was nowhere to run to.

"Now!" Sela cried.

The fear in her eyes stopped Larkin's questions. She gestured frantically. "Everyone, inside. Now! Talox, help Denan."

Caelia took off at a run. Talox hauled Denan over his shoulder. Hagath was frozen in terror. His wounds still bleeding, Ture picked her up and sprinted for the dome. Ramass stumbled after them.

The moan came again. And seeing the four Valynthians' dread, Larkin suddenly remembered where she'd heard it before: her vision of the curse first coming into being. The torn shadows with hungry mouths had ripped apart the domes of those defending the White Tree like they were made of wet paper. She started to leave the dome to assist the others.

Eiryss's hand locked around her wrist. "You can't help them."

She was right.

Breathless, Caelia stepped inside. "What's wrong?" she asked.

No one bothered to answer.

"Will it hold?" Larkin asked Eiryss in a shaking voice.

Ramass reached the dome first, Ture carrying Hagath a step behind. He set her down and steadied her against him.

"Flare," Eiryss said. "Every last one of you flare."

The Valynthians didn't hesitate. Caelia followed a beat later. Larkin's sigils glowed silver and gold. Eiryss grasped their magic. Hagath played her pipes, her notes as carefully placed as a surgeon's blade. The two of them fed the magic into the dome, which gleamed brighter by the moment.

Denan and Talox stumbled into the dome. Talox laid Denan down next to Tam, who was completely unconscious.

Denan wiped sweat from his reddened face. "Water. Does anyone have water?"

Ture handed him a waterskin. He drank greedily.

A smell permeated the air. The smell of an open grave.

"Hurry," Ramass whispered. "Oh, light, Eiryss, hurry."

"I'm trying!" Sweat ran down Eiryss's temples.

"What is it?" Talox asked.

The Valynthians didn't answer. They didn't seem capable of it.

Larkin had seen the curse's origins, but it wasn't the same. She hadn't been in any danger, and she hadn't had to watch her friends—most of her kingdom—die.

Larkin swallowed hard. "Can't you smell them?" Tam looked at her blankly. "He's called back the shadows from the White Tree." Had the Black Tree called back all of them? Some? Were their people still being attacked?

She should have planned for this. But she hadn't even considered it.

"Does that mean our people are safe?" Denan asked.

"Only if we defeat the Black Tree," Ture said.

Eiryss finished her weave and flared it into place. Hagath stopped playing as Eiryss circled it, smoothing a line here, straightening another there.

"Will it hold?" Ramass asked.

Before she could answer, there was a sudden ripping sound, as if the night itself had been broken in two. And then the shadows were there. They took the shape of formless, torn shadows filled with tearing and screaming mouths of endless black.

The weave rippled violently. With a cry, Eiryss dropped and began shaking uncontrollably. Blood leaked out her nose. Her ears. Ramass pulled her into his lap.

"You idiot," Hagath cried. "You didn't tie it off."

Larkin didn't understand. All she knew was that the attack on the dome was somehow affecting Eiryss. Larkin rushed to help her.

Hagath intercepted her. She pushed her toward the weave that was falling apart. "You're a weaver. Take it!"

Larkin grabbed the flailing threads and held them steady, wishing she'd paid more attention to the visions. "What do I do?"

"Just hold it." Hagath pulled out her pipes and played, the strands shifting back into place. "Toss it up—it'll tie off when you do."

Larkin lobbed the magic, as she'd seen Eiryss do. It melded with the dome, which shimmered. Behind her, Eiryss stopped shaking.

Ramass knelt beside her. He gently stroked the hair from Eiryss's forehead. "Three hundred years, and you still don't tie them off fast enough."

Eiryss didn't open her eyes.

"Will she be all right?" Ramass asked Hagath.

Hagath glanced up at the dome. "Her chances are as good as any of us."

Larkin couldn't look up at the shadows anymore. It was too terrifying. She tried to take stock of everyone. They seemed all right, if battered and bruised.

"How long will it hold?" Talox asked.

Above, cracks formed, spreading and widening.

"Not long," Ture said.

"All of you flare." Hagath drew a fortifying breath and began to play.

Larkin flared her numerous sigils. The ones from the White Tree felt warm, while the new ones flared cold, though both buzzed uncomfortably under her skin. But the more Hagath drew, the less they felt like anything at all.

Above the hole, the orb growing from the combination of black, silver, and white magic reminded her of ominous storm clouds, lightning arcing throughout. The cold emanating from it made the sweat freeze on her skin. The orb grew to the size of a wagon wheel by the time the last of Larkin's magic had been drained.

Larkin went to the font. Her sister still lay motionless. "Sela, if you can hear me, it's now or never."

CHAPTER

50

INTO THE DARK

S ela's eyes opened, the iris the disconcerting opalescent of
the White Tree.

"Did you reach the heartwood?" Larkin asked.

"The edge of it," the White Tree said.

"Will that be enough?" Ramass asked.

"I don't know." The White Tree sat up, sticky sap streaming
from her body. From her torso, a white root half again as wide as
Larkin disappeared into the font. It cracked along the seam of
Sela's skin. Her back was an open wound that closed off in the
next moment, leaving a horrible scar.

Larkin was horrified at how her sister's body had been used
in such a manner, just like the Black Tree had used her. The
White Tree reached for Larkin, who lifted her down. The root
the White Tree had left behind cracked down the middle. The
cracks spread until it was nothing more than dust. Sap dripped
into a deep, black hole.

"Everyone step back," Ramass said.

They all clustered around the perimeter of the dome as the shadows tore at it from above. The orb shifted like liquid clouds, lightning flashing. Hagath's song shifted. The spinning orb dropped out of sight.

They all waited, breath held. And then, from deep beneath, a boom echoed. The tree shook violently, throwing Larkin to the ground. Above, the shadows ceased their attack and wailed. Branches cracked and fell. The sound grew deafening, until Larkin had to cover her ears and curl into a ball.

The violent shaking shifted to tremors. Larkin dared to peek around her. The platform was littered with branches of varying sizes. The dome was gone. There was no sign of the shadows. She felt for Denan's hand and squeezed. "Are you hurt?"

He shook his head and looked around. "Everyone all right?"

"I'm never going to be all right again," Caelia groaned.

Tam mumbled and shifted in his sleep.

"Caelia and I are fine," Talox said as he helped her to her feet.

"We're still here," Hagath said of the Valynthians.

Eiryss sat up. "Light, my head."

Hagath smacked her arm. "Tie off your cursed weaves, then!"

Larkin had no idea what they were talking about. There was still so much she had to learn about magic. Ramass jogged to where Vicil had been.

"Ture," Ramass said. "Help me get this branch off Vicil."

"Are you sure that's a good idea?" Denan said.

Larkin agreed with him—let the branch pin the man so he couldn't attack them again.

The two men didn't respond, but soon came the sounds of men straining and the rush of leaves as the branch moved.

Larkin realized Sela hadn't answered and pushed to her feet. On the right side of the font, the White Tree knelt with both hands pressed to the bark, her eyes closed in concentration.

AMBER ARGYLE

"Did the orb destroy the heartwood?" Larkin asked.

The White Tree didn't answer.

"Hagath," Ramass said, a note of panic in his voice.

"What?" Hagath said. "It's just Vicil."

Panic stole over Ramass's features. "He's not healing."

Hagath hustled over to them.

Not healing. That wasn't possible. Unless... Larkin stepped past Ramass and Ture. Vicil lay unmoving, the side of his head caved in. Larkin watched, waiting for it to fill out. Nothing happened.

"What's going on?" Eiryss called. Her hand was still pressed against her head, her steps unsure. She wasn't healing either. They moved aside. "Vicil?" She looked at Ramass in bewilderment. "Why isn't he healing?"

"Because the Black Tree is too injured to heal him." The White Tree stood behind them, her curls a clumpy mess. "You've grievously injured him."

A ragged cheer rose from the Alamantians. Not the Valynthians. Not Larkin. Eiryss dropped down beside Vicil and scooped his body into her arms. "Vicil! Oh, Vicil. I'm sorry. You didn't deserve this. Any of it. I'm so sorry."

Denan made a slicing motion for the Alamantians to be quiet. He didn't need to. They all watched Eiryss shamefacedly.

"So we just wait for our magic to come back and send another orb down the hole?" Caelia was clearly trying to contain her excitement.

"I'm afraid not," the White Tree said.

As if to punctuate her words, a low moaning sounded. Everyone stilled, their gazes shifting, watching for the shadows.

"Even now," the White Tree said, "he's rallying."

"We don't have enough magic for another dome," Hagath said in a whisper.

The White Tree's solemn gaze shifted to Larkin. The moment had come, then. The orb hadn't been enough. It was time for Larkin to use the enchantment the White Tree had taught her.

"All my magic is gone." Larkin didn't want to admit her relief at this. *I don't want to die.*

Denan shifted so he was between the White Tree and Larkin, as if he could protect her from this. "What's going on?"

The White Tree didn't take her gaze from Larkin. "The rest of you need to get as far away from here as possible."

"Why?" Denan demanded.

Denan. Light, he was going to lose her again. Forever this time. This would break him in a way he would never recover. She couldn't do that to him. She didn't have a choice.

Another moan sounded, louder this time.

The White Tree's gaze shifted to Denan. "Larkin isn't cursed. He can't stop her."

"Stop her from what?" Denan was dangerously close to losing his temper. Larkin tried to take his hand, but he jerked free.

The White Tree's eyes slid to the font.

"You want her to go inside?" Talox asked, incredulous.

"She's the only one—" the White Tree began.

"I'll go." Eiryss struggled to her feet.

Ramass hurried to her and braced her up. "I just got you back."

"I've had two lifetimes," Eiryss said with a gentle smile. "Larkin has barely begun one."

"You don't have barrier and warrior magic," the White Tree said. "She'll need both if she has any chance of succeeding."

Another moan, louder than before. The White Tree glanced up and then around at the Valynthians and Alamantians. "Do you want to live or die with her? Because if you don't leave now, you won't have a choice."

So many people had already given their lives for Larkin. So many more had been willing to. How could she not do the same for them? Calmness stole over her. "Go. All of you. Let me do this for you. Let me save you the way you have all saved me."

"But we're supposed to protect you." Caelia's eyes were round with tears.

Larkin wanted to hug them. Say goodbye. But the first of the shadows appeared, lunging for their heads. Caelia flared, but the thing was already chewing through her magic.

"Go!" Larkin backed toward the font. "Live!"

Talox moved first. He ran to pick up Tam and headed across the platform. "Caelia!"

Caelia gripped the gold chain around her neck, her eyes wide with understanding. She nodded to Larkin—that simple gesture conveying respect and a goodbye. Ture grabbed Hagath by both arms and hauled her after them.

She reached back. "Larkin!"

Ramass pried Eiryss away from Vicil. "Come on, love. We have to go."

"It's not fair," Eiryss cried. "It should be me. It should have always been me."

Like Ture, he picked her up and carried her the rest of the way. The carriage was far too loaded, but it started down anyway.

Eiryss gripped the bars. "You are exactly the queen your people need, Larkin!"

Larkin let the words wash over her. Let herself feel the truth in them. Then she faced Denan and the White Tree. Denan set his chin, his gaze resolute. And she understood. He wouldn't leave without her. He would stay here and die beside her.

She couldn't let that happen.

She went to his side and pressed her hand to his chest. "I'm giving you a gift. Don't waste it."

He set his jaw. "I can't lose you again."

Anger flared inside her. "If you stay here, my little sister dies with us. Sela doesn't deserve that."

He wavered.

"I won't be there to take care of my family."

"Talox and Tam will do it."

"They have their own families. Like it or not, my family needs you." He still didn't waver. "We don't sacrifice out of duty," she repeated Denan's words. "We do it for love. My sacrifice is dying. Yours is living without me."

Larkin saw the moment that he realized he would leave her. His eyes slipped closed, pain washing over him.

Tears threatened to surface, and her throat tried to close off. She swallowed hard. "I want you to be happy. To be whole. Marry and have children. Understand?"

He didn't answer. But that was all right. Because he was going to live.

The White Tree stood before Larkin and motioned to her amulet. "Squeeze it in your fist until it breaks skin. Channel all your magic into it."

"But my magic is drained," Larkin cried.

The White Tree pressed her hand to Larkin's stomach. Magic flowed into her in a rush. Too fast. It was too fast! But Larkin couldn't reach the words to protest. Her sigils gleamed so bright her skin appeared translucent.

For a moment, Larkin was at one with the White Tree, as she had been with the Black Tree. And she understood. The White Tree was giving up every last ounce of her remaining magic so the enchantment would be strong enough. To save mankind, the White Tree was dying. She had known this moment would come. And she'd gone into it willingly.

I'm sorry, Larkin thought. *Sorry I was so angry with you for joining with Sela. You were only doing it to save us.*

In return, music rushed through her. Birdsong, gentle wind through branches, rich soil in her roots, the connection to thousands of trees throughout the forest. For a moment, she knew what it was like to truly belong. The way Sela must have felt all these months.

A vision flashed in her mind—one she'd had long ago. She stood in the White Tree's dead boughs, shedding her garments one by one. She wove a barrier over herself, a kind of armor with pockets of air. Then she pointed her hands over her head and dove.

From there, the old vision became new. She cut through the water, her magic lighting her way all the way to the bottom of the lake. She took a locket from around her neck and popped it open, taking a glowing seed from within.

The vision faded as fast as it came, leaving Larkin reeling as she tried to understand what it meant.

"There's a chance," the White Tree's voice echoed through her. "If you can weave…"

But then the voice was gone. Sela collapsed. Denan caught her. Larkin stumbled as the rush of magic stopped. The White Tree was dead.

Denan's gaze met Larkin's, his eyes filled with so much sorrow it broke Larkin's heart. He couldn't bear to leave her, but he would do it anyway.

"That's why I love you," she said. "Because you do what you must. You always have." They were kindred spirits in that.

He pressed his lips to hers—a desperate, frantic kiss. A shriek tore them apart. One of the shadows dove for them. Larkin flared her shield. More appeared, swooping at them.

Denan hunched protectively over Sela. "It's too late now. We'll never make the carriage."

Except Larkin had barrier magic now. And she'd had enough visions and real-life experience of Valynthian magic that she created the weave from memory. In moments, the three of them were encased in armor.

"Go!" she cried, as more of the dead screeched and tore at them.

Denan sprinted across the platform. Larkin turned in the opposite direction, stood over the font, and gripped the pendant in her hand. Below her was the black nothingness.

She glanced over at Denan just as the carriage started down.

His gaze locked on her. "In this life or the next, I will always find you!"

Then he was out of sight.

Bracing herself, Larkin launched into the dark.

CHAPTER

LIGHT

Larkin fell fast and hard, her hair and clothes whipping upward. Shadows dove after her, ripping out chunks of her hair. Until they yanked her to a standstill in the center of the tree. She lifted her arm to flare, but one clamped its teeth down on her sigil. More tore into her, their teeth biting, claws shredding.

But the damage wasn't to her flesh, but her soul. Larkin lifted her head to scream, and they dove down her throat. Larkin saw hundreds of nightmarish memories. Assassinations, rapes, mass murders, kidnappings, robberies, tortures… so much evil that her mind broke, shattering into a thousand pieces. Only then did the assault cease.

The sigil at her wrist flared silver beneath her skin. With its light came its purpose. The ahlea flower. She was the bearer of the seed. She saw herself then. Planting sacred trees in all the forests of all the world. Revered as a mother by the forests and sacred trees alike. Immortal. Beloved.

The Black Tree would be the king of them all. He would rule his children. Teach them to gather the souls of the dead and twist them to shadows. Mankind would end. But she never would. Nor would Denan, for he bore the ahlea of the White Tree.

She would be with him. Forever.

All she had to do was embrace the darkness.

She hung suspended, knowing nothing but the wicked beauty unfurling before her. A breath away from accepting the only option she'd ever known. And then a tiny speck of light appeared. A flower floating amid torn shadows. It gleamed opalescent, colors dancing along the edges.

She reached out, touching it.

"Use my light," a masculine voice echoed down through the ages.

More light flared, spearing into the dark. Flooding her with bright memories. Beginning with an ancient king dying to create the amulet she held. Eiryss, working to build a new kingdom for her broken people and the child she believed would one day come. Hagath and Ture and even Vicil fighting back the poisonous shadows for centuries.

More recently, Mama and Sela, who'd never stopped protecting her. Bane and Joy and Venna and Daydon, for their generosity. Tam for his humor. Talox for his gentle strength.

Denan. For his determination and unconditional love.

So many small kindnesses, from a simple smile to the grandest act. So many had made her life better, even going so far as to lay down their lives for hers.

Outshine the darkness.

She'd thought it a metaphor. But Sela had meant it literally.

I choose light, she thought.

"Then we will both die," the Black Tree screamed. "And all the sacred trees with us!"

The moment Larkin had slipped into the abyss, the White Tree had known this would happen. Known her kind would not survive if mankind did. She'd chosen to save them anyway. Duty hadn't driven her. Love had.

How could Larkin do any less?

She fisted the amulet, feeling the point enter her skin. She channeled all her magic into it, her whole body buzzing. Light flared.

So bright that even through her closed eyes, she could see all the bones in her body.

So bright she hung suspended within it.

So bright it hurt.

That light drove the darkness from the shadows. Without the Black Tree's malice to blind them, the shadows remembered something other than darkness.

The boy remembered his newborn sister's shock of red hair. Fishing in the lake on hot summer days with his father.

The grandmother remembered dancing with her husband for the first time. There were flowers in her blonde hair, and her cheeks hurt from smiling so much.

The bride remembered laughing with her father.

The thief and his sister remembered eating with their parents at a dinner table, their bellies full and their feet swinging.

So many memories. Hundreds. Thousands. Tens of thousands. So much light.

"You're free," Larkin cried. "He can't hold you."

Then they were gone.

The Black Tree was not. Still, he pressed against her, trying to penetrate her light. She had freed the souls trapped within him, but she had not killed him. She flared all her sigils, silver and white. She took the magic between her hands.

She was a weaver. She could shape it.

She was a warrior. She could wield it.

She wove warrior and barrier magic into her weapons sigils, shifting her swords into thousands of scythelike blades that curved around her in a tight spiral. She pulsed the scythes. A crack like the earth splitting in two, like thunder resonating in her head.

The Black Tree broke, cut into thousands of pieces that exploded with her as the epicenter. For a moment, all around her was falling and noise and chaos. And then it was simply gone.

She hung suspended in the light. Below her, the fen was a turbulent mess of chunks of the sacred tree. The wood was no longer black, but a glittering silver. The first row of hometrees was broken to splinters. A huge wave rode outward, bending other trees so they bowed away from her. Would her friends survive it?

The Black Tree was gone.

The magic around Larkin was fading, and she was falling. Faster and faster. Toward a churning mass that would crush her.

There's a chance, Sela had slurred. *If you can weave...*

Weave what?

The answer came at her in a rush. She was a fool for not seeing it earlier. Using the last of her magic, she wove a dome around herself, remembering to tie it off moments before she hit. Still, the impact dropped her legs out from under her, her head cracking against the bottom. Then there was nothing but darkness.

Pain throbbed in Larkin's head, and her stuffy ears rang. A hard, glass-slick surface was beneath her. A surface that rocked rhythmically. The dome. She was still inside the dome, floating somewhere in the fen. She had survived. Had Denan? Sela? The others?

She forced her eyes open. It was early morning. There were branches above her, and bright green leaves. A bird hopped from one branch to another, its brilliant copper beak snatching at a bug before flitting away. Debris choked the water—only, the wood glittered silver instead of black.

He really was dead. She didn't find joy in that. Only relief. She had to find the others.

She banished the dome and plunged into the water. She tried to swim, but it was more flotsam than water, making swimming impossible. She finally calmed enough to let herself float to the surface. She managed to grab hold of a large enough branch to keep her head above water and kicked for the tree roots.

She pulled herself partway up and rested, breathing, trying to adjust to the fact that she had survived. To outlast the dizziness making her sick. But then came the horrible sounds of sobbing, of a heart being broken.

"Hello?" she called, but her voice was weak and didn't carry.

It had to be one of her friends, mourning someone's deaths. Who? Not Denan. Not Sela. Not any of them.

She had enough strength to get her knees under her. After a moment, she pushed up and stood, wavering. Leaning against the tree for support, she crossed the sloping roots.

Around a bend, she caught sight of her friends. They were all huddled around one another. She made a quick count. Caelia rocked Sela in her arms. Hagath held Tam, who was sobbing uncontrollably. Ramass, Eiryss, and Ture huddled together.

Talox stood at the edge of the water, his gaze fixed on something.

"I promised my wife I'd bring her back," Tam cried. "She's going to kill me, and I don't blame her."

Light. Where was Denan? *Light.* She tried to speak, but the words came out as a squeak quickly swallowed by the sound of the lapping water. Her head swam, and she nearly fell.

"She's gone," Talox said.

"No," said someone from above.

Larkin knew that voice. She took two more trembling steps and looked up. Her husband stood in the first level of branches and scanned the water where the Black Tree had once stood. His side was dark with blood, but he was alive. Her relief was so profound her legs cut out from under her.

"Denan." The word came out in a choked whisper that no one heard.

"No one could have survived when the Black Tree exploded," Talox said gently.

"I saw her in the light," Denan said through gritted teeth. "I know I did."

Larkin finally found her voice. "Denan!"

His head jerked, and his gaze locked on hers. "Larkin."

He dropped from one branch to another. Larkin tried to stand, only to fall back. He grabbed her, holding her tight.

"You're hurt," she protested.

"I'm fine." He stopped and cradled her head. "You're all right?"

The spinning hadn't helped her headache. "I hit my head." She rested it against his chest.

Tam held out a vial of sap. Larkin drank it in one swallow—resin and minerals—and looked back to the place the Black Tree had once stood. There was nothing left of it. Her gaze went back to the Valynthians. Their sigils were silver, not a trace of shadow to be seen.

They'd done it.

The Black Tree was dead.

The curse was broken.

Something gripped her leg. Larkin glanced down to find Sela wrapped around her, eyes a beautiful, heartbroken green. "She's gone. It took the last of her magic." Tears streamed down her cheeks. "I lost my friend."

Larkin wasn't strong enough to lift Sela, so she and Denan dropped to their knees and pulled her sister into the embrace. "I know. You're not alone, Sela."

Tam gave a whoop and joined in. The others soon followed, and they were a laughing, weeping family. When the hug finally broke apart, Tam played his pipes, and the others danced. Denan wrapped an arm around Larkin's shoulders and held her tight against his chest.

Sela moved to the edge of the water, her gaze fixed on the emptiness where the Black Tree had once stood. The White Tree was gone, and for Sela, she'd just lost her dearest companion.

Denan helped Larkin move to stand beside her sister. Amid all the joy, there were pangs of sorrow. West and Atara were gone. As was Garrot. Larkin was surprised at how sad that made her. Nesha had been right. Garrot had done the wrong things, and he'd gone too far. But he really thought he'd done them for the right reasons.

Denan came to stand beside her. "The last of the sacred trees are gone. The magic will die as our generations do. The hometrees will eventually fall, and the forest will lose its wakefulness. It's the end. The end of everything. The end of magic."

Larkin traced the ahlea on the inside of his wrist—the sigil that mirrored the one on her own wrist.

"No," Sela said. "It's the beginning."

EPILOGUE

ONE YEAR LATER

J ust after nightfall, Larkin stood on her family's land on the banks of the river Weiss. Mama, Nesha, Caelia, Alorica, and Sela stood on her right, Tam on her left. In their hands, they held paper lanterns tied to boards.

Tam went first, crouching to set the lantern into the river. He gave it a little push. "Goodbye, West."

Larkin went next, setting Maisy's lantern in the water. She'd tried to protest—to insist that someone else should place her lantern. After all, it had been Larkin who'd killed her.

"She was glad it was you," Tam had insisted. "I saw it in her eyes at the end. And besides, she didn't have anyone else."

Certainly not her rat father.

Choking back a sob, Larkin gave the lantern a little push. Mama set Papa's lantern into the water and stepped back quickly. Nesha set down Garrot's and then broke down sobbing. Larkin wrapped an arm around her sister's shoulders and held her tight.

Nesha hadn't been surprised when Larkin had told her that Garrot had given his life saving hers. She wiped her tears. "He made it right in the end."

Larkin kissed her head. "He did."

Sela set Raeneth's lantern afloat. Caelia released Bane's. Alorica sent Atara's lantern off. The little lanterns spun and bobbed before joining the thousands of others, each one for a soul who died when the shadows were unleashed.

Most of the Alamantians had found shelter within their chambers or beneath interlocked enchantress shields. But when the barrier fell with the White Tree's death, the Idelmarch hadn't had those protections. It had been a wholesale slaughter; every inhabitant of Cordova was dead. A good number in the other towns and cities too.

The weight of those deaths pressed heavily on Larkin.

As if sensing that weight, Mama pulled Larkin close. "You saved thousands more. Remember that."

Larkin still had nightmares. Still woke panting and horrified in the middle of the night. On those nights, Denan held her as she cried. Sometimes, Larkin found herself so irrationally angry that the only thing that helped was sparring until her anger was spent. Afterward, Mytin usually made a big dinner. Wyn regaled them with stories of his antics in the training tree. Aaryn sent her home with something she'd made.

She wasn't jumping at every shadow anymore, and the setting sun no longer sent her into full-blown panic. Magalia had given her some herbs that helped with sleeping and her moods.

Nesha cried hard. They all held each other and cried until the last of their tears were spent.

"Mama!" At eighteen months, Soren escaped his minders and toddled down the hill, an enormous frog in his little hand, its eyes bulging at how hard he squeezed it.

Rushing up to him, Nesha caught him just before he fell. He grinned up at her. "Look!"

She kissed his cheek. "Let it go in the river, baby."

Instead of setting it down, Soren threw it. It tumbled end over end, sat for a moment, as if dizzy, and then plunked into the river.

"Atara and I used to catch frogs by the river," Caelia said.

"I know," Alorica said. "I used to bawl until Mama made you take me."

"I remember that!" Caelia said with a laugh.

"Come on, Larkin," Sela said from behind them. "The moon is almost spent."

They climbed the embankment to those waiting for them. Denan stepped forward to help Larkin up the steep part. Bane and Caelia's father, Lord Daydon, wrapped his coat around Mama's shoulders, though it wasn't cold. She smiled up at him with a soft shyness that no one else had been able to draw from her. Eiryss passed a sleeping Brenna to Mama; the toddler's breathing didn't even shift.

Tam kept shooting terrified looks up the rise to Alorica's family, who stood on the other side of the bridge.

"Your father-in-law won't eat you," Larkin teased.

He swallowed hard. "It's the mother-in-law I'm afraid of." His voice dropped. "She's worse than Alorica."

"What?" Alorica shot back at him.

Tam put an arm around her and rubbed her growing belly. "Nothing, dear."

She huffed. Tam winked at Larkin.

Talox held Venna with one hand and Kyden with the other. The boy had fallen asleep with his hand fisted around Talox's hair. The boy loved the big man almost as much as he loved Denan. "I'll just keep him for now."

Larkin nodded in relief. She and Denan had been raising the boy since he'd been weaned. If he woke up now, he might be awake for hours. The whole group crossed fields of rye, wheat, barley, and oats. They passed Larkin's family hut, which was used for storage now.

Venna drew even with Larkin and held out her fist. "I have something for you."

Larkin placed her open palm beneath the other woman's. The ahlea amulet Eiryss had given her dropped into it. It was scorched and a little cracked but otherwise intact. And it hung from the chain Caelia had tried to give Larkin before. "How did you—"

"One of the Valynthian settlers drew it up in a net," Venna said with a smile. "We bought it."

Larkin blinked back tears. "That must have cost a fortune."

Talox shrugged. "It was yours. We just got it back for you."

Larkin dropped it over her head. It felt good having it. A reminder of all they'd overcome.

On the far side of the fields, beneath the spreading branches of the Forbidden Forest, Ramass, Hagath, and Ture were waiting. Mama had become fast friends with Hagath and Eiryss. The two groups merged, making a little circle with Larkin and Denan in the middle. They came to a stop beneath the tree Larkin stood beneath the day Sela had disappeared inside the Forbidden Forest and Larkin had gone in after her.

"Are you sure you want to do this?" Larkin whispered to her husband.

He raised an eyebrow. "We've been over this. The council approved it."

Larkin shifted her weight uneasily. "I know. But after we do this, there's no going back."

He reached forward, tucking a stray strand of her wild hair behind her ear. "Their kind deserves to live every bit as much as ours."

She knew this. Of course she did. It was just the nerves. He held out the arm with the ahlea sigil. She took hold of his forearm, so the sigils on their wrists pressed together. Denan lit his first, and Larkin could feel the warmth and gentle vibration through her connection.

Hoping against hope that they weren't repeating the mistakes of the past, Larkin opened her sigils. Between them, light flared, blinding their night eyes. Larkin blinked as her eyes adjusted. Something grew between them. Pain flared. Blood dripped. She hissed but didn't pull away—after all, there was always pain at a new beginning.

The light flashed, forcing them all to look away. There was the smell of minerals and starlight. The smell of a living sacred tree. Larkin almost wept at the familiarity of it. When they pulled apart, a small seedpod dropped to the ground. It gleamed silver and opalescent on the dark ground.

Sela broke ranks, squeezing the pod in her fist so it split open. Inside were rows of silver and opalescent seeds. Sela gripped one in her fingers and held it up to Larkin.

Larkin blinked back her tears. "A female."

Sela tucked the rest into her pocket. After this, they were going to the Alamant and then Valynthia. After that, who knew?

Sela flared her magic. "Make it grow."

Save Daydon and the babies, everyone lit their sigils. Larkin took their magic and wove the enchantment for growth. Denan's hand over hers, they pressed it into the soil.

Larkin felt it then, a new consciousness coming to life, reaching out to sense them. The seed split, two new leaves stretching toward the moonlight. The branches were opalescent and edged in purple, the leaves a rich green and teardrop in shape with lovely scalloped edges that curled to and fro like Larkin's wild hair.

It grew taller still—leaves branching apart until it was taller than Larkin—before the magic gave out. She reached up, running a finger along a velvety leaf. She wondered if this was what it felt like to hold your child in your arms for the first time. Flaring a little knife, she nicked her finger and the bark until a bead of blood and a bead of sap welled.

It was all in the blood, after all.

She pressed her finger to the nick. "You're going to need to build yourself a lake." Larkin imagined it, shining waters with this tree in the center. Warmth stretched toward her from the sacred tree. Warmth and awe. "And link up with the forest to the west. They've been lonely without a queen." She imagined the roots stretching until they brushed against the others. Music filled her ears, a crystalline singing. "And fill it with trees for people to live in." She imagined hometrees filled with people. "When you're ready, you can give people thorns for enchantment, and we will give you movement and sight. There are going to have to be a lot of rules and laws, though."

Larkin sighed, loath to leave the tree. She dropped her hand; the crystalline singing abruptly cut off. They'd done it. Resurrected a species. Set a new course for the future. For a moment, everyone was silent and still as the magnitude of what they'd done crashed down on them.

Sela turned and ran back toward the village. "Come on!" she cried. "Or Venna's rolls will be cold!"

Venna tipped back her head and laughed, the sound rich and boisterous.

Tam shot a determined look at Alorica. "I've been hearing about the things for over two years. I am not missing out now."

Alorica rolled her eyes but allowed him to hurry her along back the way they'd come. The others meandered after them. Larkin made to follow, but Denan held her back. She peered at his face in the moonlight. This man who always came for her.

She stretched up and kissed him. "Denan?"

He pulled her close; they'd had very little alone time with all the rushing around replanting trees in the Alamant and Valynthia. Judging by the way he was looking at her, he had some plans that involved hiding in the Forbidden Forest.

He'd clearly never had Venna's rolls. She darted out of his grasp. He lunged for her.

She spun out of his reach. "You'll never catch me!"

He grinned a wicked grin. "You haven't escaped me yet."

Then she was running, and he was chasing her.

I hope you loved Larkin and Denan's story!
If you're dying to learn more about the origins of the curse...

A highborn lady. An unrequited love. A cutting betrayal...

The path of a warrior enchantress is bathed in blood and magic. Born to one of the most powerful families in the kingdom, Eiryss lives a life of luxury and magic. Until her father commits the ultimate act of treason.

Treason that sparks a war.

The life Eiryss knew is over. Her one-time friends are gone. All but Ramass. And if he would just look at her—touch her—the way she longs for, she might be able to bear it. But his heart belongs to another. There is only one path for Eiryss now: become a warrior enchantress and fight for what's rightfully hers. And if the powers that be deny her, well...

If they won't give Eiryss magic, she'll steal it.

If you love stories filled with swoony romance, dark magic, and wicked curses, order your copy today!

Still not convinced? Keep reading to try the first few pages...

CHAPTER

REVENGE

High Lady Eiryss slipped around dancing pairs, narrowly avoiding Lord Darten's gaze—if she met his gaze, propriety would demand she dance with him. She didn't have time for another dance. Not before the toasts. And she could not endure another hour of his droning on and on about the cursed history of magic.

She reached a table set along the perimeter, slipped the vial from the folds of her skirt, and poured the colorless liquid into two glasses. The champagne bubbled and foamed before settling again. She dropped the vial to the bark and crushed it beneath her boot—she couldn't be found with it later.

"What are you doing?" came a voice, the breath warm against her neck.

She whirled to find Ramass directly behind her, one eyebrow cocked. His curly red hair had been mostly tamed into a queue at his back. He wore royal black, which complemented his pale skin and freckles and made his gray eyes almost appear blue. His shoulders were wide and muscular, his waist narrow.

497

"Light," she swore. She grabbed his sword-calloused hand and pulled him away. "We can't be seen here."

"Eiryss," he said warningly.

Back amid the dancers, she placed one of his hands onto the curve of her hip and lifted the other into position. "You danced with me the entire song. At no point did you see me go anywhere near Iritraya or Wyndyn's glasses."

He rolled his eyes and took the lead, maneuvering them around the dais at the center of the kaleidoscope of dancers. The font, with its wicked sharp thorns, sparked in the middle and was guarded by sacred tree sentinels in their silver and white livery. Only royalty, the Arbor, or an initiate receiving the thorns that would form sigils were ever allowed upon the dais.

"What did you do?" Ramass asked.

She smirked. "You'll see."

He made a sound of exasperation. "Eiryss, now is not the time for one of your pranks."

Oh, it was the perfect time. No way either girl could best this.

"Why do you insist on this childish feud?"

She leveled a stony gaze at him. "You haven't had to endure them." The two cousins had been insufferable for the entire year. Ever since Hagath had graduated from the Enchantress Academy a year ahead of Eiryss, leaving her outnumbered and alone.

He looked away from her. "Don't turn those brown eyes on me."

Why not, when they always worked? She sniffed and changed the subject. "Where's Ahlyn?"

Ramass's jealous gaze immediately zeroed in on their princess, where she danced with the Alamantian king. "Busy being a princess."

Where the princess's features were light, the foreign king's were dark. Where her dress was suitably sober as the night sky, his layered tunic was a garish shade of green. All the Alamantians wore bright colors and laughed too loudly—like flashy birds screeching for a mate.

Not that anyone could blame the king for wanting to monopolize Ahlyn. The princess had rich gold hair, sapphire eyes, a slim build, fine features, and perfect, dainty teeth. Not to mention unending power. Half the Valynthian aristocracy was in love with her.

The truth was Eiryss didn't really like Ahlyn. Certainly not because the princess was beautiful or because she spent more time with Eiryss's friends than Eiryss did—especially since Ramass had decided he'd fallen in love with her. But because the girl was sulky and delicate and never did anything wrong. And worse, the Silver Tree had chosen her to become the next queen.

Eiryss pinched his arm to get him to stop glaring daggers at the visiting king. "I might be able to scrounge up another vial." *Maybe some could accidentally end up in Ahlyn's glass as well.*

Ramass huffed a laugh, one side of his mouth quirking up. "Things are tense enough as it is."

Feeling like she'd won a victory with that lopsided smile, she swirled under his raised arm, her skirts flaring, and came back to his embrace. "My father won't let the wicked Alamantians hurt you."

"Your father isn't infallible."

"Of course he is." Her father was a legend. No one had bested him in any test of skill in twenty-five years.

As the last song faded to silence, the pair of them reached their own table—the plates of food having been cleared away by the servants. Champagne sparkled beside her name card. She sighed. She would never be able to drink from an unattended glass again. She took it in her hand.

Hagath slipped in beside her and picked up her own glass. Her friend was the female version of her twin, Ramass, right down to the blue eyes, freckles, and wild red hair—though she made every effort to tame it. She wore her dress healer robes—

dusty blue with silver embroidery. Her boots were wet, which meant she'd only just arrived, and in a leaky boat at that.

"Couldn't your father get you out of working tonight?" Eiryss asked. He was the king, after all.

"I didn't ask." Hagath always insisted on doing everything on her own merit, which was silly. Let one of the lower-caste healers take the night rotation—they needed the money, after all. And she had proved her merit a hundred times over.

"Couldn't miss the ceremony, dear sister?" Ramass asked.

Hagath waited until an Alamantian woman passed out of earshot before leaning close and dropping her voice. "I promised Ahlyn I would be here if I could manage to slip away. You have no idea how nervous she is."

Ramass's expression immediately soured. "Had I been forced to play hostess to that vile king, I would be nervous too."

Accompanied by King Dray, Ahlyn moved past them. As high nobility, Eiryss and her friends would normally have a place at the base of the dais, but her father had insisted they stay by the tables to the right—just in case anything went wrong. It wasn't ideal, but they were still close enough to hear the princess murmuring politely to a question Dray posed.

The king's eyes flicked to Eiryss, who dropped his gaze like she would a hot coal. She pushed her fingers down the plush skirts that began as the deepest navy and darkened to black at the base. She wore sapphires and diamonds at her ears and wrists. Her thick blonde and silver hair had been twisted into a prim knot, a glowing lampent flower tucked behind her ear. If she moved too fast, she caught flashes of color chasing each other along the edges of the petals.

Her attention was drawn back to Ahlyn and Dray as they climbed the dais to stand before the wicked thorns surrounding the font and took their place next to King Zannok. Like his children, the king's hair was red, his skin freckled, and his eyes blue, though wings of white framed his temples and lines bracketed his mouth and fanned from his eyes. He had aged well, his body still strong and honed from years of weapons training.

"On behalf of Valynthia," Zannok said, "I am pleased to welcome King Dray and his delegation to our beloved city."

Delegation, ha! There wasn't an enchanter among the Alamantians under fifty—the older ones always had the strongest magic—while each of the enchantresses was in their fighting prime. More an army unit than a delegation, they could easily assassinate the king or the princess, though they would all immediately die for it.

Of course, Eiryss's father, Undrad, had prepared for just such violence. Her brother and cousin, Rature and Vicil, had followed Princess Ahlyn all night as "chaperones." Undrad trailed the king—as the son of the previous queen, it was his duty and his honor. And there were far more honed Valynthian enchanters and enchantresses than even Dray had brought.

The men of her family were a fine sight in their best tunics, their leather mantles—peaked at the front, back, and shoulders—proclaiming their house and status. Mantles nearly identical to the one Eiryss wore, aside from the differing jewels that hung at each of the peaks.

Her father's hair was pure white. Vicil's and Rature's blond hair had already started to gray at the temples. It was a common family trait—one Eiryss hadn't escaped. On her brother and cousin, it somehow lent them an air of authority, while she just looked odd.

Her father nodded to Jala, the strongest enchantress in decades, though as queen, Ahlyn would soon surpass her. The faint silver gleam of her sigils showed that she was ready to shield the king at a moment's notice. She didn't look worried though. If anything, the woman seemed bored.

If the Alamantians tried anything, they'd find themselves outmaneuvered and outmagicked. Though Undrad doubted they would attempt anything tonight; he wouldn't have let Eiryss attend otherwise. He'd seen to it that she had weapons training, but she'd decided long ago to be a healer. She'd realized it after she lost her second batch of abandoned baby birds and cried for three days straight. She simply wasn't made for killing.

King Zannok raised his glass to Princess Ahlyn. "And to our princess, at the approach of the first anniversary since the Silver Tree chose her as my heir."

King Dray lifted his own glass. "To the princess." He was in his mid-thirties with sharp features, dark skin, and straight black hair. Even tied, it hung halfway down his back. His mantle was peaked at the shoulders, the jewels at the four points fire opals. The White Tree had been beautifully wrought at the center of the mantle in opal and gold. His ring bore a green serpent, knotted and eating its own tail. The symbol for his line.

Ahlyn inclined her head. King Zannok tipped his glass to his lips and drank, the cue for the rest of them to do likewise. Eiryss took a sip while looking toward Iritraya and Wyndyn, who tasted their own champagne, none the wiser. Suppressing a grin, she quickly looked away again.

King Dray took Ahlyn's hand. Her magic flared, the raised lines of her sigils gleaming silver.

If Dray was bothered by her obvious mistrust, he didn't show it. "I have heard rumors of your strength, Princess Ahlyn. They have said that your monarch sigils have grown strong and true—that after a few months more, they will have grown strong enough for you to become queen."

All this was true, yet it wasn't seemly for Dray to say it. For as Ahlyn's power grew, Zannok's faded. He'd been a good king—a great one, even—and like a dear uncle to Eiryss. He deserved more respect than to have his swift fall from power flaunted before the most powerful people in two kingdoms.

To his credit, King Zannok showed no outward signs of the insult, except for perhaps the tremor of champagne in his glass.

Dray went on—he was either oblivious or indifferent to his gaucherie. Eiryss would bet on the latter. "After spending this evening with you, I can see that those rumors are true. I have come to make an alliance with the Valynthians, one that will bind our kingdoms. No more Alamantians. No more Valynthians. But a new people."

He reached into his pocket and withdrew something. Valynthian guards and magic wielders tensed. He opened his hand to reveal an opal the size of a small bird. Eiryss's mouth fell open. King Dray wasn't going to attack. He was proposing, offering Ahlyn a jewel to hang from her own mantle. She gaped at the opal, then at Dray, before her frantic gaze landed on Ramass.

Ramass was already moving. Hagath snatched his arm and shot Eiryss a look. Catching her meaning, she grabbed his other arm, spilling most of her champagne on his sleeve in the process.

"She's not going to accept," Eiryss hissed through clenched teeth. Of course she wouldn't. No Valynthian would debase themselves by marrying an Alamantian. Especially not their blasted king.

"Release your sigils before you start a brawl," Hagath whispered.

Eiryss hadn't noticed the buzz of his sigils under her palms, but she felt them now. Ramass hesitated, clearly torn.

"Ahlyn can take care of herself," Eiryss said.

He eased back a step, his sigils going dark a moment later. Eiryss didn't trust him enough to let go of his arm. Her gaze swung back to the dais. To the king who dangled peace between their kingdoms. For a price.

"You think to force our hand?" King Zannok said coldly. "Bully our princess into marrying you?"

The Alamantians were already pressuring King Zannok into giving magic to the rabble. Imagine, their next monarch could be wallowing in the mud right now. And Eiryss would have to bow and scrape before them. Such debasement wouldn't stand. Not in

Valynthia. Especially not after one of their cities, Oramen, had tried to secede from Valynthia to join the Alamant.

And the Alamantians had welcomed Oramen with open arms.

That had set off skirmishes and threats until the Alamantians had decided to back off and offer these peace talks. *They thought to make Valynthia and the Alamant one?* Eiryss snorted. *More like destroy us from the inside out.*

"War between our people is coming. You know it as well as I." Dray eyed the males of Eiryss's family as if he'd seen right through their fine clothes to the soldiers beneath. He looked back at Ahlyn. "We can still stop it."

The princess took a step back. "I will never marry you." Her eyes again shifted to Ramass.

Dray followed her gaze, moved closer, and said something Eiryss couldn't make out. Then he lifted his glass. "To Ahlyn—a queen who holds the future of our kingdoms in her hands."

He drained his glass. For a time, there was silence. Belatedly, everyone realized they were supposed to drink after the monarch's toast. Instead, Eiryss set down her mostly spilled glass in disgust. People murmured, some in outrage.

King Dray bowed to King Zannok. "My delegation thanks you for your hospitality. Please accept our gifts of friendship." He gestured, and men came in, bearing casks. "Wine from our best vineyards."

Ahlyn opened her mouth, closed it, and cleared her throat. There was still protocol to observe—the girl knew it better than any of them. With a deep breath, she regained control over herself. "We have gifts for you as well, King Dray."

Bolts of finely woven material, far superior to anything the Alamantians had, were brought out. All of them were in suitable somber colors, as well as royal black—a great honor that the foreign king didn't deserve.

"And now," the king's scribe said with a pointed look at Iritraya and Wyndyn, "as a show of good faith, two of our girls will sing your Alamantian anthem." Both girls hurried to the front of the crowd and stood before the dais. As the band began the boisterous anthem, the cousins opened their mouths to sing, exposing azure teeth and indigo tongues. Unabashed as their singing was, they clearly didn't know.

Despite everything, a wicked grin spread across Eiryss's mouth, her crooked teeth bared for all to see.

Ramass's head whipped toward Eiryss. Hagath narrowed her gaze. More and more people turned to look at Eiryss, whose lips slammed over her teeth. She adopted her most innocent expression. Curse the light and all who followed it. Her reputation ruined her even without evidence. She shifted uncomfortably— she hated the attention of so many people.

Clearly baffled, Iritraya and Wyndyn belted out all the louder. People, Alamantian and Valynthian alike, began to laugh. The tension eased, seeping away like snow before the hot sun. Confused, the two girls exchanged baffled looks. Their eyes widened as they took in the other. Both pointed. Iritraya's hand slapped over her mouth, her singing dying with a clap. Wyndyn followed a beat behind. The two girls rushed toward the bathrooms on the upper branches.

They could scrub all they liked. The blue wouldn't come all the way off until sometime tomorrow. It took everything Eiryss had to hold back an unladylike snort.

King Dray held out his hand to Ahlyn. Biting her lip to keep back her smile, she took it. The two danced, and even Eiryss had to admit they made a beautiful couple who would probably make even more beautiful children.

Movement caught her gaze. Her father's eyes locked on her. He said something to one of his soldiers in brocade velvet and headed toward her.

"Time to go," she said.

"Eiryss," Hagath hissed after her.

But Eiryss was already a quarter of the way to the stairs that would take her to the dock at the base of the tree. Moments before she reached the archway, her father's hand locked around her arm, and he pulled her up one of the side branches until they were out of sight and out of earshot.

He released her. "Eiryss," he said firmly. "You're seventeen—far too old for such pranks."

She kept her gaze fixed on her feet, shame swirling inside her. "They deserved it."

"And now they will retaliate. Then you will retaliate. On and on and on. When will it end?" He looked out over the water beneath them.

Above them, the vault shone like a bead. Through Valynthia, cities gleamed under the domed vaults, so named for their impermanence. Eiryss imagined that from above, they would look like pearls strung through a necklace, with the capital city of Hanama the largest and most lustrous.

With the vault in place to keep out the weather, the lake was like black glass, reflecting the tree perfectly. Only the rainbow-pulsing fish swimming among the branches distinguished the truth from its reflection. If she unfocused her eyes, she could almost pretend they were birds.

The shadows in the hollows of Undrad's face made him look haggard. If there was a war, her father would lead it. And instead of protecting the king, he was chiding his wayward daughter.

"I'm sorry," she muttered.

"What have you been training for years to do?"

Here came the lecture. "To serve our people."

"And why must you serve them?"

She sighed in exasperation. "Because I'm in a position of power."

He pulled her into his arms, holding her tight. "Ah, my girl. I'll speak with Iritraya's and Wyndyn's fathers tonight. We'll make sure a cessation of hostilities is negotiated and sealed with iron."

She buried her head into her father's chest and let the familiar smell of him—like old books, steel, and magic—comfort her. "I should have come to you."

He chuckled. "Sounds like you were dealing with it pretty well on your own."

She sniffed and wiped her eyes. "Of course I was."

He tugged the flower from behind her ear. She'd crushed it when she rested her head against him. "You're going to be a formidable woman. I'm a little worried for your enemies."

She smiled, and for once she didn't worry about keeping her teeth hidden behind her lips. They matched his, after all. He motioned for her to follow him.

"Just give me a moment," she said.

He studied her before handing her the lampent. "You have to stay at least a couple more hours, but don't wait for me after that. I imagine the council will be chewing at Dray's proposal all night."

The Council of Lords and Ladies—a bunch of old men and women who had nothing better to do than stir up trouble.

He left her. She released the flower, watching as it fell helplessly toward the dark water. It landed, spreading ripples that changed the tree's reflection, then bounced back and changed it again. A discordant ripple, and the flower was pulled to the depths by an unseen predator.

Taking a deep breath, she went back to the gala and came face-to-face with Ramass.

"Did your father toss you into the lake?" he asked.

"Clearly."

"You deserve it."

"Always." She looked about for Hagath and found her hurrying toward the exit, a flushed acolyte beside her. A lower-caste acolyte. The girl definitely hadn't been invited to the gala, which meant she'd come to fetch Hagath.

Eiryss's heart sank. She'd hoped to spend the evening with her friend. But clearly, one of her patients had taken a bad turn. With Hagath working all weekend, Eiryss didn't know when she'd see her friend again.

"Come on." Ramass took her hand, and she sighed.

At least I still have Ramass.

He led her to where everyone was dancing. They hadn't finished their rotation when King Dray approached them, Ahlyn's hand slipped through the crook of his elbow. He was more than ten years her senior and a widower. Rumor had it that his two sons were the terror of the Alamant. He bowed to Ramass. "Lady Eiryss, might I have a dance?"

Ramass abandoned her like she'd suddenly turned rancid. He and Ahlyn were dancing before Eiryss could formulate a protest. King Dray held out his hand.

Light, she couldn't think of a way to politely decline. She pressed her palm into his, wincing a little at his moist grip. He spun her about, clearly an excellent dancer.

"I'm surprised you remembered my name," she murmured to his chest. He'd met all the high nobility before dinner, but there were a lot of them.

"I wanted to thank you."

She resisted the urge to shoo his hand off her hip. "For what?"

"Lightening the mood earlier."

He was thanking her for easing the tension with her prank. Heat climbed up Eiryss's cheeks. Who had told him? Ahlyn? The little traitor. "I don't understand your meaning."

His eyes flashed with amusement. "I'll take what help I can, even if that wasn't your intent."

What harm was there in admitting her guilt to a foreigner? "Had I known that, I would have saved my revenge for later."

He tipped his head back and laughed. *He really isn't too bad looking,* she admitted ruefully. But his flawless, dark skin and black eyes only made her distrust him more, and she hadn't thought that possible.

Eiryss caught sight of her father watching them from where he stood next to the king, his expression dark, one hand on the hilt of his sword. She flashed a smile at him to let him know she was all right.

Dray followed her gaze. He spun her deftly and then pulled her back into his arms. "Your father is a legend, Eiryss, even among the Alamant. Is it true that he is as honorable as he is skilled?"

You have no idea. "Why don't you ask him yourself?"

"I would, but he never leaves the king's side."

Her eyes narrowed. "And what would you have to say, King Dray, that you couldn't say in front of my king?"

He twirled her again and again so that her head spun, before settling her against him—close enough that the line of her hip touched his. "Just a friendly meeting between commanders."

Mercifully, the song came to an end. She backed away from his arms, relieved to be free of his touch. He caught her hand. She felt the press of paper between their palms. "Will you give this to your father?"

This was not the first time someone had used her to gain access to her father, and she had strict instructions to always pass the information along. "Very well," she sighed. She slipped the note into her pocket and bowed only as low as she had to. "King Dray."

He inclined his head. "I hope to see you again soon, Lady Eiryss."

She gave a tight smile and backed away to the outskirts of the dance floor. With Hagath gone and Ramass occupied, she scanned the room for someone else to spend the evening with. Instead, her gaze snagged on Wyndyn and Iritraya, who shot daggers at her. Biting her lip, she caught sight of a familiar figure moving along behind the tables. Her gaze lightened on Kit in his Silver Tree guard uniform.

He was her brother's age, a good dancer, an excellent kisser, and very pretty—even if he was far enough beneath her station to never be an equal. There were a very select few of acceptable rank to court her. Lord Darten and his droning, for instance. *Gah! I'm never going to marry.*

Judging by the way Kit was heading toward the exit, he'd just ended his shift. Eiryss angled to intercept him. She timed it so she popped out in front of him, her grin so wide it was hard to keep her lips together over her teeth.

He started and began to smile before glancing around nervously. "Eiryss."

She grabbed his hand. "Come on. We're going to drink all the king's wine and dance until they make us go to our hometrees." She picked up a glass and pushed it into his hands.

He looked around nervously. "Eiryss, you know I'm not high nobility."

"I am." She tipped the wine to her lips. It was actually very good—hints of rose and apples—so the Alamantians could at least do one thing right. "Only the king's and Ahlyn's family outrank me. None of whom will bother with me bringing a friend."

He didn't look certain. She lifted the bottom of his glass. "Come on. It's hours yet before I can go home." She watched his mouth pinch in uncertainty. Watched as he finally gave in, lifting the glass to his lips and licking the traces of wine away.

She smiled, planning to take full advantage of those lips later. She finished the rest of her glass and pulled him among the other dancers.

For Eiryss, everything changes in the very next chapter...

If you love stories filled with swoony romance, dark magic, and wicked curses, order your copy today!

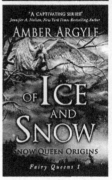

ACKNOWLEDGMENTS

Thanks go out to my amazing editing team: Charity West (content editor) and Jennie Stevens (copyeditor); and my talented design team: Michelle Argyle (cover designer) and Bob Defendi (mapmaker).

My everlasting love to Derek, Corbin, Connor, Lily, and God.

ABOUT THE AUTHOR

Amber Argyle is the bestselling author of numerous fantasy and romance novels. Her award-winning books have been translated into several languages and praised by such authors as NYT best-sellers David Farland and Jennifer A. Nielsen.

Amber grew up on a cattle ranch and spent her formative years in the rodeo circuit and on the basketball court. She graduated cum laude from Utah State University with a degree in English and physical education, a husband, and a two-year-old. Since then, she and her husband have added two more children, which they are actively trying to transform from crazy small people into less-crazy larger people. She's fluent in all forms of sarcasm, loves the outdoors, and believes spiders should be relegated to horror novels where they belong.

To receive her starter library of four free books,
simply tell her where to send it:

http://amberargyle.com/freebooks/

OTHER TITLES BY AMBER ARGYLE

Forbidden Forest Series

Lady of Shadows
Stolen Enchantress
Piper Prince
Wraith King
Curse Queen

Fairy Queens Series

Of Ice and Snow
Winter Queen
Of Fire and Ash
Summer Queen
Of Sand and Storm
Daughter of Winter
Winter's Heir

Witch Song Series

Witch Song
Witch Born
Witch Rising
Witch Fall

Made in the USA
Coppell, TX
01 March 2021

51061631R10292